Will there b
These three men will decide.

Harris—captain of the nuclear submarine's Gold Crew. Cool, distant, unapproachable, secure in his own sense of leadership and control.

Van Meer—the executive officer, sensitive and so oppressed by guilt for his wife's death that he is secretly taking a tranquilizing drug.

Schulman—the psychiatrist whose assignment is to observe the reactions of the crew who have been programmed to believe that they must fire the final missiles in a nuclear war the Russians have begun.

> Only these three men aboard the sub
> Alaska know the real truth about the
> mission, but they too are cut off from
> reality. Who can stop the inevitable...
> now that the unthinkable is just a
> matter of time?

ABOUT THE AUTHORS

In *The Gold Crew*, as in their previous best-sellers, *The Glass Inferno* and *The Prometheus Crisis*, Thomas N. Scortia and Frank M. Robinson draw drama from the dangers inherent in present-day technology. Mr. Scortia's years of experience in aerospace research and development and Mr. Robinson's editorial background in news and science have given them unique expertise and awareness of the possibilities. Both have written in areas ranging from science fiction to film scenarios. Their earlier novels have been translated into major films.

THE GOLD CREW

Thomas N. Scortia
Frank M. Robinson

WARNER BOOKS

A Warner Communications Company

For Skip Steloff,
whose nightmare has become our own

Foreword

The first operational Trident submarine is now at sea, the forerunner of a fleet whose destructive powers are unparalleled in history. It has been said that a single Trident could destroy the major nations of the world. A fleet of these weapons represents such an awesome collection of power that the consequences of their full employment in a nuclear exchange are truly unimaginable.

The Gold Crew, like *The Glass Inferno*, *The Prometheus Crisis*, and *The Nightmare Factor* before it, came into being because of our concern for the dangers inherent in today's sophisticated technology. It is a "What if?" book, depending for its drama on the terrifying consequences of an error or a breakdown in this technology.

The research for the book led us into many strange areas and frequently unearthed information we suspect may be sensitive or even classified. We have, for this reason, deliberately omitted details of the layout of the real Trident. For the same reason, we have avoided discussing the communication and ranging devices aboard a Trident, as well as its maneuvering ability and operational speed, range, and depth. We have also referred to the loss of the *Thresher* and to other accidents only in the most general terms. The reader should bear in mind, however, that the basic idea of the book has its counterpart in reality.

The idea that the Trident submarine may be designed as a first-strike weapon is our own, and one that we think worth examining in light of the weapon system's extraordinary capabilities. If a potential enemy should become convinced of such a design intention, the present relatively stable balance of power among today's nuclear states might well be seriously menaced.

A number of people were of great value in the research for the novel and during its writing. We would like to thank Larry Arnett, Ray Butters, Paul Boulanger, Ron Finley, Frank Kelly Freas, Bill Fuller, Nicholas J. J. Scortia, Tim Knowlton, Frank Olynyk, Edward Wood, and Bill Ewing, as well as a number of other helpful people who have asked to remain nameless. Our particular thanks go to Academy graduate and former fleet officer Arthur "Skip" Steloff for coming to us initially with the project and to his partner, Carl Munson, who spent a great deal of time finding knowledgeable people for us to interview.

We have, in the interest of verisimilitude, used the names of many real institutions, companies, restaurants, and hotels. Beyond the use of such names, all names of personnel, description of policies, and incidental details were invented by us and do not, to our knowledge, have any counterpart in reality.

August, 1979

THOMAS N. SCORTIA
Los Angeles, California

FRANK M. ROBINSON
San Francisco, California

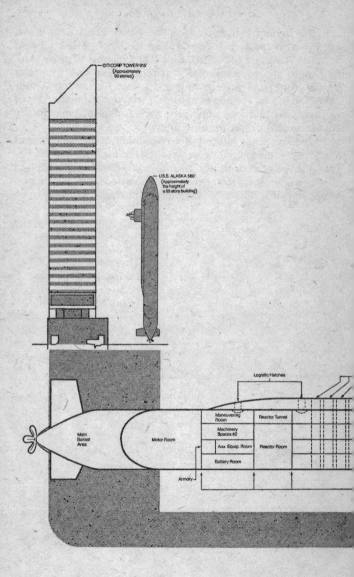

CITICORP TOWER 915'
(Approximately
90 stories)

U.S.S. ALASKA 560'
(Approximately
the height of
a 55 story building)

Logistic Hatches

Main
Ballast
Area

Motor Room

Maneuvering
Room

Reactor Tunnel

Machinery
Spaces #2

Aux. Equip. Room

Reactor Room

Battery Room

Armory

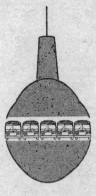

42' IN BEAM WIDTH
COULD ACCOMMODATE
THE WIDTH OF FIVE
NEW YORK CITY BUSES

U.S.S. ALASKA SSBN 737

560' IN LENGTH
42' IN BEAM
COMPLEMENT: 140

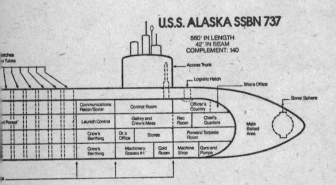

Tuesday, June 16

1

DAVID INGE shifted the coil of cable over his shoulder and glanced back at the ominous bulk of the nuclear submarine behind him. Its twenty-four muzzle hatches looked cold and forbidding in the bright sunlight. The hatches marched in serried rows up to the sail, faint indentations in the flat-black hull. He stared at them for a long moment, lost in thought. His mood dissolved as a small wave slapped against the ship's side, sending a ripple of water over the sloping deck to dampen his safety shoes.

"Hey, Inge, we don't have all day."

Thatcher was standing in the afterhatch, looking annoyed. Inge shifted the cable again, grunted, and started for the hatch, testing his footing on the wet metal of the curving pressure hull. He was getting too old for this sort of thing, he thought. He hesitated at the hatch and looked back. The *Alaska* was enormous, more than half again the length of the old *Sterlet*, on which he had served in World War II. More than two football fields in length. And more than forty feet in beam. You could stick a three-story house inside, stand on top, and still not hit your head. It dwarfed the other submarines at Electric Boat.

Thatcher gave him a hand down the stairs. A grim, silent, beefy man in his mid-thirties, Thatcher was his Navy watchdog in mufti. His assignment was to get the job done, then get out and make damn sure Inge kept his mouth shut. . . .

"There's no crew on board?"

Thatcher shook his head, frowning at the question. He didn't like curious people. "They've all been assigned elsewhere. Come on, the others are in the mess compartment."

Inge paused again in the passageway at the foot of the stairs.

Stairs. Not a ladder but *stairs*, by God, with treads and risers, not rungs. He glanced down the fluorescent-lit corridor and for a moment thought again of the old *Sterlet*. He still vividly remembered the stink of hot diesel oil and perspiration and the passageways in which two men had to turn sideways to pass. You became immune to the smell within a day or so; you never noticed how bad you and the others stank until you surfaced and opened a hatch. Then the smell was enough to turn your stomach.

This passageway struck him as eerie: You lost the sense of being surrounded by steel. The colors were muted, the bulkheads covered with Formica, the deck a tasteful, patterned tile. It was like a corridor in a hotel or a passageway on a cruise ship.

"You okay, Inge?"

"Just thinking. I was on a diesel electric in World War Two. Nothing like this." He glanced around again. "With nobody around, it's spooky."

"You served on the *Sterlet*," Thatcher recited dryly. "Drafted in '41, honorably discharged in '45. I suppose it brings back memories." There was no empathy in his voice.

That was more than forty years ago. But the time spent aboard her was still bright in his memory; those had been among the happiest years of his life. By *God*, they had made a great crew. How many commendations had the boat received? Then: you couldn't call them boats anymore. The *Alaska* was a ship—and a huge one.

"It reminds me of the *Bellamya*," he said, following Thatcher down the passageway. "I once helped set up a master engine computer aboard her."

Thatcher stopped. "The *Bellamya*?" he asked suspiciously. "That's not one of ours, is it?"

"It's a tanker," Inge said, smiling slightly. "Half a million tons. Registered to French Shell."

Thatcher grunted and turned into a shorter corridor with the familiar trefoil on the bulkhead, indicating a radiation source nearby. This corridor would be off limits to most of the crew. A moment later, Inge sidled gingerly around a thick glass disk set in the deck. There was a muted blue glow far below: Cherenkov radiation, the signature of a nuclear reactor ...

They climbed down another flight of stairs. He caught a glimpse of the huge turbines in the engine room before Thatcher muscled open another hatch. Inge stepped through into an enormous compartment, the bulkheads covered with meters and dials. Thick, stubby tubes—each a good eight feet in diameter with piping encircling them like the serpents crushing Laocoön—marched down the middle of the compartment in two files of twelve each.

The compartment itself was two hundred feet in length, almost two-thirds the length of the old *Sterlet*, and it was a good ten feet from deck to overhead. What did the crew call it? Sherwood Forest? Inge blinked, the fond memories of the old *Sterlet* evaporating. There was nothing romantic about the *Alaska*; it had looked enormous and forbidding topside, like some dull-black monster hunkered low in the water, waiting for its prey. The brightly lighted missile compartment only added to the feeling of hopelessness. At the very least, if the *Sterlet* had torpedoed your ship in World War II, you had a chance, even with the sharks and the ice-cold water. There would be no chance for anyone on the receiving end of the *Alaska*'s missiles. This one boat could devastate half the world. . . .

He was suddenly glad that he was an old man, that he had already lived most of his life in a gentler age.

"Inge." Thatcher was irritated now. "Let's hop to it." He glanced at the missile tubes around him without visible emotion, then trotted toward the far hatch. Inge shrugged and walked after him, not bothering to keep up. He was sixty-two years old and twenty pounds overweight, and hurrying was something he hadn't done in years.

The next passageway was carpeted. Thatcher suddenly stopped, a confused look on his face. They were lost, Inge thought, glancing inside an open cabin door. The cabin must be the captain's. It had a sense of luxury that he couldn't reconcile with memories of the *Sterlet*. By God, they *did* live like kings . . . and would probably die like dogs.

"I think you're lost, Thatcher," he said. "The crew's mess certainly isn't in Officers' Country."

"This way," Thatcher snapped. He hurried through another hatch and into the control room. "Keep your eyes to the front, Inge," he said in a surly voice. "Normally, all this classified stuff is covered before an outsider comes aboard. But we couldn't tell them to cover the gear this time—it would have given us away."

He had probably worked on more secret installations than

Thatcher had ever seen. He glanced quickly around, despite Thatcher's warning. It was more like a spaceship than a submarine.

He suddenly shivered. The brightly lit passageways and the echoing emptiness were starting to get to him. It was like walking through a futuristic museum. Or, more accurately, a futuristic killing machine. But that's what it was, a killing machine. . . .

Then they were in the mess compartment, where Captain Larson and the others waited, looking impatient. "It's a big ship," Inge apologized, ignoring Thatcher's quick glance of disapproval. "We got lost."

Larson shrugged. Inge could never get used to how young the officers were now. Larson was probably the same age as the old man on the *Sterlet* had been but he seemed a teenager. They were handing the world over to a bunch of kids.

Larson cleared his throat and waved at the equipment on the table in front of him. Inge forgot his memories of the *Sterlet* and his awe of the size of the *Alaska* as he took a quick inventory of the gear. It was all there, the special cassette and the miniaturized, exquisitely constructed tape player with the special sensing devices.

Larson said, "We'll have to hook up the player to the working Fathometer in the attack center and wire the output to the different installations in the radio shack. Both the switch box and the player will have to be hidden—that's your bailiwick, Inge—and all the cabling will have to be painted and aged to match the others."

Inge frowned. You couldn't get away with that; somebody was bound to notice the cabling and wonder about it. Unless the *Alaska* wasn't going to be out very long. That jibed with the other scuttlebutt he had heard.

Larson cleared his throat again. Inge wondered why he was so nervous. "We have about three hours to do it in." Larson paused. "There can't be any slipups or any delays."

Inge, only half listening now, glanced around the mess compartment and tried to reconcile what he had just seen with the diagram of the ship he had studied earlier. They had agreed on the location beforehand. It seemed reasonable. It was the last place anybody would look, if only because it was the most logical. Like the purloined letter.

They finished at twenty minutes after four. Captain Larson personally checked that no betraying scraps of wire or bits of insulation had been left behind. Inge picked up the unused cabling, packed his small screwdrivers and pliers, and followed Thatcher back through the ship to the afterhatch.

Once on the pier, he turned back and studied the *Alaska*. The fading sunlight was already casting shadows over the water. The ship couldn't be seen at all at dusk; the dull black of its sail and sides would blend right into the night and the ocean.

"You aren't to talk about this," Thatcher said quietly at his side. "At all. Not to your wife or your co-workers or your foreman or the people you drink with. Ever."

Inge knew more about the operation than Thatcher suspected. You looked at the equipment, considered the security precautions taken and the fact that no crew members were aboard. More than that, he had heard part of the tape during a test. It hadn't been that hard for him to figure out the rest of it.

"Right," he agreed laconically, picking up his tools and following Thatcher back to the nearby trade sheds. "Nothing. Ever."

It was a dirty trick to play on the crew. He was mildly surprised at his own resentment but the memories of the old *Sterlet* and her crew were crowding back again.

A dirty trick. And goddamned dangerous . . .

Tuesday, June 23

2

ADMIRAL STEWART CULLINANE shifted uncomfortably in his chair and fished in his pocket for a cigar, ignoring the light hastily offered by his aide, Lieutenant David Chavez. He hated these endless conferences. Everybody chewed and re-chewed the same cud of data, hoping to extract some new juice of meaning that would make a decision easier. There were never enough data for a sure decision and no one seemed to have the courage to risk making a mistake. But, then, staff officers never did take chances.

He looked down the long conference table, squinting against the glare of the afternoon sun shining over the roof edge of the Pentagon's inner court. He was trying to catch Admiral Howland's eye but the Chief of Naval Operations had lowered his head and his features were lost in the deep shadows cast by the back lighting.

Cullinane shrugged, thinking once more of how much he dis-liked these meetings, especially when Oxley was giving the brief-ing. Today, Captain Oxley, looking very nervous, was standing before his chart easel and droning endless figures on the near-readiness of the ARGUS array. ARGUS was the third generation of submerged listeners, a complex system of underwater micro-phones, noise discriminators, and rapid computers that had a range of ten thousand miles. When the system was finally activat-ed, there would be very little going on in the oceans of the world that the Navy's experts could not detect and identify. Its readiness was long overdue, and now . . . Was it ready or not? Oxley, as usu-al, couldn't quite make up his mind.

Cullinane leaned back in his chair, hid behind a small cloud of cigar smoke, and studied the captain. He didn't like Oxley. He didn't like the man's delivery, which was condescending and pedantic, and he didn't like the man's face, which was lined with a hundred tiny capillaries ready to burst through the florid skin. Nor did he care much for the fact that Oxley's stomach was so large that the cloth of his coat was tugging at the buttons. But most of all he didn't like Oxley because the man had a computer for a heart and a budget for a brain and was more a politician than a Navy officer.

He wondered idly if disliking Oxley had become a vice in which he was indulging himself. . . .

He listened a moment longer, then couldn't resist interrupting. "Captain Oxley, what you're actually telling us is that you have no idea as to the present status of ARGUS. Now, you've either solved the problem of the interface with the SOSUS and CAPTOR surveillance systems or you haven't. Which is it?"

Oxley cleared his throat and nervously pulled at an earlobe. "I thought I had made myself clear. We've modified SOSUS by expanding the hydrophone network and adding new discriminatory circuits so it can now handle the entire Baltic region. But the response is still slow compared to the ARGUS response." He glanced around the table, hoping that there were no more questions.

Three chairs down, on the other side of the table, Caleb Warden, the President's National Security Adviser, pulled out a blue bandana and blew his nose. Cullinane groaned softly. Did Warden have to carry the dirt-farmer image that far? Everybody at the table knew better.

"What's all the fuss about, gen'lemen?" Warden asked, the hard consonants in his voice buffed down to an oily smoothness. "Once SOSUS detects an enemy submarine leaving the Baltic, Admiral Cullinane's boys don't seem to have any difficulty keeping track of it in the Atlantic."

Pillsbury, the elderly Undersecretary of the Navy, had been quiet up to now, his parchment-lidded eyes giving the impression he was dozing. He suddenly leaned forward, looking like a falcon ready to strike. "With what degree of effectiveness, Admiral?"

"We're running ninety-three percent—SubPac hasn't been quite so lucky."

"Our boys follow them just like a houn' dog nosing a rabbit's trail," Warden added jovially. He folded his pudgy hands over his paunch and glanced smugly around the table, his eyes lingering for a moment on Cullinane.

Cullinane stared back and mentally reviewed Warden's career. Caleb Warden: mid-forties, brilliant, deceptively soft, ambitious. A recent addition to the President's staff. Nobody you wanted to antagonize. There wasn't much Warden wouldn't do to become the next Secretary of State, and the number of shattered careers around the Executive offices testified to his skill at political infighting. And he was close to the throne. The President made up his own mind but Caleb Warden's opinion was one of the few that carried weight. Too much weight.

In the shadows by the windows, Admiral Howland cleared his throat. "Without ARGUS, Stew, there'd come a time when we couldn't keep track of all the Soviet ships—and that would be intolerable."

Damn, didn't Howland see where this was leading? ARGUS was a sideshow. "I wasn't questioning the system itself, just whether or not it's actually ready."

Pillsbury's voice was querulous. "If the new system is effective, Admiral, will it eliminate these chicken-of-the-sea tag games? Every time there's one of these incidents Defense has to answer to State for it."

Cullinane had wondered when Pillsbury would bring that up. Pillsbury was pushing seventy but his mind was quick and incisive. He had been a small-town lawyer from upstate New York before coming to Washington, and he was awed by neither the military brass nor the politics of the place.

"There isn't any sure way of eliminating them, Mr. Pillsbury. If there was, they would have been. Most of the incidents don't originate with us anyway."

Warden now interrupted, his eyes bright. "Chicken of the sea? I'm afraid that's something new to me."

Caleb Warden had been appointed National Security Adviser six months before, and in that time he had managed not only to bypass State but to establish himself as de facto Secretary of Defense. There was very little that was new to Caleb Warden.

"Potential rammings, Mr. Warden. Sometimes an enemy sub you're tailing will become aware of you and try to ram you. And sometimes there'll be simultaneous contacts that become a game of—well, chicken."

"You mean that sometimes we initiate the game?" Warden

had made a steeple of his fingers before his face, so Cullinane saw only traces of an ironic smile. "You've got some mighty frisky boys there, Admiral."

The patterns of antagonism had shifted subtly and Cullinane noted a look of relief spread across Oxley's face as the captain realized he could slip into the background while the giants battled.

They were throwing him off-balance, and Cullinane knew he couldn't depend on Howland to come to his rescue. "What we're really discussing is the degree of risk we're willing to take to maintain our attack credibility. If we back off from these undersea confrontations, the Soviet subs will get bolder and eventually there'll be a full-scale incident." Warden suddenly pursed his lips and Cullinane realized with a jolt that the man must be privy to one of the best-kept secrets in the Department of Defense: the loss of the nuclear attack submarine *Blowfin* in a chicken-of-the-sea underwater ramming by an unidentified Soviet submarine the year before. "In the meantime, we have to maintain close surveillance of their subs until ARGUS becomes fully operational, which, praise God and Universal Telephone, won't be too long."

Two birds with one stone, he thought, reaching for a glass of water. Oxley had flinched when he had brought the subject back to ARGUS and Warden had looked momentarily unhappy at the mention of its prime contractor, UT. He had once headed a New England think tank supported largely by grants from UT. Then Cullinane felt faintly ashamed of himself. It had been a cheap shot. Anybody could be tarred by the conflict-of-interest brush these days. Even he had had several inquiries about his employment availability three years downstream, when he would retire. The mere inquiry was a subtle form of bribery.

Warden turned to Oxley. "Admiral Cullinane has a point, Captain. Yes or no on ARGUS? Is it fully operational and, if not, when will it be?"

Cullinane was suddenly as alert as if he had just heard a diving Klaxon. The good-ol'-boy accent had vanished and Warden's voice had all the authority of the chairman of the board, which he had once been. His eyes, half buried in the fleshy folds around them, were diamond hard. There was a stir among the junior aides around the table. This was the Warden they had heard about.

Oxley's face was shiny with sweat. "Considering the factors—"

"Get off the dime, Captain," Warden said curtly. "Yes or no? And, if no, how long will it be?"

Oxley licked suddenly dry lips. "No, it's not exactly ready now. But within three to six months—"

Warden ignored him and swung back to Cullinane. "Speaking of credibility, Admiral, since ARGUS will be ready in its own sweet time, I suggest we take up the next item of business—specifically, the *Alaska* and Operation Fire. I hope for the last time." Warden lowered his voice to a confidential level. "I don't have to tell you the President's rather interested in this one."

It was his turn to sweat now. Cullinane chose his words carefully. "I think we ought to reconsider the operation. There's no reason to doubt that the crews of our missile subs will follow through if they're given a launch order. They conduct regular drills on precisely this."

"That's the point," Warden said sardonically. "They're drills and everybody on board knows they're drills."

Cullinane could sense his own voice go flat. "That's not true, Mr. Warden. There have been a number of instances in which the captain didn't identify the drill as such."

Warden smiled slightly. "The world doesn't go to hell in a hand basket all at once, Admiral. You've lived long enough to know that. There's always a buildup. Without it, a man would have to be out of his mind to imagine that a launch order was anything but a drill, unannounced or not."

"I've heard this argument a dozen times," Pillsbury complained, "and it never leads anywhere."

"Like a little ol' houn' dog chasin' its tail," Warden agreed, smiling at his own deliberate lapse into the good-ol'-boy accent. The smile faded. "The Russians have done their studies and my own alma mater, the Yonkers Institute, recently released its study and, frankly, there's room for doubt. Missile submarines are a second-strike weapon. By the time they get their launch order there's no more war left to win. The only motive remaining to the crews would be one of revenge, and for some crews I don't think that would be enough."

"The crews have been trained—"

Warden interrupted, his eyes crystal. "To respond like Pavlov's dogs when they hear the bell? My objection, Admiral, is that I don't think they'll salivate on cue."

There was a shocked silence. Warden stood up and leaned his knuckles on the table, turning to glower at Cullinane.

"Those damn submarines aren't worth a fiddler's fuck if they have to launch a single missile, Admiral. We know that—what makes you think the crews don't? We've got twenty billion dollars' worth of hardware resting on the shaky premise that its mere existence guarantees it won't have to be used. Maybe you think that's a dandy way to run a railroad but I sure don't. I think we ought to firm up that premise. If it's going to work, fine. If it isn't—then I think we should know it."

"Even if we run the drill," Cullinane said, angry, "how will the Russians—"

Warden interrupted again, waving an arm at the corridor outside. "Are you really that naive, Admiral? You couldn't walk a stone's throw from this room without running into a Russian mole. And if it served our purposes, we could leak the results to the papers. Hell, the Department of Defense has been run by leaks for years—for example, every time your damned appropriations come up."

The silence was heavier this time and Pillsbury said thinly, "You're calling names, Mr. Warden. We're here to make a decision."

Warden shrugged and sat down. "The admiral still has his objections. We've gone over them before but I suppose we'll have to give him another hearing."

Chavez had warned Cullinane that he would be out of his class if he got into a fight with Warden. But it was too late to play it cool. He had his own friends on the Hill but you could use up an entire bank of goodwill rather quickly fighting men like Warden. And there was no way he could ask for outside help with this problem anyway.

For a moment he wondered if he wasn't being too hardnosed about this. He tried to imagine himself stationed on one of the new Trident submarines during the next war, not as an officer but simply as an enlisted man. The world outside had erupted and there was precious little left of the green earth and all that he loved. Knowing this, could he force himself to deliver the coup de grâce to a world near death simply for revenge? Simply because this was what he had been trained to do if the nation were attacked? It would be very easy to believe that a small enclave of murdering humanity surviving somewhere in the world was better than no humanity at all. But that was falling into Warden's hands. By doubting the system, he was agreeing that the system must be tested. And the dangers of *this* test, Operation Fire, were just too great.

He cleared his throat and spoke, ticking off the objections on his fingers. "One, it's risky politically and diplomatically. Two, we're playing with the lives of a submarine crew—perhaps indirectly, but playing with them nevertheless. Three, the gun is loaded." His voice thinned. "We're deliberately going to mislead the crew into thinking that a war is on and give them orders to launch four dummy missiles. Let's not forget that the other twenty warheads are live."

"I thought you were going to come up with something new, Admiral," Warden said with contempt. He held up his hand. "Do you mind? Of course it's risky politically and diplomatically. So are the near-rammings we talked about earlier, of which you seem to approve. As for the men in that submarine, they enlisted; they weren't drafted. They know damned well they run the risk of getting shot at. And finally . . ."

Warden paused, his hand still outstretched. "You, of all people, should appreciate the lethality of a Trident submarine, Admiral. There's even a formula for it, figuring the warhead yield in megatons and the accuracy in nautical miles. You take one Trident submarine loaded with twenty-four Trident missiles, each with seventeen seventy-five kiloton MARVS, and you wind up with a lethality for one submarine that you wouldn't believe.

Cullinane felt his face grow red. Warden was lecturing him. "I'm familiar with the figures. That's part of the point I'm trying to make—"

"The point *I'm* trying to make, Admiral, is that it would be foolhardy to take that much punch out of circulation, even for a short time. And I can tell you right now, the President wouldn't approve."

And that was the name of the game, Cullinane thought bitterly. "I'm sure you reminded the President that any submarine-based missile system is capable of operating independently of him or any commands from Washington? It's the only system that can, Mr. Warden, and if something went wrong with the drill, it just might." He paused, taking care to emphasize his words. "The President has no control over it, Mr. Warden," he repeated. "None whatsoever."

There was a nervous, almost hostile silence now. He had reminded them of something they didn't want to think about. And there was nobody present who was about to thank him.

"There's no way we can maintain constant communication with our submarines at patrol depth, Mr. Warden. Water is opaque to radio waves beyond a minimal depth. To receive, a submarine has to rise to a certain depth. To transmit, they have to be on the surface or send up a wire—an antenna, if you please. To be effective as a weapon, the crew has to have complete control of the nuclear devices on board." He let his words sink in for a moment. "Washington can command but it does not control, Mr. Warden. In the final analysis, it's the captain and his crew."

Warden looked shocked. "I can't believe you're saying this, Admiral. What you're implying is that our crews might be uncontrollable. I think that I and your compatriots here"—he waved his hand magnanimously at the others around the table—"have more faith in them than you do."

Then Warden dropped his mask of feigned outrage. His voice was tight. "The operation is necessary, Admiral. There are no ifs, ands, or buts. If the Russians doubt our determination to retaliate when attacked, then it's all over but the shouting. We not only have to prove it to ourselves, we have to prove it to them. Frankly, we don't have a choice."

There was a lengthening silence. Admiral Howland glanced around the table. "Mr. Pillsbury?"

Pillsbury hesitated, dabbed at his mouth with a handkerchief, and said in a firm voice, "I've been authorized by the Secretary to give State's approval."

Howland shrugged. "The President's for it and State's for it. I'm inclined to agree with them, Stew. I'm afraid you're outvoted." He turned his shadowed face to Warden. "Navy agrees that a credibility problem exists, Caleb, and that we should determine how the crews will actually respond."

"Or perhaps find a better solution," Warden said casually.

The decision made, Howland was all business. "Stew, you've gone ahead with the preparations?"

"Yes, sir," Cullinane said. "The *Alaska*'s been in Groton undergoing a retrofit. The Blue Crew, under Captain Renslow, manned her for her last patrol, so the Gold Crew, under Captain Harris, was due to take her out for the next one."

Warden frowned. "Why the Gold Crew? Seems to me that

since the Blue Crew was out last, they'd have the most recent experience on her."

Cullinane shook his head. "The Blue Crew is scattered for leave and further training. To call them back now would arouse too much suspicion." He hesitated. "Considering the psychological nature of the drill, I don't think that's advisable."

"Tha's right," Warden said brightly, relapsing into his good-'ol-boy role. "No sense arousin' suspicions. You real confident of this Captain Harris?"

"All my commanders are capable," Cullinane said. "Otherwise, they don't command my ships." He softened his voice, realizing how abrasive the last remark had sounded. "The modifications of the *Alaska* were completed a week ago. She puts to sea tomorrow."

Warden raised an eyebrow. "I've received no operation plan."

"None were distributed," Cullinane said grimly. "The President has one copy and the Secretary of Defense has one, with the third under lock and key in the CNO's office. If it should leak, not only would the operation be compromised, the diplomatic repercussions would be . . . unacceptable. Not my decision alone, Mr. Warden—State wouldn't have it any other way."

Warden looked as though his nose were out of joint and Cullinane felt better. This was one brouhaha that the sick old man who headed State would have to handle.

"The nature of the modifications of the *Alaska*?" Warden sounded sulky.

"Principally the installation of an automatic tape deck that will—in effect—substitute for the radio transmissions that the *Alaska* would normally receive the first ten days of patrol. When she rises to receive, the first incoming signal will trigger the tape deck. The tapes are programmed with a scenario of increasing crisis, leading the crew through a yellow, blue, and red alert to the final launch order." He hesitated, aware again of just how risky the plan was. "Only three men aboard will know it's a drill: Commander Harris, the captain; Lieutenant Commander van Meer, the exec; and Lieutenant Schulman, the medical officer."

Pillsbury looked baffled. "Why the medical officer?"

"In addition to being a qualified MD, he took his residency in psychiatry at Columbia. He's our observer—the man who will write the report we receive." He paused. "In the interests of objectivity, ordinarily he wouldn't know the nature of the drill. In this case it was deemed too dangerous for him not to."

"No other members of the crew know?"

Cullinane shook his head. "To the rest of the crew the drill will be reality. They'll be led to believe via the tapes that world tensions have escalated to the point of a nuclear exchange. And, finally, they'll be told to launch their missiles against prearranged targets in the Soviet Union."

"And the launch itself?" Warden asked with a faint smile.

Cullinane couldn't make up his mind whether Warden was enjoying his discomfiture at having to relate the details of a drill he didn't approve of, or whether the man loved the vicarious thrill of forcing a dress rehearsal of Armageddon. What was the word the Germans had coined? *Schadenfreude*—the joy of destruction.

"There'll be four launches down the Atlantic range. At the conclusion of the fourth launch the drill will be terminated and the *Alaska* will return to port for a debriefing of the crew."

There was another silence when he finished and he wondered if the gravity of the situation was sinking in. Some decisions were made in such a hurry that you didn't realize their importance. Well, if he hadn't done anything else, he had managed to get that much across.

The meeting started to break up and Cullinane handed his conference folder over to Lieutenant Chavez, who stowed it in the heavy leather briefcase chained to his wrist. They stood up to go and Cullinane thought wryly that he might have to find another aide—the young lieutenant towered a full head above him.

"Are all top-level conferences like this, sir?" Chavez asked, curious.

Cullinane shook his head. "No, occasionally I win one."

Warden met them at the door, all smiles, and, as usual, Cullinane was faintly surprised. Warden was not much taller than he was—a short, pudgy man with none of the air of the corporate bully that he projected at the conference table. He wondered for a moment if Warden had done any acting in college, then realized that projection and presence were tricks he had probably learned in the boardroom.

"What time will the *Alaska* put to sea, Admiral?"

Cullinane forced himself to sound pleasant. "She's at Charleston now. She'll slip anchor early tomorrow morning."

"Mind if I join you all in Flag Plot during the drill? I've heard a lot about that Buck Rogers Situation Room of yours."

Admiral Howland, at the door now, cut in. "Our pleasure, Caleb—I think it's the only spot in Washington you haven't seen."

Cullinane would have been happier if it had been a forced acceptance but Howland seemed genuinely pleased. The next chairman of the Joint Chiefs, he thought, even if Howland had to sacrifice the submarine service to get it. But he was being unfair again. What he desperately needed was to take a look at the world through the bottom of a martini glass.

A pat on the back from Howland, who was slipping through the door. "Don't worry, Stew. In ten days it'll all be over."

Warden was still standing belly to belly with him, the odor of after-shave losing the battle with the stink of perspiration. "You shouldn't take me so all-fired serious, Admiral—mah bark's a hell of a lot worse than mah bite." His face was sweating pure friendship. "We'll have dinnuh some night and have a meeting of the minds." A light tap on the arm. "I admire a fighter, Admiral. I truly do."

Then Warden's aides were pulling him away, leaving Cullinane and Chavez and Pillsbury alone at the door. Cullinane picked up his hat to go, then paused. Farther down the hall, there was the sudden sparkle of flashbulbs where a small circle of reporters had surrounded Warden.

"What's that all about?"

Pillsbury shook his head. "Among other things, probably the threat to religion in modern life. Funny how a man can talk so much about morality in public and be so slick at slitting your throat in private."

"I've been to four meetings with him and he still surprised me in there," Cullinane said, the resentment showing in his voice.

"Roughed you up a little, didn't he? Somebody should have told you he plays dirty."

Cullinane recalled Chavez's memo. "My own fault—somebody did."

"He was an honest-to-God poor Southern boy when he started," Pillsbury continued thoughtfully, watching Warden disappear down the hall. "Four years of Georgia Tech and a master's from Tulane added the polish—if that's what you call it." He nodded good-bye, took a few steps, then looked back. "I wouldn't believe that friendly malarkey if I were you, Admiral. He's out to get you—and he probably will."

Cullinane grimaced. "I wouldn't bet on it, either way." He returned the salute of the security guard and stepped out into the corridor, Chavez faithfully dogging his heels. He'd stop at Hogate's on the way back to the city; he really needed that martini.

Then, bleakly: Ten days and it would all be over. Ten days of increasing hell for the crew of the *Alaska* and ten days of having to live with his own conscience and growing anger.

An anger mixed with just a touch of . . . what?

3

IT WAS ONLY a matter of time before he killed her. . . .

Ernie Gradow blinked, confused and frightened, and stood stock-still for a moment, as if he were listening. Where had that come from? He shivered, then shook his head and finished drenching the charcoal in the barbecue pit with starter fluid. He lit it and stumped back to the card table set up under the elm tree a few feet away. Florence had piled the steaks on huge platters and Ernie did a quick count, then swore silently to himself. Dammit, there weren't going to be enough. Half the Gold Crew of the *Alaska* had shown up. Already he'd had to tap another keg of beer and that would be gone in an hour.

But the party was still a great idea, one of Florence's better ones—if only the steaks and the beer held out. There wasn't a cloud in the sky and the kids were screaming and shouting, running through the lawn sprinklers and tumbling into the wading pool. Most of the crew had stripped down to cutoffs and were gathered around the kegs of beer stacked under the back steps. Their wives and girlfriends were on the porch, catching up on the latest gossip, the sound of their giggling shimmering across the lawn like heat waves.

Great party, Ernie thought again. Even the Old Man and the exec had shown up, and when was the last time both of them had gone to the same blowout?

"How're they coming, Chief?" Lieutenant Tony Cermak waddled over to the card table and hefted one of the steaks approvingly. "Good two-pounder there—looks like Navy prime to me."

Ernie managed an uneasy smile. "Enjoy 'em, Lieutenant, I paid a fortune for them at the commissary."

"Just puttin' you on, ol' buddy." Cermak liked to think of himself as one of the boys and Ernie wished he wouldn't try; it embarrassed him.

There was a splash from the wading pool and they turned. Animal Meslinsky was being pulled out of the pool by Russo and Bailey, both of them doubled up with laughter. Even at a distance, Animal looked huge. Two hundred and fifty pounds of coal-miner muscle topped off by a face that would frighten a gorilla. His saving grace was that he had the most easygoing disposition of anybody on board.

Cermak turned back to Ernie. "Not sorry you'll be sitting this one out, are you, Chief?"

It was suddenly hotter under the tree than it was in the sun. If Cermak hung around any longer, he might see the boxes the steaks had come in with u.s.s. ALASKA stenciled right on top. "C'mon, Lieutenant," Ernie protested, "I didn't break my leg on purpose."

"That's *your* story." Cermak turned to look in the direction of the beer kegs. "I think Animal needs help with the booze."

Ernie wiped the sweat off his forehead and watched Cermak hurry away. The lieutenant wasn't a stickler but he sure as hell wouldn't cover if he knew about the steaks. . . .

"Great party, Chief."

Glenn Bailey was tall and thin, his New York–sharp features framed by a pair of horn-rimmed glasses. It made him look like a younger, skinnier version of that old-time movie actor, Ernie thought—Harold Lloyd, that was it. A bright kid with a big mouth that would probably get him into trouble someday.

He squinted and glanced at the far end of the yard again. Who the hell was in the pool now? "Yeah, it's not a bad blowout at all."

"Mind if a nuke helps a forward puke?"

Ernie laughed, handed over the fork, and stumped back to the shade. "Just make sure none of them get well done. . . . Christ, it's hot."

Bailey carefully tested the steaks and occasionally turned one. After the sixth he shot a cautious glance at Ernie. "I hear Olson's going to be chief of the boat."

Ernie glanced toward the back porch, where Ray Olson was talking to Florence. Olson seldom talked to women at all but he'd always had a thing about Florence.

"Only this once. He gets off when the *Alaska* returns."

"I didn't know he was a twenty-year man."

"He's smarter than some of us."

Bailey grinned. "Cut the shit, Chief—you wouldn't know what to do without the Navy."

Ernie took a gulp of beer. "Try me," he said, but there wasn't much force to his voice.

A sudden ripple of laughter rolled from the other end of the yard. Meslinsky had hoisted an almost empty keg and was letting the beer foam down his face and chest.

"They don't call him Animal for nothing," Ernie said with a combination of disgust and admiration. Another swallow of beer and a suspicious look at Bailey. "He really fell in the pool? He wasn't pushed?"

Bailey smothered a smile. "*I'll* never tell."

"Animal would make two of you, kid. Don't ever get him steamed."

"C'mon, Chief, he's a baby. You know that." Bailey turned the last of the steaks, then gave the fork back to Ernie and wiped his hands on his cutoffs. "Need more help, just whistle."

Why didn't everybody just go home and let him paint his boat? The goddamned party hadn't been his idea. . . .

Now, what the hell had made him think that? He was having a great time.

It was dusk when the party began to break up, leaving a small knot of die-hards around the last keg of beer: Cermak and Animal and Billy Russo and his date—where did the kid meet those knockouts, anyway?—and Costanza, the navigator, and his wife. Olson was still finding Florence fascinating and Edith Olson was doing a slow burn.

The Old Man came over to say good-bye. "Sorry you won't be going with us, Ernie. Olson tells me you're going to spend the next ninety days working on your boat."

Stephen Harris was the picture of a submarine captain: dark hair, stocky, a bachelor who had a way with women. He also had a knack for making the crew like him even though there was a hint of prep school and the Ivy League in his manner that sometimes seemed out of place aboard a submarine.

"It's my new baby, Captain—an eighteen-foot day sailer."

"I wondered what was keeping you out of trouble." A firm handshake and that Burt Reynolds smile, which Ernie always resented because he couldn't help reacting to it. "See you in three months, Ernie. Take care of yourself. We need you."

Ernie watched him walk to the gate and compared him to the exec, Mark van Meer, a tall, thin man with a floating Adam's apple and wire-rimmed glasses that seemed about to fall off the end of his nose. Harris was born to command. Van Meer, on the other hand, always seemed uncertain of his next move, as if he were never quite sure it was the right one.

He wondered what had been bothering van Meer that day. The exec had been unusually quiet and had left early, but in the hour or so he'd been there, he'd put away a respectable amount of beer. He'd left without staggering but it had been a close one.

Most of the crew had gone now and Ernie hobbled over to the empty beer kegs, where Olson and Meslinsky and a few other die-hards were trading sea stories for the benefit of Bailey and Russo, the radioman striker.

". . . so you take three of the Q-three cores and pressure-tape them together, then feed in a couple pounds of marshmallows, put some foil over the firing end, and hook up the other to a hundred pounds of air. Did you ever get hit with a nine-foot marshmallow?"

There was a roar of laughter, then Animal had drained the last of the beer and a glum Edith Olson had given the nod to her husband. Ernie lingered awhile at the gate, listening to the chatter and gossip fade as the last car drove away. Ninety days. He was sure as hell going to miss them. Tonight they'd fly down to Charleston and tomorrow they'd head out to sea.

Florence and the boys were already cleaning up the yard, picking up the empties from beneath the trees and bushes, and throwing the greasy paper plates on the fire in the barbecue pit. The plates blazed up, then Florence chased the kids to bed and she and Ernie were alone in the cool evening.

"The boys are really tired, Ernie. I'm sure they went right to sleep."

Why the hell didn't she go to bed? Why was she hinting around?

"I'll be right in, Flo," he said slowly. "I want to check the boat."

"Don't work too late," she said, disappointed, and disappeared inside. Ernie thumped out to the garage. He opened the door and flicked on the light. A sudden gust of wind made the overhead bulb sway slightly. Shadows chased themselves around the corners, then gradually settled down.

He closed the door behind him and stared proudly at the boat. It was a little blue beauty, gleaming in the yellow light. He opened a can of paint, then balanced himself on his crutches while he dunked the brush in the small vat of blue. She was a beauty, a real beauty.

He had forgotten the afternoon party already.

It was nearing ten o'clock; he'd been working for almost two hours. Another hour and he'd have finished the cabin, then he'd knock off. He wondered if an old Carson rerun was on the tube that night. Florence usually stayed up to watch the show but tonight he hoped that Florence had gone right to bed. He was too tired to make love to her. . . .

Christ, it was stuffy in the garage. But if he left the door open, some cat would sneak in and get paw marks all over the bright blue trim and he'd worked on the boat too long to allow that.

He hoisted himself out of the small cabin and carefully climbed down the ladder to the garage floor. Funny how things had gone downhill in one week. Nothing he did seemed to please Florence anymore. She especially hated the boat, had hated it since he had first laid down the keel in the garage.

It took time away from her; that was probably the reason. Tonight she'd even implied he would rather work on the boat than go to bed with her. Well, she might be right at that. . . .

He put the crutches under his arms and thumped over to the corner, then gingerly lowered himself to the floor and opened up the second can of paint. It was the same gorgeous shade of blue. Even in the overhead light of the garage it had a subtle sheen to it, a gleam.

Warm, really close . . . He pulled out a handkerchief and wiped his forehead. Odd how the shadows in the corners seemed to be crawling even though the overhead light was stationary. Then he caught his breath at a scurrying sound in the far end of the garage. Out of the corner of his eye he could see something run across the floor and disappear into a pile of rubbish against the opposite wall.

He pulled himself to his feet, stumped over to the wall, and swatted at the pile with a crutch. The litter of papers and cans clattered but nothing else moved. He stood there, holding his crutch and listening. For a moment he wasn't sure what he had heard or seen in the first place.

Goddamned rats . . .

He turned back to the boat, thinking he was tired and ought to go to bed. But he didn't want to go to bed with Florence. He was uncertain for a moment, then decided he would climb back up and finish the cabin. Might as well get it over with; it wouldn't take long. . . .

Eleven-thirty. He hadn't realized it was that late.

The shadows in the garage were moving again and Ernie blinked, trying to make then stand still. On top of everything else, he knew he was going to have nightmares again that night. He had been having them regularly the past week.

He glanced at his watch again. The sensible thing to do was to knock off and go to bed.

Which meant going to bed with Florence. She would probably complain about how he'd behaved at the party, then she'd get amorous and end up acting more like an elephant in heat than a woman wanting to make love. Even the thought turned his stomach.

Florence.

Forty years old and where the hell was he? Ernie thought savagely. Stuck with three kids and a mortgage and a fat shrew of a wife. Florence had finally succeeded in making him as unhappy as his old man had been. But maybe that's what she'd wanted to do all along. How did the insurance read, anyway?

He hobbled back to the can of paint and tamped the lid down with the end of his crutch. Many more years of this kind of life and something would go wrong with the ticker, sure as hell. It ran in the family; his old man had died of ticker trouble at the age of forty-nine and he was getting up there himself.

A nice Navy pension and she was young enough to marry again. . . . Oh, she was capable of it, all right; she had probably been planning it from the day they got married. Like most guys, he had been a pushover; he'd have done anything to get into her pants. . . .

A final look at the boat behind him and he limped over to the garage door, knocking over the empty paint can. The noise was

frighteningly loud and he stood there in confusion, trying to remember what he had been thinking about.

Florence—that was it.

He tipped the can upright with his foot, leaving a small trail
of blue on the concrete floor. Then he flicked off the light and
opened the garage door to look out at the night sky dotted with
stars. The dark bulk of the house loomed in front of him and he
stared at it for a long moment. There was a small light in the upper bedroom window.

Florence was waiting for him.

A bum leg and crutches and he'd have to climb the flight of
stairs to the second-floor bedroom. A little slip—or a little push—
and Florence would have the insurance and be free as a bird.
Maybe she'd even marry Olson. He'd always been hot for her. Olson would ditch Edith in a minute. . . .

He blinked and shook his head and stepped back into the garage, his right hand brushing a baseball bat leaning against the
wall. He cleared his throat. That's what he'd do. He'd call Flo out
to the garage and settle things once and for all. . . .

The third time he called her, the lights came on in the kitch-
en. Then she opened the screen door and stood on the steps,
clutching at her bathrobe.

"Ernie?"

"Out here, Flo."

She came slowly down the walk, feeling her way in the dark,
her bedroom slippers making shuffling sounds on the flagstones.
She hesitated a few steps away. "Ernie, is there something
wrong?"

In an oddly excited voice: "I need some help."

She came closer, apprehensive. "What's wrong with the
lights?" He didn't answer. A little squeak of hysteria edged into
her voice. "What's wrong with you, Ernie?"

She took one more step, craning her head to see into the
shadowed doorway, and he stepped out, swinging the bat.

She was still screaming when the lights started to go on next
door.

4

POLICE SERGEANT Herb Jeffries held the light steady and said, "Can you find the pressure points?" There was so much blood, he didn't see how Finley could manage.

A grunt. "Yeah, I think so." There was some feeble thrashing and a low moan from the woman lying on the wet flagstones. "For Christ's sake, when are the medics coming?"

"We only radioed in a few minutes ago."

"A little lower with the light, will ya?"

Jeffries knelt, looking at the woman clinically. She was still alive but just barely; whoever had worked her over had done a thorough job. Probably a set of fractured ribs, a broken arm, maybe a broken leg, blackened eyes, and a heavy bruise along the left side of the head that had to be the most serious injury. A bloody bat was lying next to her, its handle covered with prints. Whoever had used it on her had sure left a calling card.

Somewhere in the distance, there was the wail of sirens. Finley sighed with relief. "Go out in the street and hustle 'em back here, Herb."

When he got out front, the ambulance crew had already unloaded a gurney. By now a crowd of neighbors had gathered, their faces pale and waxen in the light from the streetlamps. Jeffries jerked a thumb at the sleepy medics. "In the back." They nodded and hurriedly pushed through. Another police car drove up and two more patrolmen got out. Four cars now.

He turned to the crowd, waving his flashlight. "Okay, folks, let's go to bed. You can read about it in the morning paper. C'mon, kids, past your bedtime."

The crowd slowly broke up, then the ambulance crew came out in a hurry, pushing the now-loaded gurney. The thing under the sheets had started to whimper and Jeffries thought of a dog he'd had that had been run over. It had made the same kind of noise, trying to pull its broken hindquarters across the street.

Adams was just putting his notebook away when Jeffries walked over. "What'd you get?" he asked.

"Standard stuff. It was probably the husband who assaulted her. Somebody thought he heard him calling her from the garage, where he'd been working on his boat. You check that out?"

Jeffries nodded. "Yeah, blue trim still wet, overhead light bulb still warm. That's what he'd been doing, all right."

"So she went out and *bam*, she almost bought it. Or maybe she did buy it. How'd Finley do?"

"He stopped the bleeding. The ambulance crew got here soon enough. Maybe that'll make the difference."

Adams yawned. "Hope so. They had three kids—all boys. The neighbors took 'em in for the night."

"He must've really hated her."

"Wrong. According to the neighbors, he was crazy about her. They never had a cross word and he couldn't keep his hands off her."

"Jealousy?"

"Doubt it. Neither one of them was a prize." A shrug. "I used to see these all the time in New York and I still don't have any answers."

Finley came around the corner of the house, the front of his uniform wet where he'd tried to hose off the blood. "Anybody search the house, Adams?"

"Simmons went through it fifteen minutes ago."

"He couldn't find lettuce in a salad. Why don't you guys take some lanterns and go through it again."

Adams hesitated. "The neighbors said his car's missing."

Finley sounded exasperated. "But nobody heard anyone drive away. We went through that. Maybe he didn't get his usual parking place on the street and had to park around the corner. Go through the house—and watch it; we got a nut."

They started in the basement, swearing quietly as they climbed down the creaky stairs. A stack of boxes looked like an ideal hiding place and Jeffries kicked at one of them to bring the pile down. A frightened cat and that was it. Another minute of looking and he knew instinctively that no one was there. The first floor was as empty as the basement, the darkened living room looking oddly museumlike as he flashed the light around. Then there was a sudden flare at the end of the room and he ducked, realizing a split second later that it was his flashlight reflecting off the television screen.

"Hey, look here." Adams was out in the kitchen and had opened the refrigerator door. Jeffries caught it immediately: the bags of ice, the huge mixing bowl of potato salad with only a spoonful or two left in the bottom. "They must have had a party."

Jeffries recalled the barbecue pit in the backyard. "Yeah, they did. Maybe he got loaded and somebody made a pass at his wife. That might've done it."

"Done *that*?"

The upstairs had a lived-in look, Jeffries decided. The fan in the bedroom window still whirring, the rumpled bedclothes, a toothpaste-splashed sink . . . He glanced at the bedtable. She had been waiting up for him. And he had called her out to the garage and tried to kill her.

Why, for God's sake?

He almost missed it on the way back down the stairs. The chair in the hallway, just before you came to the staircase. Coming up, he hadn't thought anything about it; they had three kids: You could have found a chair almost anyplace, including in the bathtub. He flashed his light around, then held it on the ceiling. The trapdoor leading to the attic. It was painted the same color as the ceiling but whoever had used it last hadn't centered it right and some of the natural wood was showing around two sides.

Bingo.

"You want to cover me, Adams?"

Adams glanced up at the ceiling. "Watch your head going through—if he's laying for you, that's when you'll get it."

Jeffries stepped on the chair, then suddenly pushed the trapdoor back and muscled up into the attic, scrambling to get his shoulders through so he could use his gun.

Then he was in and crouching on the floor, moving his light frantically around the low room, the beam flashing past the batts of insulation tacked between the studs and finally resting on a pile of suitcases and wicker trunks at the far end. He knelt there for a moment, listening. The sound of crickets and the murmur of the police radios in the patrol cars outside.

And, inside the musty attic, the sound of somebody breathing hard.

He walked toward the trunks, the flashlight in his left hand and his police special in the right. Behind him, he could hear Adams hoisting himself through the trapdoor.

"Okay, c'mon out, hands above your head."

Even though he was prepared for it, he was still taken by surprise.

There was the scraping sound of a trunk being pushed aside and suddenly a pudgy little man was rushing at him, waving a tire iron high above his head. He was stark naked, his face and hands smeared with dried blood.

His eyes, Jeffries thought, were as empty as any he had ever seen.

5

THE TRUCK SEEMED to roar out of nowhere and Captain Allard Renslow yanked hard on the steering wheel of his Buick, fishtailing along a hundred yards of shoulder before he could get the car back onto the highway. *Goddammit*, the red-necks didn't know how to drive.... He swore again at a red Audi that cut him off, then fumbled out a cigarette to soothe his nerves. The day was really getting off to a lousy start. First, the early-morning simmer-and-sulk session with Elizabeth and then some cracker trying to cream him with a semi.

He was still stewing when he bumped over the rusty railroad tracks at the south gate of Electric Boat. It was barely eight o'clock but the nearby yards were already filling up with men in oil-smeared overalls and hard hats. A hundred feet away, yellow forklifts were clattering down the dusty service roads, an occasional harsh clang of their reverse bells warning when they had dropped a load and had to back up into the right-of-way. In the distance there was the steady burp of a rivet gun and the warning buzzer of a traveling crane while over all was the ever-present hum of the yards: the stutter of pneumatic hammers, the harsh whir of grinders, the hiss of air hoses, shouted curses and conversations, and, farther off, the whistles of boats on the Thames.

Behind the dirty walls of the trade sheds, Renslow could see the roofs of some of the storage and transportation warehouses, their outlines fogged by the morning mists rising from the river. Electric Boat always reminded him of some of the smaller steel mills around Pittsburgh and he recalled one summer when he had worked as a boilermaker's assistant. He smiled, remembering a teenage Allard Renslow hiding behind the boilermakers' shed on Monday mornings so he wouldn't have to buck rivets for the

weekend drunks, still bleary-eyed and somewhat uncertain in
their aim with a sledge.

"Where's your badge, buddy?"

Renslow flipped open his sport coat and was waved through
the gate. He turned right and drove slowly down the service road,
past the machine shops and the toolsheds, the freight cars on
weed-choked sidings and the storage area for Port-O-Sans, the
portable toilets, and past innumerable rusting fifty-five-gallon
drums containing rough castings ready to be machined, nuts and
bolts, or just oil-drenched metal scrap.

Then he was on the riverfront road, driving north past the
graving docks and the Nuclear Repair Facility. He parked in front
of the yard office and got out, standing for a moment in the warm
sun, enjoying the smell of the river laced with the acrid odor of
welders' torches.

There were days when he regretted ever having left the mills.
Pittsburgh had been home, more than any other city since. But
life at the Naval Academy had changed all of that and now there
were two worlds in which he didn't quite fit. Who was it who said
you couldn't go home again?

Donaldson, the yard super who had been in charge of the
work on the *Alaska*, had his offices in the battered wooden annex
at the rear of the yard building. Once inside, Renslow could hear
his voice booming over the partitions that separated his cubby-
hole from the others. "Dammit, I want it *now* and I want *you* in my
office in ten minutes. Now, snap it up."

Renslow pushed through the door just as Donaldson
slammed down the phone. Burly-shouldered and fiftyish, Donaldson had once worked in the Pittsburgh mills, too, and considered
Renslow his partner in a two-man plot against the inequities of
both Electric Boat and the Navy. An occasional after-hours drink
had cemented a casual friendship.

He stood up, smiling, and thrust out a thick-fingered hand,
the black hairs on back as thick as bristles. "When did you get in
from Charleston?"

Renslow shook hands, winced, and eased his own slight
frame into a nearby chair. "Late last night. We finished loading
the birds yesterday afternoon."

"Why the hell didn't you stick around another day? I hear it's
a pretty town this time of year."

Renslow was mock-serious. "I had to come back and check up on you guys."

Donaldson rolled his eyes. "Check up, Jesus . . . How's it feel to be back from patrol?"

"Just like it did the last time. You get self-conscious because you discover you're pasty-white compared to anybody else. If the kids have the sniffles you immediately come down with pneumonia. Anytime it's above seventy-two degrees you burn up; anytime it's below, you freeze to death." Renslow shrugged. "Takes time to adjust."

"I work on the bastards but you couldn't get me to go on a patrol for all the tea in you-know-where." A heavy wink. "You and Betty getting reacquainted?"

Renslow forced a smile. "Elizabeth is fine. She wants you and Anne to come over for a drink some night."

Donaldson looked embarrassed. "She'd really hate me if I called her Betty, huh?"

Renslow shook his head. "She'd think it was cute. She only hates it when *I* call her that. How were things with the *Alaska*?"

"Piece of cake." Donaldson fished in his out box for a thick folder and shoved it across the desk at Renslow. "Here're the work sheets. I checked and initialed them as we went along." He stood up and glanced over the top of the partition. "Use the office at the end of the hall. I'll tell the switchboard you're here." He looked at Renslow, suddenly curious. "How come you get stuck with all the paperwork? Why don't they send over a yeoman or something?"

"Because I'm the guy responsible, Jerry. The *Alaska* belongs to me as much as it does to Harris and when he brings her back, then it's my turn to live with the mistakes you guys make."

"Mistakes, my ass." The phone rang and Donaldson reached for it, waving Renslow out of his office. "Any problems, just yell."

Renslow picked up the folder and walked to the last office on the floor, one with a grimy window overlooking the yard and the river. He worked at the lock a moment, then yanked the window open and stood staring at the water and the huge bulk of another Trident looming over the ways. Maybe when he was through here, he and Elizabeth could visit her parents in Virginia. A week away would do her good. Then he thought that it probably wouldn't do any good at all, that whatever was wrong with their marriage was terminal. . . .

He sat down and opened the file folder. At least two hundred pages of forms covering everything that had been done to the *Alaska* during the two-week retrofit. And, God, how he hated paperwork . . .

He sat there for a minute fingering the sheets, then decided to proceed day by day on the job orders, checking the numbers against his own on-board inspection notes. He took a file from his briefcase and set it on one side of the desk, then placed the Electric Boat file on the other side. Mix and match. Two, maybe three days of work. But first he'd have to make sure all the EB dates were sequential. . . .

By noon he was leaning back in his chair, puzzled. Everything seemed in order except for one not-so-minor detail. Electric Boat had no forms for Tuesday, June 16. He drummed his fingers on his desk for a moment, then placed the papers in the folder and walked back to Donaldson's office. Donaldson was leaning over a drawing table against the far wall, unrolling a set of Ozalid white prints still reeking of ammonia. He looked up, surprised, when Renslow entered. "You through already?"

"Got a problem." Renslow spread the papers out on Donaldson's desk and pointed an accusing finger at two sheets. "The last of the fifteenth and the first of the seventeenth. What the hell happened on Tuesday, the sixteenth?"

Donaldson frowned. "Damned if I know." He flipped through a daily reminder jammed with notes, then hesitated. "Tuesday. They pulled me off for a rush job on the *Jacksonville*."

"Aw, c'mon, Jerry—didn't anybody cover? They must've had somebody there signing out the job."

"Lemme check." Donaldson dialed a number, then said sharply, "Joe, look up the flow chart on the *Alaska* for Tuesday, the sixteenth. What'd they do?" He tapped a pencil against his teeth for a moment, then looked surprised. "That all? Yeah, I get the picture." He hung up, looking relieved. "I was right. I wouldn't have forgotten it if it had been important. Routine housekeeping. That's what the man says."

Renslow looked at him blankly. "That's hard to believe; we were crowding the calendar as it was."

"Believe it. Maybe they had a delivery foul-up so they went in with a housekeeping crew. It happens all the time. The welders can't work until the metal cleaners get through and the grinders come before the cleaners and if they're hung up then so are the welders. You follow me? We got a union shop here, Commander, and don't you forget it." He waved a paw dismissively and flipped the pages of the reminder back to the current date. "What are you and Betty doing for dinner tonight?"

Renslow hit his head. "Christ, I almost forgot—going to dinner with Harris and some girl from a Washington embassy."

Donaldson looked disapproving. "He's getting a little old for that, isn't he? Besides, you don't get to be admiral by chasing the embassy whores. What about later on?"

"No dice—have to take Harris and van Meer to the airport at one in the morning."

"You're all heart, aren'tcha? How about saving us a spot on your dance card for next week?" He stood up and stretched. "Incidentally, the Groton Motor Inn has a new menu and a new chef. And speaking of food, it's time for lunch. Want to join me? On the company?"

After lunch Renslow leafed through the work sheets once more, slowly reading the pages and checking them against his own notes. The third time that he found himself turning back to the missing day, he paused, the seeds of suspicion growing in his mind. Donaldson lived with his jobs; he shouldn't have had to check the calendar to find out what they'd done that day. And nothing was so unimportant that he would forget it, not even a routine housekeeping job. Not when it had been within the last week or two.

Except, of course, that Donaldson wasn't that good an actor and it would be easy enough to check if he had been called in on the *Jacksonville.*

He was chasing his tail, Renslow thought. He took an address book out of his coat pocket and thumbed through the pages. Maybe nobody from the yard except a housekeeping crew had been aboard the *Alaska* but somebody from the Gold Crew sure as hell must have been.

His hand hovered over the phone. He could call Harris. Then: To hell with Harris. Some of the junior officers must have been poking around the boat that day and there would have been the regular work details. The IC electricians would have been crawling through her for sure. . . .

An hour later, Renslow tilted his chair back on its legs and stared out the window at the river and the skeleton of the newest Trident, huge against the skyline.

According to Donaldson, nobody from the yard had been on board the *Alaska* that Tuesday except the housekeeping crew—despite the fact that their retrofit had had a priority. Furthermore, nobody from the Gold Crew, so far as he could check, had been aboard her, either.

And that was flatly impossible.

6

"ONE MORE DRINK and you won't be able to walk out of here."

Mark van Meer swirled the Scotch in his glass, squinted through it at one of the dining-room chandeliers, then put the tumbler back on the table. "It shows that much?"

Cheryl Leary nodded. "It shows."

Well, it ought to, van Meer thought, slightly fuzzy-headed. He had been drinking steadily most of the afternoon to dull a series of anxiety attacks that not even his Equavil tablets had been able to touch. He glanced up at Cheryl, who was pointedly ignoring him and studying the other diners in the room. He knew she was more concerned than she looked but nobody loves a lush and that's what he had been turning into lately. He started to feel maudlin. Their last dinner together before he flew to Charleston to catch the *Alaska* and he was going to screw it up, sure as hell.

He fumbled with the menu, glancing without interest at the list of entrées. He wasn't particularly hungry but, then, he hadn't been particularly hungry all day, just particularly thirsty. Then he caught himself wishing they had gone somewhere else for supper, maybe even driven up to New Haven or Hartford. The dining room at the Groton Motor Inn was nicely done in dark-wood paneling with a heavy-beamed ceiling and thick carpeting but there was still something about it that reminded him of the Navy. And God would forgive him, but he'd had enough of the Navy.

He closed the menu and shoved it away from him. "You've eaten here before. What's good?"

"David used to like the stuffed jumbo shrimp."

For a moment he wondered if she was trying to get even because he had shown up at her apartment drunk. Shortly after they had met, they had made a pact. He wouldn't mention Maggie if she never mentioned David. It hadn't been a matter of jealousy, just acknowledgment that at one time each had meant too much to the other and neither of them could handle the separation yet.

She suddenly realized she had broken their agreement. She reached over and touched his hand. "How long do you think you'll be gone?"

That was one of the things he wanted to talk about. To hell with the restaurant; what he really wanted to do was sit in her living room clutching a bottle with both hands and talk his heart out to somebody who was interested enough to listen.

"Ninety days," he lied without hesitation. "It'll give you that much longer to make up your mind." He had meant to speak lightly but hadn't and he thought once again, Christ, I'm going to screw up the whole evening.

She was absorbed in her salad for a moment, then: "You don't need another wife, Mark. Not when you still can't forget the first."

He sobered a little. "Low blow, Cheryl."

Another soft touch on the hand. "I don't mean it that way at all. Maybe what I'm trying to say is that you're too nice a person."

"You mean it's too soon for you."

Her face was shadowed. "Perhaps."

It wasn't what either one of them had wanted to say. He wondered again if they had hit it off in the first place for the wrong reasons: He had lost Maggie in a plane accident and Lieutenant David Leary had been caught in an undertow off a Spanish beach. Both tragedies had happened about the same time.

Or maybe it was something more than that. Like what kind of man had David Leary been and just how did Mark van Meer stack up against him?

His hand drifted over to the glass of Scotch and Cheryl said quietly, "I'm not nagging but I'd like you to be able to at least kiss me good-bye." She glanced at her watch. "We don't even have that much of the night left. When do they pick you up?"

"Renslow said midnight."

"That doesn't give us much time."

Time enough, he thought, to say what was on his mind. And also time enough for him to ruin an evening . . .

The waitress came with the entrées and van Meer discovered he had an appetite after all. Surprisingly, the shrimp were of excellent quality. He was on his third when Cheryl glanced at the entrance of the dining room and said, "Speak of the devil . . ."

Van Meer looked in that direction. Renslow and Harris, both of them in civvies. He recognized Renslow's wife, Elizabeth—a tall, slender woman with a deep tan and sun-bleached hair. The woman with Harris he had never seen before. She was a small, delicate-featured woman, faintly exotic in the way she dressed. Chances were ten to one her father held a diplomatic passport.

Cheryl said softly, "She's very striking."

"Did you ever want to be a woman like that?" he suddenly asked.

"That's not a casual question, is it?"

"I'm serious."

She went back to cutting her shrimp. "The answer is no. I'll admit to a certain curiosity but I'm quite satisfied being myself." Later, over coffee, she said, "I'm curious about Captain Harris. You never talk much about him."

He glanced over at the table where Renslow and Harris were sitting. Harris was husky, with black hair and mustache and a narrow, ascetic face. Except for the shorter hair, he was a double for a photograph van Meer had once seen of John Wilkes Booth.

Allard Renslow wasn't as tall as Harris and on the slender side, a man who might have been a diver or a gymnast in college. Reddish-brown hair, craggy features. Not what you would call handsome, not in the way Harris was. Self-confident, competent, not as formal as Harris, more of a tendency to bull his way through . . .

There was something about Renslow and Harris that made him want to compare himself to them and when he did, he found himself wanting. In one sense, he had been through more than both of them put together—and maybe that was the difference. He knew exactly how weak he was, not only physically but psychologically.

Neither Harris nor Renslow had really been tested yet. What galled him was that he knew instinctively both would come out on top.

"Care to let me in on it?"

He drained the tumbler and started to signal the waitress for another. Cheryl caught his hand and he shook it off in annoyance. "For God's sake, I know my limit."

She shrugged. "Alcohol reacts with the Equavil. You know that."

It took him a moment to calm down, then: "Stephen Poindexter Harris. Patrician. Old money, one of Massachusetts' leading families. Appointed to the Academy because of family background and connections. He had enough generals and admirals in his family tree to staff an entire war, both sides. But he really didn't need pull; he was honor man in his class."

She studied the far table. "I know Al, but not really well. From what he's said, I assume he came up the hard way."

"You're right. Comes from a blue-collar family in Pittsburgh; his father was an industrial engineer for one of the steel mills. He's hardly what you'd call a sophisticate. The tea dances at the Academy never took."

"Honor man?"

"No, but he did all right."

She was suddenly curious. "How come you know all this?"

"I was in the same class. Old four-eyes van Meer, the class historian."

Again that somewhat hidden, speculative look in her eyes and once more he wondered how he was stacking up against her memories of David Leary. He had a sudden image of himself at six two, a hundred and fifty pounds, beanpole-thin, with a weak chin, and pale-blue eyes hiding behind wire-rimmed glasses. Another minority heard from: the ectomorphic scholar.

"You and Harris don't get along, do you?" she asked quietly.

"No, we don't." Then he clammed up. It was half an hour too soon and hardly the right place. He shot Cheryl a covert glance, wondering if she was sorry she had brought the subject up, but she was still looking at the far table. Light laughter floated over to them.

"They certainly seem like friends."

He fumbled out a cigarette. "You're wrong. They hate each other's guts."

She glanced up at him, surprised by his sudden vehemence. "Why?"

He shrugged. "It's not important; it's just gossip."

"I used to be a Navy wife, remember?"

He ordered an after-dinner liqueur, toying with it when it finally came. "I don't think Harris hates Renslow," he said. "I don't think he hates or loves or fears or despises anybody. He's above most emotions. Al Renslow would like to be but isn't."

"So Al hates Harris? There's got to be a reason."

"There is. Two of them. The first is that Harris once had an affair with Elizabeth Renslow; he went with her before Renslow did."

She looked surprised. "Al never talked about it." She went back to picking at the remains of her shrimp. "I suppose Elizabeth didn't realize it was the hunt and not the quarry that moved your Captain Harris. When she figured it out, she married Al out of spite and made sure he never forgave Harris for spoiling the merchandise."

She held out her glass for more wine. "That's a lot more believable in a television soap opera than it is in real life."

"But you're right on—that's the story." Then: "The submarine Navy's a pretty small world, Cheryl. Everybody knows."

"What's the other reason?"

"Renslow was accused of cheating at the Academy; Harris testified in his behalf."

She frowned, puzzled. "Sounds noble enough."

The sweetness of the liqueur wasn't sitting well; van Meer suddenly wanted to get out of there, to go to her place and take off his shoes and loosen his tie. He was sick to death of eating in a dining room with a hundred other Navy men and their dates. And he was bored with talking about Renslow and Harris.

"The hearing was behind closed doors and nobody talked after that. The charges were dismissed."

"Because he was innocent or because Harris testified?"

"God only knows," he muttered. "I sure don't." He stood up, pulled a roll of bills from his pocket, and peeled some off.

Cheryl glanced up at him, worried. "You feel all right?"

"I've felt better." Then, sarcastically: "You're absolutely right, Cheryl—I've had too much to drink and I can't hold it. They ought to cashier me from the Navy for that reason alone." He was talking too loud and some of the diners at nearby tables were glancing his way. He nodded at the table where Renslow and Harris were eating, then Cheryl grabbed his arm and steered him out of the dining room.

Outside, he took a deep breath of the cool night air and tried to get his eyes to focus. It was chilly and the sweat on his forehead turned clammy. He started to shiver.

"You'll have to drive."

"The boy's gone to get the car," she said quietly. "It'll be here in a minute."

"You know what I want?" he suddenly asked.

"I've been wondering most of the evening."

He grinned. "Another drink."

She had changed into a nightgown, pink and frilly and revealing. For a moment van Meer was torn between a desire to talk to her and a desire to take her to bed. There wouldn't be time enough for both. She was thirty and maybe ten pounds overweight but she had the muscle tone of an active woman and she was tall enough to carry the extra poundage. It made for a sensuous figure rather than an athletic one, he decided. With her dark-blond hair and wide cheekbones, she was actually an earth-mother type. The sort of woman you could lose yourself in, one who was comfortable and deliberate in her lovemaking and had an intuitive knowledge of the needs and passions of men.

Or at least of his needs and passions.

He poured himself another drink from the bottle on the sideboard and slouched back to the sofa, watching her as she stacked his briefcase and small overnight bag near the front door.

"When are you going to marry me, Cheryl?"

"We've been through that. Did you pack your pills?"

"Yes, I packed my goddamned pills," he mimicked. He took a sip of the Scotch, then put the glass on the table and made an exaggerated show of pushing it away from him. He had reached the liquid limit; one more swallow and he'd be sick all the way to Charleston.

"You know you're going to hate yourself in the morning."

"Did you hear me?" he said truculently. "I was talking about marriage."

She walked over and sat next to him on the couch, tucking her feet beneath her. "I heard you. And someday I might be very interested—when I'm sure I'll be something more than just an echo of your first wife."

He could feel the emotions start to bubble up, and spent a

minute fighting them. "I don't have to forget Maggie to remember you."

"That's not what I meant. It's when you quit blaming yourself for . . . for what happened."

Low blow again, he thought. But, no, not really. She was trying to open him up, to lance the boil. He held his head with his hands and leaned his elbows on his knees. Now was the time and now was the place and he could feel the sweat start on his forehead.

She put a hand on his shoulder, watching him with a mixture of compassion and reserve. "If you want to talk, Van, I'm certainly willing to listen."

Friends had said that before and so had lovers and he had come to distrust the invitation. But, with the exception of Maggie, nobody had ever been as close to him as Cheryl.

He took a deep breath and reached for the Scotch again. "I'm no longer fit for command," he said. "If I ever was."

Her face was expressionless and he didn't know whether she felt surprise or shock or disgust or understanding. Maybe she thought he was just a maudlin drunk. But it was too late for him to stop; the flood of words was already forming in his mind. He could no longer help himself and it didn't matter whether it was a question of security or not. He was going to say far more than he should and far more than Cheryl wanted to hear.

He was even going to tell her about Operation Fire.

7

"Y OU'RE PRETTY QUIET tonight," Renslow said.

Harris shifted in the backseat, turning his face away from the window. "You've got something against silence?"

"Just trying to make conversation. You were pretty talkative at the inn." He shoved a sleepy van Meer back onto his side of the seat. "I know what happened to Van but what happened to you? Yvonne go back to Latvia?"

He meant the question to sound funny and was shocked when it came out sour.

"Martinique," Harris said curtly. "The date was an official arrangement with the State Department."

You can't have them all, Renslow thought. Then: How old was Harris now? Thirty-six? Thirty-seven? He was still a handsome man but the crow's-feet were starting to show around his eyes and five miles of jogging and a workout in the squash court every day wouldn't hold off time indefinitely. So far, Annapolis' number-one stud had won all the battles but eventually he was going to lose the war.

"Good-looking woman," Renslow said, swinging the car onto the airport cutoff. "She'll make somebody a fine wife." Then he realized that could be taken the wrong way, too.

"I'm sorry Elizabeth couldn't make it to the airport," Harris said, distant.

"She didn't want to come along. We're not seeing eye to eye these days—as you probably know." Navy wives must have passed along the gossip, he thought. When you married Navy, you moved into a glass house.

"She seemed all right at dinner."

"That's because you were there." Then he swore silently at himself. Why the hell couldn't he keep his mouth shut? Why was he always throwing down the gauntlet? Elizabeth and Harris had been a number years ago; that was ancient history. Or was it?

"Keep it light, Al." Harris sounded tired.

Van Meer suddenly stirred. "Are we there yet?"

"Just a few minutes more."

When he had seen van Meer at the inn, he had looked a little unsteady on his feet. Now Renslow knew why. He must have been drinking all day. He frowned, vaguely troubled. Van Meer hadn't been the same since Maggie's death.

The lights of the small terminal building were showing in the distance now. In the backseat Harris yawned and said, "The plane won't be leaving for half an hour, Al. You don't have to stick around. I imagine Elizabeth is waiting up."

Elizabeth hadn't waited up in years, Renslow thought. He pulled into the airport parking lot and said, "I'll help you with your bags." Harris started to object but he was already out of the car, searching for the keys to open the trunk.

Harris helped van Meer out and turned to Renslow. "Thanks for the lift." A polite handshake and a glimpse of an expressionless face half hidden by his cap, then Harris was striding toward the terminal building. Renslow watched him go. He was never sure if Harris gave a damn whether he lived or died. Maybe that was part of his mystique of leadership. Or maybe, he thought uneasily, it was just that he really wanted Harris to care, one way or the other.

They were almost to the doors when Renslow said, "One thing, Steve." Harris turned. "I was going through the work sheets for the retrofit and Electric Boat screwed up. Donaldson told me they didn't do any work on the sixteenth, that nobody was on board except a cleaning crew."

He hadn't intended to mention it, but Harris ought to know. Harris froze for a second, then shrugged. "If that's what Donaldson told you, then that's what happened."

Renslow cocked his head. "It doesn't make sense. We were on priority."

"Look, I don't know what the hell happened," Harris said, angry for the first time that night. "I wasn't there. Some secretary must have screwed up."

He turned on his heel and Renslow said quietly, "Good luck on patrol."

Van Meer came to life then, still half drunk. "Brother, are we gonna need it."

"Shut up, Van," Harris said sharply, then they disappeared through the doors. Renslow stared after them, puzzled.

When Harris had told him to shut up, van Meer had looked both angry and afraid, as if Harris were reprimanding him for something he shouldn't have said.

But what the hell had van Meer said?

Renslow drove back to Groton, his mind filled with the memories of an earlier argument with Elizabeth. He could go home but he really wasn't that sleepy and if Elizabeth were still awake, they'd probably pick up where they had left off. The alternative was to stop at the inn for a drink but he was in no mood for late-night drunks and he hated to drink alone.

He glanced at his watch. One o'clock. There was a chance Cheryl was still up and if she were, maybe he could beg a cup of coffee and talk to her for a while. He hadn't dropped by for a long time, even though he'd been a good friend of David's. He'd felt guilty about it but neither he nor Cheryl had wanted van Meer to get the wrong idea. . . .

There was a light on and he parked and rang the doorbell. She answered, wearing a battered green bathrobe pulled tight around her waist. There was a touch of something pink beneath it and he guessed that she had dressed for the occasion when Van was there.

"I saw the light. Glad I didn't wake you."

She grabbed his arm and pulled him inside. "God, it's great to see you. Come on in. You're just in time for *Annie Hall*."

"I've seen it. Three times. Hated it; loved her."

"Drink? Coffee?"

"Coffee would be fine." He followed her into the kitchen and sat down at the table in the breakfast nook, watching her as she measured out the coffee and put the pot on to brew. Even late at night, walking around the kitchen in worn mules and a ragged bathrobe, she was a good-looking woman. She was heavier than he liked but, on the other hand, she didn't have Elizabeth's air of fragility, either. And he felt at ease with her.

She sat down opposite him and closed her eyes. "Ten seconds of silence," she pleaded, "and I'll be right with you." After a moment she sighed, opened her eyes, and said, "I don't think I can ever get used to this."

"Get used to what?"

"Saying good-bye forever twice a year."

"You used to do it with David."

She shook her head. "No, my dear, airedales lead a far different life than submariners do. Believe me." A timer announced the coffee was ready and she filled two mugs, then rummaged in the refrigerator for milk. "You lose your home?"

"Elizabeth and I have been locking horns."

She raised an eyebrow. "You've got a girlfriend?"

He grinned. "Pow, right to the point. But you lose—no outside interests."

"Then she's got a boyfriend."

"Elizabeth?"

"She's a very attractive woman. I'm sure she's had her offers." She laughed at the expression on his face. "Oh, come on, now. Don't look so gloomy. I didn't mean it. Tell Sister Cheryl your problem."

He sipped at his coffee, not smiling. "It's serious."

She leaned back in the booth, making herself comfortable, her mood changing subtly to fit his. "You're among friends. You know that."

Now that he had the chance, he found it difficult to find the words. "We argue," he said slowly. "Almost all the time. Especially in the past six months."

Casually: "Why?"

"A standard reason—I want children, she doesn't. And she's in her middle thirties now. If she doesn't have them soon, the argument becomes academic."

"She didn't tell you how she felt about children before you married her?"

He shrugged. "I come from a background where having kids is one of the reasons you get married. I assumed everybody else felt the same way."

She was silent for a moment. "That's only part of the problem, isn't it?"

He was getting in deeper than he had intended; she was too receptive, too open, too much of a good listener. He suddenly felt embarrassed. "Look, I didn't come here to dump on you." He held up his cup, deliberately breaking the mood. "Any more coffee?" Then, somewhat reluctantly: "How are things with you and Van?"

The barest suggestion of a shadow fluttered across her face. "I don't think he can shake his feelings about Maggie."

"Did you expect him to?"

She shook her head. "I phrased it badly. Maybe I should have said he's never going to shake his feelings about himself."

"The accident?"

"He's never forgiven himself."

"But it wasn't his fault."

"Try to convince him of that. He won't accept it. He'll go on blaming himself for the rest of his life." Then, half angry: "Why do people talk about things at night that they'd never mention in the morning?"

Renslow smiled cynically. "So they can go to bed and forget them before they wake up." He finished his coffee, then excused himself and headed for the bathroom. That was another thing you could say for Cheryl, he thought a moment later—she didn't use the shower rod as a clothesline. He rinsed his hands in the sink, and wondered if she had any aspirin in the medicine cabinet. He opened the door and started to poke around among the small bottles lining the shelves. Nobody ever threw away a prescription, he mused. The average American medicine cabinet held enough drugs to cure a small town of plague.

He knocked a bottle off the shelf and grabbed it, then, curious, read the label. Equavil—whatever that was—prescribed by a Dr. Rosenberg for van Meer. He felt vaguely embarrassed, remembering the time at a married friend's house when he had wanted aspirin and run across the familiar green bottle of A-200. The small tin of Bayer was hiding behind a bottle of mouthwash. He spent a moment prying it open, then shook out several of the tablets.

Back in the kitchen, Cheryl had refilled his cup. He took a sip to wash down the aspirin. Still thinking of van Meer, he said, "Maybe you should try to get Van out more—get his mind off himself."

He was ready to go and she got up to walk him to the door, showing a flash of firm, shaved leg.

"Already thought of that—we're going to take a trip to New

Orleans when he gets back, bum around the French Quarter for three or four days. And I told him I'd get tickets for *Hi, Lily* and we'd make a long weekend of it in New York. For once, he thought it was a great idea."

She gave him a thoughtful look at the door. "You really wanted to talk more about Elizabeth, didn't you?"

"I did and I didn't—you've got your own problems; you don't need mine, too." He shrugged. "Maybe some night we'll both let our hair down."

She laughed. "Sure. Come earlier, stay later."

He kissed her lightly on the forehead. "You're a sweetheart. You also make great coffee."

In the car, he glanced back and saw her framed in the yellow rectangle of the door. She was the best thing that had ever happened to van Meer. And she had come along at just the right time.

It wasn't until he was almost home that he remembered something she'd said that had bothered him. He had spent most of Sunday browsing through the New York *Times*, and in the entertainment section he had seen the ad for *Hi, Lily* with a LAST THREE WEEKS notice emblazoned across it. Cheryl must have been thinking of something else. She knew Van wouldn't be back for three months . . . .

Lucky bastard, he thought. Cheryl was a real winner.

Wednesday, June 24

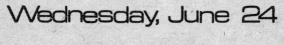

DAY ONE

8

THE CAB DROPPED them off at the main gate to the Charleston Naval Shipyard. Harris gave the cabbie a bill and waved him off and van Meer thought fuzzily, Who's he trying to impress? He struggled out of the cab, winced at the bright lights around the main gate and in the shipyard beyond, then shivered as the chill night air hit him. The nausea he had felt during the short plane ride had left him but now he was suddenly conscious of how tired he was. He couldn't hold his liquor. How many times had Cheryl told him that?

He took a deep breath of air and shook his head, trying to clear it. The air itself smelled of the ocean, laced with the heavy odors of diesel oil and rotting fish. It was a smell he had grown to love and for just a moment he thought of how much he was going to miss it during patrol.

"Let's go," Harris said curtly. "We can't stand here all night."

Van Meer drew himself up and grunted, "After you." Did Harris ever get drunk? he wondered sullenly. Come to think of it, he'd never seen him drunk, had never seen him out of control. When Harris was fifty, they'd probably be calling him Old Iron Pants.

He blinked at the lights, took another deep breath of decaying sea bass and bunker oil, then followed Harris through the gate, returning the salute of the marine guard as he entered. There was a small guardhouse twenty feet beyond the gate and, just behind that, a long wooden bench and lean-to that served as the base's bus shelter.

Some liberty parties were still straggling back and the enlisted men huddled silently in the lee of the shelter, the collars of their pea coats turned up against the night air. One of the men at

the far end of the bench was holding his head in his hands, occasionally retching and shuddering.

"There but for the grace of God," Harris said, looking at van
Meer.

A reference to himself, van Meer thought querulously, or was
he being touchy? He hunched his shoulders against the chill, then
squinted again at the sick sailor. "I think it's one of ours."

They walked the length of the bench and van Meer shook
Meslinsky roughly by the shoulder. "On your feet, Animal."

Meslinsky didn't move for a moment, then finally looked up,
his eyes slits in his puffy, bruised face.

"Who the hell—oh, Christ, sorry, C'mander." The big man
got to his feet and van Meer and Harris took him by the arms and
walked him over to the fence.

"Fresh air do you good," van Meer said. It was an effort to
keep his own voice from slurring.

Meslinsky clutched the fence and shook his head. "No, it
won't. Oh, Jesus . . ." Some of the spatter caught Harris on the
shoe. He looked disgusted and took out a handkerchief and
scrubbed at the leather.

Van Meer held Meslinsky up against the fence. "Let it all
come up, Animal."

More retching, and Meslinsky sagged against him. "Ain't
nothing left."

"Bad booze'll do it every time." Van Meer's stomach started
to feel queasy. He walked Meslinsky back to the shelter. God help
him if Animal passed out. He would be a bitch to try to handle as
deadweight.

"Not bad booze," Meslinsky mumbled. "Just too much of it."

"Must've been some party."

Meslinsky shook his head, his mouth having difficulty fram-
ing the words. "Jenny sent me a 'get lost' letter." He shuddered
again. "Oh, God : . ." One more session of dry heaves and Animal
would be bringing up the green stuff. Some of the other men on
the bench were staring at them now, dull-eyed. They probably
didn't feel much better.

He caught Harris looking slightly offended and withdrawn,
and guessed he had detached himself from the whole situation—
that Harris had decided Animal was his, van Meer's, charge.

There was a squeal of brakes and the base bus pulled up. Van

Meer helped Meslinsky stumble over to the door. "Did they move the *Alaska* yet, Animal?"

Meslinsky wiped his mouth with a sleeve of his pea coat. His voice was a mumble. "Day . . . day before yesterday. She's outboard the *Simon Lake*."

"You gonna be okay?"

Meslinsky nodded. "Jus' open a window so I can . . . hang my head out. Jesus, do I feel *awful*."

Ten minutes later, he was trying to steady Meslinsky while he saluted the sleepy officer of the deck on the *Simon Lake* and requested permission to come aboard. A mess cook had just brought up a pot of coffee and some sweet rolls, and van Meer realized how desperately he needed a cup of coffee.

Meslinsky smelled the coffee and started to make noises and van Meer hastily steered him into the tender and down a maze of ladders to the deck that opened out on the *Alaska*, moored alongside.

He paused at the edge of the gangplank, as awestruck as he had been the first time he had seen the giant submarine. Grab ropes had been rigged leading to the forward hatch, a circle of light in an otherwise dull-black hull that seemed as long as the *Simon Lake* itself. There was a slight chop on the bay and small phosphorescent waves curled over the bow. He couldn't make out her outline below the water; the ocean was black and the hull was black and the *Alaska* vanished at the waterline. Even above the waterline, the submarine was almost invisible: the silhouette of her sail, the faint outline of the twenty-four muzzle hatches that covered her missile tubes, the light from the forward hatch, and that was all.

She was enormous, van Meer thought, sobering. And she was terrifying.

Behind him, Harris said curtly, "Let's go, Van—you've seen her before."

Meslinsky stumbled across the gangplank, van Meer holding on to the collar of his pea coat to steady him. Then they were on the rounded hull, clutching the safety lines that ran to the open hatch. The deck watch snapped to attention and Harris said, "At ease, Baker. Ask the OD to send up a couple of men to take care of Meslinsky."

Baker, a third-class lab tech who had yet to qualify for his dol-

phins, didn't noticeably relax. "Yes, sir, right away, sir." He
opened a small hatch in the sail and spoke briefly into a battle
phone. Then, somewhat tentatively: "Request identification
check, sir." Van Meer and Harris produced IDs and Baker
glanced at them, then nodded at Meslinsky, who had one arm
draped around van Meer's shoulder and was half asleep. "Him,
too, sir."

Van Meer shook his head in mock dismay. "You've forgotten
who we are already."

Baker didn't appreciate the joke and looked uneasy. "I'm sorry, sir. Orders."

Van Meer dug through Meslinsky's wallet and pulled out his
ID at the same time two seamen showed up to help Meslinsky go
below. For just a moment van Meer caught the look on Baker's
face as he watched Meslinsky disappear through the hatch. East
was East and West was West and the nukes were never going to
understand the ops and vice versa.

"Don't go down yet, Van." He turned and Harris motioned
him back toward the gangplank from the *Simon Lake*, out of ear-
shot of Baker. The wind had come up and the small waves cream-
ing over the bow had become larger. They were slapping against
the hull as they broke and raced over the forward part of the ship.
Harris was standing with his back to the bow, clutching the safety
lines and staring at the sail. But that wasn't what Harris was actually seeing, van Meer thought. In his mind's eye, Harris was con-
templating the twenty-four muzzle hatches just beyond and thinking of the missiles below.

Harris glanced over at him. "You know," he said quietly, "if
Hitler had had one of these, we'd all be speaking German now."
He smiled. He had a face that smiled easily, but the cold glare of
the lights from the *Simon Lake* made him look slightly satanic.
"Scary stuff, huh?"

"I think about it at times," van Meer admitted. What he wanted to say was that he thought about it a *lot*.

Harris shrugged. "If we ever have to launch them, we launch
them. As simple as that. No thinking allowed." It sounded pompous and it suddenly occurred to van Meer that Harris played at
being captain as if it were a role in a movie. Then, casually: "Meslinsky always drink that much, Van?"

"He was upset about his girlfriend."

"What about the other times?" Harris looked reproving. "It's your job to get to know the crew, Van, at least as well as they know you."

He didn't need this. He was sick of mini-lectures from Harris, sick of being terrified by the potential of the *Alaska*, sick of the Navy.

"Everything all right between you and Cheryl?"

"That's personal," van Meer said tightly.

An edge crept into Harris' voice. "It is and it isn't. No more so than Meslinsky's drinking. Anything that affects how you function aboard the *Alaska* affects one hell of a lot of people. You know, at Gradow's party you were hitting the bottle pretty hard yourself." He paused. "The drinking doesn't worry me, Van. What worries me is that you're not a happy drunk."

Harris turned back to the hatch, ignoring the spray blowing over the hull. "When we get under way, I want you to take the maneuvering watch." He hesitated. "I want you to take her down, too. Spencer will be your diving officer."

Van Meer watched him go and wondered about the special emphasis on giving him the maneuvering watch and making him OD to take the *Alaska* down. Maybe Harris was worried that a man with a hangover couldn't navigate the *Alaska*. Or maybe it was more involved, something that would eventually wind up in his fitness report.

As if he gave a good goddamn.

He hung back and for a moment after Harris had disappeared he was alone topside except for Baker, a small, quiet figure shivering by the open hatch twenty feet away. There was scud on the ocean and van Meer turned into the wind and let the spray hit his face. He could make out the lights of several freighters out in the bay and, a mile or so beyond, a carrier standing out to sea.

The drill was going to be a bitch, he suddenly thought. The only blessing was that it wouldn't last long.

He went below, the ladder emptying into a corridor a few feet from Officers' Country. The passageway was rigged for red and he waited a moment for his eyes to adjust, then went to the compartment he shared with the ship's new doctor, Abe Schulman, and the navigator, Mike Costanza. It was empty. Convenient, he thought. It would give him time to hide the small bottle of Equavil tablets.

He pulled the compartment door shut, then turned to inspect the small room. The bunks were racked three high against the far bulkhead, each with its own reading lamp and air vent. The bulk-heads were covered with a walnut-patterned Formica and there was soft brown carpeting on the deck. He smiled. A Pullman berth a thousand feet down.

To his left, a small metal desk sat at right angles to the bunks and above it were three shelves, one for each of them. Schulman's held a book on submarine medicine, a copy of the *Physicians Desk Reference*, and a photo of his wife and four kids—a surprisingly young wife and children for a man who looked as old as Schulman did. Schulman was in his early forties but prematurely graying, and apparently loving every strand of it. The older you look, the more people trust you, he claimed.

Trust? Schulman was going to betray a lot of it during the drill.

Costanza's shelf was bare except for a paperback Western. That's all that would ever be on it, one paperback. A new title every three or four days as Costanza methodically read through the ship's library.

To his right, opposite the desk, was a small floor safe and above that a fold-down stainless-steel sink. There was a tiny mirror for shaving and then cupboard space to the overhead. Between the sink and the cupboard and extending right up to the door opening was the built-in wardrobe.

Not much hiding space at all. He frowned. Then he had an idea and opened the wardrobe. Their dress shoes were on the bottom shelf: his to the left, Schulman's in the middle, and Costanza's to the far right. He took out his own left shoe and removed the metal shoe tree. It was perforated and hollow; the bottle of Equavil fit very comfortably beneath it.

He put the shoe back and closed the cabinet. So much for the cloak-and-dagger routine. But the compartment was too small to hold secrets and Schulman would have too many questions if he came across the tablets. Of all the men on board, he was the one who would know what they were for.

He glanced at his watch, then changed into his working uniform, a blue Dacron jump suit. Oh-three-hundred and he wanted to go through the ship before they got under way. And, Christ, he could use some coffee. . . .

He walked back into the dimly lit corridor, then noticed a light in the wardroom and ducked in. Cermak was sitting in the captain's chair at the far end of a table, a stack of requisition forms spread out before him. The compartment looked like the boardroom of a small corporation. The chairs were upholstered in earth tones, the table and bulkheads of wood-patterned Formica. A battery of intercoms and battle phones were racked on the bulkhead to Cermak's left. On his right was a seventeen-inch radar repeater that showed the *Alaska*'s position and the surrounding area when they were at sea. Next to it were a compass repeater and instruments indicating the ship's course, depth, and speed.

The only thing that looked inefficient and unmilitary was Cermak himself.

Chips Okamoto was seated opposite Cermak, making notations in a red spiral binder stamped SECRET. Affable and easygoing, Okamoto had only two faults. The first was a tendency to pull out the family photograph album at the slightest show of interest. The second was that the missiles on board were his hobby as well as his profession and he talked about them incessantly.

He was too engrossed in the binder to look up when van Meer walked in.

Cermak waved at a coffeepot and a plate of sweet rolls in front of him. "Have some coffee. You look like you could use some." He finished off a roll and licked the frosting off his fingers. "The sticky buns aren't bad, either."

Van Meer imagined a dozen requisitions all stuck together with traces of Cermak's nighttime snack. "Those reports were supposed to be in two days ago, weren't they?"

Cermak shrugged, helping himself to another roll. "Come off it, Van. Neither you nor the captain was here to countersign them. Don't worry. They'll get off in time. Sure you won't have a roll?"

Van Meer shook his head and sat down, ignoring Cermak. "What're you reading, Chips?"

"Specs on the new birds." Okamoto put down the binder and

yawned. "My God, you won't believe them. I think they could hit a fly on a screen door in Moscow."

Van Meer was suddenly wide awake and alert. Chips would have overseen the on-loading of any new birds. If anybody had spotted the dummies, it would have been him.

"You'll have to tell me about them some other time." Chips's yawn was contagious and van Meer realized he desperately needed to take on some coffee.

Okamoto glanced at the chronometer set in the bulkhead and stood up. "Time for my beauty nap." Then, to van Meer: "How's the captain?"

"Fine. Same as always," van Meer said ironically.

"What's fine about that?" Okamoto clapped the binder under his arm and stumped out the door.

"We got lucky," Cermak said after Okamoto had left. The last roll on the plate was already in his hands.

Van Meer stopped, halfway through the door. "How do you mean?"

"Ordinarily he'd spend half the night telling us what the birds can do. Christ, Van, I know the world's going to blow up someday but I hate the instant replay ahead of time."

"Tune him out. The rest of us do," van Meer murmured. He left, wondering if he shouldn't try harder to like Cermak. The food on board all submarines was excellent but on the *Alaska* it was superb and the reason was Cermak, in charge of the supply department and the cooks and bakers. Nobody loved to eat better than Cermak, and he was eating all the time. You could track him through the ship by the trail of crumbs and crumpled napkins. . . .

The crew's mess was pleasantly warm and smelled of hot coffee and rolls. Van Meer slipped into a chair at one of the tables and poured himself a cup, then huddled over it, letting the aroma wash over his face. It would be another six hours before he could log any sack time and by then he'd be a wreck.

Halfway through his second cup, he began to feel more human and looked around. There was a scattering of crew members at other tables; a few had glanced up at him when he came in, then ignored him. Others, he knew, resented his presence. He noted that the booths had been reupholstered in light green and yellow vinyl so the compartment now had the overall effect of a pleasant hometown diner. Along both bulkheads were hung photographs of ports they had been to, including one shot of the Auld Hoose in Holy Loch, the only bar he had ever been thrown out of. It was right after Maggie had—

His mind suddenly froze. *Mustn't think about that, not now, not here* . . .

"Does he always drink like that?"

"Stuff it, Bailey."

In another booth Glenn Bailey, one of the lab techs, was eating a sandwich and staring at Meslinsky, still in his dress blues, across from him. Nick Geranios, the hospital corpsman, was patiently holding a cup of coffee for him while Meslinsky, his eyes half closed, tried feebly to shove it away.

"Another cup and I swear to God I'll be sick all over again."

"You're on duty in two hours, Animal. Drink it down and keep it down."

"It's your fucking funeral."

Bailey was fascinated. "You figure his weight and blood volume, he must have drunk a full liter."

Meslinsky lifted his head and held up two fingers. "Two liters. Count 'em."

"That's impossible," Bailey said, indignant. "The human body—"

Leggett, the first-class baker, came up to the table with a tray of hot rolls and set them down in front of van Meer, then turned to Bailey. "Drop it, motor mouth, the man is suffering."

"Two to one a certain lab tech doesn't make it through the whole patrol without losing at least two teeth," Geranios said.

Leggett slapped his hand. "Even odds and you're covered." Then, turning: "We don't hate you because you're one of the nukes, Bailey—we just hate *you.*"

Van Meer finished his coffee and left, squeezing past the small booth that served as projection room and entertainment locker. He took the ladder down to crew's berthing and stood for a moment in the red-lit gloom, listening to the quiet breathing around him. Even with the blowers going, there was a faint smell of feet and perspiration, laced with the vague odors of the sea and the docks. Funny how sensitive you got to smells and changes of temperature, he thought. Once on patrol, the temperature would be a constant seventy-two degrees and the air would become as odorless as in a vacuum. He glanced around again, feeling vaguely uneasy. He was responsible for the crew and the ship . . . and he was no longer up to it.

He looked at his watch. Another hour and it would be time to set the maneuvering watch.

Dr. Abraham Schulman was in sick bay, leaning back in his chair with his hands crossed over his stomach, staring intently at a calendar on the opposite bulkhead. Van Meer touched the doctor on the shoulder. Schulman didn't move; the only indication he was awake was the sudden focus of his eyes.

"You do that very well," van Meer said.

Schulman yawned. "If you had to listen to some of my patients, you'd learn how to sleep with your eyes open, too."

"The captain might not appreciate it, Abe."

Schulman looked properly penitent. "That's what too much shore duty does to you. I guess I've got a lot to learn, huh?"

Van Meer nodded. "Especially about the captain."

There was a sudden glint in Schulman's eyes. "A little professional jealousy, Commander? Care to tell me about it?"

Schulman was a psychiatrist and there were a lot of things he'd like to tell him, van Meer thought bleakly. He made a joke of it. "I'd look you up but New York's too far for commuting."

Schulman sat up and made a stab at looking professional. "What about illnesses on board? I've been briefed but I'd like to hear it from you."

Van Meer was surprised, though he knew he shouldn't have been. "You've never been on board a Trident before?"

Schulman took off his glasses and polished them, staring nearsightedly at van Meer. "A dozen patrols on early Polaris subs; nothing since then."

Van Meer shrugged. "It's not that much different. You'll spend most of your time logging in film badges and checking radiation levels. And you'll keep track of the air. The first few days out, you'll have the ordinary run of colds and respiratory infections. After that—nothing. The air's recycled and nothing new comes in from the outside. A decade or so ago, you'd expect three or four cases of clap in the first week. Crews are older now, the ops are mostly married men, and the nukes . . ." He shrugged. "God knows what they do on liberty. Probably spend it all in the local library."

"Radiation?"

"As I said, it's not that much different. Levels are high in the reactor room but when the reactor's operating, it's bare of personnel anyway."

"What about drugs?" Schulman looked over the tops of his glasses. "I mean dope, Van."

"With a closed air loop, it's hard to smoke pot without somebody knowing."

"Coke? It's popular among some of the brighter boys."

"I doubt it. Too expensive. Same goes for the harder stuff—and it's tough to support a habit a thousand feet below the nearest source, let alone a thousand miles away. I don't know about pills." Which was a lie, he thought grimly. He knew a lot about pills, but nothing he was going to tell Schulman.

"Which leaves booze."

Van Meer sighed. "There's liquor on board, Abe. Most of it's under your lock and key. Medical stores."

Schulman half smiled. "You're trying to tell me that the duty's going to be a snap."

"Maybe we can arrange an emergency appendectomy."

Schulman looked apprehensive. "You wouldn't kid an old broken-down doctor, would you? The only thing I've cut into lately is a steak."

Van Meer looked thoughtful. "Accidents are always a possibility—falls, finger mashings, high-frequency burns, that sort of thing. Appendectomies, we'd surface and call for help. But I'm not so sure we would *this* time."

There was a subtle change in Schulman's expression now; his voice was suddenly firmer—and disapproving. "We'll have a discussion about that later with Captain Harris. But aside from that meeting, Commander, I don't think we should ever talk about . . . the drill . . . Operation Fire . . . or allude to it, even among ourselves. Once we're under way, the situation should be as real to us as it is to the rest of the crew."

"If we don't believe in it ourselves, the crew will pick up on it. That it?"

"As my more moneyed colleagues might say—precisely."

Van Meer couldn't resist making a stab in the dark. "I take it the drill was partly your idea."

Schulman studied him for a long moment and van Meer suddenly realized that Schulman undoubtedly was familiar with most of his medical history and probably knew much of his personal history as well. He was tempted to ask Schulman point-blank if he knew of his prescription for Equavil, then thought better of it.

"I won't ask your opinion of the drill," Schulman said slowly. "You're responsible for carrying it out. But I think you should know that *I* didn't approve, that I consider it extremely dangerous. That's one of the reasons they asked me to be the monitor. They knew that I would be a severe critic."

Van Meer felt cold. "What are your objections?"

Schulman laced his fingers behind his head and leaned back in his chair, his face set and grim. "Simple. There are only three men on board who know what's going on, who could stop the drill if something went wrong. You and I and Captain Harris. And I don't count."

The missile control center was one of the larger compartments aboard, with missile tube, missile launch, and missile fire controls concentrated in the same area. But the larger the submarine, the more the Navy found to put in it, van Meer thought. The bulkheads were a maze of dials and buttons and computer controls, the center of the compartment itself dominated by the computer consoles. Even the overhead was covered with rivers of cables and piping.

Patrick Moskowitz, assistant weapons officer and professional New Yorker, was seated at a console in the corner, working a keyboard and watching numbers come up on a CRT display. He glanced at van Meer, made an adjustment on the board, and swiveled around. "I was looking through the ops schedule. They're going to keep us hopping, aren't they?"

Moskowitz was one of the younger officers, one who van Meer had figured as a transient and who would leave as soon as his obligation was over. Maybe for that reason van Meer had never really gotten to know him.

"Better than being bored to death, Pat."

Moskowitz seemed preoccupied. "Funny thing about the Navy," he mused. "I thought I'd be bored when I joined up but I never have been. It surprises even me."

"When's your time up?"

"One more patrol after this." Moskowitz laughed without humor, shaking his head. "I've got a real problem—I like the Navy."

He glanced up at van Meer. "Hardly the type, am I? I should have ended up a lawyer like the old man."

Four o'clock in the morning must be the time for confidences, van Meer thought, faintly embarrassed. "How come you didn't?"

A shrug. "A free education and, at the time I applied, I figured the Academy would have a quota for instead of against and they'd be glad to take me—and after all, Rickover made admiral, so there was hope for the future."

Van Meer paused a moment at the hatch. "Those the real reasons?"

The light from the readout terminal made Moskowitz look somber. "I didn't want to chase ambulances or hang around the divorce courts or play mouthpiece for minor hoods." He sounded bitter. "I imagine I would have been good at that." He swung back to the terminal, his mood suddenly lighter. "I understand Dr. Schulman's a landsman from the land of egg creams and chestnuts in the park."

Van Meer smiled. "He didn't say." He turned and stepped through the hatch into the huge missile room, waiting a moment for his eyes to adjust to the overhead fluorescents. He stared in silence at the two rows of tubes that filled most of the compartment. Each of the twenty-four tubes was more than eight feet in diameter and cut through all four decks of the *Alaska*. Piping and cables wrapped around them like parasitic growths on the trunk of a tree, giving them a gnarled appearance. The tubes themselves, thick with insulation, were painted a light cream; the decks were tiled in a neutral beige.

The *Alaska*'s Sherwood Forest—the killing ground, van Meer thought bleakly. Each tube held a Trident II missile with a range of six thousand miles, and each missile contained seventeen individually targeted warheads—408 in all. What was the punch that each warhead packed? Five times that of the Hiroshima bomb?

The silence was oppressive and he walked down the center aisle toward the afterhatch, nodding at a missile tech working on a control panel. At the end of the aisle he paused for a moment, surrounded by the four tubes containing the dummies. The Grand Deception, he reflected darkly. Then: Schulman was right. It was risky, far too risky.

He shivered, glanced back again at the tech, a blue-suited

troll working silently in the glare from the fluorescents, then climbed through the hatch and headed aft.

In the maneuvering room Harold Stroop, the chief engineer, was in tense conversation with three assistants. He raised a pair of shaggy white eyebrows when he saw van Meer and waved to an empty chair. "Have a seat, Van. Maybe you can shed some light on this."

Van Meer poured himself a cup of coffee from the pot on the nearby hot plate and straddled his chair. "What's up?"

Stroop held up a sheaf of papers in one huge paw and looked at van Meer expectantly. "Where were you on Tuesday, the sixteenth?"

Van Meer felt his stomach lurch. "Alive and well and living in rotten Groton. You serious?"

Stroop nodded, his mane of white hair flying about like the strands of a mop. He turned to Frank MacGowan, the main propulsion assistant. "Okay, Frank, tell the man where you were."

MacGowan, a younger, paunchier version of Stroop, rubbed his nose and looked annoyed. "I told you, Hal—I drew a one-day refresher at diesel school."

"Learn anything you didn't know before? . . . Didn't think so. Earl, what the hell did they assign you to?"

A wiry little man with a pencil-thin mustache, Earl Messier was the electrical officer and, more importantly, a drinking buddy of both Stroop and MacGowan. "Same thing—ordered to sit in on a course on new electrical systems."

"And nothing of any particular relevance to the *Alaska*, right? Jeff?"

Jeff Udall, the young reactor control officer, was slouching against a panel board that ran from the deck to the overhead, covered with temperature gauges and warning lights. His eyes were half closed but van Meer guessed he could repeat the conversation verbatim if he had to.

"Nothing mysterious." He looked faintly embarrassed. "An invitation to play golf."

"From a Navy Department flunky who sails a desk in Washington and snowed you into thinking he was somebody important. Think you'll ever play golf with him again? . . . I doubt it, too, Lieutenant."

"He was hot-boxing me," Udall explained. Like Moskowitz,

he was getting his share of job offers, van Meer thought. Udall was a top man with reactors and the Navy had tried to keep him but he'd already made up his mind. He now considered himself apart from the rest of the crew, a civilian in military clothing. Harris detested him because he proselytized the other nukes for the Good Life ashore.

"He wanted to pitch you. On Tuesday," Stroop added sarcastically. He turned to van Meer. "Well, how about it, Van? Where were you?"

Van Meer buried his face in his coffee, thinking very fast. He finally looked up. "Right here," he lied, looking Stroop in the eye. "Captain Harris and myself and half a dozen vendors went over some preliminary work for next year's retrofit."

Stroop stared at him, frustrated. "If you and the captain were aboard, then I swear to God you were the only two. They pulled me out for a physical. Some bullshit about a suspicious spot on a lung X ray. The next day, I checked the engineering log to see what had been done while I was gone and nobody had filled it in. Nobody was *here* to fill it in. Can you beat that?"

Van Meer shrugged. "So the ways of the Navy are mysterious. You can't make a federal case out of coincidence."

MacGowan cut in, truculent. "Maybe it was coincidence but it sure seemed like somebody wanted us off the ship." He was eyeing Stroop as he talked, putting into words what he thought Stroop was thinking. A natural-born toady, van Meer thought. MacGowan was one of the few men on board whom he actively disliked, and one of the few who disliked him.

Stroop fluttered his huge hands helplessly and dropped the papers back on his desk. Most of the steam had gone out of him. "If that's the way it was, then that's the way it was. But, goddammit, it sure looked odd."

Van Meer yawned and stood up. "Any trouble with the beast?"

Stroop shook his head. "There's never any problem. You know that. She's simple to operate and easy to maintain and there's no coolant pumps so she's quiet as a whisper. The evaporators are more of a pain."

"You should catch some Z's," van Meer said, yawning again. "Reveille's at oh-five-hundred."

Stroop shrugged. "Why bother?"

Van Meer climbed through the hatch and took the ladder down to the engine room. A quick tour of the huge compartment that housed the turbines and the electric motors that drove the screw and a fast check of the emergency diesel and the battery room. If the reactor ever had to be scrammed, they'd have to limp home on either the diesel or emergency-battery power. The main compartments left were the auxiliary machinery room and the forward torpedo room; he'd hit those on his way back to Officers' Country.

But all the time he was inspecting the rest of the ship, he couldn't forget the look of bafflement on Stroop's face and the skeptical expression on Messier's. Stroop might have found his story about what happened on Tuesday a little hard to swallow but he had swallowed it.

Messier, on the other hand, was convinced he had lied.

9

THE ALARM WOKE him at six but Renslow lay on the couch five minutes longer, half dazed with sleep, listening to the tinny sounds of the small clock radio. His back ached and he considered briefly how much more comfortable it would have been to have slept with Elizabeth. On second thought, he reflected, each of them would have hugged his respective side of the mattress, avoiding any possible contact with the other. . . .

He washed and shaved in the downstairs bathroom—it had lately become his personal john—then put on his clothes, clipping the red-striped EB badge on his shirt pocket. The work sheets had been preying on his mind ever since he'd left Cheryl's and he wanted to get to Electric Boat early and go over them. There had to be some clue indicating why the slowdown had occurred or why there had been a hang-up in deliveries, some reason the housekeeping crew had come in early. . . .

Elizabeth was waiting for him at the breakfast table, wearing a blue silk kimono he had never seen before and the silver-and-turquoise necklace he had given her two years ago when they had been on vacation in Arizona. She was also wearing full makeup except for lipstick. He tried to remember the last time he had seen her without it. It had become one of the things that annoyed him most about her: She always looked her best but it had been at the expense of some of her humanity. He never saw her combing her hair or shaving her legs or staring in the bathroom mirror, wondering what had caused that first wrinkle.

"You're up early." Her voice was flat, moody.

The water in the teakettle was hot and Renslow made himself a cup of instant coffee. He wouldn't bother with breakfast. He'd pick up orange juice and a sweet roll from one of the lunch wagons at EB.

"I've got to check on a problem at Electric Boat."

He watched her as she stubbed out a cigarette in the ashtray and promptly lit another one. What a difference eight years had made. She was still a beautiful woman but she was in her mid-thirties now, trembling on the brink of becoming a matron. In a few years the marriage would shrivel completely and she would become absorbed in the Navy Officers' Wives Club, spending her days running the thrift shop and her nights in silent communion with the tube or playing cards with the other wives. . . .

"I heard you come in last night." She didn't ask why he had slept on the couch; they had battled that one out the last time he had returned from patrol.

"I had to drive Harris and van Meer to the airport." Maybe he should pick up his coffee at the lunch wagon, too.

"The plane left at one," she said. A stream of smoke and another look of cool appraisal. "Did you stop at the inn for a drink?"

"Why the third degree, Liz?"

"This is a pretty small town." She picked up her coffee and Renslow couldn't help contrasting the elegant china cup with the mugs that Cheryl had set out.

"What's that supposed to mean?"

"People talk."

The network of Navy wives couldn't have reached her this early, he thought. She was being bitchy for the sake of being bitchy.

He leaned against the sideboard, wondering where she had picked up the trick of holding her elbow with one hand and the cigarette with the other and blowing smoke out, just so, through flared nostrils. Did they teach them that in the Eastern finishing schools or was it something inherited? However she had learned it, it was pure Bette Davis. He knew if he wanted to throw her into a screaming rage, all he had to do was tell her that.

"I stopped at Cheryl Leary's for a drink," he said sarcastically. "You remember the Learys? I was David's best friend." He paused. "She's currently going with Mark van Meer, Harris' executive officer. They're what used to be called a number."

Her expression was suddenly bitter. "I suppose they taught you that at the Academy," she said, her voice tight. "That the best defense is a good offense." She savagely stubbed out her cigarette. "I was worried," she said. "That's my privilege, isn't it—to be worried?"

She got up and walked into the bedroom, closing the door behind her. She had sounded troubled rather than bitchy, and Renslow felt vaguely guilty. He had loved her once, not too long ago, but that was before they both had agreed that her only problem in life was that she had married the wrong man.

Then he wondered suspiciously if the "best defense" accusation didn't apply more to her than to him.

It was seven-thirty when he checked in at Electric Boat but Donaldson was already in his office. Renslow paused at the door. "How's it going, Jerry?"

A nervous glance. "You're a little early this morning, aren't you, Al?"

"I wanted to get a head start."

"Everything's just as you left it. Nobody's touched anything. They only clean in here once a week." He sounded jittery.

What the hell was eating him? Renslow thought. He walked to his office and threw his coat at the hook on the back of the door, then jerked open the window and filled his lungs with the breeze off the river. June, the best month of the year in Groton.

He took the work sheets out of his briefcase and stacked them in two piles on his desk, stretched for thirty seconds, then carefully started reading through the stacks. Within an hour he was up to the fifteenth and seventeenth, still without a clue as to what had happened on the day in between.

Bits of conversation now bobbed to the surface of his mind. Last night, saying good-bye to Harris and van Meer . . . What was it van Meer had said just before Harris told him to shut up? That they were going to need good luck on the patrol? What was so special about that? You always needed luck. . . . And Donaldson's nervousness, like a little kid who had been found out. . . . What was bugging him? The only thing Renslow could think of was his inquiry about Tuesday, and why should that upset him?

He glanced down at the sheets again, feeling uneasy. What the hell was going on—or was there anything at all going on? He and Harris and van Meer were all under pressure for different reasons. Maybe he was the one who was cracking up, becoming paranoid.

He fingered the forms for a moment, then made up his mind.

Nothing was ever done in the yard without being written up in triplicate—and usually more. Somebody, somewhere, had to have a record.

He found a company phone book in a bottom drawer and started running down the listings. . . . An hour later, he totaled up the score: The good guys hadn't scored a single run. The first call had been to Accounting, asking for the charges levied on Tuesday and precisely what they had been for. According to the secretary who answered, the *Alaska* had been billed for a housekeeping crew. A check with their foreman confirmed it. Calls to the different trades buildings were also a zero. Nobody had been signed out to the *Alaska*. Other calls were just as fruitless.

So nobody had been on board the *Alaska* that Tuesday except a housekeeping crew. Period.

But he still couldn't understand why nobody from the ship's crew had been on board, either. He had another thought, glanced through the phone book for an address, then reached for his coat. Donaldson spotted him on the way out.

"What's up, skipper?"

"Personal business. Thought I might take the day off."

"Still not worried about Tuesday, are you?"

Warning flags went up in Renslow's mind. "Didn't you say a housekeeping crew had been in?"

Slowly: "That's right, a housekeeping crew." Then, suspicious: "The switchboard has some messages for you. They said your line's been tied up."

"Family problems," Renslow mumbled, and wondered if the switchboard had been listening in on his calls.

Central Issue Point for Radiological Control was located a block away. A name tag identified the college type on duty as Mr. Swanson. Renslow showed his ID, then asked how far back their records went.

A quick smile. "We never throw them away, Commander. Government rules. If somebody gets sick ten years from now and blames the radiation he might have absorbed while working here, we can always refer to the dosimeter readings for the total exposure he received. That's for the government's protection as well as our own."

Renslow lowered his voice to a confidential level. "I'm curious about Tuesday, the sixteenth, on the *Alaska*. We think some members of the crew might have been subjected to a higher-than-usual level."

Swanson blinked, looked serious, and said, "Let me check."

He came back reading an open folder and frowning. "No dosimeters were issued that day to any crew member, Commander. Apparently nobody was working in a radiation area."

"What about yard workers?"

Another shake of the head. "No yard workers were issued dosimeters that day, either." Renslow had shrugged and turned away, disappointed, when Swanson, still reading the folder, said, "The only dosimeter issued Tuesday to anybody going aboard the *Alaska* was a TLD to Mr. Thatcher."

"Thatcher?"

"Yes, sir, a Mr. William Thatcher. He came in with a group of six from Washington. He requested a thermal luminescent dosimeter; said he had been accidentally exposed on a job once before and was playing it safe. Nobody else asked for any."

"What firm were they with?"

Swanson looked surprised. "No firm, sir. The Department of the Navy."

Somebody had to have seen them, Renslow thought, somebody had to know. . . . "Where's your phone?" Swanson pointed and Renslow dialed yard security, asked his question, gave his name, rank, and need to know, then waited while they checked the records.

Jackpot.

Well, not quite. There *had* to have been one man from the *Alaska*'s crew on duty that day: the military guard posted at the gangway to keep off unauthorized visitors. But Bailey, the crewman who had drawn the duty, had been replaced in midmorning by a quartermaster from the *Will Rogers*. And the *Will Rogers* had sailed two days ago. . . .

Why had Bailey been pulled? And why had he been replaced by somebody from a different ship? One thing for sure, he couldn't find out from the replacement.

It was a long, dusty walk to the south piers. Renslow stopped in the shade of a nearby building and mopped at his face with his handkerchief; it must be in the eighties, he thought; it was hot enough to soften asphalt.

An attack submarine was now moored where the *Alaska* had been. A barge carrying retention tanks was tied up outboard, red rad lines strung around the tanks themselves, designed to hold the radioactive water pumped from the ship's reactor system. Renslow glanced at the barge, then turned back to the wharf, searching for the shack used by the roving company guards. He spotted it sitting in the shadows of a toolshed, a small, wooden shack about as big as a Port-O-San with a phone line leading from it to the shed.

The man inside looked about sixty, with a two-day growth of white stubble. He inspected Renslow's badge and grudgingly put aside the clipboard he had been reading.

"Something I can do for you?"

"I'm from the *Alaska*'s—"

"The *Alaska* left Groton nearly a week ago."

"—Blue crew," Renslow finished curtly. "There was a crewman named Bailey standing gangway watch on the sixteenth."

The guard looked blank. "So?"

Renslow let a little stiffness creep into his voice. "He's been accused of misconduct on duty, an incident involving a yard worker. I'm supposed to look into it."

The guard picked up a small notebook and thumbed through it. "Anything we report, we make a note. . . . Here it is, the sixteenth." He chewed his lip, then looked up, frowning. "Your man Bailey was relieved at ten o'clock. He didn't stand watch the rest of the day. Guy named Simmons from the *Will Rogers* took over for him. That's all I've got down here."

"Were you on duty that day, too?"

The guard nodded, closing the book. "Every day, seven-to-three shift."

"And you didn't notice—ah—any incident?"

Firmly· "If I had, I woulda made a note." He leaned out the door and spit in the dust. "I remember your man Bailey, though. Smart-ass kid—somebody's going to pound him one day."

"You sure nothing happened?"

"Couldn't have. There weren't no yardmen around for Bailey to mouth off to. Nobody but some Puerto Rican housekeeping crew "

Renslow looked surprised. "That was all?"

"I just told you," the guard said curtly. "Nobody but the housekeeping crew and some electronics team."

"I don't remember electronics being scheduled," Renslow said, deliberately looking confused.

The guard was disgusted. "I thought the Navy kept better records than that. Had to be electronics. About half a dozen guys and a couple of them were carrying coils of cable."

"I was off that day," Renslow murmured, lost in thought. "I just got the report on Bailey this morning."

"Well, there wasn't any incident here." The guard went back to his clipboard. "Next time you see that Bailey, tell him to watch his mouth; someday somebody's going to slug him." A shake of the head. "Smart-ass kid." 　　　　　　　　　　　　　　　-

Captain Hubert Manley, the yard captain and liaison between the Navy and the Electric Boat Company, was a small man with thinning white hair and a bantam-rooster manner. He had long since been resigned to a desk command. "We also serve . . " had become not only his personal motto but part of his character. With the years, he had learned to suffer complaining ship captains, not gladly but as part of the cross he had to bear.

"I've met your other half but it seems every time you're in the yard, I've been away."

Renslow shook the proffered hand; the captain's grip was almost offensively firm and uncomfortably sweaty. Manley waved him to a chair and went through the coffee ritual, then settled back and waited for Renslow to start the conversation.

Renslow hunched forward in his seat. "I hate to bother you, sir, but there's been some inconsistency in the work sheets on the *Alaska*."

Manley paused with his cup halfway to his mouth, then set it back down on his desk blotter. From the expression on his face Renslow guessed that he was going to take it personally.

"In what way?"

Renslow pulled the work sheets out of his attaché case. "There's a gap in the retrofit log for Tuesday, the sixteenth." Manley obligingly cleared a place on his desk so Renslow could spread out the papers. "Apparently nothing was done on the sixteenth except housekeeping."

Manley looked bored. "That sometimes happens. A ship comes in on a priority schedule and everything is rush and then there's a delay we can't help and we'll send in the housekeeping crew ahead of schedule, especially if there isn't too much work left to be done." A small smile. "Most ship captains seem to have the same complaint."

Captain Manley was probably convinced the Navy hadn't changed much since Farragut's day, Renslow thought. "I said apparently, Captain. Something was done on the sixteenth, but it was never written up on the work sheets."

"What makes you say that?"

"Radiological Control issued a TLD to one man in a group that went on board that day. And the guard in the guard shack a hundred feet off the pier remembers a group of six going on board. He thinks they had something to do with electronics."

Manley pursed his lips in sudden remembrance. "That was probably the group I was with."

Renslow stared. "I don't follow you."

"A team came in from the inspector general's office to check out dock facilities. We gave them a quick tour of the *Alaska* as a courtesy. I think some deliveries were made while we were on the pier. I could probably have them traced down, though I'm not so sure they'd show up on invoices for that day." He hesitated. "If you insist."

"Would you advise it?" Renslow asked.

Manley picked his words carefully. "It means devoting a lot of clerical man-hours to it at a time when we're shorthanded on staff." A wary glance. "I guess it's not up to me to say. It depends on how important you think it is."

It wouldn't be worth it, Renslow thought. Manley would make sure of that. He stuffed the papers back into his attaché case. "Thanks for your time, Captain."

"Think nothing of it." Manley walked him to the door. "That's what I'm here for, Commander." A quick handshake and the captain retreated behind the doors of his office.

Outside, Renslow took off his suit coat and started walking back to Donaldson's office. Manley had been too quick and too glib with his explanation. And the guard hadn't seen three groups; he had seen two—the housekeeping crew and then the electronics team, or what he thought had been an electronics team. The guard certainly would have known a group of VIPs when he saw them. . . .

And why had Bailey been pulled off guard duty and replaced by a crewman from a different ship? And why had no crew members been aboard the *Alaska* that day?

Manley had come up with his explanation on the spur of the moment and it didn't hold water. Harris, Donaldson, and now Manley. In one way or another, they were all covering up. But why should Manley and Donaldson be privy to information about the *Alaska* that was being denied to him? Then he realized that of the three, probably only Harris knew the whole story. Manley and Donaldson had just followed orders.

Something had been done to the *Alaska*, something so secret that they wouldn't brief even him, the captain of the Blue Crew.

But, goddammit, the *Alaska* was just as much his command as it was Harris'.

10

H E HAD JUST closed his eyes for five minutes when the intercom burst into life: *"Reveille! Reveille! Up all hands! Up all hands!"* Van Meer rolled into a sitting position on the edge of his bunk and sat there for a moment, holding his head in his hands. He had been dreaming and right then Groton and Cheryl were far more real in his mind than the flight down to Charleston or coming aboard the *Alaska* a few hours before. . . .

The smell of coffee and toast drifted into the compartment and he struggled to his feet and splashed cold water on his face from the sink. He had the small room to himself; Schulman had probably slept in his chair in sick bay and Costanza, as usual, would show up just before muster.

He stretched and scratched himself, then toweled his face and followed his nose to the wardroom. Okamoto and Cermak were already there—Cermak obviously on his second order of ham and eggs—and Udall and Spencer came in a moment later. They all looked as bad as he did, van Meer thought righteously—with the possible exception of Spencer, who was a physical-culture freak and managed to look as if he had just jogged a bracing two miles.

He grunted a good-morning and choked down three eggs and two slices of toast, trying desperately to focus his thinking. The *Alaska* still wasn't for real. . . .

"More coffee, Commander?"

He waved away the little steward. "No thanks, Perez. I'm wired already."

"It'll heighten your consciousness," Udall said without a smile.

"And shorten your life," Spencer added.

"All hands muster on duty stations in working blues."

Ten minutes later, Olson knocked on the wardroom door and brought in the muster reports. "Mr. Costanza's not on board yet, sir. Neither is Russo."

Van Meer frowned. "Who's Russo?"

"New man—radioman striker."

Van Meer had a vague impression of a Peter Pan build and a baby face. A little young, he thought. Too damned young.

"Set the maneuvering watch, duty section three. Commander van Meer, lay up to the bridge."

He initialed the muster reports, then grabbed his hat and a foul-weather jacket. He guessed from the slight roll of the ship that it was blowing topside. Harris was already on the bridge, along with Gerassi, the telephone talker.

"Good morning, sir." Harris looked withdrawn and detached, nodding perfunctorily at his salute. Van Meer turned to Gerassi. "Have all compartments report when they're ready to get under way."

"Aye, aye, sir."

The sky was a streaked, charcoal gray, the clouds low and threatening, with a broad hint of sunrise in the east. The air was chilly and the wind was stronger now. Waves were rolling across the bow and slapping at the bottom of the sail. Van Meer stared blankly at the sea for a minute and then Gerassi started to relay "condition normal" reports from the compartments below. "Engineering reports answering all bells on the reactor, sir."

"Have the radio shack pass the word to the squadron commander that the *Alaska* is ready to get under way."

There was a sudden scramble on the ladder below and a hurried "Request permission to come up, sir." Poletti and Morrison, the port and starboard lookouts. Van Meer nodded and looked over at Harris, still staring at the sea. It was getting crowded on the bridge but Harris showed no sign of going below.

Somebody was shouting on the *Simon Lake* and van Meer turned to watch the deck crew disconnect the last of the utility lines. Two crew members had just started to hoist in the brow when a man rushed over the small gangplank. Russo, van Meer thought cynically: a quickie before returning to ship.

He was suddenly aware that Gerassi was talking to him. "Permission granted to get under way, sir."

Van Meer nodded. "Pass the word: All stations stand by to get under way." Gerassi repeated the order into his battle phones and van Meer cupped his hands and leaned over the edge of the sail.

"Stand by your lines."

There was a flurry of activity by the special sea details standing along the sides of the *Alaska* and the *Simon Lake*.

"Cast off number four line." Then: *"Cast off the spring lines."*

The deckhands on the *Simon Lake* started taking in the now-slack ropes.

"Cast off the stern line."

The stern of the *Alaska* drifted away from the tender. Van Meer waited a moment, then: "All back one-third."

"All back one-third, aye," Gerassi repeated.

Three blasts on the ship's whistle and a slight turbulence behind them.

"Cast off the bow line."

The bow of the *Alaska* started to swing out and come parallel to the *Simon Lake*.

"All stop." Pause. "Left ten-degree rudder, all ahead one-third."

"Left ten-degree rudder, all ahead one-third."

"Steer one-five-zero."

"One-five-zero, aye."

"Rudder amidships."

"Rudder amidships, aye."

The *Alaska* was headed into the river now, the *Simon Lake* dwindling behind her. Ahead were the gray waters of Charleston Harbor, dotted with warships and freighters; beyond lay the seven-mile expanse of the bay and then the wave-torn Atlantic. Van Meer kept up a steady stream of commands to the helm, then they were passing Folly Island into the bay proper.

He half closed his eyes for a moment, feeling the wind and the spray against his face and watching the wheeling gulls circle the wake. Soon he would be completely surrounded by plastic and metal and Formica, locked into a world where there were no birds overhead, no wind, no waves, no sky, not even a sense of motion. The air would be a constant seventy-two degrees and the only distinction between night and day would be when the ship was rigged for red or white. Aside from the members of the crew, there would be no other life aboard. Not so much as a cockroach or a canary . . .

They were hitting the swells running up the bay now and the *Alaska* had started to wallow. "Secure the anchor detail."

Gerassi passed the word and a minute later relayed, "Deck secured. All personnel clear, sir." Van Meer caught a glimpse of Gerassi's face and felt a brief surge of sympathy. Submariners seldom, if ever, got their sea legs; there was no need to. A thousand feet down, where the *Alaska* was in her natural element, there was no pitching or rolling.

For the next twenty minutes he stared out at the bay and gave Gerassi orders to pass on to the helm. Then he turned to glance back at the receding Charleston skyline and was startled to see Harris studying him. Harris had been watching him, he realized, almost the entire time he had been on the bridge. He suddenly felt like an ensign who had gotten a ship under way for the first time. "Any comments, sir?"

A thoughtful look. "Were you expecting any, Van?"

"I thought you might have something on your mind," van Meer said curtly.

"I do." Harris studied the sea a moment, then: "I'm going below. Let me know when we clear the last channel buoy."

Van Meer watched him disappear through the hatch, then turned to glare at a gull wheeling overhead. Poletti and Morrison were suddenly busy with their binoculars while Gerassi stared at the sea and looked miserable. He had no idea what was eating Harris, but he'd tough it out for the ten days and after that it wouldn't matter anymore. . . .

The clouds in the eastern sky had turned a dull gray and the dark shapes of ships that had anchored out were starting to etch themselves against a lighter background. The gulls were dropping behind now, cawing their disappointment at not finding any garbage bobbing in the *Alaska*'s wake. The waves had become larger and van Meer almost smiled at Gerassi, standing with clenched jaws, his face pale. There'd be no cure for Gerassi until they had submerged. . . .

They had cleared the bay and the coastal flats had begun to disappear in the distance when Morrison suddenly said, "Last marker buoy, sir."

It took van Meer a moment to locate the black can bobbing in the waves. He flicked on the ship's intercom and hit the stud for the captain's quarters. "Last marker buoy sighted, sir." Harris acknowledged and van Meer pressed the remaining studs. *"Secure the maneuvering watch. Set the regular sea detail. Section one has the watch."*

A grateful Gerassi disappeared below and van Meer went back to staring at the green-black sea. Someplace out there, just a few miles off the coast, was a Soviet Aggie, an intelligence ship, carefully noting all departures from Charleston. If the scuttlebutt was right, she was due to be relieved that morning. With luck, they'd crept past without being seen.

"Request permission to come up, sir." Costanza climbed out of the hatch, looking cheerful and alert despite the puffiness around his eyes. He yawned, filling his lungs with the ocean air. "God, I hate to say it but it's great to be back."

Van Meer shivered. "Maybe I'm not enough of a masochist."

There was an amused look in Costanza's eyes. "You look like your motor's going to freeze, Van. You should've taken on more alcohol."

Everybody was starting to sound like Harris, van Meer thought. "Maybe you're right. This is the only ship in the squadron that runs on booze."

Costanza looked at him sharply, suspecting a dig, then shrugged. "Permission to leave the bridge, Commander." He lowered himself through the hatch. "On second thought, maybe you should've taken on less."

Harris' right-hand man and shadow. They didn't look alike but they sure sounded alike. . . . He wrapped his jacket tighter around him. It would be another two hours before they would be out of the shallows and could take the *Alaska* down. You always felt more secure if there were a hundred extra feet of water beneath the keel. But it was frustrating; if you could submerge, you could "fly" the *Alaska* off the continental shelf in less than half the time than if you remained on the surface. . . .

After an eternity of staring at a gray sky and a gray ocean, he flicked on the intercom again. *"Rig for dive."*

In his mind's eye, he could see the crew locking up loose equipment and dogging down compartment hatches, checking the emergency lighting—would Schulman remember to check the battle lanterns in sick bay?—and doing the hundred and one other things that needed doing before the *Alaska* sank beneath the waves. As diving officer, Spencer would be inspecting the ship from bow to stern and God help them all if he overlooked something. . . .

Readiness reports began to come over the intercom from the compartments below.

"Ventilating secure . . ."

"Snorkling secure . . ."

". . . outboard induction and exhaust valves shut and locked . . . inboard induction and exhaust valves shut, recirculating . . ."

". . . stern planes tested satisfactorily . . ."

". . . fair-water planes tested satisfactorily . . ."

And, finally, the word from a nervous-sounding Spencer: "Ship rigged for dive, Commander."

"Stand by to dive. Clear the bridge. Clear the bridge." Poletti and Morrison promptly ducked down the hatch.

Van Meer waited until the lookouts had cleared the ladder, then sounded two blasts on the diving Klaxon and shouted into the intercom, *"Dive. Dive."* A moment later, he had secured the hatch behind him and was half climbing, half sliding down the twenty-five feet of ladder into the control room.

Even after three patrols in the *Alaska*, the control room was still intimidating—the cockpit of an airplane gone mad. The bulkheads were covered with gauges and dials, the compartment itself crowded with the duty section. Directly in front of the diving stand, Clinger and Sandeman, the inboard and outboard helmsmen, were sitting in bucket seats behind aircraft-type controls. Spencer slouched in the diving officer's chair between, his eyes glued to the bank of instruments directly in front of him.

Gurnee had drawn the duty as chief of the watch in charge of flooding the ballast tanks and was seated at the vent manifold to the immediate right. A wiry little man, he could have run the control room by himself if he'd had to. In the compartment's aftersection, radar and sonar crews watched multicolored beams paint oscilloscope pictures of the surrounding area. Close by, two quartermasters studied the tiny dot of light in the DRT—the deadreckoning tracer—as it traced the *Alaska*'s position on a chart of the Carolina coastline.

Harris was sitting in the captain's chair at the far side of the control room, watching him. Van Meer nodded and stepped onto the diving stand, ordering, "Up scope." He grasped the handles, then pressed his face to the eyepiece and twisted the periscope

around. There was nothing visible in the lens except the leaden
sky and the black waters below. Then something caught his eye
and he twisted the right handle to bring the scope up to full power. A lone gull hovering against the threatening clouds . . .

"Periscope depth, Mr. Spencer."

Tension in the compartment thickened now. Spencer nervously cleared his throat. "Periscope depth, sir."

From somewhere there was the sound of rushing water as the
ballast tanks continued to fill. On the closure panel the last of the
small circles that indicated hull openings winked out, the red bars
behind them lighting up.

"Straight board, sir."

Spencer nodded. "Pressure in the boat." There was a hiss
and van Meer could feel his ears pop. "Secure the air."

Gurnee studied the internal-air-pressure gauge. "Pressure
holding."

Through the periscope, van Meer saw the waves start to roll
over the bow of the *Alaska* and then cover it completely. On impulse, he tilted the periscope lens slightly. The gull was fading in
the distance, circling slowly back to the mainland.

There was a slight slope to the deck now and van Meer followed Spencer's eyes to the bubble gauge in front of him. Spencer hesitated, then: "Close all vents. Ten-degree down-bubble."

Clinger eased his aircraft-type steering wheel forward. "Ten-
degree down-bubble, aye."

The tilt of the deck became more pronounced as van Meer
watched the depth gauge climb to sixty feet, seventy feet. . . .

Spencer glanced up. "Periscope depth, sir."

"Have all compartments check equipment and spaces, Mr.
Spencer. Cycle the vents."

Spencer passed the word, then went back to staring at the instrument panel in front of him, his forehead shiny with sweat.
Even Harris felt the tension. He had been leaning comfortably
back in his chair, hands folded over his stomach; now he was sitting up, concentrating on the sounds of the ship around him.

Had it been like this on board the *Thresher* in 1963 just before
she slipped to the bottom and imploded? van Meer wondered.
One hundred and forty Jonahs in the belly of the whale. Then: He
was getting morbid; he was past due for his tab of Equavil. . . .

All the "condition normal" reports were now in and there
was silence in the control room except for the faint whir of equip-

ment fans and the quiet sound of water being pumped back and forth between the trim tanks.

"Periscope down. Make your depth one hundred feet, Mr. Spencer."

"One hundred feet, sir."

"Down easy, Mr. Spencer."

Spencer's eyes were glued on the bubble gauge. "Hold five-degree down-bubble."

Clinger eased back slightly and the bubble climbed in the tube. "Five-degree down-bubble, aye."

"One hundred feet, Commander. Trim satisfactory."

Another check of all compartments. "Two hundred feet, Mr. Spencer."

"Two hundred feet, sir."

The rolling of the ship had stopped minutes before—the last connection with the surface. They were locked in now, van Meer thought, alone with one another and the whispering machinery around them. He thought of the gull again, its wings outspread, climbing up into the muddy sky.

"Two hundred feet, Commander. Zero bubble."

Van Meer glanced at the compass. "Come right to zero-nine-zero."

"Zero-nine-zero, sir."

Well, she was down. They would stay at two hundred feet until they were off the continental shelf, then go to operating depth. He asked for compartment reports once again, then: "All ahead standard, Mr. Spencer."

"All ahead standard, sir."

He sensed that Harris was standing at his side and turned. "We're at two hundred feet, course zero-nine-zero, Captain. Standard speed and answering bells on the reactor."

Harris nodded absently. "Mr. Spencer, you've got the con," he said, surrendering control. Then, to van Meer: "My cabin in five minutes. Have the word passed for Dr. Schulman."

Van Meer stared after him, desperately trying to conjure up the gull again. But all he could visualize was a rolling black ocean and an empty sky.

Harris' cabin was luxurious. The bulkheads had been covered with walnut-patterned Formica and there was an orange-and-brown throw rug covering the carpeting between the small wood-grained desk and the single bunk, which looked more like a Danish-modern sofa. Several repeater scopes were built into the far bulkhead, and just over the bunk was a large color photograph of an Alaskan glacier with towering mountains in the background. With only the desk light on, the effect was that of the captain's cabin on a luxury liner. The few snapshots on the shelf above the desk were obviously of Harris' parents, Back Bay and regal, then van Meer noticed with something of a shock that one of them was of Elizabeth Renslow—a younger, happier Elizabeth than the one he knew. Harris wasn't the type to carry a torch and he wondered if the photograph was more in the nature of a trophy. He decided it probably was.

Harris leaned back in his chair and smothered a yawn, then nodded to them to take seats. "We were all briefed by the admiral, so I won't bother with details. But if there are any questions, now's the time to ask them." He paused, looking at both van Meer and Schulman with a tired stare. "This is probably the only time we'll discuss the drill, for all of the obvious reasons. In case you're wondering, there are no written orders—either here or any other place. The drill is as top secret as you can get."

There was a knock on the door and Harris swore quietly. "Come the hell in and then get the hell out."

Perez, the small steward, cracked open the door, his face impassive. "The coffee you ordered, Captain." Harris nodded and cleared a spot on his desk. Perez put down the tray and poured three cups, then set the pot on a nearby hot plate. Harris waited until Perez had left before continuing.

"The drill will last for ten days. On the third day, we rendezvous with the attack sub *Chicago*." He glanced at Schulman. "Captain Blandini knows all the details of the drill. So do his exec and navigator. Any communication with the *Chicago* will be through them. In any contact with crew members relaying messages, they'll verify our so-called worsening international situation." He sipped his coffee. "They'll monitor the drill; they'll be on our tail at all times. And that *will* be standard operating procedure."

He hesitated, losing his train of thought for a moment, and Schulman asked, "When do the tapes start?"

"The goddamned tapes." Harris closed his eyes. "I'm repeating the admiral now, Doc. You weren't listening. We'll be out of radio contact with everybody except the *Chicago* for the entire time of the drill, part of the electronics jiggering that the Washington boys did. The only exception will be a one-a-day ship's status report we'll send via FasTrans. . . . There's an override in case of dire emergency"—he opened his eyes—"which pray to God won't happen. All transmissions we receive will be simulated transmissions from the on-board tapes, including several familygrams. The first transmissions will be received today."

Schulman still looked unhappy and had started to chew on the frame of his glasses. "And the missile teams won't find out?"

Harris shook his head. "Not unless they physically open up the dummy warheads. The computers have been programmed to give all the right responses to any panel checks."

"Which leaves only the crew to worry about," van Meer said quietly.

There was a moment of heavy silence. "You've got something you want to say, Van?"

He hadn't wanted to get into it, van Meer thought glumly. Cheryl had been right a second time. He not only drank too much, he talked too much. And it was too late to shut up. "We spend ten days programming the crew to believe the world is coming to an end and then we launch four missiles. Just like that."

Harris nodded. "That's right, Van. Barring any emergency transmissions, we launch four birds with dummy warheads. Just like that. On the afternoon of the tenth day."

"And then?"

Harris sighed. "We tell the crew it was a drill and go home."

"What do you think their reaction will be?"

"I'm not good at guessing games, Van. Are you trying to make a point?"

"I'm serious," van Meer said stubbornly. "We put them through ten days of hell, then we tell them that it was all a drill, that their homes really weren't blown away, that everything is still coming up roses. I think they'll have pretty strong reactions."

Harris swiveled his chair toward Schulman. "Doctor?"

Schulman studied his chewed frames for a moment. "I should think there would be vast relief, maybe even some euphoria or minor hysteria." He hesitated. "There might be some bitterness, particularly among family men."

Harris shrugged. "I think you're too close to your own specialty, Doctor. I agree that they'll be immensely relieved. After the drill we return to Charleston for a debriefing and they'll get an unexpected week's liberty before going back out on patrol. That should take out most of the sting, if there is any."

"And during the ten days?" van Meer persisted.

Harris looked disgusted. "Weren't you listening, either, Van? That's what this goddamned drill is all about. That's what we're supposed to find out." He turned to Schulman again. "What do you anticipate?"

Schulman looked thoughtful. "Prior to the launch, I would expect increasing levels of depression and anxiety, undoubtedly some anger, and probably a feeling of hopelessness. Beyond that, I'm tempted to think they'll react precisely as they've been trained, with overlays of the emotions I've mentioned."

"Any tendency to violence?"

"Among the crew members? I rather doubt it."

Harris stood up. "Anything more, Van?"

Van Meer started to say something, then thought better of it and shook his head. Schulman suddenly asked, "Where's the tape deck?"

Harris half smiled. "Where you'd least expect—" The phone buzzed and he picked it up, listened for a moment, then said, "Give me a minute," and hung up. He shook his head. "Stroop wants to go over some spec ops." A sour smile. "I guess that will be the game for the next ten days—pretending that we're really on a regular patrol." He nodded at Schulman, dismissing him. "Van, stick around for a moment."

After Schulman had left, Harris toyed with a pencil, not meeting van Meer's eyes. "Once the drill is over, I want you to request a transfer. And, frankly, I think I'm anticipating you."

He was, but van Meer didn't want to admit it. He hadn't expected Harris to initiate it. He had wanted to do it himself. "Any reasons why?"

Harris looked up, his face expressionless. "Simple. We don't get along and there's no sense in pretending that we do. The crew knows it and it's only a matter of time before some of them try to use it. I'd just as soon avoid that. It would make it difficult for both of us."

He admired Harris for his honesty but he still couldn't help reacting angrily. "Anything specific?"

Harris sighed. "A lot, but frankly they're not the sort of thing I could put in a fitness report and then defend. You brood a lot; your mind wanders; you're not happy. I don't think you really give a damn about the Navy." His voice hardened. "I don't trust you anymore, Van—not as an officer and certainly not on board the *Alaska.*"

Van Meer felt the warmth at the back of his neck. "I'll think about it."

Harris shrugged. "We'll have to stay out of each other's way for a few weeks."

Van Meer got up to go, then stopped at the door, suddenly curious. "What do you think of the drill?"

"I think it stinks," Harris said quietly. "Just like you do. That's probably the only thing we both agree on."

"But you went along with it."

The pencil snapped. "For Christ's sake, Van, I was *ordered* to. I don't make policy; I carry it out—you know that. If and when you get your own command, you'll carry it out, too. Besides, you could have objected. Why the hell didn't you?" He glared for a moment, then burst out: "I don't *like* being an errand boy for the politicians. I don't *like* being experimented on. Did it ever occur to you that Doc's report on us will probably be as extensive as that on the crew?"

The phone rang again and he ran a hand through his hair in frustration, then waved van Meer out. In the passageway van Meer thought that for one brief moment he and Harris had almost communicated. If Harris hadn't been so tired, if Stroop hadn't called from the maneuvering room, if he hadn't been so out of it himself, maybe for the first time they might have understood each other. . . .

His compartment was still deserted. He pulled the door shut behind him and stood there for a moment wondering if he should hit the rack or write a letter. He sat down at the desk. Cheryl hadn't been too happy when he left. He hadn't solved any of his problems but he had certainly added to hers. . . .

He had filled half a page with apologies when it hit. He had paused for a second to yawn and massage the bridge of his nose when once again he was lying beside a private landing strip in Pennsylvania, feeling heat at his back; hot oil ran in rivulets through the grass. Somebody, somewhere, was screaming and something thick and viscous was dripping down his face and dampening his shirt. . . .

He had staggered to his feet, suddenly aware that his coat had started to scorch and his skin to blister. Behind him was the wreckage of his small Cessna 152 and inside it, somebody was screaming. He had stood there in shock, trying to remember how he had gotten there, to remember what had happened, to remember who was in the plane. . . .

He couldn't—not now—recall how long he had stood there while somebody screamed in what was left of his plane. Rosenberg had told him it couldn't have been more than a second or two. But he didn't believe that. He knew damned well he had stood there for minutes, doing nothing, while the person closest to him had burned alive.

Maggie.

But it had been too late, much too late. He had dashed for the plane but the heat had been too intense and then some people had run up and pulled him away. And the screaming had stopped before then, anyway. . . .

Van Meer shuddered, picked up the sheet of stationery, and tore it into small pieces. The least he could do was be loyal to her memory.

He was tired now, and smothering in a black depression. He felt like crying but he was too old for that and there was nobody around whom he could hit. He walked over to the wardrobe and fumbled out a tablet.

It was a good twenty minutes before he managed to blot out the vision of the burning plane and drift off into an uneasy sleep.

11

NY VISION PROBLEMS, dizziness? Any headaches? They're common when you first come back."

Renslow shook his head. "I feel fine, Doctor. If it were up to me, I wouldn't be here at all."

"We're almost through." Captain John Hamady pulled his stool closer to Renslow, who was sitting on the examination table. He took an ophthalmoscope from the pocket of his smock and held it up to Renslow's face. "Consider a physical as preventive maintenance, Commander. Maybe we can catch something before it gets serious. If anything goes wrong with you when you're a thousand feet down, you're stuck. Now look straight ahead and don't blink."

"What's the light for?"

"So I can see the network of tiny arteries at the back of the eye. It's a simple check for arteriosclerosis."

"Christ, I'm not even forty yet."

Hamady peered intently at something two inches past the base of Renslow's nose. "Arteriosclerosis is no respecter of age, Captain." He shifted the scope to the other eye. "Ever had difficulty moving your fingers? Any pain in your hands? . . . Okay, that's it. Put on your clothes." He snapped off the scope and walked back to his desk.

Renslow pulled on his pants. "So how am I?"

"A lot sounder than the dollar." Hamady started to write on his prescription pad. "You have the usual colds?"

"I always come down with one after a patrol."

"Try these; maybe they'll help."

"They're really good?"

"The best that money can buy."

Renslow shoved the prescription into his pocket and sat down again on the examination table to put on his shoes.

Hamady's hands, Renslow observed, were huge and powerful for a man who was five seven and had the build of a bookkeeper. Hands that were surprisingly gentle and precise.

"How come you stuck with the Navy, Doctor? You could have had a rather cushy practice in civilian life."

Hamady shrugged. "Maybe so, maybe no. Here I'm a big frog in a small puddle—an expert in submarine medicine and, if you'll pardon my modesty, one of the best there is. I deal with inner space rather than outer space but it's just as fascinating: life a thousand feet down, life under pressure, what stress will do to the human mind and body . . . It's a great field."

Renslow knotted his tie. "Many guys crack up?"

Hamady leaned forward, ready to jot down notes in the medical folder in front of him. "Pressure getting to you? Any night sweats, nightmares, any tendency to argue over little things?"

Renslow laughed and slipped on his coat. "Just curious. There's a lot of strain when you're down there."

"I wouldn't know about that," Hamady said sarcastically. "To answer your question—sure, men have cracked up. But surprisingly few. The Navy's pretty good at weeding out those who can't take it."

Renslow picked up his briefcase. He was going to be late getting back. "Did you ever prescribe Equavil for crew members who might be under stress?"

Hamady glanced up, startled. "Anybody who's a candidate for Equavil wouldn't be allowed on a submarine at all."

It was Renslow's turn to be surprised. "I thought it was one of the minor tranquilizers."

"Sounds like but isn't. You know someone who's taking it?"

Renslow lied instantly. He wasn't prepared to answer that one. "No. What's so special about it?"

"It's a drug for people suffering from severe cases of reactive depression. The FDA just recently approved it—some controversy over side effects. Where'd you hear about it?"

Renslow shrugged. "It came up in conversation."

Hamady shook his head. "If you know somebody who's on it, you know somebody with serious problems. During a bad siege of depression, he can become suicidal. He also won't hesitate to take other people with him." He glanced down at the folder again. "Speaking of problems, any difficulties with your wife? You've been back three weeks now. That's a peak time for friction."

"No problems to speak of," Renslow murmured.

Outside, he sat in his car and thought hard about van Meer. Serious problems, Hamady had said. Which was no surprise; van Meer's problems had been staring them in the face for months now. He frowned, trying to recall the bottle of tablets that had fallen off the shelf. They hadn't come from the base pharmacy and the name Rosenberg didn't ring a bell. He had to be a civilian psychiatrist. A Navy shrink would have relieved van Meer of active duty. . . .

He could feel the moisture start to gather on his forehead. Some new equipment had been installed in the *Alaska* that nobody knew anything about except Harris and van Meer . . . and presumably somebody high up in the Navy Department. Anything new and secret aboard the *Alaska* would involve her combat potential. Great speed, greater silence, greater . . .

Greater what?

But part of the *Alaska's* upcoming patrol would have to be devoted to testing it out. And the one thing nobody knew was that the executive officer was a manic depressive, taking large doses of a new drug. Harris didn't know about van Meer; if he had, he would have beached him. And nobody above Harris knew. Any superior officer would have done the same. Only Van himself knew. And now he knew.

And Cheryl must have known.

He drove back to Electric Boat, preoccupied with thoughts about van Meer. What if something happened to Harris, and van Meer had to take over? How badly would the side effects of the drug influence his judgment, his mental alertness? How much could he endanger the *Alaska*?

At three o'clock he called Cheryl. Could she meet him after work? Groton Motor Inn, between five-thirty and six . . .

He left early and drove to the inn. She walked through the door five minutes after he had but not before he had managed to kill one Scotch.

"If that's your second, you're turning into a heavy drinker. Tough time at the office?"

"It's after hours; it's allowed." Then, without preamble: "I'm more interested in talking about your troubles than I am about mine."

She signaled the waiter, then faced Renslow with a trace of coolness. "I take it this is about Van. Right?"

He found himself reacting to the hostility in her voice. "Wrong. It's about Van and the *Alaska*."

Her knuckles whitened around her glass. "I think you're going to have to explain that."

He hunched over the table. "Cheryl, did Van ever talk about the responsibility he carries? It's not as if he sells insurance or holds down a nine-to-five job. He's second in command of the *Alaska*. That's a Trident submarine, the biggest there is, which carries a complement of twenty-four missiles, each of which has seventeen warheads. It's the equivalent of the third most powerful nation in the world, all by itself. Running it is what Van does for a living."

She sipped her drink and said quietly, "The *Alaska* could be carrying thirty-six missiles or forty-eight; it wouldn't mean anything to me, Al. I know what you're trying to say but don't quote figures and expect me to have an emotional reaction. That's your game, not mine." She fumbled out a cigarette. "I know what Van does for a living. And I'm very proud of him."

"I'm glad you're proud," he said with a touch of sarcasm. "But that's not the point. The point is that Van is supposed to be at his peak, both physically and mentally, when he's on patrol. That means emotionally, too."

Her face was expressionless. "You're trying to tell me that he isn't."

"You *know* that he isn't. Van's on Equavil; it's what they prescribe for people suffering severe reactive depressions."

"You found the tablets in the medicine cabinet," she said accusingly.

"By accident; I don't ordinarily snoop."

For a moment he was afraid she was going to walk out. "I thought you were his friend."

"A friend is one who wouldn't report it, right? What's a friendship worth, Cheryl? Van is the executive officer of . . . the . . . *Alaska*. It's not exactly a tin can or a freighter."

Her face was expressionless. "What are you going to do?"

He ran a hand through his hair. He hadn't given much thought to what he was going to do. Report it, yes, but to whom or when, he wasn't sure. Van was on a three-month patrol. They were hardly going to recall the *Alaska* because its executive officer was popping pills.

"I want to know how bad it is with Van."

She finished her drink and signaled for another. "He's been seeing Dr. Rosenberg for six months now. He broods about the accident. He blames himself—and so does Jimmy. The boy hasn't spoken to his father since it happened. He's living with Van's sister now." She paused. "Is there anything else you want to know?"

"How he acts."

There was sudden color in her cheeks. "For God's sake, you want me to tell you he acts crazy? He doesn't. He's as sane as you or I. So he drinks too much. Right now we're not doing so bad ourselves."

"The medicine?"

"It helps him sleep; maybe it calms him down some. I can't see inside his head."

Which told him everything . . . and nothing at all. "Why did Van keep it a secret?"

"What would you have done? If Van tells the Navy, he'll get a medical. On top of everything else, that would kill him."

"You sure he would mind a medical discharge that much?"

"If he really didn't mind, he would have resigned."

"Maybe that's what he should have done."

"Really?" She was antagonistic now, her face tight. "The Navy means as much to him as it does to you, Al. For better or for worse, he measures himself against you and Harris. He couldn't bring himself to quit, to admit that he was less than you." She hesitated. "So he has periods of deep depression. Under the circumstances, I think he's entitled."

He toyed for a moment with his empty glass. "You're looking at it from the personal side, Cheryl. But it concerns a lot more people than just Van. His . . . condition . . . could be dangerous not only for himself but for the ship and the crew. And maybe for a lot of others."

She was quiet for a moment, then burst out bitterly, "I don't give a good goddamn about the ship and the rest of the crew. How selfless is somebody supposed to be in this world?" She stubbed out her cigarette. "You still haven't told me what you intend to do. Or what you want me to do."

He was back to square one. They wouldn't recall the *Alaska* just to relieve van Meer of command. Without an examination by Navy psychiatrists, it was doubtful if the powers that be would do anything at all. In one sense van Meer was now an unpredictable element in a highly dangerous situation. In another sense it was just one more patrol and by now there had been hundreds. . . .

"When he returns from patrol," Renslow said slowly, "I suppose somebody should talk to him. I think maybe he should . . . ask for a medical leave, have a complete examination by a Navy doctor."

"What about you? Would you talk to him when he comes back?"

He was getting more involved than he wanted to. On several levels.

"Be glad to."

She finished her drink and picked up her purse to leave. Renslow followed her out of the booth and walked her to her car. "Maybe we should have dinner some night and just talk about pleasant things."

"That would be a first."

He helped her into her car and closed the door, then remembered the play. "What are you and Van going to see in New York?"

"*Hi, Lily.* They say it's a good show."

"The *Times* just ran the closing notice. Try the new Neil Simon; it'll run forever." He kept his hand on the door. "I'm going to hold you to that dinner, you know."

She smiled suddenly and the tension between them dissolved. "I thought I'd said yes."

A damned handsome woman, he thought again, watching as she turned onto the highway.

Then he wondered what she was hiding. There had been a false note throughout the conversation. She had opened up far too easily about van Meer, as if she were almost eager to talk about him.

The old Cheryl would have told him to fuck off.

12

"YOU SHOULD HAVE a star now."

"I have a star."

"Ready . . . stand by . . . *mark.*"

Pause. "You goofed, Gerassi—try again and this time don't screw up."

Gerassi swung around from the scope, his face white. "You want to try, Clinger?"

An abrupt silence filled the control room. Clinger, quartermaster first, said quietly, "I'll forget I heard that, Gerassi. Try again."

Van Meer stood to one side of the hatch, watching. It wasn't like Gerassi to blow up while taking a star fix, particularly since Clinger not only outranked him but also outweighed him by a good thirty pounds. Gerassi was the quiet, long-suffering type who thought twice before he said good morning. . . .

They had been under way for ten hours now, long enough for everybody to have slipped into the routine of the ship. But they hadn't and he couldn't put his finger on what was wrong.

"Do what he says, Gerassi—and do it until you get it right," van Meer ordered. He left the suddenly quiet control room and walked down to the sonar compartment just aft of the attack center. On the door was a sign: UNAUTHORIZED PERSONNEL KEEP OUT. Below it, somebody had written, "Don't go away mad. Just go away." He knocked and walked in. Olson was on his knees on the carpeted floor, a clean rag spread out before him. The piece of gear that lay disassembled on the cloth looked remarkably like an exploded-view diagram in a textbook. Olson, he remembered, was nothing if not neat.

"Will she fly, Ray?"

"Maybe. Replace one of these brushes and she'll be all set."

The sonar room was van Meer's personal hiding place. With its carpeted deck and cork-lined bulkheads, it was the quietest spot on an already deadly quiet ship, the perfect spot to sit and think. Unlike the cramped sonar rooms on older ships, the *Alaska*'s sonar room had been enlarged so there was space for a hot plate, a small desk, and an extra chair. And Olson was smart enough to ignore him when he wanted to be ignored. The chief sonar man on board, this time out he was also chief of the boat, van Meer's right-hand man and liaison with the crew—and one of the few who could talk to both the nukes and the ops.

Olson was also his best friend among the enlisted men on board, though van Meer realized that he didn't really know Olson well. There wasn't much to go on. Olson was forty years old, tall and gawky—an ex-farmboy who had kept his Southern Illinois twang. His first marriage had been brief and bitter; his second wife, Edith, had finally adjusted to the fact that her husband spent half of every year underwater.

Van Meer made himself at ease in the spare chair. "You haven't changed your mind?"

"To re-up? Sorry, Commander, twenty years is long enough. And nobody's offered me a job as a reactor salesman, either."

"Your last patrol can be a drag."

"I could do this one standing on my head."

Van Meer poured himself a cup of coffee. "How's the crew settling down?"

Olson put down the small clock motor he was holding and wiped his fingers on a piece of cloth. "Not too well. I think the last liberty was too much for some of them. They're skittish."

He hadn't been imagining it, then; Olson apparently had felt the same thing. "How so?"

"Complaints about a lot of things that don't mean diddly." Olson looked disgusted. "Baker thinks somebody stole a book of his. I told him he'd probably misplaced it. And two of the chiefs are bitching that somebody is smoking cigars in chiefs' berthing. And, finally, there's a whole raft of complaints about the coffee."

"Just gripes or actual complaints?"

Olson shrugged. "Just gripes. I wouldn't worry none. They don't like the tea or the Kool-Aid, either." He frowned. "A funny thing about the cigar bit. Humphreys and Morrison kept asking me if I could smell it and I couldn't smell a damn thing."

In sick bay van Meer ran across the same uneasiness. Schulman had half a dozen medical folders strewn across his desk and was thumbing through them, shaking his head. "I don't deserve this, Van—at least not this soon."

"Deserve what?"

"Contact dermatitis." He waved at the records. "A minor rash. Sometimes it itches like hell. So far, five men have come down with it. No reason for it. They're from different parts of the ship. They're not in any one division or working on the same sort of gear."

"Something they caught ashore?"

"Don't think so. It's the type of thing that shows up very quickly, within a few hours. These have come in since fourteen hundred."

"Allergenic reaction to something?"

"Of course. But to what?"

Van Meer shrugged. "You've got a limited environment down here. You could have Nick start running patch tests."

Schulman looked put out. "You want to switch billets?"

"I've just been on more patrols than you."

Schulman shuffled the folders together, then suddenly said, "Van, is it always like this when you first leave port?"

Van Meer thought for a moment. Within hours the *Alaska* usually sank into a sort of semisilence. Conversations grew muted and there would be only the whisper of fans and turbines or the sound of the movie being shown in the mess. It wouldn't be until the last few days that channel fever would set in and the men would suddenly realize they had seen nobody but one another for ten weeks and that had been at least one week too many.

The atmosphere on board the *Alaska* now was what he would expect it to be at the end of a patrol, not at the start.

"How do you mean?"

"The crew seems jumpy," Schulman said slowly. "If I wanted to be professional, I'd say they were having an attack of nerves."

"Maybe they are." Then: "Let me know if you come up with anything in the allergy line."

Back in his compartment, he lay down in his bunk and stared blankly at the overhead. The crew usually shook down within hours; the fine tuning of shipboard relationships took a week or more. You needed time to get used to the new men, time to remember the idiosyncrasies of the men you had shipped with before, time to figure out who were the wingnuts and who were the workers.

Then he realized what he was fighting. It wasn't just nervousness about the crew; it was also the desire for something to take the edge off the depression he could feel coming on.

Dr. Rosenberg hadn't expected that he would become psychologically addicted to the tablets. He had already, on his own, doubled the daily dosage. What was it that Rosenberg had said about the side effects? He couldn't remember. Schulman would know but there was no way he could ask Schulman. . . .

"Commander van Meer, lay up to the captain's cabin."

He rolled out of the bunk. He debated for a moment if he should take an Equavil tablet now. No, he decided, he couldn't let himself be this much of a slave to it. . . .

"Have a seat, Van."

Harris looked more rested than he had that morning but there was an air of preoccupation about him that put van Meer on edge.

"We'll be rendezvousing with the *Chicago* day after tomorrow, approximately oh-eight-hundred. Weather conditions permitting, Captain Blandini and his navigator and exec will come aboard. I'll want the *Alaska* looking smart, of course."

"It will be." Harris couldn't have called him in for *that*, he thought.

"How's the crew shaking down?"

"They're a little nervous. I'm not sure why." Van Meer hesitated, then said tentatively, "Maybe rumors . . ."

Harris looked blank. "Rumors of what?"

Van Meer froze. He recalled, too late, that they weren't supposed to talk about the drill, not even among themselves. But the blank look on Harris' face seemed oddly genuine. "Just . . . rumors."

Sarcastically: "That seems vague enough." Then: "What do you mean by 'a little nervous'?"

"Olson reports that there've been complaints about the coffee, about somebody smoking cigars on board."

"The smoking lamp is lit for cigar smoking in the crew's mess only. As for the coffee, they're right—it tastes oily." His expression turned sour. "With Cermak running things, it's a wonder we don't have a choice between espresso and cappuccino." He changed the subject. "I hear Gerassi screwed up a star fix."

"Clinger is on his case. He won't mess up again."

Harris didn't pursue the subject, which was unlike him, van Meer thought. Again there was the sense of preoccupation. . . .

"Scoma will be putting out a ship's paper starting tomorrow," Harris said abruptly. "The usual on-board bullshit plus a short summary of world news out of Washington." He slid a sheet of yellow paper across the desk. "If the crew's nervous, this isn't going to help things."

Van Meer read through it quickly. Bloody fighting in Egypt after a leftwing attempted coup . . . President Aziz Kasim fleeing the capital . . . Colonel Muammar al-Qaddafi offering Libyan support to the rebels and Libyan troops being airlifted to Cairo . . . A self-proclaimed revolutionary government repudiating the Egyptian-Israeli treaties of 1983 and 1984, and calling for an immediate state of war . . . Israeli troops massing on the Egyptian and Jordanian borders . . . terrorist activities by the PLO . . . an assassination attempt on King Hussein, and the U.S. protesting the sudden appearance of Cuban advisers in Jordan . . .

He handed it back. "It's well done. Very believable."

Harris' face suddenly looked starched. "You're taking it calmly enough."

Van Meer stared, waiting for the half smile. There wasn't any. "I meant it's a good first dispatch," he said, fumbling.

Harris glared at him. "What the hell are you talking about? Do you know what it means if we lose the Mideast oil?"

"The dispatch is part of the . . . the drill," van Meer said slowly, disbelieving. "It's the first in a series. We were briefed on them by Admiral Cullinane and Dr. Hardin."

The look of outrage gradually faded from Harris' face. "The drill," he said, troubled. Then, almost slyly: "The drill hadn't slipped my mind. It's just that if anything really big happened, a lot of things might get lost in the shuffle. There might not even be time to send us an override canceling the drill. And the messages would read just like this."

Once out in the passageway, van Meer could feel himself start to tremble. What the hell was happening?

Harris had tried to cover it but the truth was—he was starting to believe the drill was real.

13

ELIZABETH HAD LEFT a hastily written note propped up against the sugar canister. She was at the Navy Officers' Wives Club and wouldn't be home until seven. There were leftovers in the refrigerator, TV dinners in the freezer. . . .

Renslow crumpled up the piece of notepaper and pegged it at the garbage can, then defiantly opened up a can of tomato soup. There was some limp leftover salad that looked thoroughly unreliable and he added it to the note in the garbage. A slice of cheesecake from the freezer and presto, supper, he thought gloomily. The dieter's nightmare, low in almost everything but calories . . .

He was reviewing the conversation with Cheryl for the fifth time when he heard a car in the driveway. A moment later, the front door banged open and the sound of high heels echoed in the tiled entrance hall. Elizabeth crossed the living room to hang up her jacket, then walked into the kitchen. She looked surprised.

"I thought you'd be working. I didn't expect you home until late."

"You know I'd call if I were going to be working." He waved at the stove. "There's some soup left in the pot—genuine gourmet-style Campbell's."

"You're a little heavy on the irony tonight, aren't you?"

"Unlike you, I've got nothing against home cooking. How'd the meeting go?"

"As they usually do—it dragged." She poked through the refrigerator, setting small plastic-covered dishes on the table.

"Who'd you drive home with?"

"Nobody. I drove myself."

"You usually go with Susan or Diane, don't you?"

She straightened up and turned around. "Very clever but you're overdoing it, aren't you? There's a little difference between seven in the evening and three in the morning." She tried to keep her voice even but the words had an ugly edge.

"There's a little difference between leftovers and a solid meal, too." He was being petty and he hated himself for it—and hated her for bringing it out in him.

"You can hire a cook. You didn't have to marry one."

"It's an easy job," he said quietly. "You get every three months off."

She dug a fork savagely into one of the containers, her face flushed. "You know, there was a time when I couldn't wait until the three months were up and you'd come home from patrol. Little things would pile up around the house. There'd be decisions only you could make. Well, one day I realized I couldn't wait for you anymore. I had to learn to live my life without you, make my own decisions, arrange my own schedules." She looked up at him, her face tight. "When you come home now, you're a stranger upsetting my routine. I learned how to live without you—and I'm not so sure I want to learn to live with you again."

Renslow could feel himself growing angry. "You knew I was a submariner when you married me."

She nodded gravely. "That's right, I did. At least I thought I did. I'll take full responsibility for being starry-eyed and romantic and not looking at the situation closer. But I don't think that's the problem."

They enjoyed fighting, Renslow thought bleakly; they enjoyed scratching at each other until the blood flowed.

"I don't think it's the problem, either. What's *your* theory?"

Her voice was ragged, harsher now. "What you really want is somebody to get your meals, to have your kids, to make the beds and sweep the floors and empty the garbage. You're in love with the idea of marriage but I'm not so sure you were ever in love with me."

He couldn't win, he thought. She was too clever with words and she was smart enough to come close to the truth.

"You're half right. I really love the idea of marriage. Maybe it's my background. Two generations ago, all the marriages in my family were arranged marriages. You got married first, then you learned to love your wife. People grew to love each other. They didn't necessarily start out that way."

"It's the institution of marriage that's important. Your wife is just a replaceable part. Is that it?"

"I didn't say that."

"A man and wife can grow to hate each other, too," she said in a crumpled-parchment voice.

He stared at her, not answering. She was a remote, brittle, sophisticated woman from a world he didn't understand, a world he didn't want to understand. Both of them were avoiding the real issue. But once either one of them mentioned it, there would be no turning back. And neither he nor Elizabeth was willing to take that step. At least, not yet.

She looked back at him, her expression condescending, superior, and indifferent. She was in complete control of her emotions this time. He wasn't—and she knew it. He suddenly wanted to hit her, to see a look of pain, to hear her cry. And she was silently daring him.

Renslow found himself clenching his fists. The sound of the phone behind him cut the tense silence.

Elizabeth spooned some carrots from the plastic container in front of her. "You're the nearest."

He picked up the receiver and growled, "Renslow here." Then, slowly: "Yes . . . of course. I'll be right down."

"Something important?" She was still playing her role.

"They arrested Ernie Gradow early this morning for attempted murder." She looked up sharply and he added, "They're holding him at the base hospital."

It was a half-hour ride to the hospital and all the way there, his mind was a jumble of thoughts about Gradow. There wasn't much he could recall. He had an image of a small, heavy-set man in his late thirties or early forties and that was about it. Harris' chief of the boat—or he would have been if he had gone on patrol this time, but his broken leg had beached him. Married, three kids or four; Renslow couldn't remember which.

He parked in a visitor's slot at the hospital and went on in. At the front desk they directed him to the prisoners' wing. Dr. Strickland, the medical OD, was waiting for him at the nurses' station, along with a Mr. Black, a young man in his late twenties, whom Renslow guessed to be a Navy lawyer, and a Captain Fallon from the police department, a burly, graying man who looked uncomfortable in the hospital setting.

Renslow announced to nobody in particular, "I'm Commander Renslow."

Fallon looked at him curiously and said, "Gradow's one of your men?"

Renslow shook his head. "He's on the Gold Crew. I'm captain of the Blue. What happened—bar fight?"

Fallon shot an annoyed glance at Black, and Renslow guessed that Fallon had expected Black to fill him in. "Nothing so simple. Gradow was working in his garage. At midnight he suddenly called his wife out of the house and lit into her with a baseball bat."

It was a moment before the words made sense to Renslow. He looked at Strickland. "How is she?"

"Critical. Cracked ribs, fractures of the long bones in the left arm and leg, severe edema of the head and scalp."

"She'll live?"

Strickland shrugged. "Probably."

Black suddenly turned to the police captain. "You had no right to hold Gradow for as long as you did. He's an obvious psychopath; he needed hospitalization."

Fallon's eyelids lowered. "Mr. Black, I don't *know* that he's an obvious anything. We notified the base as soon as practicable."

Renslow cut in. "When did you pick him up?"

"Around midnight—the neighbors called in."

Black interrupted again. "That's well over twelve hours, that's—"

"We try to cooperate with the Navy in every way," Fallon said in a thin voice. "But this wasn't a drunken bar brawl. It was attempted murder. We thought at first Gradow was either drunk or on drugs and we held him, thinking he might sober up and be able to answer questions."

"The man had a broken leg—"

"If it wasn't for that cast, you wouldn't have noticed," Fallon said dryly. "It certainly didn't slow him down any."

Strickland cut in, a worried look on his face. "Did he talk much?"

"The usual babble. One of the reasons we thought he was drunk."

Strickland glanced at Renslow. "What's his clearance?"

"He's got a Q clearance—"

"That's one of the highest," Black interrupted, looking at Fallon. "I know damned well your department's got standing orders—"

"Nobody understood a damned thing he was saying, Ensign." Fallon had guessed at the rank and Black flushed.

"Where'd you find him?" Renslow asked.

"He was hiding in his attic, stark naked and raving. One of my men crawled up after him and Gradow attacked him with a tire iron."

"And you still took him alive?" Renslow asked.

Fallon looked grim. "He tripped over a floorboard. Otherwise he would have been shot. A man's out of his mind and rushing you with a tire iron, there's no way you're going to stand there and try to argue him out of it."

Black broke the silence that followed. "I'm sorry if I came on strong, Captain. . . ." His voice trailed away.

"Any reason why Gradow flipped out?" Renslow asked.

"Who knows? We interviewed the neighbors and they all said the same thing: devoted couple. Neither of them even looked at anybody else. You tell me. I've run out of theories. Why does somebody go up in a tower on a university campus and shoot eleven people?" He fished some papers out of his pocket and gave them to Black. "I've got some additional custody forms."

Renslow turned back to Strickland. "Can I see him?"

Strickland nodded and started down the hall. "He won't recognize you. He's not very coherent. Captain Fallon's right. He does act as if he were on some kind of drug."

"He's not the type," Renslow objected.

A marine guard was standing in front of Gradow's room; the window in the door was protected by a wire-mesh screen on the inside. Strickland nodded to the guard, who opened the door with a key. "We'll run lab tests, of course, and later we'll take his psychological profile."

Gradow was lying on the hospital bed, covered by a thin sheet. Renslow noted that he was under restraint. A nearby tray table held some plastic cups with straws sticking out of them and he guessed that somebody had to hold them for Gradow to drink, that Gradow couldn't be trusted with his arms free.

"We've sedated him," Strickland was saying, "but it doesn't knock him out, just quiets him a little."

Gradow was awake, his eyes flicking at them but giving no signs of recognition. Renslow tried to imagine a naked, screaming Gradow rushing at him with a tire iron. The picture was too incongruous, too out of character: He looked more like a trussed-up teddy bear than a dangerous maniac.

Renslow suddenly wrinkled his nose. "Was he brought in like this?"

Strickland nodded. "He's suffered a loss of control over natural functions. They hosed him down once but we don't trust him with a bedpan. Once a day, we'll have an orderly sponge him down."

Renslow felt a sudden wave of pity for the fat little man in the bed. How much of it would he remember when he came out of it? If he came out of it . . .

"Nobody's brought him any clothes or anything?"

Strickland looked thoughtful. "I rather doubt anybody will. Feeling is running pretty high against him. His wife was well liked in their neighborhood."

Renslow glanced at his watch. Not yet nine o'clock. "I'll stop by and pick up some things. I want to talk to the neighbors, anyway." Then, frowning: "Ever seen anything like this before?"

Strickland shook his head. "I haven't, but a friend of mine has. He's in the infirmary at Electric Boat. Had a case very much like this last week—straight-and-narrow guy who suddenly went off the deep end and tried to split the skull of a friend of his. No connection, obviously."

"I'd still like to talk to him," Renslow said, staring at Gradow. The man's huge eyes hadn't moved from his face in the past five minutes and he couldn't tell for sure whether there was an appeal in them or not.

"For what I think you want," Strickland said slowly, "I'd try Personnel or maybe Public Relations. I think you'd have trouble getting anything out of Joe." He looked curious. "You think you might be able to help him?"

"Who knows? But sooner or later, he's going to have to stand trial and he's going to need all the help he can get."

Strickland glanced down at the bed, thoughtful. "He really isn't the type to take a stick to his wife, is he?"

It was nine o'clock and Chestnut Street had buttoned up for the night. A family street. Bicycles lying on the front lawns, the muted sound of TV sets, the faint odor of cooking, somebody having a party down the block . . . It was chilly out and Renslow suddenly wished he owned a house in the neighborhood, with his wife curled up in an easy chair, the light from the fireplace splashing off her hair, the kids playing on the floor.

He smiled wryly. How maudlin could you get?

Gradow's house was an older tract type, with a huge yard in back and an ancient elm tree complete with tire swing in front. Surprisingly, there was a light on in the window. He pulled into the driveway and knocked on the door. The woman who answered was plump but somewhat sharp-faced; the neighborhood watchdog, Renslow guessed.

"The Gradows aren't home," she said firmly. "I'm Mrs. Padgett from next door."

A Navy wife, Renslow thought. He showed his ID. "I'm Al Renslow, captain of the Blue Crew on the *Alaska*. I just came from the hospital."

She suddenly looked alarmed. "How is she?"

He nodded reassuringly. "She'll live."

She opened the door wider. "Come on in. You don't have to keep your voice down. The kids are sleeping next door. Howie knows what happened. Jeff and Don are too young." She was suddenly furious. "That *mother*—"

"I talked to the police. They said the Gradows got along pretty well."

"On a scale of one to ten, they got ten plus—which is pretty unusual around here. When your husband goes away every three months, sometimes it gets to be a job to love, honor, and obey him when he comes back." She added cynically, "Or when he's away, for that matter."

He was the captain and she was taking it out on him. In a sense, he couldn't blame her.

"But Ernie and his wife got along."

"Florence is a lot of woman." She half smiled. "In a lot of ways. She adjusted pretty well. Some of us don't." She said it almost belligerently. Renslow remembered how Elizabeth had been and guessed that Mrs. Padgett's husband had just returned from patrol.

"It sounds as if Ernie changed a lot in the past few weeks or months."

She waved him to a chair. He was giving her a chance to get a few things off her chest and she was going to make the most of it. "You're right and I even mentioned it to Flo. Until the last few weeks Ernie was a pretty easygoing guy. He was a good one for jokes or dropping over to have a beer in the early evening. He was sort of the neighborhood organizer. All the kids liked him. He always had the time to fix a bike or work on somebody's car. But the last week or ten days, you'd think he was King Kong. He always had a chip on his shoulder."

She hesitated, searching for the words. "You know how people get when all the charge accounts come in at the same time? I even asked Florence if we could help out and she said no, that wasn't it, that she didn't know what it was."

Renslow stood up. There was probably another explanation that might be closer. The pudgy middle-aged man who's perfectly happy with his pudgy middle-aged wife meets some twenty-two-year-old who decides she wants a fling with stability for a change. Ernie's life could have turned upside down in a day.

"I've got to pick up some clothes, toothbrush, things like that, for him," he said. "Could you . . . "

"As far as I'm concerned, the bastard can brush his teeth with his fingers." Then, reluctantly: "All right, I'll get them for you."

She disappeared up the stairs, leaving him alone in the living room. It reminded him of his mother's house back in Pittsburgh. The faint odors of grease and onions and a touch of tomato, all of it still lingering from yesterday's barbecue . . . the easy chair in the corner with the upholstered arms worn down to the threads . . . the equally threadbare couch canted slightly so everybody sitting on it could watch the TV set . . . the prints of sea scenes on the wall . . . and everywhere the photographs: of submarines Gradow had served on, of captains he had served under, of men he had served with, all dutifully inscribed "For my shipmate, Ernie Gradow."

The dining room was more formal and he guessed they usually ate in the kitchen and reserved the dining room for Sunday dinners and company. There was some scrimshaw on the wall above the sideboard and a macramé divider hung between the living room and the dining room.

He turned on the light. The china on the sideboard caught his eye and he smiled. Strictly Navy heavy-duty china, the commissary special. Then his smile turned sour and he walked over for a closer look. The chest of flatware sitting on the middle of the shelf had a small plaque set in the lid and engraved on it was U.S.S. ALASKA. He flipped it open. Service for sixteen. A modern Danish design, also with ALASKA engraved on the handles. Hadn't Harris complained that they had once ordered special silver for the wardroom and had never received it?

He frowned and closed the chest, wishing he hadn't seen it. Gradow wouldn't be the first Navy man who had furnished his house from midnight small stores. . . . But maybe there was another explanation. Maybe.

"I thought I'd lost you. Think this will be enough?"

Renslow glanced at the pile of clothes and nodded, setting the stack on the kitchen table. "Mind if I take a look out back?"

She walked to the screen door with him, eager to point out where it had all happened. "They found her right over there, just outside the garage. Blood all over the place." She shivered. "You couldn't get me to walk out there."

He stepped outside. It was colder now, a damp cold; it would probably rain in the early morning. He walked down the flagstones toward the garage. It was the same route that Florence must have taken when she went out to the garage.

Actually, it was more of a large shed than a garage. He tried the doorknob and was surprised when it turned in his hand. He pushed the door open and flipped on the light switch, whistling involuntarily at the clean beauty of the sailboat up on chocks. My God, how long must Gradow have been working on it? He circled it, admiring the careful attention to detail, the smoothly varnished woodwork, and the bright blue trim. . . .

The odor of paint still hung in the air, sharper than it should be, and he glanced around. There was a half-open can of paint on the floor, a brush, its blue bristles stiff with dried paint, lying across the top. He knelt down and pushed the lid all the way on, then sealed it, using his foot to apply the pressure. Force of habit. It didn't much matter whether he saved it or not; Gradow wouldn't be using it for a while.

He stepped back to the door and for the first time spotted the faint brown spots on the flagstones just outside. Florence had probably hesitated there, suddenly suspicious, suddenly aware that something was wrong with her husband. And then, before she could run away, Gradow had beat her to the ground—the woman he had loved, who had borne him three kids, who had lived with him for fifteen years. . . .

Renslow turned off the light and closed the door behind him. Why had Gradow done it? he wondered.

14

THE FIRST SIGNS of real trouble came when they were showing an old Western in the crew's mess. Van Meer had stopped by to catch a scene or two. It was the kind of simpleminded Western that the crew usually liked, good for lots of popcorn and two hours of good-natured catcalls.

Ten minutes into the film, he was mildly surprised to realize that at least half the crew members present were watching it in dead earnest, concentrating intently on the dialogue. He had just noticed this oddity when he also realized that there was a vocal minority who weren't going to give it a break.

"C'mon, John, kiss your horse."

"What's the penalty for screwing ponies in Texas?"

"Two to one he makes Old Paint before he makes the girl."

There was a break in the catcalls and then a voice growled in the dark, "Shut up, Bailey, or we'll stuff the film down your throat."

"Hey, Longstreet, I hear you got a phone call in CIC."

And then a quiet, steely bass that filled the mess compartment: "The next nuke who opens his mouth is going to get a broken arm."

He'd know Meslinsky's voice anywhere, van Meer thought, but the tone puzzled him. He couldn't pinpoint what sounded ... different. Then he had it: Animal wasn't kidding. Van Meer shifted uneasily in his seat and drifted back into watching the film.

Five minutes later, he sensed there was something unreal about the silence. The men present weren't watching the movie; they were waiting for something. He bolted for the light switch a split second after the scuffle started in the front row. There was a sudden crash just as he flicked the lights on. Longstreet, a second-class electronics technician in his mid-twenties, was standing in a classic karate pose, looking slightly ridiculous.

Facing him was Leggett, the first-class baker, his right hand clutching a catsup bottle like a club.

Van Meer pushed his way to the front. "Okay, knock it off. Longstreet, Leggett, you're both on report. Baker, put the film away—that's all the movies today. In fact, that's all the movies until further notice. Everybody else, clear the mess hall."

They drifted out, a muttered "We'll get you, Bailey" floating back from the passageway. Baker had just started to rewind the film when van Meer saw a crumpled piece of paper on the deck and picked it up. A copy of the first issue of the ship's newspaper, headlined by the worsening situation in the Middle East and the U.S. protests about Cuban advisers in Jordan. It hadn't helped, he thought, but it couldn't have accounted for this much strain. . . .

"What was it like at the first showing, Baker?"

Baker put the reel back in the can. "A lot like this, sir. Maybe not quite as bad."

"A lot of friction between the nukes and the ops?"

Baker looked unhappy and van Meer realized he had put him in the position of informing on the rest of the crew. "Nothing really serious, sir."

Not until now. He'd have to report the trouble to Harris, along with the fact that housekeeping wasn't what it should be on board. Candy wrappers in the passageways; he had never seen that before.

He started for the forward torpedo room, detouring through the ship's berthing compartment, rigged for red as usual. Suddenly he stopped, cautiously sniffing the air. Not since he was a kid, he thought, startled. Not since his parents had sent him away to summer camp to spend the nights lying awake listening to the sobbing of the younger boys, homesick for whatever towns they had come from.

The faint, sour odor of urine . . .

Somebody in the compartment had wet his bed.

Thursday, June 25

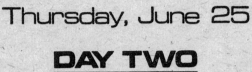

DAY TWO

15

"HOW FAR DOWN does this ol' elevator go, Admiral?"

"You'll be five hundred feet below the top of the hill, Mr. Warden."

Caleb Warden beamed. "The Russkies would have a tough time eliminating our little ol' Flag Plot, wouldn't they?"

Admiral Stewart Cullinane was annoyed. Warden knew the possibilities as well as he did; there was no need to play the country hick.

"A direct hit by a multimegaton warhead would vaporize both the hill and the installation, I'm afraid. The hill offers some protection in case Washington goes." Warden looked unhappy and Cullinane smiled slightly. Maybe that would hold him for a while.

There was a slight jar and the doors of the elevator *whoosh*ed open. A small electric cart was waiting for them.

"Flag Plot is actually cut fifteen hundred feet into the side of the hill," Lieutenant Chavez explained. "Next to Cheyenne Mountain and NORAD, it's the largest protected command center in the United States."

They were breathing canned air now, which smelled slightly damp and musty. It wasn't too much different from when Flag Plot had been located in one of the labyrinthine cellars of the Pentagon, Cullinane thought, but that installation had become obsolete years ago.

Another cart joined them briefly in the tunnel, finally turning off into one of the branching corridors. Only part of Flag Plot was devoted to the Situation Room itself. The rest of the underground establishment housed a variety of manned and automatic communication devices, together with automatic data terminals that fed into the central computer system. Cullinane had never gotten over the fact that the computers themselves occupied the smallest part of the installation, a room twenty by thirty feet buried even deeper in the heart of the hill. The outlying areas that housed the programmers and computer technicians were expendable; the computers themselves were not.

They whirred to the end of the tunnel, which opened out into a huge, brilliantly lit anteroom with fifteen-foot doors at the far end. Several marine guards were on duty in front. At the left, ten feet out from the wall, was a desk at which a pretty enlisted woman sat in front of a typewriter and computer terminal. She obviously doubled as both security check and receptionist.

"I have your ID badge ready, Mr. Warden. We heard you were coming. One for you, Admiral, and you, too, Lieutenant."

Chavez winked and pointed to his tunic. "Right there." She colored and pinned it on for him and Cullinane thought, Chavez will go far, if he doesn't get into a paternity suit first.

Warden caught the byplay and said, "You be careful, young lady, he's guv'mint propity."

"I'll handle him with kid gloves," she promised, then pressed a button on her desk. The doors in front of them rolled silently back.

"Good God Almighty." Warden gasped.

In one sense the Situation Room was outdated, Cullinane thought, enjoying Warden's awestruck expression. It was vulnerable and far too large, and its duties were duplicated by other, smaller installations spread throughout the country in less well-publicized locations. But its immense size made it an invaluable public-relations tool in impressing visiting firemen from members of congressional committees to foreign VIPs, up to and including Queen Elizabeth of England.

Cullinane had been afraid that Warden would react differently. Beneath the farm-boy façade, he was a shrewd and sophisticated executive. His association with Universal Telegraph had familiarized him with modern communications and data-processing technologies.

But even Warden was visibly impressed.

Directly in front of them was the observation bubble, which functioned as a spectators' booth. The huge Plexiglas bubble, twenty feet in diameter, was suspended twenty feet above the floor of the Situation Room proper. The walls of the room below, roughly fifty feet square, were covered with solid sheets of tiny light-emitting diodes that could be orchestrated to present aspects of the world military situation. The conductor was an officer who sat at a complex console that resembled an electric organ. During a briefing his hands flew over the console to bring to life new displays, combine old ones, make openings in existing displays so other data could be projected, outline continents, or sketch vast panoramas of fleets at sea. . . .

"Now, that's really . . . incredible," Warden said, stretching out the vowels. "Incredible, simply . . . incredible." Then: "Right out of *Dr. Strangelove.*"

Cullinane winced at the remark. It was hardly the first time that a visitor had made that observation. Watching Warden out of the corner of his eye, he said, "I'm afraid the movie set was quite primitive."

Warden walked to the front of the Plexiglas bubble and stared down at the sealed booth that served as a visitors' gallery on the main floor. He knew without being told that the observation bubble was reserved for VIPs.

Then he backed away and Cullinane watched as he inspected the observation bubble with a more calculating eye. There would be little he could find fault with—if he didn't inquire into price. The walls were transparent, soundproof plastic and the floor a slab of highly polished oak. Bolted to it was a series of bright chrome posts that supported a curved handrail of rosewood. The major piece of furniture in the bubble was an austere desk, scarcely more than a wooden surface, atop a free-form rosewood pillar. On it was a small computer terminal and a CRT display that was flush with the face. The only other items to break the simple lines of the desk were a slender chrome rod that supported a small microphone and a miniature joystick that moved a light arrow back and forth on any of the three wall displays below.

Warden pursed his lips and shook his head, half smiling. "The miracles that the Almighty has allowed men to perform . . . Admiral, just how accurate are all these data on the displays?"

"Most of the data are less than thirty minutes old. The majority are from satellite observations, radar and sonar trackings, as well as undersea sound-detecting arrays. They're less reliable but we include human-observer data as well."

"And this will all include ARGUS?"

Cullinane nodded. "It will, when ARGUS finally comes on-stream."

The doors opened behind them again and Admiral Howland walked in, trailed by the gaunt figure of Dr. Augustus Hardin, the staff psychologist who had created the tapes for the *Alaska*, and a puffing Captain Oxley, his face bright with perspiration. Oxley was finding the admiral a hard man to keep up with, Cullinane thought, but, then, Oxley would have found anybody hard to keep up with.

Howland nodded to Cullinane and shook hands with Warden. "I'm glad you've had a chance to see Flag Plot before Operation Fire begins, Caleb."

Warden leaned on the rosewood railing and stared down at the room below. "It's absolutely amazing, Admiral—right out of the future."

Howland turned back to Cullinane, lowering his voice. "Let's take a look at the Southern Impact Range, Stew. I'm getting some data I don't like."

Cullinane consulted a loose-leaf log in the single drawer of the desk, then bent down slightly toward the microphone, taking care to enunciate clearly. "Sector slash-oh-two-five-six-slash-three."

From a hidden loudspeaker in the bubble a voice said quietly, "Five seconds for cycling." In the room below, the display wall on the left shimmered as if it were being seen through heated air. Images swirled over its surface, colored symbols chasing colored symbols until the computers had assembled the needed data. The Southern Impact Range wavered, then abruptly solidified, bounded on the north by Ascension Island and on the left and right by the coasts of Argentina and South Africa respectively. The impact area itself appeared as a rectangle within a grid of light-blue dashes, its western lower corner anchored in the Falkland Islands. Just south of the Falklands was a small group of red triangles.

Howland looked unhappy. "The wolves are gathering, Stew."

Warden, who had been watching the display below, suddenly turned. "What do you mean, Admiral?"

"Russian trawlers," Oxley squeaked, then looked embarrassed.

Warden glanced back at the display wall, his eyes speculative.

"Some of them are in the impact area. That's dangerous, isn't it?"

Howland stared at the display, thoughtful. "We'll send in some small craft to play tag with them and drive them out."

"Chicken?"

"Sometimes it's necessary."

Warden turned back to the display wall again. "What are the red cigar shapes?"

"Submarines," Cullinane said. "The blue ones are ours, the reds are Russian, the yellow, French, and so on. If it's got a small box around it, that means it's running on the surface. There aren't many of those. Most of the ships out there are nuclear and running submerged."

He nearly smiled at the tone of regret in his voice. He still longed for the old Navy, he thought.

The first note of disappointment crept into Warden's voice. "Is that all the display will show?"

Cullinane stepped over to the microphone. "Full display, please."

The walls shimmered once more, then burst into a confusing blaze of colored symbols and continental outlines with white streaks spanning the full length of the walls.

"We can bring a great many more data into display at the risk of making it more difficult to read. Selective display is far more practical." Cullinane pointed. "The white streaks are projected satellite orbits, for example. We can also show most commercial and military flight paths, but then the board would be completely unreadable. If we want, we can extrapolate with the aid of the computers and predict the probable picture thirty minutes from now or one hour or—if you're willing to accept the inherent error of such a projection—as long as forty-eight hours into the future." He paused. "You can see how useful the room would be in the case of a nonnuclear shooting war."

"Considering the chances of a major nonnuclear war," Warden said coldly, "I'd say about as useful as tits on a boar hog." He squinted at the walls again. "Where's the *Alaska* now?"

"She's outside this area," Cullinane said, red-faced. "She's only one day out to sea."

"And probably dogged by at least one Russian sub," Howland added. "If she isn't now, she certainly will be by the time the mission is ended."

"We'll handle that when the time comes," Cullinane cut in.

Hardin had been staring quietly at the display walls, saying nothing. Now he suddenly looked over at Howland and said sharply, "It would be helpful for the program if we could monitor some of the psychological reactions of the crew during an actual ramming confrontation. As long as we have Dr. Schulman aboard the *Alaska*, it seems a shame to miss the opportunity."

If there was a candidate for Dr. Strangelove, Cullinane thought grimly, Hardin was certainly in the running.

"I'm sorry, Doctor, but Captain Harris has orders to avoid such confrontations. The *Alaska* is too valuable a weapons system to lose in a game of chicken of the sea."

Hardin looked unhappy behind his thick lenses and faintly rebellious. It would be just like Hardin to go to higher authority and try to get the decision changed, Cullinane thought.

"You really don't think we'd lose such a confrontation, do you?" Warden asked.

Cullinane throttled an angry retort and said quietly, "Anybody can get unlucky." Then: "I doubt the President would appreciate risking the *Alaska*."

Warden stared at him with an almost sleepy expression on his face and Cullinane realized for the second time that Warden had marked him as an enemy.

"Admiral Cullinane," a voice said over the loudspeaker. "We've just received a new transmission from the *Alaska*."

Cullinane glanced at his watch. Two o'clock; it was time for the third transmission. "Send it up."

A few moments later, a chief yeoman appeared at the door to the observation bubble with a message flimsy. Cullinane scanned it quickly, frowning.

"Something wrong?" Howland asked. The others were staring at him.

"I don't know." Cullinane handed the message to Howland. "The *Alaska* has just instituted water rationing. Apparently the evaporators are fouled. They're cleaning them now."

Warden glanced from one to the other, disbelieving. "Two billion dollars' worth of submarine and something doesn't work?"

Cullinane had no ready answer. "The backup systems should work. And the main evaporators should have been checked out thoroughly in the yard."

"It's possible, isn't it," Hardin cut in, "that somebody in the crew could have sabotaged the evaporators?"

Cullinane looked disgusted. "Are you posing a question or advancing that as a theory, Doctor?"

Hardin shrugged. "One of the crew might have wanted to get back to port early. Or it might have been just horseplay. We see that sort of thing on surface ships all the time."

"See what sort of thing all the time, Dr. Hardin?" Cullinane's voice was dangerously soft.

Howland stepped back from the bubble wall. "I'm sure Dr. Hardin didn't mean offense, Stew."

"I didn't know the good doctor's expertise was so extensive," Cullinane said. "He should know that submariners depend too much on each other for one of them to endanger the group. It would be inconceivable."

"Perhaps you've got another explanation," Hardin said distantly.

Warden had been listening, faintly amused. "You're a little on the touchy side today, aren't you, Admiral?"

Cullinane shot him a contemptuous glance, then walked over to the railing and concentrated on the display walls below. "I know my men," he said quietly. He was too angry to say anything more but in the back of his mind there was growing doubt. The latest message from the *Alaska* didn't feel right and it was more than just the fact that the evaporators were malfunctioning. Something about the message itself was wrong.

He'd have Chavez check the work sheets on the *Alaska* immediately but he already knew the answer. At the time the *Alaska* had left the yards, the evaporators must have been in top-notch shape. The ship would never have been released otherwise.

Something was wrong. Something one hell of a lot more serious than the evaporators.

16

CAPTAIN STEPHEN HARRIS signed the last of the requisition forms, then leaned back in his chair and thoughtfully massaged the bridge of his nose. Just how much was Cermak siphoning off? How many times did they have steak on the last patrol? Certainly not as many times as Cermak's requisitions would indicate. It wasn't all that unusual; there were a lot of opportunities to siphon off supplies between ordering them and stowing them on board. A venal supply officer could make a bundle if he didn't get caught. . . . And despite his congenial exterior, Cermak could be sly when he wanted to be.

Then Harris felt ashamed of himself. Cermak had his faults but venality wasn't one of them. And God knows the food had gotten better since he had come aboard. . . .

He checked through the requisitions once more, gradually feeling annoyed that he was looking at them at all. This was van Meer's job. It was up to him to make sure that the supply officer didn't line his own pockets. Except, of course, he couldn't trust van Meer these days, either. Like Cermak, the man was turning sly, becoming withdrawn. Lately, he'd had a haunted look about him, an expression of startled surprise in his eyes, as if he had never seen the *Alaska* before and everything about it was new and strange to him.

Harris checked the requisitions once more, his eyes straying occasionally to the top-secret dispatch that had been received an hour earlier. Civil war had broken out in Egypt following the assassination of President Kasim. Israeli forces had crossed into the Sinai in support of the legitimate Egyptian government, and airlifted Libyan troops were now deeply involved in fighting north of

Cairo. Jordanian troops, reinforced with Syrian regulars and backed by Russian-equipped Cuban advisers, had crossed the Israeli frontier and were engaged with Israeli tank elements.

The last items in the dispatch bothered Harris the most. The U.S. Sixth Fleet was marshaling in the Mediterranean between Port Said and Alexandria. The Russians had issued a blunt warning to the U.S. not to interfere in the fighting. In addition, Russia was sending in troops to support the Kurdish insurgents in Iran. The United States, in turn, had informed the Russians that it did not recognize their right to position troops in Iran and would take appropriate action if the Soviets did not withdraw. It struck Harris that each country was addressing the other in terms approaching that of an ultimatum.

War was coming, and there didn't seem to be anything that anybody could do about it. It was like being tied to the railroad tracks and hearing the train whistle just around the bend. He read through the dispatch once more, then made a mental note to give it to Scoma the next watch for printing in the ship's paper. There was no way the news could be kept from the crew; besides, other eyes than his had seen the message. And Admiral Cullinane had stressed that the crew should be apprised of all dispatches. . . .

Not that there was much you could keep secret on board a submarine.

He pushed the dispatch to one side and turned back to the requisitions. Since Cermak wasn't to be trusted, he'd have to institute a day-to-day mess-hall accounting system, flush out the bastard. . . .

"Captain?"

Van Meer. Couldn't the man knock louder than that? Did he always sneak up on people?

"Come on in, Van. What's the problem this time?"

Again the wounded expression. Or was it a calculating look? Van's favorite shipboard hobby, Harris thought, was trying to figure out his captain's moods. The man was always playing the angles, never relying on his own intuitive judgments. But after this patrol van Meer would be somebody else's problem. . . .

"It's important—"

Harris interrupted, impatient. "You wouldn't be here if it wasn't."

The questioning look again, as if there was something unusual about what he had said. What was so complicated about it? Didn't Van recognize sarcasm when he heard it?

"There was a fight in the crew's mess during the movies."

Harris sighed. Both Costanza and Scoma had already given him brief reports. What had taken van Meer so long?

"A real fight? Somebody actually landed blows?"

"I broke it up before then."

"Good for you," Harris said ironically.

Van Meer looked off balance now but, then, the man was always off balance.

"I had the feeling that one minute more and the entire compartment would have been at one another's throats. It was an ... odd atmosphere."

Van Meer was becoming paranoid, Harris thought clinically. "Who against who, Van?"

"The usual—the nukes versus the nose-coners."

"You're saying there might have been a riot?"

Van Meer looked stubborn. "That's exactly what I'm saying."

Harris suddenly felt tired. Goddammit, not only was he responsible for the ship and the crew, now he had to baby his executive officer. "Van, granted their training differs and they are, essentially, two different groups of men. Nevertheless, there's more holding them together than driving them apart. If you really want to check out their morale, send them out on liberty together and let somebody from some other ship pick on one of them."

Van Meer was looking at him strangely. "They never go on liberty together. You know that." Then, grimly: "The crew's not shaking down, Steve. And I don't know why."

Harris suddenly stood up behind his desk, leaning on his knuckles, his face inches from van Meer's. "Morale's *your* problem, goddammit; don't come bitching to me about it. If something's wrong, then find out what it is and do something about it. Don't keep telling me you can't maintain discipline in the ship."

He sat down again, suddenly exhausted. "How're Stroop's men doing with the evaporators?"

"They've torn them apart and reassembled them." Van Meer hesitated. "They couldn't find anything wrong."

"The coffee tastes like hell," Harris said slowly. "So does the drinking water." Something else was lurking in the back of his mind but he decided not to confide in van Meer. At least, not yet. If it wasn't the fault of the machinery, then it had to be the fault of the people who ran the machinery. Somebody who deliberately— He throttled the thought. "I don't suppose you have any ideas?"

Van Meer shook his head and looked faintly guilty. "I'm probably the only one on board but . . . it tastes all right to me."

"You're right; you're the only one on board," Harris said sarcastically. Then: "Have you been keeping an eye on Udall? I know he's got a job offer. That's his business. But I don't want him recruiting my crew."

"I've warned him."

"For all the good it will do." Harris fumbled for the dispatch on his desk and threw it at van Meer. "I'm afraid all of us have more important things to worry about than what happens at the movies."

Van Meer leafed through the dispatch, then went back to the beginning and read it more thoroughly. He glanced up, his face white. "But—"

Harris held up his hand. "Van, I know what you're going to say. We never got the release code canceling the drill. But can you imagine what kind of madhouse Washington must be right now? They're too busy wondering which ball is going to go up—a little one or the big one—to worry about us. We just got lost in the cracks. I remember the dispatches very well and this isn't one of them. Yesterday's and today's—they form a pattern."

Harris took the dispatch back and read it again, slowly, then shook his head. It was genuine; there wasn't any doubt about it.

"Back in New London, I used to follow developments in the Middle East." He tapped the dispatch. "This isn't exactly unexpected."

Van Meer looked desperate. "They're *supposed* to sound real. That's part of the drill itself—"

"*Goddammit*, Van, that'll be all," Harris roared. "I don't want arguments about the dispatches. And I don't want to be bothered with details of a fight that never happened or a riot that might have occurred if only God knows what. Crew discipline's *your* problem. *You* handle it."

Van Meer left and Harris read the dispatch again, searching for any hidden wording that might label it as part of the drill.

There was nothing strange about it; it all seemed straightforward. . . .

Then he thought about what would happen if war came. New London and Groton would be the first to get it, ahead of even the silos in the Middle West. Or cities like New York and Washington, D.C. The Russians would want to take out as much of the second-strike force as possible and that meant New London and Charleston and Bangor and Guam and Holy Loch—all the bases for the missile subs.

Which meant not only the yards and the sub pens and the repair facilities but everybody he knew and loved. Friends, neighbors, relatives, Elizabeth . . . No, that was over with but he would still feel regret.

Well, what would happen would happen. He wasn't helpless; that was for sure. He was in command of the *Alaska*, the most formidable weapon on the face of the earth, and he wasn't about to forget it.

He shuffled the requisitions, then stuffed them and the dispatch into his out box; Scoma could take care of them. In the meantime, he had to go over the ops sked for the rendezvous with the *Chicago* tomorrow. He'd pass the word for van Meer.

Van Meer. The man was acting strangely; he'd have to watch him.

He massaged the bridge of his nose again and hoped to God his headache would go away. He'd had it almost since the day he'd come back aboard, a constant, throbbing, splitting headache. And something more than that, too. A feeling that the world around him was growing fuzzy at the edges, becoming shadowy and indistinct. A feeling that in some unknown fashion he himself was changing, that somehow he was saying good-bye to a part of himself, a part that he cherished . . .

17

HARRY ANDERSEN had worked as a supervisor at Electric Boat for twenty-five years and when it came time to retire, management had asked him if he'd like to work part time in press relations. He knew the yards, he knew the foremen, he knew the men, and best of all, he knew the language. He also knew where the bodies were buried and who had buried them, and when the time came in the late seventies to trim the fat and squeeze out the grease, Andersen's suggestions had become law. More than the corporate money men or practically anybody else in management, Harry Andersen was the spirit of Electric Boat.

And as acting head of press relations he had also become chief protector against congressional committees, media exposés, and curious submarine commanders who wanted to know more than Andersen thought was good for them.

"Our files are like a doctor's or a lawyer's," he explained patiently to Renslow. "A man's working life is his personal life and he's got a right to his privacy. You wouldn't like it if some stranger came to your doctor and the sawbones promptly spilled his guts about you."

He sank back in his chair and lit his pipe and waited for Renslow to offer an argument as to why he should loosen up. He knew precisely how diplomatic to be, aware that in the long run it would take an order from the chairman of the board to countermand any decision he might make.

Renslow wondered whether Andersen was waiting for him to be threatening or charming, then realized that Andersen would be contemptuous of either approach, that the man would play with him for half an hour and deliver a flat "No" just in time for lunch. Or maybe he'd try to con a free meal, then drop the other shoe.

"I could make this official," Renslow said, and watched the interest suddenly flare in Andersen's face. A fight, by golly, and at his age ... "But I won't. I'd probably get more static from my own superiors than I would from you."

Andersen nodded, the barest flicker of disappointment on his face.

"The reason I want to know is that it might save a man's life," Renslow said.

Andersen thoughtfully dug the crust out of his pipe bowl. "I don't follow you, Commander."

"I've got a man in my crew"—it was Harris' crew but once removed was removed too far—"who tried to kill his wife the other night. It wasn't a crime of passion. He wasn't drunk; he wasn't high on drugs. Both he and his wife are in their forties and they've got three kids. He's been in the Navy for eighteen years and if he had his druthers, he'd probably rather die on board than onshore." Renslow smiled bleakly. "He's a company man."

Andersen frowned slightly and Renslow caught his breath, hoping he wouldn't consider that phrase a dig. Andersen filled his pipe and tamped the tobacco down, then lit it and took another slow puff. Renslow guessed that Andersen had read him the moment he had walked in the door and knew he wasn't the type.

"The only thing I've got to go on is that the admitting doctor at the Navy hospital said a friend of his had told him of two similar cases at Electric Boat. I thought"—he shrugged—"that maybe there might be a common thread."

"You haven't told me why you want to know."

Renslow frowned. "I thought I had. He's in my crew."

"I don't think so. You're worried, but you're not indignant and you're not climbing all over my desk." Ice-blue eyes stared at him for a moment. "He's a member of the other crew, isn't he?" A sudden change of subject before Renslow could wriggle out of that one. "Did you ever sail on a diesel boat?"

Renslow shook his head, bewildered. "No, I've been nuclear all the way."

"Damn shame. There was nothing like serving on a diesel. . . . I was on the *Tang* during the war." Any reference to "the war" obviously meant World War II. "Every time we came back to port we used to take the town apart. Great bunch of steamers in that crew. Guess there aren't many like them now. All college kids, right?"

"A lot of them are," Renslow admitted. He hoped to God that Andersen didn't want to reminisce about the war.

"Biggest damn war there ever was," Andersen continued casually. "And the less said about it, the better. Fifty million people died and some jerks still think it was glamorous." He pressed the intercom buzzer on his desk. "Bring in the poison files, Marie— all four of them."

"There weren't just two," he explained to a startled Renslow. "There were four. Happened about a month ago. You were still at sea then, weren't you?"

Marie brought in the files just then and Renslow's first shocked response was that the old man could still pick 'em. From the expression on his face, Andersen thought so, too. Marie was nearing fifty but there was no doubting either her charm or her vivacity.

Andersen opened the top folder. "The first two were painters and we thought for sure we had something. You know, fume intoxication, working in an enclosed space, that sort of thing. Never had any trouble with them before and then suddenly both of them were up to their ears. One of them attacked another painter with a putty knife. We had to call in the local cops. The other got in a fight with a machinist at a lunch wagon and came out second best—though it wasn't for lack of trying. Little guy— didn't look like he could punch his way out of a paper bag."

Andersen shoved the top two folders aside. "And then the paint theory went up the flue. The next two were a machinist and a pipe fitter. No connection at all with the first two."

Renslow looked disappointed. "Any medical reports?"

"Sanchez was the examining doctor but he won't tell you anything. At least, I don't think he will." Andersen tugged at the white fringe of hair that circled his scalp. "All four cases were characterized by extreme violence at the start. The men attacked anybody around them. It didn't matter whether it was a friend or a stranger. Afterward, two of them—the painters—became completely withdrawn and had to be hospitalized. Four days later, they recovered. No memory of the incident and neither of them could give any coherent reason why he had gone off the deep end." He fingered the reports, puffing thoughtfully on his pipe. "That was a month ago and there haven't been any incidents since. We followed up on it for the obvious reasons."

Renslow stared blankly. "Which are?"

"If you're in industry, you can't be too careful, Commander. There's a little town in Italy named Seveso, just twelve miles northwest of Milan. The ICMESA chemical plant blew up there in 1976 and released between one and fifteen pounds of dioxin, a potentially fatal poison. They eventually evacuated the whole town and currently it's surrounded by six miles of barbed wire, with all the roads nearby posted to read POLLUTED AREA." A slow puff on his pipe and a thoughtful look at Renslow. "So when these cases came up, we were more than ordinarily interested. I still don't know what happened—and I'd still like to find out. Call it enlightened self-interest."

Renslow pointed at the files. "Could I have copies?"

Andersen shrugged. "Why not?" He turned to his secretary. "Make me half a dozen Xeroxes, Marie. Block out the names."

After she left, Renslow said, "You don't have any theories?"

"I don't believe in the phases of the moon, if that's what you're driving at. I think it was something environmental but I'll be damned if I know what the hell it was. It didn't repeat, though—cross your fingers."

Marie came back with the Xeroxes and Renslow held out his hand. "I thought you were going to give me a hard time."

Andersen chuckled. "Everybody knows the story but you, Commander. You were away when it happened. Some of the local environmentalists tried to make a case out of it and the papers had a field day. I would've looked bad if I had tried to be coy about it."

Renslow left with the manila folders containing the work records of the four men, now anonymous, and drove to the Groton Motor Inn for lunch. Half an hour later, his lunch was cold but he was convinced that he had something Andersen had missed. The painters had been the first to come down with whatever it was, followed a week or so later by the machinist and the pipe fitter. But both of them had been working in the same areas where the painters had been.

Andersen had discounted fume intoxication too soon, Renslow thought. All four men had worked in an enclosed area they were either painting or that had been painted the week before. Most paints continue to give off solvent fumes even after the paint has supposedly set. In this case, after a week the concentration had still been high enough to have an effect. After two or three weeks, since there were no further incidents in the yard, the concentration must have dropped below the critical level. Or perhaps the area was no longer enclosed. . . .

Which still didn't tell him what solvent could cause a paranoid reaction in the people around it or where Ernie Gradow came in.

He stopped with his cup of coffee halfway to his mouth. Ernie had cadged half the furnishings in his house. It wasn't unusual for Navy crew members to make a deal with yard workers for small tools or some home-repair work. . . . Or maybe a couple of gallons of paint.

Ernie had been working alone in the garage for two weeks painting his boat, probably with the door closed. And it had been in those weeks that Ernie's basic character had changed.

It was a great theory, Renslow thought. All he had to do was prove it.

Friday, June 26

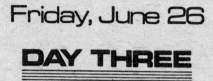

DAY THREE

18

VAN MEER FINISHED going over the morning muster report, initialed it, then asked, "Why are so many men reporting to sick bay?"

Olson ticked the reasons off on his fingers. "A few have reported in with chronic headaches, some of them still have rashes, and Russo was turned in for—ah—urinary incontinence."

Van Meer looked up from the muster report. "Urinary what?"

"He was wetting the bed," Olson said succinctly. "And I don't think he's the only one."

Van Meer had noted the odor of urine a day ago. Incontinence used to be a guaranteed way to get a medical discharge but he couldn't imagine anybody deliberately bed-wetting on board the *Alaska;* the loss of face would be too great.

"Everybody's coming down with a bad case of nerves," Olson continued, his moon face looking pinched. "And nobody seems to know what the hell's wrong with the water."

"They took the evaporators apart, Ray. There wasn't anything wrong with them."

Olson shrugged. "Water still tastes oily, sir. I haven't had a good cup of coffee in three days now."

It tasted strange to everybody but himself. Maybe he, van Meer, was the odd man out.

"Sir, if there's a war ..." Olson's voice was suddenly strained. "If there's a war, they're going to hit the New London area, aren't they?"

Van Meer was surprised. It was something that was always on

your mind but you never talked about it. "I can't think of many places they wouldn't hit, Ray."

"It's kind of unfair in a way, isn't it?"

"That's war," van Meer said, then realized it wasn't what Olson was thinking.

"I mean, they're a lot more exposed back home than we are. We're supposed to be protecting them but we're the ones who are relatively safe. They're the ones who are going to get it."

Van Meer wished that Admiral Cullinane and Dr. Hardin could listen. This was the kind of agony they should hear. . . .

"We do our job and that's it, Ray. Thinking about it won't do much good."

He put the muster report in its folder and slid it back on the shelf. Olson stood up, knowing he was dismissed.

"It's too bad I can't trade places. Edith would be safer here than there."

Van Meer watched him leave, thinking that Olson was probably the most phlegmatic man on board but the situation was still getting to him. . . . Scoma, who had been typing at the other end of the small ship's office, suddenly stopped and glanced at him.

"This Egyptian thing's going to tie a can to it, isn't it, Commander?"

"I've got no idea, Dom," he lied. "Things will probably get worse before they get better, though."

He walked out into the passageway. He had disliked the whole idea of the drill before; now he was growing to hate it. And when he saw Admiral Cullinane and that bastard Hardin again, he'd tell them—rank be damned.

In sick bay, Schulman had just put a bottle of pills down on his desk and picked up a small paper cup of water when van Meer walked in.

"I didn't know you were popping pills, Doc."

Schulman threw the pill in his mouth, took a gulp of water, and swallowed. "It's the schoolteacher's aspirin, Van—five milligrams of Valium. Good for headaches and anxiety, and, besides, it makes you sleep better. Which is something I haven't been doing lately."

Van Meer straddled an examination chair. "I understand from Olson that you've been getting a lot of customers."

Schulman took a notebook off his shelf and flipped through

it. "I'm not the only one on Valium. At the rate we're going, we won't have enough to last until we get back."

"We took on enough for a ninety-day patrol," van Meer said slowly. "We can't be using it up that fast."

"We'll run out in about sixty," Schulman said. "Simple extrapolation."

"We'll be back in ten," van Meer said.

Schulman blinked at him, owllike. "Ten." Pause. "Of course. But we don't talk about that, right?"

The incident with Harris had made him jumpy. "What's wrong besides your headaches, rashes, and kids who can't hold their water?" van Meer asked.

"Tachycardia." Schulman looked worried. "Not exactly the sort of thing I would expect on board."

Van Meer cocked his head. "What's tachycardia?"

"Rapid heartbeat. Usually found among the elderly, common with many types of heart disease. It can also be produced by stress. Or drinking a lot of coffee. Caffeine's a strong stimulant and if you hit more than four cups or so a day, your heart can start doing double time."

"So the men shouldn't drink so much coffee."

"They're not, Van. At least, not on board this ship. Have you tasted it lately?" Schulman made a face. "I've had castor oil that tasted better."

"It's got to be a selective sort of thing," van Meer said slowly. "To me it tastes fine."

Schulman smiled. "Who said, 'There's no accounting for taste'?" Then he became serious. "I might expect a few cases of tachycardia among the older chiefs. I wouldn't expect a dozen or more, including young men."

"Crew still has its case of nerves?"

Schulman polished his glasses. "I'd say so."

There was no avoiding it, van Meer thought. "Have you talked to Harris lately?"

"We went over the sick-bay roster together."

"He seem all right to you?"

Schulman looked curious. "He asked the same about you."

"He thinks Washington's canceled the drill," van Meer said bluntly.

Schulman turned away to put the bottle of Valium back in the supply cabinet. "I wouldn't be surprised if they did, what with the trouble in Egypt."

Van Meer stared. He'd have to talk to Schulman, but not now. Something was wrong, drastically wrong. . . .

He was ducking through the hatch when Schulman suddenly said, "Van?"

He turned. "Yeah?"

Schulman looked faintly embarrassed. "Just between us, is there any reason why Costanza should dislike me? Any latent prejudice that you know of?"

"I think you're getting paranoid, Doc."

"You're probably right. But if he says anything to you, let me know, huh?"

Van Meer slipped out, frowning. What the hell was happening? Schulman wasn't the type to imagine something but, on the other hand, although Costanza had his faults, religious prejudice wasn't one of them.

Doc was feeling the stress, too. Except that Schulman knew all about the drill and, like Harris, he should be prepared for it. But Harris had been acting strangely and now Doc was, too.

All the world is strange save me and thee, and I'm not so sure about thee. . . .

Van Meer was cutting through crew's berthing after lunch when the fight started. Several of the bunk lights were on in the far end and four crewmen were playing cards, with Longstreet dealing. He looked up as van Meer approached and said, "Hearts, Commander."

"If I can't see the money, I can't report it," van Meer said easily. An edge of the blanket was folded back, hiding the pot, but he wasn't about to investigate. He was just leaving when he noticed Longstreet glance over at Russo, putting some laundry away in his locker.

"Hey, Russo, you got any nude pictures of your girl?"

It was obviously a joke, and van Meer paused to watch Russo's reaction.

"Hell, no, man, I respect her too much. She's the marrying type."

Van Meer almost groaned. Longstreet now said in a voice deliberately thick with innuendo, "Would you like to buy some?"

"You son of a bitch."

It happened so fast that later van Meer wasn't quite sure of the sequence of events. Russo had been standing in front of his locker and Longstreet had been lying on his bunk, dealing cards. A moment later, Russo had pulled Longstreet by the feet and they both crashed to the deck. There was a flurry of arms and legs as they rolled into the lockers and bunk lights started to go on around them.

"Hit him again, harder, Russo."

"For Christ's sake, will you guys knock it off—I got the watch."

"Where the fuck's the master-at-arms?"

Van Meer ran back toward the locker area and spotted Olson coming in from the other side.

"Jesus *Christ*, I'm bleeding. He *stuck* me."

There was blood on the deck and on Russo's T-shirt and a lot more on Longstreet, who was looking pale and frightened. Van Meer bulled through the circle of men surrounding them. "Okay, back to your bunks. Clear the area."

He ripped Longstreet's T-shirt off, revealing a small puncture wound in the shoulder, blood welling out of it. Thank God it hadn't been the stomach; he wouldn't have wanted to push Doc's dimly remembered surgical skills too far.

"McCune, Sullivan, take him to sick bay." They left, Longstreet holding his ripped T-shirt to his shoulder to stanch the flow of blood.

"You can't take a joke, Russo?"

Russo was shaking. A jockey's build with a jockey's temperament, van Meer thought. "I didn't mean to do it, Commander. I didn't mean it."

He was holding something in his hand and van Meer held out his own. Russo dropped a small penknife into it, the blade bloody up to the hilt. It was too small to do any damage at all except for a small puncture wound. The blade was the type used to clean fingernails or slit open envelopes. Nobody in his right mind would think of using it for anything serious, least of all in a knife fight.

"Olson, search his locker; confiscate any other weapons. Russo, you're confined to your working area and your bunk space until further notice."

Russo had started to cry now. "Honest to God, Commander, I've never even been in a fight before."

Van Meer turned away, shaken. *Nobody in his right mind . . .*

In the wardroom, Harris was holding a briefing on the morning rendezvous with the *Chicago*. "Something detain you, Van?"

Always the slight hint of sarcasm. Van Meer slid into his chair. "A knifing in crew's berthing."

They were all ears now. Harris looked mildly surprised. "Who was knifed and how badly was he hurt?"

"Longstreet. Not badly. Small puncture wound."

"Who did it?"

"Russo. They were having an argument over Russo's girl."

Cermak frowned. "Russo doesn't hang around with Longstreet; he's in my division. I know."

"It started with a joke," van Meer explained. "You know the one that goes, 'Do you have any nude pictures of your girlfriend?' And when the mark gets indignant, you say, 'Would you like to buy some?' I think I heard it on my first patrol."

They were staring at him and nobody was smiling. Van Meer experienced an odd flash of panic. It was an old gag; they must have heard it.

"Russo will have to go to mast," Harris said quietly. "Keep me informed about Longstreet."

Costanza shook his head. "Longstreet didn't use good sense. For all he knew, the girl could have been cheating on Russo."

Chips Okamoto nodded in agreement. "If Longstreet had actually pulled the photographs out, Russo would probably have killed him. What the hell is he doing peddling porno on board anyways?"

Van Meer looked at them with growing amazement. "It was a joke. A lousy little joke. Longstreet was kidding Russo. He didn't have any photographs. It's a very.... old ... joke."

"Russo didn't think it was a joke," Harris pointed out quietly.

Stroop cleared his throat and they turned to listen to him. "You're away so long, a woman can take advantage," he growled. "I once knew a woman who had a husband in the Blue Crew and another in the Gold Crew. One would leave on patrol and she would hide his clothes and his toilet articles and bring out the clothes for husband number two. Smart woman—she was good at keeping accounts, so both of them trusted her with their allotment checks. Then, one day, the boomer came back early for reactor repairs—it was the old *Thomas Edison*—and both husbands met at the front door." He shook his head solemnly. "Talk about a misunderstanding."

It was an apocryphal story that everybody had heard and nobody believed. Told right, it could be very funny.

But nobody in the wardroom was laughing.

Perez came in with a tray of hamburgers and another pot of coffee for the hot plate. Spencer poured himself a cup and made a face. "Goddamned coffee still tastes like there's oil in it."

Across the table, Udall nodded in mournful agreement. "So does the drinking water and the pop."

Van Meer started. There were rumors that somebody had tampered with the evaporators but it wasn't likely they had gotten around to the canned soda.

He suddenly caught himself staring at Harris. The captain had sprayed one of the hamburgers with catsup and had splashed his coat sleeve. He absently wiped at it with a napkin, then went back to reviewing the upcoming drills. Van Meer recalled himself and Meslinsky standing by the fence at Charleston and Harris wiping off his shoe. He was a fastidious man. Ordinarily he would have sopped a napkin in cold water and sponged out the spot immediately.

Van Meer jotted down a few more notes about the drills and glanced surreptitiously around the table, trying to figure out what had struck him wrong when he had first walked in. Maybe it was that nobody had shaved. Not even Harris. Which wasn't a big deal; a lot of crew members didn't shave when out on patrol.

But Harris always did.

Harris was changing. He was becoming more human. Or, more accurately, simply less like Harris . . .

At the end of the briefing van Meer went back to his compartment to get some sleep, first sitting at the desk to write a letter to Cheryl. He wrote one a day, usually destroying it the next morning. They were about what he really thought and really felt but he had never had the courage to let Cheryl see him quite so naked. . . . The letter was brief this time and, when he reread it, frightening. The *Alaska* was drastically different from the last time he had been on her. The crew was becoming strange, reacting in ways that would normally be foreign to them. Russo had never struck him as being the violent type, nor had Longstreet seemed quite so malicious. And Harris . . .

What was happening to Harris?

And there were other things that worried him. The ship was a pigsty, crumpled papers and matchbook covers lying in the corners, cleaning rags left on top of equipment.... And then there was the water. There was nothing *wrong* with the water, at least nothing he could taste. The evaporators were in top working order, always had been.

But the coffee tasted oily to everybody on board except him.

He finished the letter, saying the *Alaska* was becoming more oppressive by the day and the sanest men on board were himself, Doc Schulman, and Olson. Then he smiled and wrote a PS, saying he wasn't too sure of Doc and Olson.

He yawned, fumbled in his shoe for the bottle of Equavil, hesitated, and finally put the bottle back, unopened. Rosenberg had warned him about the side effects and considering what was happening aboard the *Alaska*, he couldn't afford to be anything but clearheaded. He'd have to go cold turkey and it wouldn't be easy. He crawled into his bunk, still in uniform, and turned his face to the bulkhead. He fell asleep almost immediately....

"Van, wake up. What's wrong?"

He blinked and found himself staring at Schulman, standing by the side of his bunk, shaking him. The next impression he had was that his uniform and the mattress cover were wringing wet. He mumbled, "Bad dream," and sat up on the edge of his bunk, shivering. Bits and pieces of the dream came back and for a moment he was terrified by their reality.

"Maggie?" Schulman asked gently. "You talked a little in your sleep last night and I thought you were having the same nightmare."

Van Meer shook his head. It hadn't been about Maggie; it hadn't been about the accident and the fire. It had been about life on board a submarine, a dream accompanied by a terrifying, suffocating sense of claustrophobia. It was the kind of nightmare he used to have when he first started serving on board submarines. He'd had difficulty recalling the precise details but had been left with the emotional shock of seeing pipes burst and rods of high-pressure water shoot across compartments, of watching bulkheads crumple and walls of water and mangled men and equipment come smashing at him, of being crushed under thousands of tons of sea.

He hadn't had a nightmare like it in years.

19

D R. JOHN HAMADY glanced at the clock. Nobody was waiting and his appointment for ten had canceled out. Which gave him, for the first time since he could remember, fifteen minutes of absolutely nothing that he *had* to do. He stepped out into the reception room and shifted some chairs back against the wall, then pulled his bag of golf clubs from the closet and took out his putter. A ball from the side pocket of the bag and a glass from the washroom and he was all set. The first thing he noticed about the office when he had moved in the year before was the indoor-outdoor carpeting in the reception room. It was relatively new and it made a dandy putting surface.

"Patti—"

"—please hold your calls and let you know if anybody important is coming."

"Right on both counts. For fifteen minutes."

"Yes, sir."

Patti would never know how eagerly he had looked up her term of enlistment after her first week in the office, how jealous he was of her dates, how fearful that she might get pregnant. There wasn't much worry about the latter but she was as popular as she deserved and if she ever got married, he knew damned well he would never find another yeoman in the entire Navy who was as pleasant, efficient—and pretty—as she was.

She knew how to put patients at their ease, kept his files in A-1 order, and looked more feminine in a uniform than anyone he had ever seen. In addition to all of that, she had one asset that automatically placed her head and shoulders above anybody else who had ever worked for him.

She could read his mind.

He sank three putts in a row, then missed, the ball rolling behind the scale in the far corner. He retrieved it and lined it up for another putt at the glass.

"Patti." Her typing stopped. "You remember Commander Renslow?"

She shook her head of close-cropped blond hair and thought for a moment. "Thirty-seven, captain of the Blue Crew of the *Alaska*, unhappily married."

"How the hell do you know that?"

"Nothing mysterious. I've met his wife. She's not his type and he probably doesn't thrill her." She frowned. "I take that back. At one time they were probably great in bed together but he never should have married her."

She shifted in her chair, Hamady covertly watching her. Patti had the greatest thighs and he was really high on thighs. . . .

Another putt. Renslow had asked about Equavil and what it was prescribed for and, of course, the answer had been stored in his memory. . . . What he didn't have an answer for was why Renslow had wanted to know. It hadn't been for himself. Hamady had checked Renslow's psychological evaluation sheet immediately afterward. So why had he asked? Renslow's question had bugged him for days now. . . .

"Patti, you've been regular Navy for quite a while, right?"

"I wouldn't say *quite* a while."

"I mean, you know line officers pretty well." He didn't wait for her answer, which would have been defensive anyway. He lined up the ball and sank it, then leaned the club against the wall and walked into her office.

"Why would Renslow ask me about a dangerous drug, the kind a psychiatrist might prescribe, when he's not taking it himself and has no need to?"

She didn't hesitate. "Because he knows somebody who's on it but couldn't or didn't want to ask the person about it." She thought for a moment. "Since he asked you about it and not him, Renslow must have stumbled across it by accident and didn't want him to know."

"Could be somebody in the family, right?"

She shook her head. "Probably not. Chances are that if it were family, gossip would have filled him in or he would know the person well enough not to be surprised by it. There's no such thing as a private prescription in a close-knit family. If it were distant family, he wouldn't have been interested enough to ask."

Patti Smith was a whole lot smarter than he was in some areas, Hamady thought. "So he has a friend who's on it."

She nodded. "Somebody in the service."

He looked surprised. "You're guessing?"

"No, it's the same thing. He's a submariner, so most of his friends are probably submariners or service connected."

Hamady felt frustrated. "I'm still curious why he wanted to know. Renslow's no gossip; he didn't want to know for gossip's sake."

A calculating look. "Do I get a free lunch out of this?"

The thought hadn't occurred to him but it wasn't a bad one. "Base cafeteria, nothing fancy."

"He asked because he's worried, because it's important to him."

"Important to Renslow?"

She hesitated. "Not necessarily. Probably important to the service."

"He could have given me more information, like a name."

"He's no snitch."

He had her. "Not good enough, Patti. Not if it's for 'the good of the service.'"

"You're right." She frowned, then: "Maybe it would have been pointless to give a name. Maybe his friend's on patrol and won't be back for ninety days."

Bingo, Hamady thought, brightening. "You're absolutely right."

He started to reach for the phone directory and she said, "There're only two of them worth bothering with. Rosenberg and Ewing."

"Two what?"

"Psychiatrists—that's what you're looking up, aren't you? They're the only two in town with a substantial Navy clientele."

Hamady didn't ask her how she knew. "See if you can get me lunch with"—he chose one at random—"Rosenberg. Sing 'The

Star-Spangled Banner' if you have to but try to make it for today."

"The base cafeteria?"

Hamady put the golf clubs back in the closet and sighed. "Okay, Patti, make it the same place you'd like to go."

Dr. David Rosenberg looked younger than he actually was and Hamady wondered if his patients had trouble relating to him. He was also a little heavy around the hips and pectorals and had an essentially beardless face. A eunuchoid type; he should be seeing an endocrinologist. Physician, heal thyself. . . .

"Another drink?"

Rosenberg shook his head. "It'd ruin my business—two drinks for lunch and I'd talk instead of listen." The voice that went with the baby face was shockingly deep and, above all, authoritative. He glanced at his watch. "I think we both have appointments and I certainly don't want to miss mine." He took a guess. "You've got a problem that concerns my practice?"

Right to it, Hamady thought. "You have a patient from the regular Navy?"

"More than one. No offense intended, Captain, but sometimes there are things too personal to take to a Navy doctor."

Hamady half smiled. "I can think of a lot of things." Then: "The man I'm referring to is in the submarine service, probably an officer, and you're treating him with Equavil."

Rosenberg's expression became faintly hostile. "You know that a patient-physician relationship is confidential."

"Would it violate a confidence if you confirmed that you have such a patient?"

"Probably. Is this inquiry official?"

"It will be, sooner or later."

Rosenberg hesitated, then took the bait. "All right, for the moment let's assume that I have such a patient."

He wasn't sure what key it would take to unlock the pudgy doctor. Then Hamady decided the only effective approach was bluntness.

"I'm afraid all of us have a problem, then. I have to assume this hypothetical patient of yours is emotionally disturbed—disturbed enough so that he sought professional help outside of Navy channels. You have him on a drug regimen that is a specific for intense, pathological depressions." He stared pointedly at Rosenberg. "I am correct, am I not?"

"Captain, I can accept or reject a patient," Rosenberg said slowly. "After that my ethical position is clear."

Hamady shrugged. "This particular patient is no ordinary one. He's an officer on board a ballistic-missile submarine, presently at sea."

"I'm aware of that," Rosenberg said curtly. "Why are you so interested?"

He wasn't getting through to Rosenberg. "He has to make critical decisions, and many of those decisions can mean the difference between peace and war. I guess it's that simple. And that important."

Rosenberg looked bored. "Captain, the decisions of our Presidents affect peace and war, too. And at least a few of those Presidents have been under psychiatric care, or should have been. But nobody removed them from office for that reason."

"You keep calling me 'Captain,' " Hamady said curtly, losing patience. "I happen to be a doctor also. I'm responsible not only for the man who's under your care; I'm responsible for everybody else on board that ship. I'm not going to fence with you about the sanity of Presidents or bums. I'm concerned with the sanity of one man."

He lowered his voice. "I wasn't being rhetorical when I said *we've* got a problem. It's as much your problem as mine. Maybe more so."

Rosenberg looked supercilious. "In what way?"

"If you protect him, if you keep his identity secret, then in a very real sense the decisions he makes are also your decisions. You're the one who's certifying him as being fit for service, fit for combat. You're taking that responsibility on yourself." He leaned closer, bearing down on Rosenberg. "And no offense intended, Doctor, but you're not qualified to make that decision."

Rosenberg stared down at his empty glass. "I wouldn't hesitate to make that decision for a man in civilian life. Every psychiatrist has to weigh the patient's good against society's good."

"That's right," Hamady agreed. "Only in this case the stakes involved don't allow for any consideration to be shown the patient at all. Society can't afford that gamble." He paused. "Do I have to tell you what the stakes are?"

Rosenberg's face was strained. "You're pressuring me. You know that, don't you?"

Hamady leaned back and signaled the waiter for another

drink. "Doctor, all I'm asking for is assurance that your patient's condition isn't likely to affect his judgment in a critical combat situation. That isn't asking for much, is it?"

Rosenberg wiped a suddenly sweaty forehead. "I can't do that," he said finally.

Hamady stared at him bleakly. "Then you'd better tell me his name."

Rosenberg was having trouble controlling his voice, keeping it in the bass register. "Van Meer," he said. "Lieutenant Commander Mark van Meer."

Hamady had guessed that it was a senior officer on either the Blue Crew or the Gold, and probably the Gold, since that was the crew at sea. But he hadn't suspected the executive officer; he hadn't suspected van Meer.

"Tell me about the case, " he asked gently.

Patti was late coming back from lunch and for the first time Hamady quietly cursed her. When she did come in, he was short. "Do we still have the psychological screening files on the *Alaska's* Gold Crew or were those shipped to Washington? You know, the ones Dr. Hardin developed."

She interpreted the tone of his voice and immediately became crisply efficient and military. "They're still in the classified safe. They're due to be sent out by courier tomorrow."

"Bring me the folder on Mark van Meer."

She redeemed herself by placing the folder on his desk in less than thirty seconds. He spread out the evaluation sheets. It was outside his specialty but he had studied testing data as part of his interest in stress medicine and it was easy to spot the discrepancies in van Meer's file. Why the hell hadn't Hardin's men seen them?

The test responses were classic, obviously studied. And there were delayed responses to both the thematic apperception test and the Rorschach. Not outside the experimental limit, but all seconds over the average—as though van Meer had cautiously considered his responses before making them. He was well aware he had problems and had tried very carefully to hide them.

Hamady closed the file folder and stared at it. Was the information important enough to bring to the attention of ComSubLant? The admiral might think he was an alarmist.

Then he knew he had to buck it upstairs, no matter how trivial it might turn out to be. He had forced the information from Rosenberg on the grounds that if Rosenberg withheld van Meer's name, then van Meer's decisions were essentially being made with Rosenberg's okay.

The same reasoning applied to him. He had to pass the buck. He had no other choice.

20

THE STAFF CAR dropped Admiral Cullinane in front of the Cosmos Club, at Florida and Massachusetts, just before six. Drinks and dinner and a chance to talk with Caleb Warden without an audience. It might not be pleasant but it was bound to be fascinating.

"Do you want me to pick you up, sir?"

Cullinane shook his head. "I'll cab it; thank you anyway."

He stopped for a moment to stare at the massive four-story house occupied by the club. Few of the politicians who were transient on the Washington scene ever made it past the blue-silk–jacketed Indian doorman except by invitation of one of the active members.

But somehow Warden had become a member in nothing flat.

He walked up the stone steps and nodded to the doorman, surrendering his uniform cap. "Has Mr. Warden arrived yet?"

"He's waiting for you in the sitting room, Admiral."

If Warden had wanted to impress somebody, he couldn't have chosen better, Cullinane thought. The Cosmos Club was one of the few truly luxurious private clubs left in the United States. The floors were of polished Vermont marble, the rugs thick Persians, the walls were hung with tapestries, and the rich smell of leather sofas and chairs filled the rooms.

Warden was standing before one of the giant marble fireplaces that flanked the living room fore and aft, studying the portrait of Charles E. Monroe, one of the early members. He turned as Cullinane walked up, his fleshy face folding into a thick smile. "I'm delighted you could make it, Admiral. *Dee*-lighted. How do you like my little club?"

He waved a hand expansively and Cullinane winced. The voice was too loud for the club, the good-old-boy routine completely out of place. "I've been a member for years. I first came here with my father."

Warden's smile froze. "I should've had my staff research you a bit more carefully, Admiral."

He was off to a bad start. Warden sprawled out in one of the easy chairs and motioned to him to take the one opposite. A moment later, a quiet, unobtrusive waiter appeared and Warden ordered two bourbons, straight up. Cullinane wondered if Warden would order dinner for him as well. "A fine place to take people to, Admiral. Nice genteel establishment like this always impresses them. Great sense of decorating—who would've thought of using steel plates for a room divider?"

Cullinane wasn't sure whether Warden was putting him on or not. "Those are pieces of armor plate from Charles Monroe's workshop—you were looking at his portrait a minute ago. They illustrate the 'Monroe effect'—the effect of shaped charges, bazooka shells, that sort of thing. You'll note how some are dented and perforated."

"They had the military-industrial complex even then, didn't they?" Warden said with a sly smile. He was showing off, letting Cullinane know that the country-bumpkin act worked even when his audience knew it was an act. Then he wondered if Warden was letting him know that on purpose, was allowing him a privileged glimpse of the real man behind the façade.

Or maybe Warden was just showing his contempt. But, then, why invite him to dinner at all?

Cullinane sipped at his drink while Warden drained his and ordered another. He couldn't criticize; he didn't know anybody in D.C. who didn't drink as if there were no tomorrow.

Warden smacked his lips and swirled the liquor in his glass. "To enjoy good sippin' bourbon, you got to lay down a foundation first." He fought his way out of the easy chair and hunched forward, his elbows on his knees. "I got to thinkin' the other day after our meetin' and I realized I really didn't know you, Admiral. I sort of thought we should get together and maybe exchange views on the whole spectrum of events, not just Navy affairs."

Cullinane nodded a tentative agreement. Warden definitely wasn't interested in where their disagreements lay; for reasons of his own he was trying to find out in what areas their views were parallel.

The Parker House–roll smile again. "You know, with SALT Three upcoming, I've been figuring that we just don't have enough input from the men in the field, so to speak."

The steward appeared discreetly at Warden's elbow, coughed, and announced that their table was ready. "Right on time." Warden beamed. "Best service in Washington, Admiral." Their table was against the far wall, behind some potted plants. The most private table in the room; it would be difficult for anyone who wasn't looking for them to recognize them. He glanced around, noted several senators and a gaggle of generals, then looked down at the other end of the room, where a huge marble fountain, surrounded by a jungle of broad-leafed tropical plants, splashed streams of water into the air. He suddenly felt nostalgic, remembering when his father had first taken him there, shortly after the club had purchased the Townsend House. He was a young Navy captain and his father a prominent naval architect. He had, as he recalled, been very impressed—and very proud.

"Something wrong, Admiral?"

Cullinane spread his napkin on his lap. "Sometimes a sense of history catches up with us, Mr. Warden."

Warden looked at him curiously, then ordered red snapper for both of them and a bottle of Chablis. "You know, Admiral, I was speaking of the whole spectrum of events a moment ago. You look at any map of the world, you can see that it's split right down the middle. The Russians on one side and us on the other. They have their client nations; we have ours. And then there are a few nations that sort of sit in the middle."

He was plowing through his salad automatically, his eyes fixed on Cullinane. They were, Cullinane admitted, very watchful, intelligent eyes. "That's a little simplistic, Mr. Warden."

Warden shrugged. "Doesn't matter. What's important is the overall picture, and especially the fact that those nations in the middle are the ones with most of the world's remaining resources—the oil, the iron ore, that sort of thing."

Cullinane waited for Warden to come to the point. "That's the big prize, Admiral, and if we lose it, we don't stay a first-rate power for very long." Cullinane was noncommittal and Warden hesitated a moment, watching carefully for any response. Warden was sounding him out but he didn't know what for, and he felt uneasy.

"We're committed to a balance of power, Admiral. But that stays a balance only so long as both sides *think* it's a balance. Show weakness and the other side won't hesitate to take advantage of it. We can't afford that."

"On the other hand, if you show overwhelming superiority, a desperate nation might be tempted to land the first blow."

Warden's eyes glazed. "I've heard that argument, Admiral. Do you really believe it?"

Cullinane suddenly felt the conversation had become treacherous. "I don't mean that as a political statement, Mr. Warden."

"Nowadays, I think a good military man is also a good politician, Admiral," Warden said, eyeing Cullinane.

Warden was drawing a line, Cullinane thought coldly. You were either for him or against him and there wasn't going to be any middle ground.

"I'm not so sure I agree with that, Mr. Warden." Cullinane looked down at his plate and speared another forkful of snapper. "I guess it all depends on how it's meant."

Warden's expression was guarded once again. Cullinane realized that Warden had just offered him a chance at . . . something . . . and he had turned it down.

Warden abruptly changed the subject. "You haven't liked Operation Fire from the start, Admiral." A bland look. "Could you tell me the reason why? I mean, the real nitty-gritty one, leavin' out all the politics you don't approve of."

Whatever had been offered to him had been withdrawn. Now they'd get down to the whipping session. "I can't go along with any operation when I feel there's a measurable and avoidable hazard to my men—and the return doesn't justify that hazard."

"Are your feelings based on intuition, Admiral, or facts?"

"The failure of the evaporators is fact," Cullinane said curtly.

"I don't think you're being entirely truthful, Admiral," Warden drawled. "I think there's more to it than that. You'll pardon me for saying so but I think your view's a trifle restricted. Don't get me wrong—it *should* be restricted. You have your job and the CNO, for example, has his. And the President and I have ours. You're not as concerned with our overall world posture as . . . well, we are."

Cullinane reddened. "I try to have a world view."

Warden slipped back into his accent. "At the risk of repeating mahself, Admiral, we've been gettin' disquieting reports from intelligence and our embassy in Moscow that the Russian military journals are speculating our crews won't go through with a launch order once a shooting war starts. That American education and outlook are so basically humanitarian, American crews would accept a Soviet world rather than no world at all."

"Better Red than dead? I thought we had put that one to rest long ago."

Warden patted his thick lips with a napkin. "We did; we sure did. But the Russians didn't. They think we really believe that slogan and, frankly, the President is afraid a lot of Russian top brass are prepared to act on it. We've got to disillusion them and Operation Fire will do just that."

Cullinane shoved his plate back in anger. "Mr. Warden, we're deliberately developing a war psychosis among the crew members of the *Alaska*. That in itself is dangerous."

Warden studied him for a moment. "Admiral," he said softly, "just what the hell do you think this drill is all about? It's to see how the crew will react if they think there's a war on."

Cullinane got to his feet, dropping his napkin on the plate. "This isn't a game of solitaire, Mr. Warden. What happens when the Soviets send an attack sub to trail the *Alaska*? And what do you think the *Alaska*'s reaction will be when it discovers the Soviet sub is out there?"

Warden looked up at Cullinane, his smile jovial, his eyes almost twinkling. "You really shouldn't get so excited, Admiral." He took a sip of wine. "I thought the snapper was excellent, didn't you?"

Saturday, June 27

DAY FOUR

21

IT WAS NEARLY dusk when Renslow finally made it to the hospital to see Florence Gradow. She was still on the critical list but she could talk and see members of the family. Renslow showed his ID and the nurse hesitated, then gave him the room number. "Don't tire her. She's been through a lot." He took the elevator to the second floor and, after a false start in the wrong direction, located her room at the far end of a corridor. A dinner cart was outside but it was stacked with soiled dishes; apparently Florence had just finished eating.

The room contained two beds, the farthest of which was partly hidden by a curtain suspended from a curved chrome rail. Renslow rapped his knuckles lightly against the wall and peered around the curtain. Mrs. Padgett was seated in a chair by the window, holding a can of diet cola for Florence Gradow, who was sitting up in bed. Her chest was bound with a tight elastic wrapping and her left arm and leg were in white plaster casts. Her head was almost completely swathed in bandages, an ugly bruise discoloring one puffy eye.

Mrs. Padgett nodded at Renslow and stood up. "You've got company, Flo—Captain Renslow. I'll see you later."

Renslow smiled. "They made a big deal about relatives only. How'd you sneak by?"

Mrs. Padgett grinned back, the open appraisal in her eyes making Renslow nervous. "I told them I was Flo's cousin from California. You don't think they were going to check, do you?" Then, to the figure on the bed: "You need anything, Flo, just call."

Renslow pulled the chair closer and sat down. Florence put a hand up to her face, as if she were trying to brush some hair away from her eyes. "I look such a mess," she mumbled. She didn't part her teeth when she talked and Renslow realized with a shock that her jaw must have been broken and had been wired shut. The dirty dishes on the meal cart had been somebody else's; Florence would be sipping her meals through a straw for weeks.

"How you coming along, Mrs. Gradow?" It sounded inane but he didn't know what else to say.

There was a bare whisper of a chuckle. "Dr. Strickland says I'll live." She plucked at the sheet. "Your wife . . . was by this afternoon."

"The crew's like family, Mrs. Gradow." He knew from past experience it was the sort of thing she would want to hear.

Some of her anger spilled over into her faded voice. "Not . . . all of it. This is one family that's splitting down the middle." She turned her face away from him. "I never did anything to Ernie," she whimpered. "Nothing to make him do this to me . . ."

Renslow stood there for a moment in embarrassed silence. "Exactly what happened, Mrs. Gradow?"

"Just what you probably heard. I had gone to bed and he called to me from the garage. I sure as hell knew something was wrong—" She broke off to control her voice. "He hadn't been the same since . . . since . . ."

"Since he started painting his boat?" Renslow suggested.

She sounded tired. "About then, I guess. He started spending more and more time out there. Everything had to be just right. If the paint bubbled, he'd be out sanding and buffing the area and polishing it like it was the Hope Diamond. The kids didn't dare go near him; he'd bite their heads off. One night he threw a bottle of turpentine at Don, the youngest."

Renslow gave her a minute to rest, then: "Was he that way all the time?"

"No. After he broke his leg, he hung around the house a few days and drank beer. He seemed . . . in a pretty good mood. Then . . . back to working on the boat again and everything changed. For the worse."

"Did you ever try to get him to see a doctor?" Renslow asked gently.

"He saw one when he broke his leg—"

"I didn't mean that kind of doctor."

"You mean a shrink?" She sounded querulous. "He talked with one of them last month, one of the ones from Washington."

Renslow was suddenly alert. "What was that all about?"

She sounded sleepy now. Renslow guessed she'd been given a sedative. "They talked with everybody on the crew, even with the wives. One spent a whole afternoon with me, asked me about my home life, how I got along with Ernie, all about the kids."

"Everybody on the Gold Crew?"

"I think so." Her voice started to fade. "What's going to happen to Ernie, Captain?"

Renslow smiled faintly. "Do you care?"

She was crying quietly now, the tears streaking the bandages that covered the bottom part of her face. "Oh, sure," she whispered. "I could brain him . . . but I care."

He met Elizabeth in the lobby, coming in as he was going out. Trim, natty, high-fashion. She made all the other wives present look dowdy. For a moment he felt ill at ease; she was too much the society matron come to visit the poor. But Elizabeth didn't know any other way. Going to the hospital was still "going out" and one always dressed to go out. . . .

"How is she?"

"Probably the same as she was this afternoon. She's a . . . strong woman."

"I've brought her a small radio she can listen to." She hesitated. "Al." It was the voice she used when she wanted something and Renslow was mildly surprised; she hadn't used it for months. "They have three children. We discussed it at the club and I offered to take the oldest, Howard. He's twelve—I don't think I could've handled either of the younger ones. I tried to get hold of you and couldn't locate you."

"I was out in another part of the yard." He was tempted to tell her about the paint problem at Electric Boat, then changed his mind. Visiting hours would be over in half an hour, which wouldn't give her much time with Florence. "I'm proud of you for offering to take care of Howard." Then, without meaning to be sarcastic: "It'll probably be as much fun as having one of our own around the house."

"Don't start," she warned. "Don't needle me, Al."

"I'm sorry," he said stiffly. "I didn't mean it that way."

She started to turn away, then said, "You got a phone call. From somebody in Procurement at Electric Boat. I meant to leave a note and then got rushed."

Joe Gilchrist, he thought. Calling him about the paint.

She disappeared into the elevator, his last glimpse of her as she smoothed the wrinkles in her skirt and tugged the glove off her left hand. There were times when he looked at her and couldn't believe they had ever slept together or were even married. She had become that much of a stranger to him.

He forced thoughts of Elizabeth from his mind. Florence Gradow had mentioned that psychologists from Washington had talked to both her and Ernie, had talked to everybody on the Gold Crew.

But to the best of Renslow's knowledge, nobody had talked to anybody on the Blue Crew. . . . Still another difference between the Gold and the Blue. But one that he could check.

It took him half an hour to talk to the wives of five of the crew chiefs. From the sound of their voices they were splitting their time between the bottle and the tube. All of them confirmed Florence's story of the teams that had descended on them from Washington. The odd thing was that Renslow hadn't heard about it before via the grapevine. They must have been sworn to secrecy. The psychologists must have convinced them that loose talk could endanger the crew members on board. But there was no reason for members of the Gold Crew to assume that the members of the Blue hadn't also been tested.

But why hadn't the psychologists talked to anybody on the Blue? Why hadn't they interviewed him or Elizabeth?

He made up his mind then and called Captain Pierce, the squadron commander. Five minutes later, he hung up, frowning. It was a purely routine study . . . interviews with the Blue Crew would be upcoming . . . and there was nothing at all strange about the *Alaska*'s patrol. Didn't Renslow have a copy of her ops sked?

"Have a drink and forget about it," Pierce had said brusquely, and hung up.

Renslow stood there, staring at the silent receiver. *No, Captain, I'm not going to forget about it. I've known you too long and there's something you're not telling me.*

The facts were all connected but he had no idea how. The

Alaska had been visited during retrofit by an electronics team from Washington, which had installed *something* aboard—something that apparently even the crew wasn't supposed to know about, though it was obvious that both Harris and van Meer did. And a group of psychologists had interviewed the members of the Gold Crew and their wives for . . . what? A study, as Pierce had claimed? And there had been the slip van Meer had made just before taking off for Charleston. That they were going to need luck. Again, for what?

And it was not alone that something had been done, but that it was so secret that even he hadn't been told. Records had been falsified; officials had lied; there was a curtain of silence.

And now it was obvious that Captain Pierce knew what was going on. But like the others Renslow had talked to, he was also under orders not to talk. To anybody, not just to him.

Well, for the moment, at least, it would have to keep. There was the even bigger mystery of the man who hadn't gone along, Ernie Gradow. Disgraced, apparently a would-be murderer, with no cause for his actions.

Except, possibly, the paint that he had been applying to his boat.

22

I'VE GOT a faint contact," McCune sang out. "Bearing three-five-zero."

"Put it on the speakers," Harris ordered tensely. McCune flicked a switch and the usual sounds of fish and porpoises floated from the loudspeakers. Along with the others, van Meer caught himself straining to sort out the different sounds, listening for the faint *whop-whop* of a distant submarine's screw. In the compartment itself there were only the sounds of breathing and the quiet twittering of the machinery.

"Try the computer, McCune." Another flick of a rocker switch. Van Meer walked over with Harris and leaned over McCune's shoulder to stare at the CRT display. One minute. Another minute. The screen remained blank.

McCune's black face relaxed. "Contact's gone, Captain."

"It's gone now, McCune?" Harris said tightly, his voice thick with sarcasm. "Was it ever there in the first place? What the hell do you think you're listening for, the tappita fish? There are lives depending on your ears, man. When you pick something up, put the computers on it immediately—for God's sake, I shouldn't have to tell you that."

There was a shocked silence in the compartment. Van Meer stared at Harris, astonished. Harris was the most phlegmatic captain he had ever served under. Harris never chewed ass in public; he never embarrassed a man in front of the rest of the crew.

"Promotions go through me, McCune. You want your dolphins, you're going to have to earn them." Harris abruptly turned and walked out.

After he had left, Clinger said quietly, "I don't believe it."

Van Meer glanced around. Half the crew looked sullen; the other half had thinly disguised smiles on their faces. Then Sandeman said, "Just because you're black doesn't mean anybody's going to show you any favors, McCune." He almost sounded like a Southern cracker.

Van Meer was astonished again. Sandeman was black, too.

Van Meer left the control room and took the ladder down to the crew's mess for a cup of coffee. It was between meals and several men were sitting in one of the booths, playing cards. Fuhrman, who ran the small machine shop in the engine room, was sitting in another, tinkering with a collection of cogwheels and tiny metal rods, carefully laid out on a paper napkin. Van Meer watched, fascinated. The small cogwheels had been drilled and the rods threaded, and Fuhrman was carefully screwing them together.

"Whaddya making, Fred?" Meslinsky was watching from the booth behind, leaning his huge arms on the back.

"A mechanical man." Fuhrman screwed a thick rod for the body onto another, more slender rod designed to be the hips. It was delicate work; the diameter of the hole in the smaller rod was almost the diameter of the rod itself.

"They'll be a hot seller when your wife opens up her gift shop."

Fuhrman's thin face grew somber. "She'll probably never get a chance to, Animal."

Meslinsky nodded. "Yeah, I know what you mean. My sister and her family are visiting the in-laws in Montana. If anything happens, at least they'll be safe."

Bailey looked up from the book he was reading, blinking behind his thick glasses. "That's probably the worst place they could be, Animal. They've got at least fifty silos in Montana. It'll be the first state to catch it."

"Who told you, four-eyes?"

Bailey shrugged and went back to his book. "I read it someplace."

Meslinsky smashed his cup of coffee on the table, a look of hatred in his eyes. "You didn't have to tell me that, Bailey, you know that? You might be right, but you didn't have to tell me." He stood up and walked out, almost knocking over the booth as he got out.

Fuhrman frowned. "You're living dangerously, Bailey."

"But it's true," Bailey insisted.

Furhman added another small cog for a hand. "Where's your home, Bailey?"

"Chicago. Why?"

"Maybe they'll get the Montana silos first, but you can bet your ass they'll get Chicago second." Bailey opened his mouth to say something, then shut up. "Didn't like that one, did you?" Fuhrman murmured.

Nobody had noticed van Meer standing quietly in the corner and he left the mess compartment as silently as he had come. He had been in crew's berthing earlier and there had been knots of crew members talking. They had shut up when he had walked in and he had wondered what they were talking about. Now he knew.

At oh-one-hundred they surfaced and van Meer went up to the bridge to watch Captain Blandini and his men come aboard from the *Chicago*. The ocean was glassy smooth, the air humid and warm, with a thick fog bank lying a mile or so off to the north. The *Chicago* was fifty yards away, its bridge and decks crowded with men watching as a small boat was launched. It bobbed slowly over to them, and Blandini and his men hauled themselves aboard via the grab ropes that led down to the waterline.

There was a short tour of the *Alaska* and van Meer found himself looking at the ship through Blandini's eyes. He was appalled. There were crumpled papers lying in the passageways, an oil spill in the engine room that nobody had bothered to clean up, and electronic testing gear sitting unsecured on top of one of the transmitters in the radio shack. If Blandini noticed, he didn't say anything.

At oh-two-hundred they had a meeting in the crowded wardroom, where Blandini confirmed their worst fears about the international situation. He was a short, stocky man with a habit of pounding one hand against the other to emphasize a point. Van Meer wondered idly if he had ever coached at the Academy.

"I guess the bottom line is that we can't tolerate another oil embargo like the one in 1981. Washington can't stand further cuts in the national energy reserve, now that they're phasing fission plants out of the national power picture."

MacGowan leaned forward, his thick features intense. "The Russians can't do anything in the Mideast. They don't have ports on the Mediterranean and we can bottle them up in the Black Sea."

"They're already in the Med," Spencer said quietly. "Tenders, boomers, support ships, the works."

It was Okamoto who said, "We've got four hundred MARV warheads on board. If there's any such thing as target number one, we've got to be it."

There was sudden silence in the wardroom. Not target number one all by itself, van Meer thought. The *New York* and the *Michigan* were in port for retrofit; the *Indiana* was at Holy Loch for rotation of crews. That left ten first-generation Tridents on station, plus the *Alaska.*

But Okamoto was essentially correct. The *Alaska* and the other ships were *número uno* when it came to targets; they were the sources from which the second strike, the retaliatory strike, would come.

"We'll go through the scheduled exercises," Captain Blandini continued, "but after that, unless our orders are changed, we'll be acting as point."

The guard sub, van Meer thought, to draw off any Soviet attack subs that sought to trail them . . .

There was general agreement around the table, then van Meer caught himself watching Blandini intently. The heavy captain had suddenly dropped out of character, trying to catch Harris' eye with a look that said "How'm I doing?" Their eyes met and locked but there was no change in Harris' expression. For a moment Blandini looked puzzled, then shrugged. He probably thought that Harris was just sticking to the act. . . .

Van Meer now felt himself playing more and more the role of observer, the odd man out watching the others around the wardroom table. There was a striking difference, he noted, between Blandini's men and the officers of the *Alaska.* Harris' beard was more obvious, his shirt rumpled and sweat-stained. Stroop was looking grizzled and Udall and Moskowitz oddly intent and warlike, like photographs van Meer had seen of submarine officers on duty in World War II.

Captain Blandini and his men, on the other hand, were clean-shaven, their uniforms neat and trim, only slightly damp from the few minutes spent in the boat. And, most important of all, they looked relaxed.

The meeting broke up and Blandini went topside to return to the *Chicago*. Van Meer watched from the bridge and wondered what Blandini would report back to Washington. He must have seen that something was wrong with the *Alaska*, something that wasn't due to the drill at all. . . .

Half an hour after Blandini had left, van Meer was told to report to the captain's cabin. "I was with Blandini almost all the time," Harris said after van Meer came in. "You were with the navigator and the exec. I wondered if they had anything to add to what the captain said in the wardroom."

Van Meer shook his head. "It was all pretty much the same line."

"Line," Harris repeated flatly. He frowned, then handed over several dispatches. "These were received while we were in the wardroom. The Russians are still building up in Iran and now they're massing four divisions on the Yugoslav border. They've walked out of the SALT Three talks. It looks sure as hell as if they're about to go for broke." He ran his hand through his hair. "They've been causing trouble in the area ever since Tito's death. With both Yugoslavia and Iran in their pockets, they'd have complete access to both the Mediterranean and the Indian Ocean. We could come and go only at their pleasure."

Van Meer read quickly through the dispatches. "This part of the tape—" he began tentatively.

Harris hit the desk with his fist. "For Christ's sake, Van, the drill was canceled days ago by Washington. They've got more important things to worry about. Why do you still keep referring to it? Can't you tell the difference between reality and the drill?"

It was too important to let himself be bullied. "How do you know for sure that the drill's been canceled, Steve?"

Harris glared. "What do *you* think they would have done if things had gone sour on the international scene?"

That had been covered in the briefings. The override message. But it hadn't been stressed; it hadn't been considered that much of a probability.

"Lacking any—"

There was a sudden rap on the door and Olson opened it without waiting for an invitation. "Fight in the auxiliary machinery room, Bailey and Meslinsky."

Van Meer nodded and hurried after Olson into the passageway. Down in the machinery room, Messier and Udall were holding back an enraged Meslinsky. Bailey was sitting on the deck, grimacing as Schulman bandaged his shoulder. His glasses were lying on the deck near the bulkhead, both lenses shattered.

"I caught the son of a bitch screwing around with the stills," Meslinsky roared.

"I was working on them," Bailey grunted. "For God's sake, somebody tell this slob that's what I do around here."

Van Meer knelt down by the doctor. "How bad?"

"Minor gash," Schulman said quietly. "He got pushed into a stanchion."

"Keep the bastard out of my way," Meslinsky growled. "I'll kill the little prick."

Bailey suddenly showed his teeth. "Watch it when you go to sleep, Animal."

There was a ring of crewmen around them now, some curious, others staring at Bailey with thinly disguised hatred.

"*Somebody* was screwing with the evaporators," a voice said.

Van Meer turned. "Everybody get the hell out," he said in a tired voice.

Later, in sick bay, van Meer sat at Schulman's desk and sipped a cup of coffee. He was feeling shaky, unsure of what was happening, unsure of what he should do about it. It was, he confessed to Schulman, just one more example of the general deterioration of the crew.

"What the hell do you expect, Van, when we're just a step away from war?"

Van Meer closed his eyes for a moment, surprised that he didn't feel panic at Schulman's calm acceptance of the fact that it was indeed the international situation and not the drill.

"You think it's been overridden, then?"

Schulman didn't give the question a moment's thought. "The drill? Of course it has. Be sensible."

Van Meer shook his head, still not convinced. "Doc, the men

have been trained to stand up to this kind of pressure. Even if I assume this is the real McCoy, I still can't believe the men would fall apart like this. They *depend* upon each other."

"When you've as much experience as I have, you'll learn to expect this sort of thing." Schulman refilled his coffee cup, dropping in three lumps of sugar. "Don't worry. When it comes time to launch missiles, they'll be right there. Meanwhile, they'll probably take out their fears and frustrations on each other."

" 'And I'm not so sure about thee,' " van Meer said quietly.

Schulman frowned. "What's that supposed to mean?"

Van Meer stood up to go. "Nothing, Doc. Thanks for the advice." He stopped at the hatch. "Did you notice how Blandini and his men had three cups of coffee apiece? They really loved the stuff."

Back in his compartment, he sat at his desk and started a letter to Cheryl, then tore it up. He had to do something but he wasn't sure what. Then he thought of Bailey and Meslinsky.

He'd send back a message about apprehending Bailey doing unauthorized work on the stills. Maybe somebody onshore would read between the lines.

He nodded, pleased with himself, and scratched the growing stubble on his chin. Harris usually signed the situation reports but there wasn't any reason that he couldn't step out of the chain of command for once.

He massaged the bridge of his nose and closed his eyes. The thought popped into his mind then, and he realized it had been in the back of his head all day.

Maybe Harris was right. It wasn't impossible, after all. Maybe the tapes *had* been overridden.

Maybe the Soviets *had* walked out on the SALT III talks.

Sunday, June 28

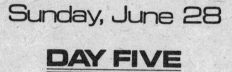

DAY FIVE

23

THE PAINT, according to Joe Gilchrist, had come from New England Pigment, a small paint-manufacturing plant in Lafayette Falls, New York. It had been a small consignment but, then, New England Pigment wasn't one of their major suppliers. Rumor had it that the state representative was a friend of a friend in management, but don't quote him. Why was Renslow so hot to know?

Renslow ignored the question, thanked Joe profusely, and agreed they'd have to have a drink some night. . . .

He hung up and tilted his chair back on its hind legs, staring out the window at the yards below but not actually seeing them. What was he going to ask? He wasn't enough of a chemist for the composition of the paint to mean anything to him. Maybe the production manager could tell him what he really wanted to know but a better bet would be the quality-control man. If something had gone wrong with a batch, that was where the buck would stop.

He dialed for an outside line, then paused. It was Sunday; nobody would be working. He shrugged and decided to try it anyway. A moment later, a female voice confirmed that this was indeed New England Pigment and that because of the press of orders, a Sunday shift was on duty. The man he wanted to speak to was Mr. Moody. She could have him paged, she added helpfully. Her voice sounded as old-line as the company, an echo from the days when you didn't call somebody; you rang them up.

Moody was cautious when he came on the line, hesitating when Renslow said he was from Procurement and wanted an appointment that afternoon. If Mr. Renslow insisted, he'd be glad to see him. Pause. But if Electric Boat provided them with the lot number, order number, and shipping date, New England Pigment would be glad to make good any consignment that had failed—

Renslow cut the call short, saying firmly that he looked forward to seeing Mr. Moody that afternoon.

Moody wasn't going to tell him anything. And maybe there was nothing to tell. It would probably be a wild-goose chase, the only good thing about it being the spring scenery along the way.

The drive took nearly three hours and when he pulled into Lafayette Falls, it was almost one in the afternoon. The town itself was standard New England with dozens of white clapboard houses, a church and steeple that could have modeled for a Christmas card, and a town square complete with a Revolutionary War cannon, flanked by a pyramid of cannon balls. Down by the river, there was a small industrial district, a huddle of aging red brick and dirty windows.

Sleepy little town, Renslow thought. New England Pigment had to be one of the major industries.

He drove slowly around the square looking for directions to the paint company, then finally drew up in front of a single-story building with a painted front window proclaiming it the home of the Lafayette Falls *Examiner*. There were lights on inside and he could see several people moving around.

Renslow parked and walked in, finding himself in a railed area separated from a "city room" containing half a dozen desks and innumerable filing cabinets. Two of the desks held computer terminals, gray plastic units each with a keyboard and a twelve-inch video screen. Two girls were working at the terminals; neither of them looked up. In the corner was a large drawing table where an older man—a well-preserved fiftyish, Renslow estimated—was working at makeup.

"Be right with you, mister . . . just as soon as I put Monday to bed." He pasted in another story, then yelled at one of the computer operators. "Mary, proof sector thirteen Charlie, then paste it up."

He stood up and came from around the table to the railing, fishing in his vest pocket for a pipe and matches. He was tall and appropriately angular, the Lafayette Falls version of American Gothic. "Sorry I had to keep you waiting—the paste-ups have to be at the printing plant by five and that's an hour's drive from here." He held out his hand. "Name's Cletus Wexler—owner, publisher, and editor-in-chief."

Renslow shook his hand and glanced around. "You don't print your own paper?"

"Haven't touched a press in eight years. Too expensive. We do camera-ready paste-ups and truck them over to Falls Church. They've got a plant that handles twenty newspapers. Saves a lot of capital investment." He stuck the pipe in his mouth and held a match to light it, studying Renslow curiously. "You don't look like an irate subscriber. What can we do for you?"

"You could tell me where I can find New England Pigment." Renslow took a chance. "Maybe you could even tell me something about the company."

Wexler smiled. "Every day perfect strangers rush up and ask me about New England Pigment."

Renslow handed over his ID and Wexler glanced at it, flipped it over, then returned it. "Just what kind of information you looking for, Captain?"

"I'm from Procurement," Renslow lied. "We've been having some . . . peculiar problems with their last shipment of paint."

Wexler jerked a thumb toward the rear. "My office is back there." He opened the gate in the railing and Renslow followed him to a small room in the rear. The main piece of furniture was an L-shaped desk, the side extension holding a battered IBM model B; the main desk was stacked high with perforated printout sheets.

Wexler sat down and pulled out a bottle of Chivas Regal and two glasses from a drawer. "Shut the door. We don't want to have to share this." He poured two hefty drinks. "You don't like fine Scotch, you don't leave this room alive."

Renslow pulled over a folding chair from the corner and stretched out, sipping at his drink. Wexler took a sip himself and swished it around his mouth with obvious pleasure. "I like you already, Captain. You're a gentleman and a scholar." His eyes were frank and innocent. "But you're no more a Navy procurement officer than I am. What's your game?"

Renslow tried to bluff it. "What makes you think—"

"Come off it. Full captains in the submarine service don't get butt procurement jobs unless they've screwed up. And I don't think you've screwed up."

"Shrewd deduction," Renslow said dryly.

"Not very. Got a son who's a lieutenant, jg."

Renslow took a gulp of the whiskey and let it burn its way down. "The paint company's the biggest industry in town, right?"

"Ever since the boat works closed."

"And if I go poking around asking questions, everybody's going to protect the company, right?"

Wexler shook his head. "I wouldn't say that. Company pays minimum wage, they've got no health plan, and the plant itself is falling down. To top it off, I used to be a strong union man and the paint company isn't union. It's the only game in town; they don't have to be."

Renslow finished off the whiskey, took a deep breath, and started talking. When he had finished, Wexler said, "Some story. You think there's a connection between the paint and your man Gradow almost killing his wife?"

"Maybe. Ever hear of a fluorocarbon-induced psychosis?"

"If I did, I sure as hell can't remember it now."

"It used to occur when a hot fluorocarbon resin was sprayed on frying pans, pots—you name it—to give them a nonstick coating. In poorly ventilated plants a number of the production people started acting irrationally, displaying all the symptoms of classic schizophrenia. Improved ventilation eliminated the problem but for a while it looked as if a lot of people were going off the deep end and nobody knew why."

Wexler refilled both glasses, then shook his head. "Don't think we can help you, Captain. Been some labor trouble at the plant but that's because they pay criminally low wages. A couple of bad fights—they drink a lot in this town. One stabbing, nonfatal. A guy on the line thought a fellow worker was putting something in his Thermos of coffee to make him impotent. Crazy."

"No more so than Gradow taking a baseball bat to his wife."

Wexler looked down his nose. "A lot less crazy, if you ask me. But don't get your hopes up. The same guy flipped out when he was at the boat works." He shrugged. "Some people come apart for no reason at all, Captain."

"I've got an appointment with their quality-control man anyway," Renslow said stubbornly.

"That's Ron Moody." Wexler stood and picked up his jacket

and hat from a nearby chair. "He'll be glad to see us. Break the monotony."

"Us?"

"You'll like him, Captain. Young man with bad habits. Keeps a bottle in his desk just like I do."

Ron Moody wore a lumberjack shirt, blue jeans, and crepe-soled hiking boots with rawhide laces. His badge of office was a knee-length white lab coat, starched and clean, with sleeves that acid had turned into tattered lace. A skinny redhead well over six feet two, he shared Wexler's habit of chewing on the stem of an unlit pipe.

He listened to Renslow's story thoughtfully, then shook his head. "Sorry to disappoint you, Captain, but we've had ventilating fans on the line long before we started to run your batch of paint. I've argued for air-conditioning the entire plant but at the moment it's not what you'd call cost effective."

"What do you have on the line now?"

"It's a new formulation using a chlorofluorohydrocarbon as a pigment vehicle."

Wexler looked interested. "That related to a fluorocarbon resin?"

Moody glanced darkly at Wexler. "It is and it isn't, Cletus." Then, to Renslow: "Look, there's no indication at all that the paint causes anything more than a desire to throw up after you've been smelling it for eight hours straight. Besides, with each new batch I always run animal tests. They've come up negative ever since I started."

"What do you mean by animal tests?"

"I'll show you." Renslow followed him to the rear of the lab, where Moody pointed out three tiers of animal boxes. "I paint the boxes on the inside and then put the mice in. So far as I can tell, not a damn thing has happened." He lifted the lid of the top box and one of the mice promptly stood on its hind legs and hooked its front paws over the edge. Moody scratched it behind the ear while it stared stolidly at them.

Renslow looked back in deep disappointment. He suddenly felt as if he had let Ernie Gradow down. He turned away from the animal boxes and walked back to stare out the window. It was a chilly spring day, with a faint nip in the air, a nip he could feel even in the lab. He glanced back at the animal boxes.

"You make those boxes yourself?"

Moody looked surprised, then shook his head. "I had a biology student from the high school build those a year ago."

Renslow took a sheet of paper from Moody's desk and held it over the wooden cages. The paper fluttered slightly in a draft. "He built them right over the warm-air duct—probably afraid the mice would catch cold. Your tests have been no good; the boxes have been too well ventilated."

Moody waved his hand over the boxes to feel the slight draft of warm air and cursed quietly to himself.

"Could you paint the boxes with the Electric Boat formula?" Renslow asked. "Shift the boxes and try it for a few days?"

"You could get the biology student to help you," Wexler said, smiling.

"Bug out, Cletus." Moody turned to Renslow. "I'll run it another two days, okay?"

That would be long enough, Renslow thought. He shook Moody's hand, then nodded to Wexler. "Thanks for everything."

"Anything to oblige the Navy, Captain."

Maybe something would turn up, Renslow thought when he got into his car. And then maybe, as Wexler had suggested, Gradow had gone off the deep end for no good reason at all.

Oddly, all the way home, the image of Gradow kept fading from his mind, to be replaced by that of the mouse clutching the side of the box, its whiskers twitching and its small black eyes staring up at him.

24

CULLINANE WAS WATCHING the shimmering walls of the Situation Room below when, behind him, Warden said, "The President has asked to see a briefing each morning from this point on." He said it softly, as if he were talking to himself. "Nothing more than a paragraph, you understan', but it *does* show the man is interested in what we're doing."

Cullinane turned. "I never thought for a minute that he wasn't."

Warden, his face looking faintly red and freshly scrubbed, was lounging in one of the Nelson modular chairs at the rear of the observation bubble.

"Oh, he is, Admiral. He is, indeed." There was an undercurrent in Warden's voice and Cullinane thought again of the dinner at the Cosmos Club. He shouldn't have lost his temper; he should have papered it over. Then: No, he should have said what he thought. But he should have said it long ago.

"I hope you'll include some of the evaluations from the psychology team," Hardin said.

"That's the whole purpose of the drill, Dr. Hardin," Warden assured him. "We'll certainly need your input for the next round of SALT Three. I've taken the liberty of quoting you personally when it seemed to make a point."

That could be dangerous to Hardin, Cullinane thought, and turned back to the plastic wall in front of him. Warden heaved himself out of his chair and walked over. "I imagine you're concerned about those little bogeys down there." He pointed to one of the side walls, where the *Alaska* was clearly marked as a cigar-shaped symbol without a box. Unlike the blue symbols for other American submarines, the *Alaska* symbol was gold-colored.

Several other cigar-shaped symbols were in the same general area as the *Alaska*, one of them yellow and three of them red. One French and three Soviet submarines. All of them submerged. Cullinane turned to Chavez. "Lieutenant, do we have a registry on the French ship?"

Chavez leafed through the log on the observer's desk. "There's no current entry and we don't have an update from the last watch."

Warden edged around the lieutenant. "Those Soviet subs, Admiral. How recent are the data on them and how positive can we be of their accuracy?"

"It's a comparative display," Cullinane said quietly. "The data come by cable from our shore listening arrays and are combined with satellite observations as well as information from surface ships. The computer compares the different sets of data and decides on the most probable information. That's what you see on the display wall."

Warden looked uncertain. "That still doesn't tell me the degree of reliability, Admiral."

Cullinane nodded at Chavez. "Lieutenant."

Chavez opened the drawer in the observer's desk and took out a slender black rod with a long cord at the end of it. He plugged it into a receptacle on the side of the desk. "This is a light pencil, Mr. Warden—actually, it's a small hand-held laser so there's no beam spread. You plug it into the desk and select a function by pressing the appropriate button on the small panel here. For example, I'll press function four—that's ship location—and aim the light beam at a particular symbol, and a probability percentage will appear just above the symbol."

"If the probability percentage is less than seventy-five percent, it's wise to wait for a better reading," Cullinane added. "Other settings will give you fleet designations for the vessels, surface speed, armament—almost anything you might want to know."

"Remarkable," Warden murmured, handling the light pencil gingerly. "Truly remarkable . . ."

The doors at the rear of the observation bubble opened and Chavez walked over to take a message flimsy from the yeoman.

He glanced at the heading, then hurried back to Cullinane, his face somber.

Cullinane scanned the message, then handed it without comment to Warden and Hardin. He waited until they had finished reading, then said to Hardin, "You have a file on Bailey?"

Hardin removed his thick glasses and carefully polished them with a sheet of silicone paper from a pack in his shirt pocket. He was stalling, Cullinane decided.

"Offhand, he's not the type for sabotage," Hardin said slowly. "Quick-tempered, a brilliant man, somewhat unstable childhood but nothing serious."

Cullinane wondered if he had memorized the psychological profiles of all the crew members, then decided he probably had.

"How would you evaluate this?"

"The men are always under a great deal of pressure," Hardin said slowly. "Superimposed on this is the mounting tension caused by the spurious tapes. The early false transmissions, while not terribly alarming in themselves, were designed to introduce a vague unease. One of the by-products would be increased friction among the crew. Naturally we'd expect an increase in disciplinary problems."

It was all gobbledygook designed to explain sabotage by a man who had no motive, Cullinane thought. And that wasn't even the important point.

"Disciplinary problems are settled by a captain's mast or other suitable punishment," he said. "It's not the sort of thing you send back in a situation report. It's certainly not the sort of transmission a captain would send." He paused. "Or the ship's executive officer."

Hardin grabbed the flimsy back and read the signature. "Van Meer. I don't understand that. I don't understand the significance."

Neither did Cullinane. The few FasTrans messages from the *Alaska* were to have been signed by Harris. And he couldn't understand why any transmission concerning a disciplinary problem would have been sent at all.

He shoved the flimsy at Hardin. "I want a complete file on the crewman and on van Meer and Harris, including the possibility of breakdown under pressure."

Warden had been listening and walked over. "Admiral, we're

not even halfway through the drill yet. You mean to tell me that some of your men are breaking down?"

Cullinane grew angry again. "I'm not drawing any conclusions at all, Mr. Warden. But if any of the key men *are* breaking down, we'll scrub the operation."

"That's the whole purpose of the drill, Admiral," Warden said in silky tones. "To find out if the men will hold up under the simulated circumstances or whether they'll crack. If they're going to crack, then we ought to know."

"Mr. Warden," Cullinane said tightly, "I'm not going to sacrifice a crew to prove a point."

"Nobody's asking you to sacrifice a single crew member—"

Suddenly there was a shimmer on one of the walls below and Cullinane turned away to watch as new symbols appeared. Two Soviet Victor III submarines had moved into the *Alaska*'s area.

Warden joined him at the bubble wall. "What's wrong?"

"Trouble," Cullinane said quietly.

25

VAN MEER and Lieutenant Udall were going over the results of a damage-control drill when Harris walked in and dropped a dispatch on van Meer's desk. "Give it to Scoma for the ship's paper," he said. "Then ask him to see me for comments to go along with it."

The message was stark, headlines excerpted from a longer news story with the comment "Details to follow." The Jarir government of Iran had asked for American troops, and the Sixth Fleet was airlifting two battalions of the First Marine Division to Tehran, with other elements to follow.... The Soviets had refused to withdraw from Iran or Yugoslavia and had announced the delivery of tactical nuclear weapons to the Libyans and the Jordanians "for the defense of their homeland." ... The Israelis, now forced back on two fronts, had warned that Israel would not face destruction as a state without resorting to every weapon at her command. ...

Van Meer was shocked. He hadn't thought the Soviets would go this far. It occurred to him, but only for a moment, that the message was part of the drill. Then he dismissed the idea. They had reviewed the messages with Admiral Cullinane and there had been one like it but it hadn't been quite the same; he was sure of that. This was a case of life imitating art. ...

He shoved the message across the desk to Udall, who glanced at it, then said, "How many days do you give it, Van? Two or three?"

"Before the ball goes up?" Van Meer shrugged. "Who's to say?" He added a cube of sugar and a tiny tab of saccharin to his cup. The damn coffee tasted oily; the only thing that would cut it was the saccharin. "You got a family, Jeff?"

Udall was holding his cup with both hands, his elbows on his knees. The youngest officer on board, and right now he looked it. Worried, frightened, confronted for the first time with a problem that brains alone couldn't solve.

"Just my wife, Anne. No kids yet, thank God." He stared moodily into his cup. "You know, I never *really* thought we'd actually do anything more out here than run around in circles for ninety days and then go back in."

"It hasn't happened yet," van Meer said lamely. "The politicians might still pull it out."

Udall fingered the message flimsy and read it again. "It's got a smell to it. The real McCoy." He suddenly glanced up at van Meer. "I've got a job offer from Bechtel—that really put the icing on the cake, Van. The wife, the house, the job ... The great American Dream, right?" He shook his head. "I hadn't figured on a war."

The news had hit missile control center before van Meer got there. Moskowitz and three of the missile techs, Poletti, Sullivan, and Longstreet, were checking some computer printouts. Earl Messier was leaning over them. It was Moskowitz who noticed van Meer first.

"You heard the news, I take it."

Van Meer nodded. "How'd you hear it so soon?" Moskowitz was growing a beard, too, he noticed. He looked like a teddy bear with whiskers.

"Bad news travels fast." Moskowitz folded up the printouts and stacked them in a bin by the computer console. "Think it will go all the way up to a shooting war, Van?"

He'd always wondered how the crew would actually behave when it came right down to it. What had ever made him think they would sit around in silence and go through a launch without ever talking about it? They did during drills but that was because everybody knew they were drills.

"It's possible." Then, without hedging: "Yeah, I'm afraid it will."

"Commander." Poletti licked his lips nervously. He couldn't be much more than twenty-one or twenty-two, van Meer thought. "They'll take out New London and Groton, right off. And probably Holy Loch and the other bases." He hesitated. "What do we use for a home port then? Where do we go?"

Van Meer forced a smile. "That's like asking how many pieces the vase will break into before it's even broken. Let's worry about that when we come to it."

"If I had to pick a first target," Moskowitz said slowly, "I don't think it would necessarily be New London or Groton."

Poletti glanced at him. "What's your choice, sir?"

"New York. One big one would wipe out everything from Ninety-fifth Street to the Battery."

"You say that because you live there," Messier cut in.

Moskowitz shook his head, frowning. "No, I didn't say it for that reason. It's not a big military target but it's the nerve center of American business and banking. It would cripple the entire country. Lose New York during the night and we'd sign on the dotted line in the morning."

"It won't be like that," Messier said quietly. "They'll get everything at once. They've got enough missiles to do it. New London, New York, Chicago, San Francisco, the silos in the Pacific Northwest . . . The big economy strike."

"What's the point of it all?" Sullivan suddenly said, the despair thick in his voice. "Sure, I know what deterrent is supposed to mean but I don't think I can buy it. Everything up above gets wiped out and then we're supposed to sit here and add to the general radioactivity. By that time there won't be anything worth saving anyway. But for revenge we kill a lot more innocent people and make a lot more real estate uninhabitable for a thousand years." The words came out rapid-fire; Sullivan was almost babbling. A quiet kid, van Meer thought, one who spent most of his free time reading and studying. If anyone eventually came up with the "better Red than dead" argument, it would be Sullivan.

There was sudden silence, then van Meer heard himself saying, "I don't think we ought to discuss that, Sullivan. We've got a mission and we'll carry it out. There's no choice in the matter."

Van Meer wondered how many others on board thought as Sullivan did; not many, he was sure, but Sullivan certainly wasn't the only one. . . . He caught Messier staring at him curiously. Messier looked as if he had something else on his mind, something not connected with the current discussion.

"I don't think we have to worry about home ports or even about getting all our missiles off," Longstreet said. "We launch half of them and then they'll know where we are and that's the name of the game. We'll be blown out of the water by a SUBROC before we launch all twenty-four—that's for damned sure."

"That's defeatist talk," van Meer said with an edge to his voice. "I wouldn't repeat that if I were you, mister." Longstreet reddened.

"We're all getting morbid," Messier said, standing up.

Poletti glanced at Messier, frowning. "Do you believe in God, Lieutenant?"

Messier's smile was self-conscious. "No, I don't, Poletti. I haven't for quite some time now."

Van Meer first heard the slight ringing tone in his right ear when he was walking through the darkened crew's compartment. It was very low but obviously there; a pure C-natural tone. He stopped and listened, wondering for a moment if it was someplace in the ship or in his ear, then decided on the latter. It was like coming up from a deep dive in the water, when you'd have a ringing in the ears. . . .

He shied away from a sudden shadow that seemed to be creeping out from under a bunk, momentarily startled. The combination of the red compartment lights and the white bunk lights played tricks on your eyes. But he sensed other shadows behind him and could feel himself growing nervous. . . .

He stopped for coffee in the crew's mess, just in time to hear a three-way argument among Leggett, Russo, and Olson.

"Do it again," Leggett was saying, furious, "and, goddammit, I'll see to it that you're assigned to mess cooking for as long as you're on board the *Alaska*. I don't care if you're a radioman striker or not."

"I did what you told me and that was it," Russo said stubbornly. "Nobody eats the crap anyway."

Van Meer walked over. "What's the problem?"

Olson cut in. "Leggett claims that Russo overdid the spicing of the meat loaf to make him look bad."

He'd had some that night, van Meer remembered. It *had* tasted spicy but he wasn't going to feed the argument. "It's your imagination, Leggett."

Leggett went white. "My imagination? When six crew members say it had so much pepper in it they couldn't touch it?"

"Forget it," van Meer ordered.

Outside the mess compartment, Olson nodded wisely.

"Russo has had it in for Leggett for quite a while."

Van Meer was only half listening. The C-natural tone was growing more intense. "Keep your eye on them, Ray."

Olson said, "Sure thing," and disappeared up the passageway. Van Meer watched him go. For the first time he realized that Olson was wearing cutoffs and go-ahead shoes and had a handkerchief tied around his forehead. It used to be the standard uniform on board the old diesels Olson had served on, in which both the humidity and the temperature were close to a hundred, and not just in engineering. But that had been years ago. . . .

In sick bay Schulman examined his ear with a speculum. "Ever have attacks of dizziness? Ever have an inflammation of the inner ear? Any history of tumors, head injuries?"

Van Meer thought of the plane accident two years before. "Would a blow to the head be enough to cause it?"

Schulman nodded, putting the speculum away. "You've got a mild case of tinnitus. I wouldn't worry that much about it. When we hit port, if it's still bothering you, I can give you the name of a good specialist right in New London. Divers have a lot of problems with their ears."

"How come it hasn't bothered me until now?"

Schulman looked thoughtful. "A lot of things that haven't bothered people before seem to be bothering them this time out."

He leaned back in his chair; he looked tired, worn out. "I've been running myself ragged, Van. A lot of the men are bothered with nightmares. One of the nukes—Baker—has lost his voice—"

"Why?"

"Nervous hysteria, so far as I can tell. And I'm not the only one who's nibbling Valiums as if they were after-dinner mints." He suddenly changed the subject. "You know, that was the only smart thing I ever did."

"What's that?"

"Jeanne and I have a summer home in upstate New York. We made an agreement that at the first sign of trouble, if I wasn't around, she'd take the kids and light out for it before the exodus began." He smiled. "Exodus," he repeated. "I wish this *were* the drill," he said suddenly, smashing his fist on the desk. "Why the hell can't it be the drill?"

Back in his own compartment, van Meer sat at his desk and

started a letter to Cheryl. This is what war is really like, he wrote. The preliminary period of rumors and uncertainty, the jockeying for position among the great powers, and most of all the buildup of tension among men who knew what was coming and who were absolutely helpless to stop it . . . There was nothing they could do aboard the *Alaska*. They couldn't wire their congressmen or talk to their neighbors or load up their family in the station wagon and head for the high country. They were on a one-shot retaliatory mission that lost all of its meaning the moment they were ordered to carry it out. . . .

He could feel the tension on board, not only in himself but in the crew. He hesitated, stopped writing briefly to cast a frowning glance at the shadows underneath the bunks. Something had moved. . . .

But that was impossible; there were no rats on submarines. He watched for a moment longer, then bent over the letter again. And it was hard on him, he continued, having to serve under an officer who was secretly plotting to ruin his career. There was nothing that Harris wouldn't do. . . .

Now that he was putting it down on paper, it all made sense. Harris watching him when he had taken the *Alaska* down, Harris' conversation with him in his cabin later . . . Harris was building him up as the fall guy in case anything went wrong. He started cataloguing all of Harris' sins, feeling quite righteous about it when he had finished. Then he thought about it a moment and added in the next paragraph that he was convinced the depression and the feeling of helplessness would be replaced by a desire to carry out the job, by the desire for revenge.

And finally: Cheryl, I miss—

Then he visualized Maggie, bright and smiling, and he felt that same numbing grip of agonizing depression. He dug out the bottle of Equavil and hastily opened it. He palmed two tablets and swallowed them with a handful of water from the sink.

He'd lie down for a bit, then finish the letter. . . . He dozed for what he guessed was half an hour, then went back to the desk to complete the last few lines. He started to reread the letter from the beginning and, a moment later, glanced up at the mirror above the desk in consternation.

The stubbly, unshaven face of Mark van Meer stared back at him. His shirt was dirty, rumpled; his eyes wild. He looked just like everybody else. In less than two days. He glanced down at the letter again. It had been the work of a madman. . . .

The Equavil, he thought coldly, was what had been keeping him sane. It was the one thing that had made him different from the rest of the crew. And when he had stopped taking them, he had slid into the same abyss with the others. He wasn't sure what was wrong with the *Alaska*. . . . Probably a subtle form of sabotage. Harris had convinced himself that the drill was reality and so had Schulman. The others, of course, didn't know. He'd have to get hold of Schulman and tell him, convince him, then they'd have to get to Harris—

"*Battle stations! Battle stations! All hands man your battle stations!*"

He jammed the bottle into his pocket and dashed for the control room. Harris was already there, hunched over McCune's shoulder. The sounds of fish and porpoises were coming over the loudspeaker and very faintly, almost lost in the background noise, the sound of a distant ship's screw.

"Put it on the computer, McCune."

"It already is, sir."

Van Meer stared at the faint green glare of the CRT display. The letters rolled into view. A Victor III, one of the newest class of Soviet fleet submarines. Displacement: fifty-five hundred tons surfaced, sixty-five hundred dived. Complement: ninety-two men. Speed: forty knots plus submerged. And, chillingly: armed with SUBROC-type missiles, the improved version of the SS-N-15.

The letters hung there for a moment and van Meer knew the computer was searching the ship's library of voiceprints for the submarine's identity. If the Soviet ship were a new-enough model, they might not have it.

McCune said the name aloud as soon as it appeared on the screen. "Charlie's name is the *Zhukov*."

Van Meer felt something freeze inside him.

There was no possible way the *Zhukov*'s presence could be part of the drill.

26

"I DON'T WANT excuses," Admiral Cullinane said coldly, "just an explanation."

Hardin looked both rebellious and frightened. Cullinane thought with contempt that the man was a half-breed, half Navy civilian employee and half psychologist who somehow considered himself outside the chain of command, a consultant with special prerogatives. He was also no clutch player; Hardin had covered himself sixteen different ways in his original opinions of the drill. If it came out well, he could claim credit. If for any reason something went wrong, Hardin had a dozen escape clauses.

"I didn't personally go over every interview, Admiral," Hardin said stiffly. "I'll make sure that the man responsible is reprimanded."

"You'll do a good deal more than that, Doctor," Cullinane said bitterly. He walked over to the windows and stared out at the Pentagon in the distance. Hardin's team had gradually expanded to fill a large part of one floor in the Navy Office Building and naturally Hardin's personal office was in the corner, so he had windows on two sides. How did he rate? Cullinane wondered. He turned back and caught a view of Hardin's desk as Hardin would see it if he were sitting down. He walked over and picked up the photograph on top and read the inscription: "To my good friend Augustus—Caleb Warden."

Hardin had all the influence he needed.

Cullinane set the photograph down. Hardin, he noted with pleasure, was red-faced.

"Which still leaves us with an officer suffering from acute depression—so acute he's been under professional care—in a sensitive command. That'd be alarming enough under ordinary circumstances, but in the *Alaska*'s case it's unacceptable. You've read Dr. Hamady's report?"

Hardin nodded, his eyes cautious.

"He's a highly respected doctor, probably the most highly respected in his field. He's also apparently more of an expert in your field than your assistant was."

"I said I would—"

Cullinane waved his hand in disgust. "You've examined the dispatches?"

"All those to date," Hardin said with studied solemnity. "We've applied certain semantic tests to them and discovered there's a definite and ordered logic except—"

"I'm interested in van Meer's at the moment," Cullinane said.

Hardin looked nettled. "There have been only a few but we've compared those against the records on Lieutenant Commander van Meer. These include analyses of his interviews with members of my section as well as indices of word order, stress content, and usage values from an analysis of his formal and informal written communications."

"Which means?"

"That the syntax of his recent message is atypical."

"I'm sure all of that means something to you and your team," Cullinane said sarcastically, "but I'm not getting the message."

Hardin became patronizing. "What I'm trying to say is that van Meer wouldn't ordinarily say things that way."

"You think he didn't actually author the transmissions signed by him?"

Hardin hesitated, trying to avoid being put on the spot. "Either that or he was trying to phrase them to convey a message other than its obvious literal content."

Cullinane thought about that for a moment, then: "Why would van Meer sign transmissions when the routine signer should be Harris? And if Harris is out of action, why doesn't van Meer report it?"

Hardin looked down his nose. "I think that's an extreme interpretation. It doesn't mean Harris is out of action. The few messages from van Meer seem to be in addition to those from Harris, not instead of."

Which still didn't tell Cullinane why. "You went over his interview again?"

Hardin now looked genuinely worried. "All my team members agree that van Meer's reactions to all the tests indicate unusually tight control. That's confirmed by the abnormal galvanic response of the skin. He was obviously hiding something, probably afraid that we would find out about his crippling depression."

Cullinane shoved a sheaf of papers across the desk at Hardin. "That's all in the report from Hamady—the loss of his wife and his subsequent depression, and *that*, Doctor, is something we knew about all the time."

"We're only human," Hardin objected. "We're bound to overlook a few things."

"Just a few minor things," Cullinane said sarcastically. He hated the priesthood of psychologists; they weren't much better than witches and warlocks. "So what's he liable to do?"

"Probably not much of anything. The Equavil controls these cases very well."

"Let's bottom-line it, Doctor. What would happen if he should be cut off from his medication?"

"Well, it all depends on the individual—"

"Worst-case prognosis," Cullinane persisted.

Hardin looked unhappy. "If he goes into a deep depression, it could color his whole view of reality. Things he would normally value might appear worthless."

"You mean he could be suicidal?"

"That's possible," Hardin admitted reluctantly.

"And the lives of those around him?"

Hardin was sweating. "They'd probably have no more value than his own. I have to stress, though, that this is a worst-case possibility."

It had been risky right from the start. The *Alaska* had been sent to sea on a drill designed to inculcate a war fever among the crew, culminating in the actual firing of missiles. The controls in case of a mishap were the three men on board who knew about the drill.

And now one of them was revealed as suffering from a deep depression, perhaps dangerously so.

"Any chance of van Meer cracking under pressure?"

Hardin suddenly realized he had been backed into a corner; that if something went wrong, the albatross would be hung around his neck.

"Anybody can break under pressure."

"If you were me, would you cancel the drill?" Cullinane asked quietly.

Hardin tried to smile and didn't quite make it. He was being forced to commit himself and he desperately didn't want to. Cullinane saw his eyes stray to the photograph of Warden; Hardin's Adam's apple worked spasmodically.

"I think that would be extreme. I don't think that would be advisable . . . at least under the circumstances as we know them now." There was a fine bead of perspiration on his forehead.

Cullinane nodded. "I'll be glad to quote you later."

The phone on the desk rang. Hardin picked it up and listened for a moment, then handed it to Cullinane. "It's for you."

Cullinane took the phone. "Cullinane here." Then: "I'll be right over." He took his briefcase off the desk. "The Situation Room," he told the curious Hardin. "The *Chicago* has radioed that they've identified the *Zhukov*, a Victor Three attack submarine, in the area."

"In the area," Hardin repeated blankly.

"It's getting very close," Cullinane said grimly. "You're about to have your confrontation, Doctor."

27

ALL THE OFFICERS were in the wardroom, van Meer noted, with the exception of Costanza, who had the con. Stroop looked as if he had aged five years. Moskowitz and Udall were obviously frightened; even Spencer seemed in something of a funk. Chips Okamoto's expression was ambiguous. Cermak, looking edgy, cracked his knuckles until a glance from Harris silenced him.

Watching Harris was like looking through a split-image viewfinder. There were outlines of the Harris whom van Meer had known, but only outlines, smeared now by a five-day growth of beard, the soiled uniform, and a piercing look in the eyes. The beard was actually being trimmed, if only roughly. Another week or so and Harris would finally look the picture of the dashing Civil War cavalry officer—black-haired, mustached, devil-may-care. He wondered what ancestor Harris was emulating.

Harris cleared his throat and stood up; the slight rustling and coughing in the wardroom ceased. He tapped a dispatch on the table in front of him. "Gentlemen, the shit's going to hit the fan almost any moment now." His voice was heavier, more of a growl than his usual controlled, even-tempered tone. He picked up the flimsy and started reading. " 'Elements of the First Marine Division have made contact with advance units of the Soviet forces in Iran and have suffered more than fifty percent casualties. . . . Libya has launched several tactical nuclear weapons at front-line Israeli troops. . . . The Egyptians have launched a preemptive nuclear strike with a twenty-five-kiloton missile that fell short of Tel Aviv but caused enormous casualties. . . . The Israeli nuclear counterstrike has completely destroyed Cairo. . . . Main elements of the U.S. Sixth Fleet are standing off Haifa to land troops and supplies. . . . A large Soviet force is moving rapidly to intercept the operation. . . . Four Soviet divisions are thirty miles into Yugoslavia and meeting fierce resistance. . . . The Chinese, silent up to now, are moving troops across the Manchurian border. . . . The Soviet delegates have walked out of an emergency session of the Security Council. . . .' "

There was dead silence in the small compartment when Harris had finished. Van Meer knew what they must be thinking. It was only a matter of hours.

Harris picked up another message flimsy that had been hidden by the one he had just read. He waved it at the group. "As of just before this meeting," he said in a hoarse voice, "the United States placed its armed forces on a yellow alert."

Van Meer was on his feet, facing Harris. He was going to do something dumb and they'd break him out of the service for it later, but he couldn't let the drill go on any longer. Whatever it had been meant to be, something had gone dreadfully wrong. Once the launch order came up on the tapes, they'd never stop with the four dummy missiles. . . .

"The yellow alert, Steve," he said in a thick voice. "It's on the tapes, for God's sake—"

"Shut up, Van." Harris smashed the table with his fist and leaned toward him. "For six hours now we've been shadowed by the *Zhukov.* Is the *Zhukov* on tape? Answer me, goddammit. *Is the* Zhukov *on tape?"*

The others were looking at him curiously; some of them—MacGowan and Stroop—openly hostile. "No," he said, stiff-lipped.

"Then sit the hell down, Van." Harris glared at him a moment longer, then ignored him and went back to the dispatch. "I guess we know pretty well what to expect in the next day or probably the next few hours. Some members of the crew will be upset. I don't want to hear any morbid conversations about what might happen or what might be happening back home. The emphasis should be on the fact that we've got a job to do, that any hope for the future will come from our willingness to do it. And if worse comes to worst, we can at least make sure that the enemy will regret having started it."

Cold comfort, van Meer thought cynically. Then the meeting was over and they started to drift out. Messier was waiting for him in the passageway, his thin face intense. "Whenever you've got a moment, Van, I'd like to talk to you."

Van Meer looked at him, curious. "Sure. What about?"

"About what happened Tuesday, the sixteenth," Messier said quietly. He glanced quickly around, then shrugged. "Maybe it's a natural way to react but a lot of this seems . . . unreal." He turned and walked toward the ladder leading down to the engineering spaces.

Messier was always the most levelheaded, as well as the most cynical, of those aboard. Maybe he was also . . . immune? Was that the word? He shoved his hands into his pockets, his right hand closing around the bottle of Equavil. He'd go to sick bay and tell Schulman what was happening, that whatever was wrong, somehow the Equavil seemed to act as a buffer. Maybe they could get Harris to take some. . . .

Cutting through the crew's mess, he was stopped by Russo, his apron and hands white with flour. "There's rumors going around, Commander." Russo looked ashen-faced. "Somebody said the war's about to start."

There wasn't anything he could say. He had broken silence about the drill in the wardroom but nobody had paid any attention. The chances were that Russo would think he was out of his mind.

He was trapped; he'd have to play it straight.

"Probably, Russo. Though you can never tell what the politicians might do." And that in itself was a cruel deception because he knew the contents of the upcoming dispatches and anybody who put his faith in the politicians was going to be sadly disappointed. He wondered, once the drill was over, how long it would take men like Russo to recover from their trauma. Would they just shrug and walk away and say, "That's a hot one on me"? Not much chance. They'd bear the scars for a lifetime. . . .

In a few days he would be seeing Admiral Cullinane and Hardin for the debriefing. He had a lot he wanted to get off his chest then. And if it meant getting cashiered from the Navy, so be it. . . .

Schulman was in sick bay, taking inventory of the drug cabinet. "The only good thing to be said about all of this is that pretty soon it'll all be over." He finished checking one shelf and sighed. "A lot of things will be over then, I guess."

"That was part of the tape, Doc," van Meer said quietly.

"You going to give me that again?" Schulman shook his head sadly. "Have some coffee, Van. The powdered cream's in the cabinet there."

Van Meer didn't move. "You don't believe me, do you?"

Schulman settled back in his chair and took off his glasses to polish the lenses. Without them his eyes looked weak and myopic. "I don't believe you because it doesn't make any sense, Van. To speak professionally, it's a wish-fulfillment fantasy." He put his glasses back on and his eyes were suddenly sharp and penetrating. "Harris was right, you know. The *Zhukov* has nothing to do with any tapes but it *is* doing exactly what it should, considering the imminence of hostilities."

"You think the crew's acting normally?" van Meer asked.

Schulman looked as if he were itching to get hold of a pad and pencil and take notes. "Under the circumstances, yes."

"We talked about how the crew might react the morning we left Charleston," van Meer said. "It's reacted pretty much as you predicted except for one thing: Can you explain the fights, the violence?"

Schulman hesitated. "I can explain it. I'm not so sure it would be a valid explanation."

Van Meer lowered his voice to a persuasive level. "There's nobody on board who's got a grip on reality anymore, Doc. Certainly not Harris. And not even you."

Schulman looked at him sadly. "You're the only sane one—is that it?"

"That's exactly right," van Meer said, overlooking the irony in Schulman's voice. He pulled out the bottle of Equavil. "Because of these."

Schulman took the bottle and read the label. "You're being treated for acute depression," he stated without expression.

Van Meer made a wry face. "That's right. Ever since Maggie died, I've been on Equavil for the past three months. Two days ago, I went off it. The moment I stopped taking it I began to slip." He hesitated. "I'm not sure why. Something in it protects me from what's affecting the rest of you."

Schulman opened the bottle and jiggled a few of the tablets into his hand, inspected them casually, then slipped them back into the bottle and tightened the cap. "It's a strong drug," he said coldly. "With unpredictable side effects. It's prescribed in severe cases, when a man might be suicidal or might hurt others."

Before van Meer could stop him, Schulman leaned forward and put the bottle in the still-open safe. He shut the door and twirled the combination knob.

Van Meer stared. "I need those, Doc."

"Van." Schulman's voice was thick with compassion, his eyes filled with pity. "What the hell would you do if you were me? You come in here and tell me you're the only sane man on board—and the reason is that you've been taking a dangerous drug for the past three months. What the hell do you expect me to do?" Then: "You know the rules as well as I do—no unauthorized drugs are allowed on board; it doesn't matter who they're for. Those are the rules and for my money, they make sense." He shrugged. "So in a day or so, we'll all be one with the fishes. But for right now that's the way it is. You realize I'll have to report this to the captain?"

"I really need them," van Meer repeated desperately. "If you don't believe what I'm saying, Doc, drop a couple of tablets yourself. What have you got to lose? Either I'm out of my mind or what I'm saying is the truth. A simple experiment and you'll know for sure."

Some of the compassion had gone out of Schulman's eyes and his voice was harder. "Don't push me, Van."

The words dried up in van Meer's throat. It was one thing to be reported to Harris for the possession of unauthorized drugs, quite another to be put in restraint or confined to his compartment. And if he said anything more, that's what could happen.

He still had his travel supply of twelve caps in the aspirin tin that he carried in his wallet. Now he'd have to ration those for as long as they would last.

"You're making a mistake, Doc," he said quietly, and left sick bay. He went down to the engineering spaces to watch Stroop run his officers through combat-readiness drills. MacGowan gave him a definite fish eye; Messier glanced at him speculatively but said nothing. He cut back through the crew's mess and had a cup of coffee. He listened for a few moments, feeling more uneasy all the time. A few crew members, like Russo, were still scared green and talked wistfully of home; but several others were debating just how badly they were going to hit the Soviet heartland.

The war fever would build. Nobody was going to stop them once they launched the four dummies. Certainly not Harris or Schulman.

He made up his mind then and headed for the radio shack. Dritz, the first-class radioman, was reading a repair manual.

"Send a FasTrans to ComSubLant: Yellow alert acknowledged."

Dritz blinked. "That's not standard, is it, sir? To acknowledge a yellow alert?"

There were very few things on board the *Alaska* that were standard anymore, van Meer thought. "Over my signature," he added.

"Give me a minute to code it for the can, sir."

It would be coded, along with other messages, at high speed on tape, then inserted in a can that served both as transmitter and float. Launched through a signal-ejector tube, it would rise to the surface, send up an antenna, and, in a delayed burst of high-speed transmission, send the messages off to Norfolk without revealing the location of the *Alaska*.

Then maybe, just maybe, van Meer hoped, ComSubLant would pick up on the fact that something was seriously wrong with the *Alaska*.

Monday, June 29

DAY SIX

28

RENSLOW GOT UP LATE, showered, then wandered into the kitchen for breakfast, still yawning. He glanced at the stove clock and shuddered: ten-thirty. He made himself a cup of instant coffee using hot water from the tap, gagged at the results, and put the kettle on to boil. The drive back from Lafayette Falls had taken longer than he'd planned and instead of coming right home, he'd stayed out late drinking with Donaldson. My God, the super could put it away. . . . Elizabeth had gone to bed by the time he came in; thank God for small favors.

He filled a bowl half full of cornflakes and poured in some milk, then sliced a banana on top. It had been a pretty drive up to Lafayette Falls, he thought, then wondered if Moody had moved the boxes away from the ventilating system. Like most people, he probably had a hundred and one other things to do that he considered more important. . . .

He was halfway through the bowl of cereal when the kettle started to whistle. He made himself another cup of instant and sipped at it. That helped. One more cup and his eyes might come unglued. . . .

The porch door abruptly banged open and a twelve-year-old boy was standing in the doorway of the kitchen, staring gravely at him. Renslow stared back, startled, then remembered Elizabeth saying she had agreed to take in Howie Gradow for the duration. He must have come over last night.

"Hi, I'm Al Renslow." He stuck out his hand.

The boy took it and shook it once, formally. "I'm Howie Gradow."

They sized each other up for a quiet moment, then Renslow said, "If you want anything to eat, help yourself."

The boy stared a moment longer, then turned without saying anything and opened the refrigerator. He studied it, shot a glance at Renslow, then went back to inspecting the contents.

"See anything good in there, Howie?"

"Not much," Howie said frankly. Then: "Some cherry pie."

He'd forgotten the pie. My God, how long had it been in there? They might as well finish it up now.

"How about a piece for each of us? Pour yourself a glass of milk and I'll heat up some more water."

Strong boy, he thought, watching Howie move around the kitchen. Ernie Gradow had been a small, muscular man when he was younger and Howie would grow up the same way, probably a little taller than his father. He apparently knew enough to be polite around grown-ups, though Elizabeth had said that Howie had the reputation of being the hell-raiser of the clan.

He suddenly felt wistful. Howie Gradow came equipped with red hair and freckles, probably made slingshots, got into fights, liked to go camping with his father, and undoubtedly made life miserable for his younger brothers.

Howie had finished the pie and sat staring solemnly up at him, a thin mustache of milk on his upper lip.

"How long have you and Mrs. Renslow been married?"

"Seven years," Renslow said, thinking that it seemed much longer. "Why?"

Howie shrugged. "There're no kids around the house." Then, on a subject not quite so important: "You don't have a boat, do you?"

Renslow shook his head, disarmed and defeated. "No, I don't have a boat, either, Howie."

"My dad does," Howie said with an air of superiority. "He was painting it when—"

His face went slack with the memory and Renslow stood up and caught him in the crook of his arm just in time. "Let it all out, Howie."

The boy clung to his bathrobe, sobbing, then pushed himself away. "I'm okay." He looked as though he wasn't quite sure.

"Men cry, too," Renslow said quietly. "It doesn't matter how grown up you are." He waited, then said, "I saw the boat. Your dad really did a neat job."

"Yeah." Howie wiped his nose on his sleeve. "He worked on it every night."

"Tell you what, Howie," Renslow said. "Why don't you cut yourself another piece of pie while I make a phone call? Then we'll go down to the yards and watch them make submarines."

The formality suddenly disappeared. "Hey, really? Dad always said he was going to take me but he never did. Can we go this afternoon?"

Renslow grinned. "Sure, Howie, this afternoon." He walked over to the kitchen phone and dialed Lafayette Falls and a moment later was talking to Ron Moody. Yes, Moody had moved the boxes. Yes, he had painted them the night before and put the mice back in. No, there was nothing wrong with the mice. It would probably take a few days. They were currently hopping around the boxes, obviously in the prime of life. . . .

After Renslow hung up, Howie said, "I used to raise gerbils and guinea pigs. Mom didn't like them. She didn't like the white mice I had, either." He finished the last of the pie and pushed the plate away, a ring of red around his mouth. How much pie could kids eat before they got sick? Renslow wondered.

"But your mom was nice enough to let you keep them."

"Yeah. They ran away, though. My little brother let them out of the cage."

"I've got a friend who might give you some replacements, Howie." He'd have to make one more trip up to Lafayette Falls to wind things up. Moody probably wouldn't mind giving the mice away.

Howie looked suspicious. "Why does he want to get rid of them?"

"They were part of an experiment and in a few days the experiment will be over."

"They're not going to be sick or anything?"

"I was just talking to him," Renslow said. "He says they're kicking up their heels and running around in circles in their boxes."

The look of suspicion deepened. "You mean really running around in circles?"

An alarm went off in Renslow's head. "Small circles," he said slowly. "As if they were trying to catch their tails." That was what Moody had said.

Howie shook his head. "I don't want them."

"Why not?"

"They sound like Japanese waltzing mice. There's something

wrong with their nervous system. They can't do anything but run in tight little circles."

"They were probably bred to 'waltz.' " Then he remembered the mice he had seen the other day. Curious, friendly mice that had hooked their forepaws over the edge of the box to stare up at him. They had done anything but run in circles. . . .

"Son of a bitch," Renslow said abruptly, then felt guilty for having sworn in front of Howie.

It wasn't until he was on the road that he realized Howie must have heard the words a dozen times before and had probably used them himself.

Both Moody and Wexler were waiting for him at the plant, Wexler looking curious and Moody unusually tight-lipped. At first Renslow thought Moody was annoyed at his sudden return, then decided something else was bothering him.

"Back here, Commander." Renslow followed him to the rear of the lab, where the animal boxes had been placed in a corner. Moody took the lid off the top box. Inside, the test mouse staggered around in tight circles. Its condition had obviously deteriorated since that morning; Moody hadn't sounded concerned at all when he had called earlier.

Without thinking, Renslow reached into the box to take out the mouse for a closer look.

"Watch out."

It happened so quickly that for a second he thought the mouse had grabbed his finger with its paws just to hang on. Then the pain hit and he swatted his hand against the side of the box, trying to shake off the mouse. Moody quickly reached in and, with a thumb and forefinger on either side of the tiny jaw, squeezed the mouth open.

Moody put the lid back on the box, then turned on the tap in the lab sink while Renslow held his finger under it to wash the wound. "Foolish thing to do, Commander."

Renslow shrugged. "I wasn't thinking. Naturally. What were they like this morning?"

"Not like that. A little hyperactive, some running in circles, but not that tight."

Wexler lit his pipe. "This'll make a great story."

"Print one word about it and I'll wring your neck, Pappy." Moody walked back to the boxes. "Let's try something else."

He placed a box on the floor and another box next to it, took off the lids, and covered both with a sheet of metal screening. Then he reached down carefully with a pencil and opened both slide gates so the mice could move from one box to the other.

Wexler started to say something and Moody held up his hand for silence. Renslow could feel his jaw muscles tense. He was only vaguely aware that his finger had started to throb. Finally one mouse trotted into the opposing box. The occupant of the second box stood on its hind legs, staring and sniffing the air. Then, without warning, it dashed for the first mouse and fastened its teeth around its throat.

Red blood spurted over white fur.

"Is that what you were looking for?" Moody asked.

"I guess so," Renslow said, shaken.

"Holy Jesus," Wexler said.

29

ADMIRAL CULLINANE HAD bolted his lunch and now realized he'd be paying the penalty for his haste all afternoon. He stared down at the shimmering observer walls below and tried in vain to smother a belch. Lieutenant Chavez, reading the CRT display embedded in the surface of the control desk, reached into his pocket and pulled out a roll of Tums.

"Here, try these."

Cullinane peeled off two of the white tablets. "I'll probably have an ulcer before I retire. The *Alaska*'s due to report, isn't she?"

"Scheduled contact time was about ten minutes ago," Chavez said. "We've already received the regular transmission from the *Chicago*."

The door behind them *whooshed* open to admit Warden and Dr. Hardin. Warden had a wry smile on his face; Hardin looked angry.

"Admiral, I want to lodge a formal complaint."

"What's the matter, Doctor?" Cullinane asked. He was going to enjoy this, knowing very well what was bothering Hardin.

"I understand I'm no longer to get direct copies of the *Alaska*'s transmissions."

Hardin wasn't red-faced; he was livid. "That's right, Doctor." Cullinane was almost smiling.

Hardin was close to stuttering. "Rapid access to all data, including the latest messages from the *Alaska*, is essential to my team's fulfilling its assignment."

"Security, Doctor," Cullinane assured him.

"Sir, that's ridiculous. My clearance—"

Cullinane froze him with a look. "It's a decision the CNO, the Secretary of State, and I all concurred in."

"The services take care of their own, Doctor," Warden said in an amused voice. "If it appears events aren't going to plan, don't think you'll be asked for an evaluation. You probably won't even receive the data."

The trouble with Warden was that ten percent of the time he was right, Cullinane thought. But if something really went wrong with Operation Fire, dangerous and unorthodox measures might have to be taken. And there was no sense letting documentation about them fall into the hands of a non-Navy group, no matter how good its credentials.

"From now on, all transmissions will be received here," Cullinane said, turning to Warden. "We have facilities for printout and if it's necessary, I'll be glad to provide the printouts that are needed." Then, for Hardin's benefit: "There'll be no printouts, of course, without the proper authentication code."

Warden nodded. "Which only you hold."

"Admiral," Chavez interrupted, "they're coming in now." Cullinane walked over and read the words on the CRT display: FIRE XMISSION 008#; 1350.

"Relay," Cullinane ordered. Chavez punched out the command on the recessed keyboard below the tube: VERIFY. Cullinane slipped into the console chair and typed out a string of eight symbols. SYNTAX ERROR, the screen responded. Cullinane swore under his breath and retyped the authentication code, this time adding a period. That was the trouble with machines; they were monomaniacally literal. He remembered an instructor at the Academy who had once hung a sign over his desk that read A MACHINE DOES NOT CARE.

A good thing to keep in mind, Cullinane thought grimly, particularly when you were dealing with machines as complicated as submarines.

The transmissions from the *Alaska* rolled across the surface of the display screen. Cullinane scanned them, then hunched over the screen, startled. He stopped the scrolling on the screen and commanded the machine to print. Almost immediately a perforated sheet rolled from a slit beneath the screen. He tore it off and handed it to Hardin without comment. Warden read it over Hardin's shoulder.

"It's signed by van Meer again," Warden said, puzzled.

The man was blind, Cullinane thought impatiently. "It's an acknowledgment of the yellow alert."

Warden looked blank. "I'm not sure I know what's upsetting you, Admiral."

This time it was Hardin who was impatient. "The yellow alert is programmed on the operation tapes; it's not a legitimate transmission. And van Meer knows it."

"Then there's no reason he should acknowledge it," Warden said, still puzzled.

Cullinane tapped his fingers on the desk top. "That's hardly standard operating procedure in any case. You don't acknowledge alerts unless requested."

"The man sounds like he's a little out of control," Warden said cautiously.

"He should be relieved," Hardin stuttered.

And you'd be off the hook then, wouldn't you, Doctor? Cullinane thought. "That's right," he said. "We'll message Harris that his executive officer is in the dangerous stages of a reactive depression and that they'd better slap a straitjacket on him." He looked at Hardin with disgust. "For some reason I don't think that's a very good idea."

There was a note pad on the control desk and he jotted a few words on it, then shoved it across to Chavez. "For the *Chicago*. Immediately." He turned back to Warden and Hardin. "I've asked Captain Blandini for an assessment of the combat readiness of the *Alaska*; he was on board her yesterday."

"You're sure he won't cover for a fellow officer, Admiral?"

"Not on something like this, Mr. Warden. The captain knows just how serious it is."

He turned away from the others and walked over to the wall of the observation bubble to stare at the changing symbols below. The Victor III was still out there, still nosing around, still curious about what was happening. She'd stick with the *Alaska* until she was chased away.

It was fifteen minutes later when Captain Blandini's response came through. All of them now crowded around the display screen as the message slowly scrolled up: COMSUBLANT. UNABLE TO ASCERTAIN RELIABLY COMBAT STATUS ALASKA. BLANDINI/CO CHICAGO.

Warden looked smug. "We should have made a small wager, Admiral."

"I know Blandini," Cullinane said slowly. "The word 'reliably' says it all. He's worried."

And so was he. Something was wrong. His gut feeling had been growing for the last twenty-four hours and now he was sure.

He swung around to face Warden and Hardin. "Unless somebody can convince me to the contrary, I'm sending orders to the *Alaska* with copies to the *Chicago* canceling Operation Fire."

Warden stared at him with open hostility. "I can guess your reasons, Admiral, and they're not that good."

"I'm afraid I've more experience in the Navy than you have, Mr. Warden," Cullinane said flatly.

"You'd be sacrificing your career, Admiral," Warden said thinly.

The men of the *Alaska* were more than just chips on a political chessboard, Cullinane thought. "I don't know whether I'd be sacrificing my career or not. Considering what's in the balance, I'm not sure I'd care."

Warden's thick face wore a dangerous smile. "Oh, you'd be sacrificing it, Admiral. Believe me, you would. Setting up Operation Fire has cost a pile of money—a big pile of money—and there are too many decisions riding on its outcome. The Russians will figure out what this is all about later on and they'll just laugh right up their sleeves." The smile faded. "Or it might be a good deal worse. They might figure exactly what we don't want them to think—that our crews are unreliable."

Hardin was trying desperately to find a middle ground. "The CNO should know," he said. "It should be his decision."

Cullinane glared at him. "It's not his decision. It's my decision. And the admiral will back me a hundred percent in whatever decision I make."

Warden was pleading now, in a tone of voice that Cullinane had never heard him use before. "At least go to the source, Admiral. Contact the *Alaska*. If Captain Harris can assure you that everything's all right, then certainly there's no need to cancel the operation."

Cullinane shook his head. "No transmissions have been sent to the *Alaska* since the operation started. We didn't want to run the risk of confusion between our transmissions and the taped transmissions aboard. Any simultaneous transmissions, and the radioman would have to be an idiot not to become suspicious." He hesitated. "I'll have Blandini contact them on the UQC, the underwater telephone. But we're still running the risk of compromising the operation."

Warden was jovial again. "Why, I think you've made a smart decision there, Admiral."

It was a logical one, but Cullinane still had the feeling that he and Warden were dicing with the lives of the crew. And maybe with a good deal more.

The problem with intuition, he thought grimly, was that if you put it down in black and white, it read like madness.

30

TWO CARS WERE parked in Renslow's driveway and the street itself was jammed from one intersection to the other. Renslow finally found a spot around the corner and walked back to the house, cursing. Somebody on the block was giving a party in the goddamned middle of the week. . . . Once inside the front door, he realized it was Elizabeth holding a meeting of the Navy Officers' Wives Club. He nodded at the chattering group in the living room, then, disgruntled, went back to the kitchen and made himself a cup of coffee and a sandwich. Eight o'clock; they'd be good for another two hours.

He took the coffee and sandwich, and climbed the stairs to the guest room, on the second floor. The TV set was on loud and he had to knock twice before Howie's voice piped, "Come on in."

Howie was lying on the bed, his eyes glued to a science-fiction movie on the tube.

"You object to some company, sport?"

"Heck, no, Mr. Renslow."

"Al," Renslow corrected.

Howie grinned and looked back at the screen. "It's pretty good." Then: "What are all the women doing downstairs?"

"It's a club that Mrs. Renslow belongs to. They're all Navy wives."

Howie looked bored. "I guessed. They were talking about allotment checks. Hey, watch this coming up. The special effects are great."

It was the first time that Renslow had seen a whole planet disintegrate on the screen and it gave him an odd, queasy feeling. Give them another hundred years, he thought, then corrected himself: another fifty.

The good guys had triumphed and the bad guys had fled to another galaxy by the time the cars started to leave the driveway. Renslow picked up his cup and saucer, and rolled off the bed. "You got any studying to do, Howie?"

Howie looked guilty. "Just a little."

"A little what?"

"Some reading for English."

"No TV after this until your homework gets done." It was the first time he had ever acted as a parent and Renslow couldn't keep from smiling.

"You sound like my dad," Howie said, then looked away.

"He'll be okay," Renslow said awkwardly.

"I'll never talk to him again," Howie said tightly. "Not after what he did to Ma."

"It wasn't his fault, Howie. He couldn't help himself."

Howie looked as if he were going to cry again. "You're just saying that."

Renslow shook his head. "No, I mean it, sport. And I think I can prove it." He paused at the door. "No more TV, huh? Not even with the volume down?"

Elizabeth was tidying up in the kitchen when he walked in with his dirty dishes. She was faintly hostile.

"You could have at least come in and said hello. Now they'll talk."

Renslow slid his dishes into the soapy water in the sink. "They've been talking about us for years."

She rose to the bait like a trout striking a lure. "That's more your fault than mine."

He started a hot retort, then thought better of it. He was too tired, too worn out. He wasn't expecting affection from her but neither did he want to argue. "I told Howie I could prove his father was innocent."

She looked mildly interested. "How?"

"It was the paint he was using on his boat. Residual fumes, something of the sort, caused it. The animal tests up in Lafayette Falls pretty well document that."

"Florence will be glad to know." Her lips were tight, and he knew she was waiting for the inevitable argument.

"It's great having Howie around the house, isn't it?"

"He's a nice boy," she said slowly. "But I don't think I'd want him underfoot all the time."

"For a moment upstairs, I felt like a real parent."

It was like the air just before a storm. He could feel the electricity between them.

She turned away from the sink, her face flushed. "Children are a responsibility. You have them when you have a stable environment in which you can raise them."

Renslow realized he was hooked, that they were finally going to have it out. "Sometimes children help create a stable environment."

"You think it would have helped the marriage," she said in a flat, angry voice.

"I think it might have," he said coolly.

"Keep them barefoot and pregnant," she said, swiping viciously at a dirty dish with a soap pad. "The automatic solution for the unhappy wife."

Renslow dropped the towel on the counter. "You've never told me what you have against children," he said. "Are you afraid to have them? If there's a medical reason, why the hell didn't you ever tell me?"

Small red spots were dancing in her cheeks. "You know there isn't. We both share the same doctor; I know damn well you've asked him a dozen times. The reason is I grew up in a household where two people tried to patch up a lousy marriage using me as the glue. They hated each other; they constantly fought with each other and each of them tried to turn me against the other. Nobody ever thought I might want . . . desperately . . . to love both of them."

For a moment he felt terribly sorry for her, and then the feeling was washed away by anger. "You think this is a lousy marriage?"

She was almost sobbing. "Isn't it? I know what you want out of it. But did you ever ask me what I wanted out of it?"

It came out then, and the moment he spoke he knew he had passed the point of no return. "Would you have been happier with Harris?"

"It would have been different," she mused. Then, more defiantly: "My *God*, it would have been different."

"You would've had Harris' kids," he said accusingly.

"I'm not afraid to have children. My only requirement is that I have them by a man I feel loves me."

Renslow felt sweaty and nauseated. "What do you do when

I'm not around, Liz? When I'm gone for three months, Harris is back here. Do you see him, Liz? Do you go to bed with him?"

"You're disgusting," she said tightly.

He grabbed her by the shoulders. "It's a simple question," he said thickly. "We've both wanted to talk about it for years."

She closed her eyes but the tears leaked under the lids. "I don't do anything," she whispered. For the first time she sounded broken and he thought of a kid's doll thrown against the wall. "He's not interested; he's never been interested. He doesn't want me."

"You're lying," he said, trembling.

"No." She slowly shook her head. "No, I'm not. I made it a point . . . to find out."

He let her go then and turned away. In the morning he'd talk with her about seeing a lawyer. But for tonight he couldn't stay there; he had to get away. He had finally gone too far and it had been all his fault.

Harris hadn't wanted her. But she still offered herself to him. Harris.

God, how he hated the man.

The bars closed at two o'clock and it was two-thirty when he drove up to Cheryl's. Got to be quiet about this, he thought, mustn't wake the neighbors . . . He rang the doorbell and lifted the heavy knocker, then changed his mind and lowered it carefully back into place. It was early in the morning; it'd make too much noise. . . .

On the fourth ring, lights came on in the hallway and a moment later, the door opened the few inches permitted by the chain inside.

"It's Al, Cheryl."

"Just a minute." The door closed again, then swung open all the way. "What on earth—?" Her mouth thinned and she pulled him in. "Into the kitchen. I'll put the kettle on. Jesus, you smell like a brewery."

He sank into the kitchen booth and held his head with his hands.

She brushed her hair back out of her eyes and tightened the sash of her robe. "Two cups of coffee and that's it," she said grimly. "I work tomorrow and I don't take house calls at three in the morning."

He watched her as she moved about the kitchen. The same bathrobe, the same worn mules. But without makeup she looked even more human, more approachable.

"I'll be seeing a lawyer tomorrow," he said.

She sat down opposite him. "It'll take five minutes for the kettle to boil. You've got until then."

He told her about the evening's argument. When he had finished, she said quietly, "I'm sorry, Al, I can't sympathize with you." The teakettle started to whistle and she got up to pour the coffee.

He was sullen. "I'm in the wrong?"

"Has Elizabeth ever mentioned divorce?" He shook his head. "Ever wonder why?"

"Maybe her religion."

"Come off it, Al. You'd know whether she had religious convictions about divorce or not." She set a container of milk and a box of sugar cubes in front of him. "Your marriage is important to your career. Divorced men seldom get promoted to flag rank. You know that. If your marriage broke up, you'd probably never get promoted above captain. I know of several marriages that have held together—officially, at least—for just that reason."

"You think Elizabeth is that self-sacrificing?"

"I have no idea." She hesitated. "But it's curious you haven't even considered the possibility."

"Divorce cuts both ways," he said darkly. "Liz's social circle has been the Navy for the past seven years. As a divorcée, she'd probably be dropped by most of the other wives. She might have an affair but I rather doubt that she'd be a hot prospect on the marriage market."

"At three in the morning that's pretty cynical."

"Realistic," Renslow corrected harshly.

Cheryl studied him for a moment. "You do have your unattractive side, Al." She finished half her cup, then said, "If you're high on realism, have you ever considered what's really wrong with your marriage?" She held up her hand. "I know, there are a number of things. But one of them certainly stands out."

It was argument by proxy, with Cheryl taking Elizabeth's part. And maybe that was what he needed. It wasn't that Elizabeth couldn't defend herself; it was that they didn't talk the same language. Cheryl and he did.

"What's wrong with your marriage is not that you don't love

your wife," Cheryl continued. "What's wrong is that you hate Stephen Harris more."

Renslow stood up, almost spilling what was left of his coffee. "I don't have to—"

"You certainly don't," she interrupted. "And I'm under no obligation to try to tell you the truth at three in the morning, either."

He sat down again, angry and ill at ease. He didn't want to hear what he knew she was going to say.

"When did it start? At the Academy? The kid from the wrong side of the tracks in competition with the boy who had everything, including charm, wealth, and social position. The competition was intense, wasn't it?"

He sighed, the anger starting to leak out of him.

"You two became very close, in a sense." She got up and put the kettle back on. "Harris was number one in the class and you were number two, weren't you?"

He nodded again.

"And then you were accused of . . . what, cheating?" She refilled his cup. "And Harris testified in your behalf and you were absolved."

"Van Meer told you."

"He didn't tell me much more than that. But you hated Harris after that, didn't you?"

"They didn't absolve me because I was innocent," he said harshly. "They absolved me because of Harris' testimony."

There was sudden understanding in her eyes. "You mean he perjured himself."

"There was no way he could have known the truth," Renslow said bitterly. "So he lied on the witness stand, under oath. It didn't mean anything to him."

"It was a charitable act," Cheryl said slowly.

Renslow nodded. "That's right. One more act of charity for somebody who had had charity all his life. I didn't need it again. There was no way I could repay him, nothing I could do for him, nothing that he needed. The competition was over. He had obligated me for life." He paused. His words were coming out wrong; they didn't quite reflect the way he had always thought about what had happened. "I was innocent," he said after a moment. "But I never got a chance to fight it my way."

Cheryl let out a long sigh. "I was wrong about something," she said.

"About what?"

"About Elizabeth. And about you." She looked at him with an expression of pity. "I think Elizabeth would have liked to marry Harris. At least at one time. And I think you might have loved her when you married her. But I don't think your competition with Harris was over. I think you wanted to take something away from him, something you thought he really wanted. When it turned out he didn't want her, Harris won for the last time. You never forgave him for that." She paused. "You asked Elizabeth a lot of tough questions tonight and it was really unfair. You already knew the answers."

Renslow was stone-cold sober now. "You don't always do people a favor by telling them the truth, Cheryl. And you're kidding yourself if you expect them to thank you."

He was sorry the moment he spoke but she didn't react. "We are what we are, Al. And none of us can change until we admit what we are."

"Am I that much of a bastard?"

She smiled a little wanly. "Perhaps too proud. But you were programmed for that."

He drained his coffee cup and stood up. "Thanks a lot, Cheryl." But there wasn't much force to his words.

She walked him to the door and all the way there, he was conscious of how close she was, of the hem of her bathrobe hitting against his pants leg, of the warmth of her body and her faint animal smell.

He said, "Thanks for everything," again at the door but didn't open it.

She looked at him without expression, her eyes somber. "That's all right," she said. She didn't make a motion to open the door, either.

They stood there in silence a moment and he said, "Well?"

"Al, I—"

He ran his fingers lightly over the back of her hand, then slowly pulled her close and wrapped his arms around her, feeling the heat of her body against his chest and stomach. She didn't push him away but she didn't respond, either. He fumbled with the sash of her robe to open it and pressed the palm of his hand firmly against her naked back. She started to shiver and he lowered his face to hers and forced his knee slightly between her legs. She opened her mouth and he kissed her for a long moment, then stepped back and gently closed her eyelids with his hand. The couch was only a few feet away and he swung her up and carried her over to it. Her breathing was heavier now, her hands clutching at him.

He laid her down on the couch and knelt beside her, burying his face in her hair. It was a very lonely three o'clock in the morning, he thought.

He lit her cigarette, then swung his feet over and sat, naked, on the edge of the couch. He felt sweaty and wanted to shower but for the moment all he could do was sit there and think of nothing at all.

"It's been a long time for you, hasn't it?" she asked quietly.

"Elizabeth exiled me months ago," he said. He shook his head, annoyed. "I don't want to start that again." He spotted an ashtray on the mantel across the room and walked over to get it, aware of his own nakedness and feeling very relaxed and comfortable with it. "It wasn't the same reason for you," he said.

"No," she admitted, "it was different. Call it sex without shame, sex without guilt. It's very difficult to make love with a man who feels that every time he beds you, he's cheating on his dead wife." She grimaced. "I put that badly."

He took a drag on his cigarette and let the smoke out slowly. He felt curiously detached from the situation, from Cheryl herself for the moment. She was close to Van, and he wondered what she really knew about the *Alaska*, about how much Van might have told her. There were times when it occurred to him that she might know a great deal. He took another puff and felt guilty for even thinking about the *Alaska* right then.

"I'd like to see you again," he said suddenly.

She shook her head without hesitation. "You know that's impossible. For better or for worse, I love Van. Besides, he'll be back in a week."

The statement came out naturally. She turned her face away. "Oh, Christ."

"He'll be back in a week," Renslow repeated stupidly. "What the hell are you talking about, Cheryl?"

"They're on a short patrol," she said, still facing away from him. "They'll be out for ten days, launch four dummy missiles down the Atlantic range, then come back to pick up real ones, the replacements." She sighed, her voice tired. "After that they'll go out for the rest of their normal patrol."

Renslow reached for his trousers on top of a pile of clothing on the nearby chair. The hairs on the back of his neck were starting to stand up.

"You're not making sense. I oversaw the loading of those missiles. They were real, not dummies."

She turned on the couch to face him. "Not even the crew was supposed to know about them." Then: "Van came here just before he caught the plane to Charleston. He was very depressed. He told me about the drill."

Van Meer knew what they had done to the *Alaska* that Tuesday, Renslow thought. And he had certainly known about the team of psychologists who had interviewed the members of the Gold Crew. They must have talked to him, too, and van Meer had covered up the fact that he was seeing a shrink, that he was on Equavil. If he had admitted it, they never would have let him sail with the rest of the crew.

Renslow sat back down on the couch, facing Cheryl, who was sitting up, clutching her bathrobe tightly around her.

"What drill?"

She told him everything that van Meer had told her five nights before. Renslow listened with growing fear.

"What a lousy, cynical trick," he said. And then he remembered that van Meer was in the center of the drill.

Van Meer.

Depressed . . . unstable . . . dangerous.

31

"**B**ATTLE STATIONS! *Battle stations! All hands man your battle stations!*"

The moment van Meer arrived in the control room he could hear it—the steady beating of a submarine's screw. He knew without checking the name on the CRT display that it was the *Zhukov*, circling for another look. The tension in the compartment was almost tangible—not alone because the *Zhukov* was trailing them but because the Victor III class was something of an unknown quantity. At forty-plus knots, it might prove as fast as the *Alaska*. And it was far quieter than most previous classes of Soviet submarines. The Russians were catching up fast, van Meer thought. In another few years . . .

Half an hour later, the *Zhukov* was still close on their tail. Van Meer glanced around. Even at a rock-steady compartment temperature of seventy-two degrees, the crew stank of perspiration. Gurnee's weathered face looked oiled; Costanza's shirt was plastered to his armpits. Harris stared at the loudspeaker, concentrating on the throb of the screw and looking even more the old-time cavalry officer than he had the day before.

"Thermal inversion to port, Captain."

Harris glanced over at Olson, hunched before the CRT display. "See if you can map it, Ray."

Van Meer felt a brief surge of relief. Harris was thinking of hiding. Under the circumstances, it's what he himself might do.

Dritz suddenly cocked his head, placing one hand on the small relay headset he wore. "Coded message coming in from the *Chicago*, Captain."

"They're going to chase away the *Zhukov*," Harris murmured, almost to himself. "They'll have to."

There wasn't any other choice, van Meer thought. The *Alaska* and *Chicago* could separate but the *Zhukov* would stick with the *Alaska*. The *Alaska* could devastate a continent; the *Chicago* couldn't.

He heard the sounds of two screws now as the *Chicago* moved in to play chicken of the sea. The sweat began to trickle down van Meer's neck. It must have been a lot like this during World War II, he thought, when you lay at the bottom of the ocean while they dropped depth charges on you.

Except, of course, that it wasn't wartime and there would be no depth charges. But the crew wasn't at all sure of that. . . .

Somebody giggled and van Meer glanced quickly around, annoyed. Once again the appearance of the crew struck him. Almost all the men sported beards and mustaches. Their blue Dacron jump suits were rumpled and dirty, and some men had switched to cutoffs and go-ahead shoes, shower clogs. The officers didn't look much different.

And all of them stank, including himself.

"She's moving away," Olson said suddenly. Van Meer strained to listen. The sounds of both screws were receding now. He could feel the tension drain out of the compartment. Sandeman and Clinger broke into wide smiles and even Gurnee looked relaxed.

"Good show," Costanza said in a low voice.

"She'll be back," Harris warned.

But she hadn't come back in another half hour. Harris passed the word to secure from battle stations. As he left the compartment van Meer felt a light jab in the ribs and turned to see Cermak grinning at him. "Perez has set out lunch in the wardroom. I told him to open up a bottle of Taittinger."

Van Meer was startled. "Champagne?"

Cermak winked. "What's the sense of being supply officer if you can't do something unofficial from time to time? Something to cheer us up as we all go down the tubes."

Harris was waiting for him in the passageway outside the wardroom. When the others were inside, he said, "Dritz finally got around to telling me. You included an acknowledgment of the yellow alert in the message can. That's not only against regs, mister, that's against my direct orders—no messages are sent except over my signature." Harris' eyes were a cold slate-gray. Van Meer was suddenly afraid he might flinch under the stare. "And your outburst in the wardroom the other day." Harris' eyes turned suspicious, the voice threatening. "I don't think you're well, Van." He turned abruptly and went inside the wardroom to sit at the head of the table.

For a moment van Meer considered skipping lunch, then pushed his way in and sat between Moskowitz and Udall, directly across from a somber Okamoto. The weapons officer had spent the previous watch drilling the missile techs in launch procedures and the strain was showing.

A cork popped and then Cermak was pouring the champagne. Somebody said, "Toast," and Harris stood up, a grim smile on his face. "I guess the only thing I can say is that whatever happens, we're ready, willing, and more than able. And I hope the Russians are listening."

It was MacGowan who started the cheering. Then all were standing and holding up their glasses. Van Meer felt as if he were back at the Academy, then realized that not everybody had his heart in the brief surge of warlike spirit that flooded the wardroom. Okamoto seemed tired and sad, Messier had a cynical smile on his thin face, and Moskowitz looked as if he wanted to cry.

They sat down and in the buzz of conversation that followed, Moskowitz caught van Meer's eye and raised his glass again. "Here's to my mother," he said in a low voice. "She's dying of cancer at Boston General and whatever happens tomorrow may be a blessing."

Van Meer clinked glasses, then went back to inspecting the faces around him, desperately searching for a possible ally. He had hoped his acknowledgment of the yellow alert would have served as a warning to the drill monitors ashore, but no message had come through calling off the operation. Apparently, if the drill was going to be stopped, it would be up to him. But he couldn't do it by himself.

He reached into his pocket for a handkerchief and felt the tin of twelve Equavil tablets. He'd have to slip some to one of the other officers. He glanced around the table again, taking special note of Messier, Udall, and Spencer—Moskowitz was a possibility, too—then realized it had to be Schulman. Doc already knew of the drill; he wouldn't need the explanation, which, if anything, would sound more fantastic than the situation they were already in. But he was suspicious and van Meer had been unable to persuade him to take the Equavil. . . .

The lights in the compartment now blinked in rapid succession, the ultra quiet signal for battle stations.

Udall murmured, "Here we go again." They hurriedly left the compartment. Back in the attack center, the sound of the *Zhukov*'s screw was loud and distinct. So was that of the *Chicago*.

Harris suddenly held up his hand for absolute quiet. Blotting out the sound of the screws was a harsh, grating noise, clearly audible through the pressure hull. Van Meer shot a startled glance at Costanza. He could still hear both screws but over all was the low squeal of tearing metal.

Then there was a sudden silence in the watery universe outside. A minute passed. Another. Then once again there was the retreating whir of a screw. The *Zhukov* was moving away.

There was no sound at all from the *Chicago*.

Tuesday, June 30

DAY SEVEN

32

RENSLOW'S HEAD ACHED and his tongue felt thick and fuzzy. He fumbled for the alarm clock on the floor, next to the couch, and turned it off, then closed his eyes, hoping for a blessed five minutes more of sleep. Finally, he sat up and fished for his trousers, then staggered to the bathroom. He filled the sink with cold water and plunged his face into it.

Three immersions later, he felt better and turned on the shower. Cold, he thought. Make it ice cold. . . . He was still shivering even after he had toweled down. He went to the kitchen and put on a kettle of water for coffee, hoping that Elizabeth wasn't already up. For a moment he wondered if she had fled the house as he had, then decided it wouldn't have been her style. Besides, it had become more and more her house, and in the property settlement she would undoubtedly get it. So be it; he owed it to her.

He huddled over his coffee and thought of what had happened a few hours before at Cheryl's house. He certainly had no regrets; the only residual feeling he had was of a great desire to see Cheryl again. Then he remembered that van Meer would be coming back shortly and that would be the end of that affair. What did she see in van Meer? he wondered, then decided the question was juvenile, as so much of his thinking had been.

The toast popped up and he opened the refrigerator to get some butter and marmalade. One major mystery at least had been cleared up. He now knew what had been done to the *Alaska* and what its mission was. He swore silently to himself. Of all the crazy— It had to have been some politician's idea; he couldn't imagine either Admiral Cullinane or Howland proposing it. To deliberately lead a crew into thinking a war was brewing—in fact, had occurred—was criminal. It was also a slander against their own crews. Every crew that went out was on a war footing; there wasn't any doubt that they would perform as trained.

He had also scored on another front. He now knew what had happened to Ernie Gradow and, more importantly, he knew he could prove it. And there was one lady especially he wanted to tell about it.

He finished his coffee and toast, and wondered why Elizabeth hadn't come down yet. She must be sleeping in—thank God, he couldn't go through last night all over again—and to judge from the dishes in the sink, Howie had already left for school. He glanced at his watch. Eight o'clock. The morning shift would have reported to the hospital. . . .

Dr. Strickland went with him to Gradow's room. The guard was still out front but Gradow himself was no longer under restraint. He was curled up in an almost fetal position under his thin blanket, sleeping.

"How is he?" Renslow asked in a low voice.

"It's been touch and go." Strickland frowned. "I've never seen anything quite like it. He has moments of lucidity and I think we're making progress and then he either lapses into a deep depression, when he's noncommunicative, or he's completely out of touch, much as he was when he was brought in. It's too early to tell but it seems that those periods are becoming less frequent. His depression I'd attribute to a growing realization of what he did to his wife." He shrugged. "In the long run, you could say I'm optimistic."

"Any evidence of a physical cause?"

Strickland smiled bleakly, looking even more like a mortician. "You mean, is there a biochemical cause for his behavior? That's always a possibility. I guess we'd all like to think there is." He leafed through some pages on his clipboard. "There seems to be some liver damage. Nothing significant but there are some signs of loss of function." He glanced up, suddenly curious. "Do you know if he's been near any toxic chemicals?"

"How about extensive exposure to paint solvents?"

"That might not mean too much—unless it was something chemically similar to trichloroethylene or carbon tetrachloride."

"If he had been, would you testify in court that such exposure could account for his behavior?"

"That all depends on the solvents involved and their concentration, Commander." Strickland stared thoughtfully at the figure under the blanket. "From what I know about the patient, I'd certainly be curious about the chemical end of things. People don't go that far over the edge without reason."

Florence Gradow was sitting up when he walked in. She was still swathed in bandages but much of the puffiness had left her face and her eyes were alert enough to indicate she was off pain-killers. She glanced up at him, surprised.

"How'd you get in? Visiting hours aren't until this afternoon."

Renslow smiled. "I bribed the nurses. How you doing this morning?"

"They tell me I'll live, though I'm not so sure I want to."

"The nurses say you're coming along fine."

"Nurses. What do they know?" Then a wan smile. "I'd like to go home but they tell me it'll be another week or two. And I hate being trapped in a bed." She lowered her voice to a confidential level. "You start to heal and what they don't tell you is that you start to *itch*. And there's a lot of me to itch." She patted his hand. "It was awfully nice of you to take Howie in. I can't thank you and your wife enough."

"He's a good boy," Renslow said quietly. "He looks a lot like his father."

"God forbid."

"I stopped in to see Ernie before coming up here."

There was a long pause. "How is he?" Her voice held carefully concealed interest.

"The doctor is guarded about his condition, but he thinks Ernie is showing improvement."

She turned to look out the window. "What will they do with him?"

"He'll have to stand trial."

"They'll send Ernie away for a long time," she said sadly.

"It wasn't his fault," Renslow said.

"There wasn't nobody standing behind him urging him to hit me," she said bitterly.

He told her about the paint and she closed her eyes in pain. "He couldn't help himself, then," she said when he had finished.

"I think he loves you very much, Mrs. Gradow."

She started to cry and he stood up to go. When he was at the door, she said, "Captain Renslow, please ... don't tell Ernie I ever doubted him."

He smiled. "I don't think he'd believe me even if I did."

He left, feeling a little less confident about the paint than he had sounded. He'd have to go to the Gradow house and pick up a sample, then persuade the Navy testing labs to run it through a chemical analysis to determine the composition of the fumes, what constitutes a toxic concentration in an enclosed space, and finally the effect on personnel subjected to the fumes. It would be a while yet before Ernie Gradow was completely in the clear. . . .

Scotty Black, the young Navy lawyer he had met at the hospital a few days before, was waiting for him at Gradow's house.

"I called the hospital for permission to get the keys from Mrs. Padgett. They said you were on your way over."

Renslow shook his hand. "You've been appointed counsel?"

Black looked slightly abashed. "Chief Gradow's in no condition to pick counsel and Mrs. Gradow said it was all right with her. They can choose other counsel later if they wish but I thought I'd do some preliminary work—interview the neighbors, that sort of thing."

He fished in his pocket for the keys and opened the front door. "That Mrs. Padgett is quite something."

"Don't get too close; she won't let you get away."

The living room looked different this time, Renslow thought sadly, but that was because he knew what he was looking for. The blanket on the back of the couch was Navy issue, even though there was no stencil on it. So were the ashtrays and the china. And in the kitchen both the blender and the electric mixer showed an area where a metal registration tag had been pried loose. But they'd never hang Gradow for those; chances were he had a good explanation and nobody would have any records. And Renslow himself didn't give a damn.

"Do you think you can help him?"

Black looked uncertain. "I don't know. Probably the only chance he has is to plead temporary insanity."

"By reason of solvent poisoning," Renslow said quietly.

Black stared, his Adam's apple stalling at half mast. "I don't follow you."

"He was painting his boat in the garage with the door closed. The paint fumes were vicious—it was a newly formulated paint."

"You've got a lab analysis?"

"Not yet. That's why I'm here—to pick up some of the paint."

"There's some around?"

Renslow walked through the kitchen to the back door. "Out in the garage. I almost stumbled over a partly opened can the other day; had to tap the lid back down." On the flagstone walk he said, "They found Mrs. Gradow in front of the garage door there, right next to the flower bed."

Black looked unhappy. "That's bad for the chief. If he called her out, then it was premeditated for sure."

Renslow pushed open the garage door and flicked on the light. The can of blue paint just inside the front door was gone. "*Goddammit.*"

"What's wrong?"

"The can's gone."

A voice a few feet above his head said, "What's gone?"

Renslow glanced up. Howie Gradow was sitting inside the cabin eating a sandwich. "What're you doing here, Howie?"

"It's recess time and I thought I'd show Bill dad's boat." Another face joined Howie's at the railing. "We heard somebody coming, so we hid up here."

"I was looking for the can of paint that was by the door," Renslow said.

Howie swung himself off the railing and hung for a moment, then dropped to the concrete floor. "I put it over in the corner so nobody would trip over it." He scurried into a dimly lit corner of the garage and came back with the gallon can of paint. "You need any more?"

"Sure," Renslow said. "You got any more?"

"Dad's got a whole case."

Howie ran back to the corner and tugged out an open cardboard carton. There were three cans inside, separated by corrugated cardboard dividers. Renslow took a screwdriver off the nearby workbench and jimmied one lid open. The paint inside was the same cerulean blue that had been used on the boat. He picked up the partly filled can and put it into the empty space in the box, then double-checked the serial numbers on the side. It was the same lot from New England Pigment that had been used at Electric Boat.

He started to close the cardboard flaps. There was stenciling on top that made sense only when the flaps were down.

With the box closed, the stenciled words read U.S.S. ALASKA.

Renslow felt as if somebody had kicked him in the stomach.

Gradow had diverted part of the paint shipment meant for the *Alaska*, as Gradow had diverted so many other things meant for the *Alaska*. But he would never have diverted all of it. The same paint had undoubtedly been used in the recent refurbishing and retrofit of the *Alaska*.

Renslow considered the implications. The paint was lethal. It was capable of inducing paranoid schizophrenia in personnel who inhaled the fumes. And it had been used in the self-contained environment that was the *Alaska*. It was unlikely the scrubbers would completely remove the fumes from the air. They would remain in the atmosphere and be inhaled until the crew was composed of 140 Ernie Gradows. . . .

He had a sudden image of a small mouse hanging on his finger and of another lunging for the throat of its companion. . . .

The *Alaska* was now at sea on a secret mission, and manned by a crew that was no longer completely sane and with an executive officer who had been over the edge to begin with. It was a crew that had been led to believe that World War III was due to start any day now.

And the submarine was armed with twenty-four missiles. Four of them were dummies but the remaining twenty were among the most deadly nuclear missiles made, capable of destroying any country on the globe.

What was happening on board the *Alaska*? he wondered with growing horror.

And what would happen when the *Alaska* received its false launch order?

33

THE CONTROL ROOM was quiet except for the faint whir of equipment fans and the underwater noise from the loudspeaker. They were hovering at neutral buoyancy, engines off, the men walking about on crepe-soled shoes and talking in whispers, straining to sort out the significant sounds from the noisy background of the sea outside. The *Zhukov* had left minutes before, the sound of her screw retreating into the distance. The *Chicago* was still silent and Harris had forbidden any attempts to contact her by underwater telephone, the UQC. The *Alaska*, for the moment, was hiding from friend and foe alike.

Olson suddenly turned away from the sonar station to face Harris. "The *Chicago*'s blowing all tanks. She's trying to surface."

A moment later, Dritz ripped off his headset and said, "The *Chicago* reports she's surfacing to check damage."

"Don't acknowledge," Harris said tightly.

What the hell was Harris going to do? van Meer wondered. Just sit there? Or break radio silence and ask Washington for immediate instructions? It was obvious that the *Zhukov* had deliberately rammed the *Chicago*. It would have to be reported. They would have to send a message asking for immediate help.

Weppler, the other radioman striker, hurried in with two messages. Harris scanned them and passed them on to van Meer. The first was from Admiral Cullinane, asking for a readiness report on the *Alaska*. Van Meer read it with a vast surge of relief. They had picked up on his acknowledgment of the yellow alert after all; they knew something was wrong.

Harris looked both confused and angry. "It doesn't make sense. Why ask for a readiness report at this time? And why are they asking me to break radio silence to do it? They must be mobilizing in the States now, probably evacuating government offices. Obviously all the ships at sea have been put on yellow alert." He turned the message over in his hands and read it again, the expression on his face showing that he thought there was something definitely fishy about it.

The other message was from the *Chicago*, requesting the *Alaska* to surface and lend assistance. The *Chicago* had a damaged screw and was disabled.

It was all over, van Meer thought. There was no way the drill could continue with the *Chicago* disabled. And there was no way that Harris could rationalize the messages. Breaking radio silence to send in a readiness report would reveal his position, something out of line for a fleet vessel on yellow alert. And Harris couldn't possibly believe that the *Chicago* would ask the *Alaska* to surface and lend assistance if war was close and a Soviet killer sub was in the vicinity. He would now *have* to believe the previous messages were part of the drill.

Harris would have to pick a course of action, and chances were better than even that he would surface to see what help he could render the *Chicago*. He'd *have* to.

"Captain." Weppler was back, his face ashen. Harris grabbed at the newest message, scanned it, then crumpled it in his fist.

"Blue alert," he said harshly. He turned to Spencer at the diving station. "Flank speed and maximum down bubble. Head for under the thermal inversion. That'll deflect their sonar."

Van Meer was stricken. What the hell had happened? Then he knew. Somewhere within the ship a solenoid had chosen that moment to come to life and the programmed tape had silently rolled to the next message—the blue alert.

A few minutes later, they were in the thermal inversion and Harris ordered all stop on the engines and gave the order for ultraquiet.

Then a voice came over the loudspeaker. The *Chicago* was trying to contact them on the UQC. "CO *Alaska* from CO *Chicago*. Have damaged screw. Need assistance. Acknowledge."

"That's Blandini," Gurnee whispered.

Van Meer glanced at Harris, trying to read his face. Costanza and Spencer were standing by, waiting for orders. "It's a trick," Harris said tightly. "Don't acknowledge."

"They need help," Spencer said, uncomprehending.

Harris shook his head, looking fierce. "How do we know for

sure that's Blandini? The *Chicago* isn't the only submarine in the area. Anybody could send a voice message. Anybody could fake his voice." He smiled slyly. "We don't have a voiceprint of Blandini in the computer banks."

Van Meer was in despair. They weren't going to try to help the *Chicago*. What Harris was going to do was to take the *Alaska* to a prearranged station and launch her missiles when he got the launch order on the tape. And that was only a few days away.

It was too late to stop Harris now, too late to try to convince him that the blue alert was part of the drill.

One look at his face and van Meer realized that Captain Stephen Harris had just gone to war.

34

THE FLOOR OF the Situation Room was slowly filling with the figures of silent, uniformed men hurrying from console to console while other figures bent over data boards, responding to commands whispered from small speakers on curved stalks near their ears. High above the floor, in the observation bubble, Admiral Cullinane stood watching, occasionally glancing past the restrained bustle to the glowing walls that showed the last-reported positions of the *Chicago* and the *Zhukov* and the *Alaska*.

Considering the significance of the disaster, the floor below was an oasis of calm, with commands given in low voices and acknowledgments in near-whispers.

When war comes, Cullinane thought, *it will be like this. All superficial calm and quiet . . . no obvious excitement. Just a whispery, disembodied voice spelling out the agony of a dying planet. No emotion, no histrionics, just statistics detailing the number of silos destroyed, interrupted occasionally by mention of the passing of Chicago and Leningrad and Osaka and London . . .*

He crumpled the latest message flimsy in his hand, then nervously smoothed it out and read it once more. Behind him, Warden cleared his throat and asked, "What's happening, Admiral? I think I ought to get some sort of briefing." His voice sounded oddly plaintive and too loud in the quiet of the bubble.

Cullinane ignored him and turned to Lieutenant Chavez. "Ask Norfolk again if they can confirm a ramming." Chavez spoke softly into his microphone and turned, shaking his head silently. On the floor below, Burton, the chief communications officer, glanced up at the bubble and spread his arms eloquently.

"I'm not sure you realize the diplomatic implications, Admiral," Warden said, his voice pompous.

"I'm well aware of them," Cullinane said curtly.

"If the *Zhukov* has been sunk, in plain sight of the world . . ."

Cullinane whirled around. "I don't give a good goddamn about the *Zhukov*," he snapped. "I'm worried about the *Chicago* and the *Alaska* and the crews on them."

He turned his back on Warden and stared down at the floor. It took effort but he could tune the man out. All the complaining noises Warden was making now that *his* drill had turned sour, his wheezing, his constant clearing of his throat . . . If only he could wave a magic wand and make the fat little bastard disappear completely.

"We've made contact," Chavez said suddenly.

"Get that message up here immediately," Cullinane ordered. He watched Chavez tap out the authentication code and listened to the sound of the high-speed console printer as the message was ejected. Chavez ripped the paper along the perforations and handed it to him.

"What's it say?" Warden demanded, trying to read over Cullinane's shoulder. Cullinane walked over to the first row of Nelson chairs and sank into one. "Well?" Warden persisted.

"The *Chicago* reports a grazing collision with the *Zhukov*," Cullinane said quietly. "They've been forced to surface. There's damage to her screw and apparently the shock of collision damaged her sonar. As a result, they've lost contact with both the *Alaska* and the *Zhukov*. They're shipping water but they're under way using emergency diesels."

"And the *Zhukov*, Admiral?" Warden asked, white-faced. "What about the *Zhukov*?"

Cullinane massaged his forehead for a moment, then walked back to Chavez at the console. "Message to CNO. Permission to send in another fleet submarine and any surface vessels in the vicinity. The *Chicago* may have to be towed."

He had finished a quarter pack of cigarettes when Chavez said, "Message acknowledged, permission granted." He paused. "Admiral Howland and Dr. Hardin are on their way over, sir."

"The *Zhukov*—" Warden started again.

"We'll find the goddamned *Zhukov*," Cullinane said savagely. "After that it'll be in State's lap."

He walked back to the window wall. This was what he hated most about a command position. The endless waiting for news, the frustrating attempts to second-guess a situation that was changing from moment to moment. He'd give a month's pay to be at sea and on the scene rather than sitting in a hole in the ground having to rely on electronic interpretations of events taking place two thousand miles away.

"A new message from the *Chicago*," Chavez announced suddenly. "They've requested the *Alaska* to surface and render assistance. They're not getting any response."

"Of course they're not getting a response," Cullinane said, irritated. "The *Alaska* thinks there's a war on."

Too many things had gone wrong. Harris and van Meer knew it was a drill—nevertheless, the *Alaska* had failed to respond to his request for a readiness report. The medical history of van Meer didn't ease his mind any, and the previous messages and the acknowledgment of the yellow alert had been anything but standard operating procedure. The failure of the *Alaska* to respond to the *Chicago*'s request for help was the last straw.

He turned to Chavez again. "Message to both the *Chicago* and the *Alaska*. Operation Fire has been canceled. The *Alaska* is to surface and render all assistance to the *Chicago*, both vessels to return to Charleston. Request immediate acknowledgment."

He looked at Warden with contempt. "I already know what you're going to say, Mr. Warden. But this time I'm not making a mistake. The mistake I made was not doing this days ago."

Warden turned red. "That's the sort of decision that should be made by the President or at least the CNO."

"What are they going to do?" Cullinane asked in a suddenly silky voice. "Shoot me at dawn? I'm sorry, Mr. Warden, those are *my* men out there."

Warden was suddenly remote and pious. "So be it, Admiral. It's on your head. I wash my hands of it."

Fifteen minutes later, the *Chicago* sent a message that there was still no response from the *Alaska*. "How soon before their sonar is operational again?" Cullinane asked.

Another five minutes went by as Chavez radioed the *Chicago*. Then the answer came in and the lieutenant's face went chalk white. "They've repaired the damage in part and they're operating on reduced range, conducting sweeps of the immediate area. Captain Blandini reports no sign of the *Alaska*."

Cullinane hesitated. The next decisions would be all-important and they would be all his. Admiral Howland was en route and wouldn't arrive for another hour. But they were in a situation where time was of the essence. "They've been out of sonar contact for two hours now," he said slowly. "That could mean simply that the *Alaska* is beyond the *Chicago*'s limited range. It could also mean that, for whatever reason, she's hiding." He hesitated, then said bluntly, "Or it could mean that she, too, was involved in the collision and sank."

Warden turned away from the bubble wall, his expression one of shock. "That's three billion dollars' worth of ship and missiles," he said, exploding. "That's almost ten percent of the seaborne retaliatory force of the United States."

"You forgot the hundred and forty men in her crew," Cullinane said thinly.

"What are you going to do, Admiral?" Warden demanded. *"What the hell are you going to do?"*

Cullinane ignored him and turned to Chavez at the console desk. If there had been any sounds of breakup, any obvious oil slicks or debris, the *Chicago* should have reported it. But with limited propulsion and damaged sonar, all three could have happened to the *Alaska*, and the *Chicago* might not have known.

"Ask Captain Blandini to widen his search area and continue contact attempts by underwater telephone. Request CincLantFlt to notify all surface ships in the area to rendezvous at the *Chicago*'s coordinates." He thought for a moment. "And message Norfolk to have the *Ortolan* ready for sea as soon as possible. The same for the DSRV *Avalon*. All deep-submergence rescue teams are to report immediately."

Maybe they wouldn't be needed. Maybe it was all a waste of time, energy, and money. But he wasn't going to be responsible for the sort of delay that there had been in the case of the *Thresher* years ago, the first nuclear submarine to be lost.

"What's a DSRV?" Warden asked petulantly.

"Deep-submergence rescue vehicle," Cullinane said. "They can operate at depths in excess of five thousand feet. The *Ortolan* is a surface support ship for the DSRV."

"Five thousand feet," Warden repeated, surprised.

"That should be enough," Cullinane said grimly. "It's more than the crush depth of the *Alaska*."

There was more activity on the floor below and Cullinane returned to the wall of the observation bubble and stared down. The main observers' booth was filling up. He thought he recognized some officials from State and the Executive offices of the White House among the brass. Bad news was traveling faster than usual. . . .

He stepped over to the microphone to talk to the chief communications officer below. "Please notify all guests that there will be no talking and that they are in a no-smoking area—smoke haze interferes with the visibility of the displays. A news blackout has been imposed; the media will be notified fully of the situation later." Like hell, he thought, then wondered how long it would take before somebody below leaked it.

Warden was now standing next to him, watching the displays. Cullinane could read his mind without even trying. First, there would be the long, painful investigation by a naval review board, then both of them would be put through the wringer by a congressional committee. As of right now, everyone connected with Operation Fire was walking on eggs. It wasn't going to be enough to save the *Alaska* or resolve the dangerous situation that was developing. It would have to be done exactly the way the Monday-morning quarterbacks, six months from now, would think it should have been done.

And during those six months, of course, Warden would be trying to place the blame.

A red light was flashing on the console desk. Chavez picked up the telephone, then turned to Cullinane. "We've got company, Admiral."

A moment later, the doors slid silently open and Admiral Howland stalked in, followed by Hardin and two men in mufti, one of whom looked familiar.

Howland walked over to the bubble wall and glanced briefly below. "It's all bad news, Stew?"

"No casualties aboard the *Chicago*," Cullinane said, grim-faced. "The *Alaska* disappeared three hours ago."

Howland looked at him sharply. "Any sounds of breakup, any oil slicks?"

Cullinane shook his head. "Captain Blandini says the *Alaska* wasn't involved in the collision."

"In *their* collision," Howland corrected. "It's possible there was a second one."

He was thinking the *Zhukov* might have played still another game of chicken of the sea, Cullinane thought. It was unlikely but, then, perhaps Howland didn't want to face the fact that the *Alaska* might simply be hiding, waiting for World War III to start.

But that didn't hold water, either. Both Harris and van Meer had been fully briefed on Operation Fire. Both of them had known that the patrol was actually a drill. What the hell had gone wrong?

Hardin was trying to interrupt, to get his attention. Cullinane stared at the man. The usually arrogant Hardin looked as if he were about to be sick.

"We brought along Commander Renslow," Hardin chattered. "You've got to listen to him."

Cullinane turned to Admiral Howland questioningly. Howland nodded, a worried look spreading across his face. "It's serious, Stew."

Cullinane finally recognized the man with Renslow. Captain Pierce, squadron commander for the *Alaska*. But Renslow . . .

For some reason he couldn't immediately place the small redheaded man in civilian clothes who was now walking toward him. Then he had it. Of course. The captain of the *Alaska*'s Blue Crew.

He studied Renslow's tight face and slowly held out his hand. They'd had enough bad news for one day, but he suddenly knew that what Renslow was going to tell him was much worse.

Cullinane felt his stomach knot in anticipation. For the first time since his sub was holed off the Marianas early in World War II, he was genuinely frightened.

35

THEY WERE RESTING almost on the bottom, six hundred feet below the thermal inversion. Van Meer took out his handkerchief, folded it several times, trying to find a dry spot, then mopped at his forehead. Sweat ran down the rims of his glasses, stinging his eyes.

"Anybody know anything about the Victor Threes?" Costanza asked in a low voice.

"They're fast and they're silent," Harris answered quietly. "Maybe as fast as we are. How quiet, nobody seems to know. There're rumors they've got an active sonar whose signals can't be picked up." He changed the subject. "With the *Chicago* out of action, that makes us the only pigeon down here."

Spencer said, "We're being stalked, Captain."

"Probably," Harris said in a matter-of-fact voice.

Van Meer hunched forward in his chair, glancing occasionally at his wristwatch. With an active sonar you'd hear a *ping* once it located you. Shortly after that you could expect a torpedo—they were too close for the *Zhukov* to use its version of a SUBROC, a nuclear-tipped missile. But the *Zhukov* wasn't interested in sinking them. It wasn't part of the drill and it wasn't expecting a war. It had simply gone too far in a game of chicken of the sea. . . .

Half an hour passed before the loudspeaker crackled into life once more: "CO *Alaska* from CO *Chicago*. Relay from Washington. Cancel Operation Fire. Surface and render assistance. Return base Charleston. ComSubLant."

Harris glanced around at the radioman. "Dritz, take the UQC off the loudspeaker. Any more underwater phone messages from the *Chicago*, type them up on message forms."

"What the hell is Operation Fire?" Costanza asked, frowning.

"It was a psychological drill," Harris said casually. "A reaction-time drill. It wasn't important." The sweat was glistening on his mustache and beard. "I wonder if they think we're really going to believe that. They're asking us to show ourselves when we're expecting a red alert and when there's been hostile action. If we came up, we'd be blown right out of the water."

"How do you know it isn't Blandini?" van Meer suddenly asked.

Harris' eyes were large. "You're naive, Van. They've been planning this for decades. Their files on us are probably just as complete as our files on them, maybe more so. They could have taped Blandini almost anytime, anyplace, without his knowing it. Our voices are probably on tape, too. And once you're on tape it's easy to piece together almost any transmission." He hesitated, as if he were double-checking the logic of what he had said and had found it sound. "The *Chicago*'s out of action; we know that. It's possible it's been boarded. There are undoubtedly Soviet trawlers around. There might even be Soviet agents in the crew." He glanced around and Gurnee and several others nodded in agreement.

"The Soviets planned it rather thoroughly, then," van Meer said dryly.

Harris nodded. "It's for keeps, Van. There's not going to be a replay. There isn't going to be any negotiated peace. Winner takes all." He cocked his head to one side, obviously wondering how anybody could doubt his logic. "Knowing the power of this one submarine, Van, what lengths would you go to in order to knock it out or neutralize it?"

That was the clinching argument. Harris was absolutely convinced, and to judge by the expressions on their faces, so was everybody else in the compartment. Van Meer suddenly felt very lonely. He was the only man on board who didn't believe they were on the brink of World War III.

Harris was staring at him suspiciously. "Van, you don't still believe in that drill business?"

Van Meer suddenly realized that to argue now could be dangerous for him. "No, of course not, Captain."

Harris nodded, satisfied with his answer. "Pass the word. We'll rig for quiet until further notice. Run a noise check on all compartments."

They couldn't pass the word via the ship's intercom, and it was possible somebody might miss the special pattern of battle lights that had flashed on over the hatchways. "Rigged for quiet" meant no cooking in the galley, where pots and pans might be knocked against each other; no working in the engine spaces or machinery rooms, where a wrench or a pair of pliers might be dropped; no wearing of ID tags or bracelets; no cassette players; no movies; no activity of any kind in which the sound might carry beyond the pressure hull. . . .

Van Meer hurried aft to the ship's engine room first, relaying Harris' words to a taciturn Stroop and a hostile MacGowan. "He's got a point," Stroop agreed. "It'd be worth a great deal of effort to remove the *Alaska* from the board."

"They probably had their own people on the *Chicago*," MacGowan added. Then, darkly: "For that matter, they probably have their own people on board the *Alaska*, too."

Van Meer stopped next in the electrical shop and the auxiliary machinery room. Messier's only comment was "I wonder who he's going to suspect first." A half smile. "I think it'll probably be you, Van."

Back in Officers' Country, he was passing Cermak's compartment when he heard voices from behind the door. He rapped twice, answering, "Van Meer," to a cautious "Who goes there?"

Cermak opened the door and motioned him in quickly, then locked it again. "Just in time, Van—I'm unveiling my private cache." He had opened his locker and at the bottom van Meer could see a number of bottles wrapped with thick towels and rubber bands. One of the bottles had been unwrapped and was sitting on his desk—a fifth of Jim Beam.

Udall and Moskowitz were sitting on the lower bunk, drinks in their hands, and Okamoto huddled in a chair on the other side of the desk, looking inexpressibly sad.

Van Meer started to back out of the compartment. "I don't think you want me as a guest, Tony. This is against regs—"

Cermak waved a thick hand. "For Christ's sake, Van, so's the end of the world." He poured a double shot into a water tumbler and handed it over. "Bottoms up and forget the damned war for thirty seconds."

Van Meer drained the glass in one gulp. It burned all the way down and landed with a small explosion in the pit of his stomach.

He could chew out Cermak and the others, but they were seeing things from a completely different viewpoint. And he had them at a disadvantage: He knew what was actually happening and they didn't.

"Eat, drink, and be merry," Okamoto said quietly. "For tomorrow everybody in the world dies. Or maybe it'll be the day after. Who knows?"

Udall said, "No more for you, Chips."

"In a day or two I'm going to be playing God," Okamoto said.

"You're just doing your job, Chips," Moskowitz said. Then, more belligerently: "You'll just be doing to them what they'll already have done to us."

Okamoto shook his head and put his empty glass on the table. He stood up to leave. "Somehow I can't bring myself to believe that all the housewives and the school kids and the streetcar conductors in Moscow are the ones who will have pushed the button. Good night, gentlemen."

He left and Cermak shrugged and turned back to van Meer, noting his empty glass. "I really admire a man who can handle good booze." He pulled a towel-wrapped bottle out of the bottom of the locker and handed it to van Meer. "Enjoy it while you can, Van."

"That's . . . pretty generous."

Cermak gestured at the stack of bottles. "Hell, none of us is going to live long enough for me to work my way through all of that, so why *not* be generous?" He suddenly knelt down and pulled out a long-necked bottle and unwrapped it. A bottle of Château Lafite-Rothschild, 1959. A fabulous year, van Meer thought, and glanced up in surprise at Cermak, who was regarding the bottle sadly.

"It's a good-luck piece, Van. I've taken it on every patrol I've been on, thinking I'd open it if we ever got a launch order. It was sort of like, you know, hedging my bets." He looked at van Meer with a wry half smile. "It'd be appropriate, wouldn't it, Van? I mean, it'd be time to drink the good-luck piece when we've run out of luck."

Van Meer took the bottle of Jim Beam and wrapped one of the towels around it again. "Thanks a lot, Tony." Then, hesitantly: "Maybe things aren't as black as they seem."

He ducked into his own compartment just long enough to hide the bottle at the rear of his wardrobe drawer, then checked through the remaining compartments of the ship. Something was changing. Not everybody was quiet or stoic or frightened. A few of the crew had caught war fever, calculating the time necessary to launch all their missiles and get away, and then the chances of reaching a South American port. Only Chips Okamoto seemed to feel that his actions would mark the end of all the things he knew and loved.

In sick bay Schulman was preparing for the worst, breaking out necessary drugs and other medical supplies.

He looked at van Meer over the tops of his glasses as he went through his list. "Did you ever think what it will be like to try to evacuate Manhattan, Van? The bridges and the tunnels will be jammed within the first hour. The only way you'll be able to leave the city will be to walk out and I'm not sure you could even do that." He glanced at a bottle and jotted a number down on the sheet in front of him. "Besides, if the bombs miss you, you're only buying a little time."

"What do you mean?"

Schulman's eyes were owllike behind his thick lenses. "Say you survive the first wave of destruction. Sooner or later, all that fallout is going to end up in the food chain. Then the milk, the eggs, the fried chicken you eat—that's what'll kill you."

Van Meer suddenly snapped. He grabbed Schulman by the arm. "Goddammit, Doc, it's the drill. Do you remember the drill? The *Zhukov* isn't part of it but games of chicken of the sea aren't that rare. The admiral's tried to call the drill off but Harris won't believe the message. He's paranoid. For God's sake, it's over with; it's through. There's nothing left to do but surface, take the *Chicago* in tow, and go back to Charleston."

Schulman pulled away. "You can't face it, can you, Van?"

"Oh, for Christ's—"

"Van, don't you think I'd prefer to believe it was a drill? I'd give everything I've got to be able to believe it was a drill, to think that Jeanne might be safe." He shook his head. "It's probably one of the side effects of the Equavil. It prevents you from seeing"— he paused—"reality."

Van Meer was beginning to feel like Alice in Wonderland.

Even with the Equavil, it took an effort not to become caught up in the mass delusion. . . .

"You're the only one," Schulman said. "It's got to be *you*."

Van Meer turned away; he was too tired to argue.

"Harris said there were agents on board," Schulman added as Van Meer was about to go through the hatch. "He's right, you know."

"What makes you say that?"

"I was testing a counter to see if it was in working order," Schulman said. "The ship's been contaminated."

He was paranoid, too. Like Harris. "I suppose you know who did it?"

Schulman nodded slyly. "The water chemist, of course. Bailey. He had the opportunity when he was sampling the cooling water in the reactor. And we all know he had the motive."

"Maybe he just got sloppy, Doc."

Schulman's expression hardened. "I don't think so. I think it was intentional."

"How heavy a dosage?"

"Light. Geranios and I decontaminated the spaces. But it could be heavier next time."

Why hadn't he been told? Then Van Meer wondered if it had actually happened. Suddenly, out of the corner of his eye, he caught something winking. The battle-stations light . . .

He raced back to the control room and Costanza told him what had happened. "One *ping*, Van. Loud and clear."

The single short, high-pitched note meant they had been detected; they could expect a torpedo shortly. Or so everybody else in the crew believed.

What it really meant was that somebody had a search sonar going and was looking for them.

36

T HIS WAS the point of no return, Renslow thought. From here on in, his career was on the line.

"Renslow," Admiral Cullinane said grimly, gripping his hand. "Captain of the Blue Crew of the *Alaska*, right?"

For a fleeting second Renslow was distracted by the activity on the floor below, the flow of symbols and continental outlines on the shimmering walls. Then he nodded and shook the admiral's hand. Cullinane was perhaps two inches shorter than himself, with the extra heft around the waist that went with age and a desk job. His hair was white and cropped short, his eyes friendly but shrewd. Renslow sensed drive and competence; he liked him immediately.

A man who had been standing by the wall of the observation bubble now turned and walked over to them. Cullinane deferred slightly to him. "Mr. Warden, this is Captain Renslow of the *Alaska*'s Blue Crew. Commander, Caleb Warden, the President's National Security Adviser." Cullinane's eyes narrowed slightly and Renslow took the signal to mean *Be careful.*

Warden was a smallish, round man with a florid face and the first signs of wattles at the borders of an otherwise youthful jawline. He ambled rather than walked and despite his age—probably low forties, Renslow thought—he already possessed a dowager's hump. His eyes were hard and bright and inquisitive. He made Renslow feel uncomfortable.

"It's mah pleasure, Commander."

Admiral Howland said, "You don't need me, Stew. I already know the situation. The Undersecretary from State is downstairs. I'd better get back to him." He glanced at Captain Pierce. "I'd appreciate it if you'd come along, Captain. SubLant's in this up to its

ears and I'll want your ideas." He hesitated at the sliding doors.
"You've got my full backing, Stew. This is your baby."

The doors *whoosh*ed and he was gone, leaving Renslow alone
with Admiral Cullinane, Warden, and Lieutenant Chavez, the admiral's aide, who was manning the controls of the console. And,
of course, Dr. Hardin, whom Renslow had talked to earlier. He
hadn't liked Hardin.

It occurred to Renslow that there was meaning behind all the
activity on the floor below and the growing crowd of Defense Department dignitaries. It was obvious something had happened.
He had sensed it the moment he entered Flag Plot. But busy as
the scene was, and as Admiral Cullinane must be, he had been
brought here immediately.

He froze. The *Alaska* . . .

Cullinane walked back to the small lounge area, trailed by
Warden and Hardin. He motioned for Renslow to sit in one of the
modular chairs. "You've got something to tell us about the *Alaska*,
Commander?"

"She's down, isn't she?" Renslow blurted out.

Cullinane looked at him with compassion. "We don't know
that yet, Commander. Perhaps your information will help us determine that."

Renslow tried to pick the precise words but fumbled it immediately. "If she's not down, Admiral, she's still in deadly danger."

Warden stared at him, curious. Hardin tapped his fingers
nervously on the chair arm. Cullinane kept his face carefully
blank. "Why so, Commander?"

"The paint that was used on her interior during retrofit,"
Renslow said hurriedly.

Cullinane's eyes glazed. "The paint," he said politely. Out of
the corner of his eye, Renslow could see Warden smile slightly.
They must think he was some kind of nut. . . .

"The *Alaska*'s an enclosed system," he said swiftly, "like all
submarines. A new paint formula was used but it was inadequate-
ly tested. It gives off toxic fumes that would be dangerous under
any conditions. Under the special circumstances of the drill—"

Cullinane cut in quickly. "What do you know about the drill,
Commander?"

Renslow took a breath. "The crew's been primed to believe
that World War Three is starting. Only the captain and the exec

and the ship's doctor know it's a drill. It's armed with four dummy missiles that it's supposed to launch when they receive the command."

Warden suddenly chuckled. "So much for Navy security, Admiral. Seems like it's about as effective as usin' chicken wire for window screens."

Cullinane ignored him, leaning tensely forward. "Which one of the three told you, Commander?"

Renslow hesitated. "None of them," he said slowly. "I don't think it matters how I found out, sir. It's not that important now."

Lieutenant Chavez turned from the console. "Admiral, I have a message from the CO, Eleventh Naval District. He reports the *Trieste Three* is in harbor at San Diego. He wants to know if he should initiate procedures to bring her east."

Cullinane shook his head. "No, the water's not that deep in the operations area."

She *was* down, Renslow thought.

Cullinane read his mind. "That's precautionary, Commander. You were telling us about the paint." He nodded to Hardin, who edged closer to listen. Warden shook his head, smiling again.

Renslow cleared his throat, then quietly and methodically began telling of Gradow's attack on his wife, the incidents with the shipyard workers, and the primitive experiments with the mice at New England Pigment. Cullinane listened carefully, interrupting only twice to ask him to clarify a statement. When he had finished, Cullinane leaned back in his chair, rubbing his chin and digesting the information.

Warden now interrupted, the smile smeared thickly across his face. "Commander, that has got to be the *most* fantastic piece of . . . uh . . . most fantastic story I've ever heard." He turned to Cullinane. "Admiral, you don't seriously believe any of this?"

Cullinane looked at Hardin. "What's your opinion, Doctor?"

Hardin glanced at Warden, on his right, then back to Cullinane. His hands were shaking slightly, his face sweaty. He was the man in the middle. It was obvious to Renslow that there was friction, serious friction, between Warden and Cullinane.

"I really don't know what to make of it, Admiral. I'm familiar with chemically induced psychosis, of course."

Renslow saw a flicker of disgust on Cullinane's face. "Doctor, would you be kind enough to confer with the other members of your staff? I want a preliminary opinion"—he glanced at his watch—"within the hour."

Hardin blanched. "I couldn't get to Washington and back in an hour—"

"Go down to ops and start making phone calls, Doctor— they've got a secure line." Hardin nodded, glanced briefly at Warden, and disappeared through the doors at the rear. The loudspeaker in the observation bubble came to life: "Admiral, we still have no late information on the *Zhukov.*"

Cullinane walked to the console microphone and bent over its stalk. "Check with Captain Blandini again. See if the *Chicago* can pick her up at all." He turned to Warden. "Any word on the diplomatic front? Has State heard anything?"

Warden shrugged. "I 'spect we will shortly. The Russkies are always quick to holler when we burn their fingers."

"I imagine they'll think long and hard before they protest this one," Cullinane said thoughtfully. "But that's something you and State will have to handle."

Warden picked up his briefcase. "Why, I thank you for your confidence, Admiral." His voice was thick with sarcasm. "Glad you got here in time for all the excitement, Commander. We've been goin' 'round like a houn' dog in a briar patch."

Renslow watched him leave, sensing that much of the tension was leaving with him. It wasn't just a matter of disagreement over the *Alaska.* The observation bubble had seethed with the tension of two strong-willed men with reputations on the line. He was suddenly glad he wasn't in the admiral's shoes. Then he wondered if perhaps he was. Warden certainly hadn't believed him, nor did Warden particularly like him. . . .

"We've got a message from SAC, Admiral," the loudspeaker announced quietly. "MIROS is being programmed for low-orbit–surveillance laser probe, blue spectrum. They should be in position and relaying computer-enhanced pictures within the half hour."

Renslow was alarmed. MIROS. The Air Force's hush-hush military intelligence, reconnaissance, and observation satellite. He'd once been briefed on it and knew it was equipped for blue-spectrum laser probing that could penetrate the ocean to a significant depth. How deep he hadn't been told. But it meant that the *Alaska* might be down, and 140 of his closest friends and acquaintances along with it. Or was this just one more precaution?

Chavez said, "We're getting the first transmission from the overflights from the *Hornet*. They'll be sending us summaries of negative flights."

Cullinane nodded. "Break in if there's a positive contact. Have them patch a direct line into this console if they get a live one."

It was more complicated and dangerous than just the *Alaska* being down, Renslow thought. And what the devil did the *Zhukov* have to do with it?

Cullinane walked back to the chairs and slumped into the nearest one, fatigue etched deep in his face. Renslow wondered how many hours he had been there.

"David, have them send up a sandwich and black coffee." He glanced at Renslow. "You want anything, Commander?" Then, thoughtfully: "I think you'd better order. I've a hunch you're going to be around here awhile. There are a few things you should know."

It was a little more than an hour before Hardin came back, clutching a handful of notes and looking vaguely alarmed.

"I've discussed this with the staff and we've consulted with two very prominent psychobiochemists, one of them a Nobel laureate."

"The point, Doctor," Cullinane said curtly.

Hardin looked faintly piqued. "They're of the opinion that Commander Renslow's story is possible. Dr. Paley has proposed a detailed enzymatic rationale that—"

Cullinane turned to Renslow. "You have samples of the paint?"

"There's a gallon in Captain Pierce's office."

"Good, we'll have a man pick it up. Dr. Hardin, I want your crew to take the paint and run it through every lab analysis you can think of. What about bringing in this Dr. Paley? Do you know if he has clearance?"

"Well—"

"The hell with it. Get him cleared—interim on the CNO's signature for right now. Tell him whatever he has to know. I want that analysis and I want it in hours, not days."

"I'll do the best I can," Hardin said, and started for the door.

"Doctor."

Hardin turned. "Yes?"

"Do better than that."

The loudspeaker cut in again: "Admiral, we have a signal from Captain Blandini. A Russian trawler is moving into the area. Our sound arrays also indicate another Soviet fleet submarine is in the vicinity. We have identified it as the *Vyshinsky*, a modified Alfa class."

Cullinane walked over to Chavez. "Contact State and tell them that we'll be getting offers of help from the Russians. Ask them to field the offers and warn the Soviet ships to stay the hell out, that we don't want them damaged if they get in the way."

"That'll be a little touchy, Admiral."

"Don't you think I know that?" Cullinane turned back to Renslow. "We have to work on the assumption that you're right, you know. It will be a couple of days before Hardin turns up any positive evidence."

"I'm sure of the paint," Renslow said. Then, almost plaintively: "The *Alaska* is down, isn't she?"

"You have friends on board, of course," Cullinane said sympathetically. He walked back to the lounge area and sat down, suddenly looking very tired and very old. "I think we have to proceed on the worst-case assumption."

"That the *Alaska* is down and presumed lost?" Renslow asked.

"That's not the worst case," Cullinane said slowly. "The worst case is that the *Alaska* is intact but hiding from us. That the present crew of officers and men are deep in the grip of some kind of chemical psychosis . . ."

He looked up at Renslow and for just a moment there was a flicker of terror in his eyes.

". . . and that this crew is convinced World War Three has started and within a few hours they'll receive their launch order." Cullinane paused. "At this moment nobody knows but us, Commander. What worries me is what the Russians will do when they find out."

37

FOUR HOURS AFTER the *ping* and the immediate evasive action that had followed, Harris relaxed the torpedo alert.

They could no longer pick up the *Zhukov*, though Harris admitted he wasn't certain whether the Soviet sub had moved off or whether it was lying quietly somewhere nearby, waiting for the *Alaska* to show itself. The American Tridents were superquiet but at close range the *Zhukov* would have no difficulty picking up the sound of her screw.

Van Meer was almost ready to leave the control room when Olson, on sonar watch, suddenly said, "Heavier traffic up above."

Harris ordered rig for quiet once more. For the next hour Olson read the roll call of the ships converging on the area. The old *Hornet*, a World War II aircraft carrier converted to antisubmarine warfare, a few miles away, and farther off but coming up fast, the *Kinkaid* and the *Elliott*, destroyers of the Spruance class, all of them attached to the Second Fleet. Behind them were several Russian trawlers for which they had no specific voiceprints, and a Russian submarine of the Alfa class, the *Vyshinsky*.

"They're jockeying for position," Harris said, frowning. Then: "It's bad tactics to cluster when a nuclear war is imminent."

"One missile could get them all," Costanza added.

It wasn't difficult for Van Meer to figure out what had happened. The *Alaska* hadn't answered the *Chicago*'s request for help and shortly after that they had disappeared under the inversion layer. But the *Chicago* wouldn't have been able to locate them anyway if its sonar was out. . . . The chances were that within minutes after the collision and the *Alaska*'s failure to answer, the *Chicago* had radioed Norfolk that the *Alaska* might be down.

The task force assembling above was looking for them. And the Russian trawlers would be concerned about the *Zhukov*. . . .

He glanced around the compartment once again, noting the intense look on Harris' face, an expression reflected by Costanza and Spencer and the enlisted men present. He couldn't argue with them. Not here and not now. All of them had become True Believers.

Harris now gave orders to creep farther under the thermal inversion layer and leave the area. "We've got our own mission. I can't risk the *Alaska* by getting involved in any surface action."

Spencer, who had the con, looked relieved. "They're sitting ducks up there."

Van Meer's heart sank. Harris would leave the area. It wasn't going to be easy for a task force to find them. . . .

Later, in the wardroom, Harris let the others in on his thinking and possible future strategy.

"We're on blue alert," he said, once all the officers had squeezed in. "But the situation above can change any minute . . . without warning. Then"—he spread his hands—"they'll throw everything they've got at us." He made a wry face. "And they'll throw it first."

He sat back as if he expected a response. Van Meer wondered what he was driving at. It was MacGowan who had the answer.

"You mean it might all happen so fast that we'd never receive a red alert or a launch order."

Harris nodded, pleased that somebody was following his thinking. "That's right, Mac. Theoretically, our satellites can detect their missiles in flight. That gives us fifteen minutes, maybe half an hour to launch retaliatory strikes. But that's theoretical. It might not work out that way."

There was an uncomfortable silence in the wardroom. Udall, white-faced and in a voice that was almost shaking, asked, "What would we do?"

Harris leaned forward in his chair. "If that happens, then we'll have to pick our own time, fight our own war. We'll know what's happening from the messages we get. If all transmission is cut off, or if messages change radically in character, then we'll know what's happened." He smiled grimly. "And we'll know how to respond."

Van Meer felt as if his guts were slowly freezing. Washington had finally figured out that something was wrong and had broadcast a cancellation order. But, Harris would be in no mood to believe them. And neither would any other member of the crew. The missiles would be launched regardless.

Most of the officers crowded around the wardroom table were nodding assent to Harris' logic. But Messier was poker-faced and Okamoto looked withdrawn and preoccupied.

Moskowitz, his sweaty face pale in the overhead light, suddenly said, "I don't think it's a good idea to launch without direct orders from . . . somebody."

There was sudden silence, then Harris was on his feet, hammering the wardroom table with his fist. "Mister, that's exactly what we're talking about. There may be nobody left to give that order."

"I think the lieutenant's right," van Meer said quickly. "I don't think any launch should be done without . . . direct orders. And there's always the possibility that the alerts might be canceled."

"Is that your opinion?" Harris said, sneering.

"Once the missiles are launched you can't call them back," van Meer argued, his voice harsh.

"Van," Harris said, his voice threatening, "if we get a message canceling the alerts, we'll know who sent it, won't we? But we won't rush into precipitous action. We'll wait a reasonable time and listen to reports. We'll sift what we hear and then assess it."

Van Meer hoped he might have won some time. Maybe a day or two before a paranoid Harris and crew would launch the missiles.

"I didn't think the wardroom was a democracy," MacGowan suddenly growled, his eyes on van Meer.

"Van knows I'm captain," Harris said softly. There had been something in his eyes when he spoke. Van Meer suddenly realized what it was: *He hates anybody who crosses him.*

After the meeting had broken up, Harris signaled for van Meer to remain behind. For a moment he didn't meet van Meer's eyes, then he glanced up slyly. "Van, I've mentioned the possibility of there being Soviet agents on the boomers."

"What are you driving at?" van Meer asked, then suddenly knew.

"Doc said there's been some contamination of the ship."

"The decks have been scrubbed."

"But you didn't tell me about it."

Van Meer reddened. "I thought Doc already had."

Harris nodded, dismissing the statement. "What do you know about Bailey?"

Van Meer felt uneasy. "I don't think he's a Soviet agent, if that's what you mean."

Harris looked shrewd. "I wouldn't be too sure. Neither you nor I know much about him except what's in his service record. It's possible."

"What are you going to do?" van Meer asked cautiously.

"Have him watched." Harris smiled coldly. "There may be more than one and if there is, Bailey knows that, too. Give him enough rope, he'll hang himself." He nodded, pleased with himself. "They usually do."

Harris should be surrounded by shadows from guttering candles, van Meer thought. His words would have seemed more believable coming from him under those conditions than spoken aloud in the cold light of the wardroom. He wondered if Harris was telling him this as a warning. He had crossed Harris twice now; to do so a third time would be foolhardy.

He had to do something, he thought, frustrated, when he left. He had bought some time but not much and he was without allies except possibly Doc . . . and maybe Messier. It wasn't that Messier disbelieved what was happening; it was just that he didn't quite believe it. Whatever was affecting the rest of the crew, Messier somehow seemed immune. Maybe it was his natural cynicism; maybe he simply had a higher tolerance level.

He'd have to talk to the electrician.

He was walking back through the red-lit crew's quarters when he suddenly stopped, half hidden in the shadows. Three bunks farther up the narrow aisle, several men were playing cards. He could make out Leggett, Geranios, Clinger, and McCune by the glow of the bunk light. He should walk right on past; if they saw him standing there, they'd think he was spying on them.

He didn't move.

"That's all I got," Leggett said. "Two hundred bucks."

"You want to see 'em, it'll cost you another hundred," McCune said.

Geranios said, "You heard the man, Leggett. You wanna see 'em, get it up."

"That's a lot of money," Leggett protested.

Clinger laughed. "You don't think you're ever gonna get a chance to spend it, do you?"

Van Meer edged closer in the darkness. There was a hardness to the conversation that he didn't like.

"All I got is this ring," Leggett said. The players were partially hidden by a blanket, which had been rigged to hang from the bunk above to keep the light from disturbing anybody else.

"Let's see it."

"It's . . . a tight fit. It's hard to get it off."

"Just hold your hand out so we can see it. . . . All right, you're on—everybody in?" A small chorus of agreement. "Okay, suckers, read 'em and weep. Kings over treys. Gimme the pot."

There was some shuffling on the bunk. "Hey, Leggett, how about the ring?"

"For Christ's sake, dummy, I told you—I can't get it off. You're gonna have to trust me."

"Trust you, *bullshit.*"

Then Geranios' voice: "C'mon, Leggett, hold your hand out. We'll get it off."

"What the hell you gonna do? *For God's sake.*"

Van Meer raced up the aisle. Geranios was the corpsman on board.

Leggett screamed.

Van Meer yanked down the blanket. Sitting on the bunk was McCune, a satisfied look on his face. Clinger was staring open-mouthed at Geranios, still holding the slim slash of a microtome surgical knife. Leggett was bent over, looking stupidly down at his hand.

Lying on the mattress cover in front of them, neatly severed at the knuckle, was Leggett's ring finger, the thin band of gold lightly flecked with blood.

An hour later, van Meer sat on the bunk in his compartment, trembling with fatigue and emotion. Geranios had been put under formal arrest. Schulman had done a fair job of closing Leggett's finger stump. He debated for a moment, then pulled the aspirin tin out of his wallet, squeezed it open, and took out two tabs of Equavil. And why not a whiskey chaser? To hell with the side effects . . .

He was holding the tabs in his left hand and the tumbler of whiskey in his right when there was a knock on the compartment door and, a moment later, Schulman opened it. Van Meer immediately palmed the tumbler with his left hand the two tabs sinking to the bottom of the glass.

Schulman sat in a chair and sighed. "What are you going to do with Geranios? There won't be a chance to try him until the war's over." He snorted. "Not that there'll still be courts around then."

Van Meer could argue the point, but he wouldn't win, and it would just set Schulman against him again. "That's Harris' problem. He'll think of something."

Schulman cocked his head, his eyes suddenly curious. "You sure that Leggett didn't threaten Geranios, pull a knife or something like that?"

Van Meer shook his head. "He's your corpsman, Doc. I don't blame you for defending him."

"They probably had it in for each other for a long time," Schulman said slowly. He gave van Meer a knowing look. "One thing you can say about the *Alaska:* It's easy for a man to make enemies. I think Harris is probably laying for you and I suspect Costanza has a few surprises in store for me." He looked unhappy. "I thought he'd be above the religious thing."

"Doc, why are you so sure that Costanza's prejudiced against you?"

Schulman leaned forward, suddenly the conspirator. "For God's sake, haven't you seen how he looks at me?"

Van Meer shook his head. "It's all in your mind, Doc."

"You mean it's all in his." Schulman suddenly spotted the bottle of Jim Beam on the floor next to the bunk van Meer was sitting on. "Good bourbon," he said approvingly. Then: "I know you didn't smuggle it in, so somebody must have given it to you. Cermak?"

"Shrewd guess." Van Meer unscrewed the cap and passed the bottle to him. "Help yourself. Cermak assures me that because of the international situation, good booze is perishable."

"Maybe I should see Tony—"

"And get your own? He'd wring your neck. If word gets around, Harris would confiscate it all."

Schulman poured himself a precise shot with a practiced twist of his wrist and downed it with a gulp. He smacked his lips. "Nice aroma, nice belt. Nothing like a bourbon with a punch."

Van Meer sat there, not drinking. He glanced casually down

at the glass in his hand. The two tabs of Equavil had almost completely dissolved now, leaving the bourbon slightly cloudy.

"You know," Schulman said expansively, "I can remember when you used to have to search for your dolphins at the bottom of a ten-ounce glass of whiskey."

Van Meer glanced at him curiously. "How do you mean?"

"When you qualified, they'd put your dolphins in a water tumbler and pour ten ounces of whiskey in it. By the time you worked your way down to them you needed help to pin them on." He sighed. "Then some busybody figured out that ten ounces of whiskey was a potentially lethal dose, so they stopped it. That's the trouble with the modern Navy. No traditions anymore. Washington thinks you can take the spirit and replace it with money. Won't work, Van. Man lives by symbols, not by cash."

He stood up to go, then noticed the full glass in van Meer's hand and realized van Meer hadn't so much as sipped at it.

"You're going to drink that, aren't you?"

He had him, van Meer thought. He shook his head. Schulman looked indignant. "My God, you can't waste good bourbon."

Van Meer held out the glass to him. "I was working on the bottle before you came in."

"You're a generous man." Schulman took it and slipped back into the chair. He sipped at the glass without looking at the slightly murky contents. "Did I ever tell you I've got a sister teaching biochem at Harvard? I keep thinking that if they drop one in Boston Harbor, they'll drench Cambridge and get Martha, too."

"Say something cheerful, Doc."

Five minutes later, Schulman drained the rest of the glass and made a face. "They don't make anything like they used to, not even good bourbon. Jesus, it's got a lousy aftertaste."

38

THE ROOM AT the Tabard Inn was more old-fashioned but also larger and more comfortable than one Renslow would have found at a hotel. Chavez had been right in recommending it. Renslow grinned, wondering under what circumstances Chavez had stayed there. . . .

He tipped the bellboy, then put his overnight bag on the bed and opened it. It had been packed with extraordinary neatness. Elizabeth had neither questioned nor complained when he said he had to leave immediately but had offered to pack his bag and make the reservation for him. For a moment they had been almost close and he had wondered if things could be different. . . .

But, no, there hadn't been a chance, would never be a chance. Not so long as Harris was in her life.

He turned on the television set and, without waiting for the picture to appear, took his shaving kit into the bathroom. It was a pleasantly old-fashioned bathroom, with water that was scalding hot as it left the tap. He showered and shaved, then went back to the room and dressed in the summer suit Elizabeth had packed. A hand-lettered menu card was sitting on top of the small desk and he glanced through it. The prices weren't bad at all, considering the reputation of the cooking. . . .

He had just started to lose himself in watching a senseless chase starring two motorcycle cops on a California freeway when there was a rap on the door. He hadn't called room service, and was startled, then he guessed it might be a messenger from Cullinane. . . .

Elizabeth was wearing a tweed traveling suit and carrying a small flight bag. Her makeup was impeccable as ever, her eyes cool and somewhat cautious. "May I come in?" He stood aside and she walked in, sat down in the overstuffed chair by the window, and studied him as she stripped off her gloves. "The admiral's office told me you were staying here."

He didn't want her here. She'd be nothing but a distraction and right then he had enough problems.

"Why did you come down, Liz?"

"I wanted to," she said casually. "There are friends of mine aboard the *Alaska,* too." She glanced around and noted the single bed. "I checked. They have more rooms available. I wouldn't be staying in here with you."

He wasn't sure whether there was a hesitation in her voice when she mentioned the other rooms or whether she had expected an invitation to stay with him. Unlikely, he thought.

"What about the *Alaska*?" he asked bluntly.

Her voice was suddenly brittle. "It's down, isn't it?"

"What makes you think so?"

"You took off for Washington on a dead run, with no explanations," she said, her eyes studying him for any facial giveaways. "And there are rumors."

"There're always rumors."

She sighed and shifted the window curtain to look out. "They didn't give you much of a view, did they?" Then, bitterly: "When you go to sea, I know it's wartime conditions. But it's not wartime conditions ashore and men and their wives *do* talk to each other." Her eyes filled with frustration and anger. "The wives know something's wrong. They don't know exactly what but they know that something is. There are even rumors that this is a short patrol. Some of the more worried wives called the base and got a runaround." She paused. "The Navy's not very clever at that."

"And you're worried, too."

"Of course. I know the wives. I know many of the men."

"Some of them better than others."

"That's very subtle," she said sarcastically. She stood up and opened the flight bag, taking out a small paper bag and putting it on the bed.

"I never claimed to be a subtle man," he said. Why the hell hadn't she stayed back in New London?

She was openly angry now. "We can't even say good morning to each other without arguing, can we, Al? Well, I'll put your mind to rest. Yes, I'm worried about Stephen Harris. He meant something to me once. I'm also worried about Mike Costanza and Tony Cermak—Milly Cermak's my best friend. And we've entertained Chips and his wife and Billy Spencer and his. They're my friends, too, or would you deny me that as well?"

He was in the wrong again, and perversely blamed her for putting him there.

"I'm only going to be here tonight," he said in a softer voice. "The admiral wants me back at Flag Plot early in the morning with my shaving gear. I may not be leaving there for a few days."

Her hand went to her throat, her face suddenly pale. "It *is* down," she said in a stricken voice.

"I didn't say that," he said roughly. "Even if it were, I couldn't tell you." She could interpret that any way she wanted.

She studied him, wondering whether to believe him or not. "I'll stay in town," she said after a moment. "I'll let the admiral's office know where." She hesitated at the door and said, "I was willing to try, Al."

Now was the time to say a dozen things that might make a difference for the rest of his life. But he was too tired, too distracted; there was too much on his mind.

"Bad timing, Liz."

Her eyes were bitter. "It's always bad timing with you, Al."

She was out the door then and he heard her heels suddenly pound down the carpet as she ran for the stairs. He could go after her, then he decided against it. Maybe a few days from now, another time, when the disaster involving the *Alaska* had been resolved . . .

He turned back to the room and noticed the paper bag on the bed. Inside was a handsome hand-tooled leather wallet. The workmanship was intricate, almost professional. The small, scribbled note attached read "Thanks for everything. Howie Gradow."

The TV set had been nattering in the background and he glanced at the screen. The cops had vanished and the evening news had come on. The picture on the tube showed several boomers tied to the docks in Charleston. He quickly turned up the sound.

" . . .rumors of another submarine involved in the collision in the same area. The Department of the Navy has refused to confirm or deny that the *Alaska* is down or that another submarine has suffered severe damage. Newsbreak's reporter Chuck Hambrick is in Charleston, South Carolina, where he interviewed several of the wives of crewmen on board the *Alaska,* as well as Mrs. Luisa Blandini, wife of the skipper of the *Chicago*, the other submarine rumored to be involved.''

A moment later, Luisa Blandini was on the screen. A young blond reporter with a raspy Southern accent was thrusting a microphone in her face and demanding to be told the latest news about the *Chicago.* Renslow remembered Mrs. Blandini from a dinner party a year or two back: a thin-faced, black-haired woman with a nervous laugh and a tentative smile. Her eyes now seemed shadowed, haunted. She forced a smile and said she understood that everybody on board the *Chicago* was well. No, she knew nothing about any collision. She parroted the official line that all submarines leaving port were on a wartime footing and that meant, of course, that the wives of the crew were cut off and there wouldn't be any real news until the men returned.

Renslow was furious. Some politician in the Situation Room had leaked the story to the press. Then the pathos of Mrs. Blandini struck him. It was bad enough that men went to sea realizing that for all intents and purposes they were at war; he had known—but only abstractly—that the same thing applied to their wives. Now the pain in Mrs. Blandini's eyes made it seem far more real. Then he thought, it had been that way for Elizabeth, too.

But there was also a flicker of something else in her eyes and he suddenly wondered how much Blandini might have told her. She obviously knew something she couldn't tell. The dullest viewer could see that.

It occurred to him that Cullinane and the others at Flag Plot must have talked with Blandini. The *Chicago* was involved in the exercise. Blandini could well have gone on board and seen the crew for himself. But the officers at Flag Plot might not have known the right questions to ask Blandini. None of them knew the crew as well as he did, certainly not that creep Hardin, who thought he had everybody thoroughly catalogued in the form of test results and punch cards. The only one who could really evaluate whatever Blandini might say about conditions on board was himself. And if they ever did succeed in contacting the *Alaska,* the one person the members of the crew might trust was also himself.

He grabbed his toilet kit and shoved a clean pair of shorts into the top of it. On the way out he thought for a moment of Elizabeth.

The next time he saw her, maybe it would help if he told her he hadn't spent the night at the Tabard after all. . . .

39

TWO WATCHES LATER, sonar detected another single *ping* and sounded a second torpedo alert. The *Alaska* once again took evasive action. They found shelter under another inversion layer and hovered near the bottom, the boat rigged for quiet. They sat for an hour while perspiration streamed down van Meer's forehead until the handkerchief he used for a sponge was as soaked as his shirt.

"Sonar report." Harris sounded uneasy.

Olson shook his head, puzzled. "There's nothing within miles, Captain, unless it's lying there as quietly as we are. There was nobody around when we left, either."

"Somebody could have been lying doggo," Harris said.

Van Meer found himself fighting to believe that nothing was happening on the surface except—in all probability—an intense search to find them. It was difficult not to believe that war might be only hours away.

Another sudden, sharp *ping* echoed in the compartment. Van Meer felt the muscles in his cheek jump.

"Olson," Harris snapped.

"There's nothing out there," Olson said desperately. "I'd stake my life on it."

You're not just staking yours," Harris said. He looked over at van Meer. "Have the first lieutenant search the ship."

If it hadn't come from outside the *Alaska*, then it must have come from somewhere inside. Metal striking metal in such a way that it made the same sharp *ping* . . .

An hour later, Meslinsky came into the compartment clutching a metal cross hanging from a thin gold chain. "Here it is," he aid. "I found it wrapped around the bottom of a stair railing. Anybody walking down the ladder, if the tilt of the boat was just right, made the medallion strike the metal stair riser. That was our 'sonar' *ping*."

"Anybody know who this belongs to?" Harris asked. He turned it over and read the engraving on the back. His lips thinned. "Find Bailey, Meslinsky, and tell him to report here on the double."

A few minutes later, Meslinsky dragged a swearing Bailey into the control room.

"Get your goddamned hands off me, Animal."

Meslinsky had one of Bailey's arms behind his back. He thrust the small man forward. Bailey stumbled, his glasses sliding down his nose. He grabbed for them, then straightened up before Harris.

Harris held out the medal. "This yours?"

Bailey looked sullen. "Yes, sir."

Harris held the chain and let the medallion swing free so it struck against a stanchion. It wasn't the same *ping* but it came close. Bailey paled.

"Two torpedo alerts," Harris said grimly. "Did you know it would make that kind of sound?"

"You're goddamned right he knew," Meslinsky said.

"Shut up, Animal. Well, Bailey?"

Bailey swallowed. "No, sir."

Harris' voice became harder. "I didn't know you were a religious man." He waited for an answer, his eyes cutting into Bailey's. The silence in the control room was thick and hostile; the other crew members stared at Bailey.

"I was raised a Catholic, sir," Bailey said, almost belligerently. Another convulsive swallow. "I haven't really been very religious until just the past . . . several days."

Meslinsky glanced away in contempt. "Jesus . . ."

"You knew everything was supposed to be secured against making noise, didn't you?"

"Yes, sir."

Harris juggled the cross, then flipped it back to Bailey. He looked disgusted. "You're confined to your berthing compartment, the crew's mess, and your working spaces. That'll be all, Bailey."

Van Meer caught the nod from Harris and escorted Bailey back to crew's berthing. Once in the passageway, he said, "I didn't know you were religious, either, Glenn."

Bailey's eyes were smoky behind his glasses. "I wasn't until this patrol and I swear to God that if I ever get back to the States, I'll never miss mass again."

"You're worried about what's happening topside."

"It's scaring me shitless, Commander."

Van Meer had to react the same way they would. He had to act as if war were imminent and the end of their world was near. "If the balloon goes up, we'll make them pay a pretty heavy price."

Bailey stared at him, sweat making his glasses slide to the end of his nose again. He pushed them back, then swore when one end of the wired-together frames cut his finger.

"If we have to launch missiles at all, Commander, it means we've already lost. Maybe it makes sense to you, but it sure doesn't make sense to me." Then he muttered, "I don't know what the hell I feel anymore. Part of me is bloodthirsty as hell." His eyes suddenly got large. "Animal wants to kill me, you know. You can see it in his face."

"That's your imagination," van Meer said uneasily. But the truth was that he had gotten the same impression.

He turned as the intercom murmured, *"Commander van Meer, report to the captain's cabin."*

Harris was waiting for him. He motioned van Meer to a seat, then pointed to a message flimsy lying on the desk top. Van Meer picked it up and glanced through it. The tape deck had broadcast another message. It was the final news roundup they would receive from a harried Washington.

The Aswan Dam had been bombed and the lower Nile valley flooded, causing great loss of life. . . . Tel Aviv had been destroyed, apparently by a nuclear device smuggled into the city by Palestinian terrorists. . . . The Soviets had occupied a strip along the Yugoslavian border "for the protection of Serb nationals, who are also fellow Slavs and comrades". . . . An abortive uprising by the extreme Left in France had been crushed but had left Paris in flames. . . . The United States had delivered an ultimatum to the Soviets on behalf of the legitimate Yugoslav government. . . . Navy fighter bombers were strafing advancing elements of the Soviet ground forces in Iran. . . .Chinese land forces had penetrated more than fifty miles into Siberia without major opposition. . . .The air lanes into Berlin had been closed by Soviet fighter planes and the East German Democratic Republic was mobilizing. . . .

"Somebody will make a preemptive strike," Harris said slowly after van Meer finished reading. "It won't be us." He sounded bitter.

However false the facts might be, Harris believed them. In the few days they had been at sea, van Meer had seen Harris change from a calm, rational submarine commander to a tight-lipped, suspicious warrior preparing himself for an orgy of vengeance. But it was even more than that: Harris had become an exaggeration of the wartime submarine commander, a parody. . . .

Harris unrolled a chart of the Atlantic over the desk top. "We're at our designated station right now." He put his finger on the map. "But depending on the messages received—or not received—from Washington, I propose moving up to here." He shifted his hand. A crafty look crept onto his face. "The Barents Sea, just north of Novaya Zemlya. Probably the best launch station there is."

Van Meer felt desperate. The task force searching for them would expect the *Alaska* to be somewhere around its original station. If Harris headed for the Barents, the *Alaska* would be that much more difficult to find. . .and to stop.

"Our chances of running into Russian attack submarines or coastal subs will be pretty high."

"It would be a lot riskier trying to get into the Baltic," Harris said sarcastically.

Van Meer could feel his armpits dampening again. "I wasn't suggesting that," he said soothingly. "Just that you take evasive action across the Atlantic, that you don't head for the Barents directly."

Harris continued to study the chart. "That's an obvious point."

It would at least keep them in the same area a little longer, van Meer thought. "If things are as bad as the message says—"

Harris hit the desk top with his fist, the chart sliding off onto the carpeted deck. "What the hell do you mean, 'if things are as

bad'? You've seen the dispatches. I didn't invent those alerts."
His blazing eyes held van Meer's for a moment, then he picked up
the chart and spread it on the desk again. "If we're going to fight
this ship, Van, we sure as hell better agree as to what's going on."
His voice turned deceptively soft. "MacGowan was right. This
isn't a democracy, you know. Don't try to make it one."

"I'm not," van Meer said softly, his stomach turning. Harris'
eyes were the eyes of a man who was going mad and who—someplace in the dark folds of his mind—realized it.

Van Meer left, more than ever aware that he needed an ally
and still unsure of what he could do to stop Harris and the rest of
the crew. He walked through crew's berthing on his way to the
mess hall, struck once again by the changes that were overtaking
the crew. Several tents had been rigged in the berthing compartment to provide more privacy. At the far end somebody was playing a harmonica, the sound oddly plaintive in the red-lit gloom
. . . . Van Meer recalled the string of hippie beads that he had
spotted McCune wearing in the control room. The cutoffs, the
sprouting beards, the tension, and the paranoia. . . The crew was
turning into . . . what?

He'd have to approach Messier. The electrical officer had
said he wanted to talk to him and he was obviously less affected
than the others on board. And he himself was close enough to Olson to perhaps get through to the sonar chief. But he'd have to
convince them both that the messages the *Alaska* had received
were from an on-board tape deck. And to make them believe that,
he'd first have to find it. . . .

At one of the far tables in the crew's mess a small group was
playing cards, money visible on the table. Van Meer shivered.
What would the table stakes be this time? He poured himself a
cup of coffee and sat in a corner, listening to the quiet swirl of
conversation around him. It was no longer the homogeneous
crew it had once been. The men in the mess hall kept their voices
low, occasionally glancing at other groups, their eyes narrow and
speculative.

Baker, Longstreet, and Fuhrman, all nukes, were sitting nearby; Longstreet was speaking in a whisper that carried throughout
the compartment.

"What gets me is that it happened so suddenly." He shook
his head. "I can't understand it. When we left the States they were

talking about Salt Three and there were meetings at the UN . . . ." His voice trailed off.

Baker was more sanguine. "So don't try to understand it. We get the launch order, we launch, and that's it. The next day, we have a brave new world on our hands."

"If you want to live in it, you're welcome to it," Longstreet said dryly.

Okamoto came in and sat down, Longstreet moving over to make room. Chips didn't look well, van Meer noted with shock. His eyes were haunted, his face strained. He sipped his coffee quietly, not making any contribution to the conversation.

"I don't think anybody realizes just how much nuclear destruction the *Alaska* represents," Fuhrman mused. "They wouldn't be screwing around if they did."

Okamoto came to life then, for a moment reminding van Meer of the weapons hobbyist he had been just a few days before. "It's not just nuclear," he said tonelessly.

Longstreet looked blank. "What do you mean?"

"The *Alaska*'s a bomb. Dock us at a pier and give the hull a sharp rap and we'd probably wipe out a city—without the nuclear warheads being involved at all."

Longstreet shook his head. "You've been holding out on us, Chips. I didn't think we had that kind of standard armament aboard."

Okamoto took a long sip of coffee. He looked gray. "Not talking about standard armament. The missile booster engines themselves are bombs. Each one is twelve tons of unstable propellant with a binder that's predominantly nitroglycerine. That's the equivalent of almost three hundred tons of nitro." He pushed away from the table. "Happy dreams."

Van Meer finished his own coffee and had started to leave the compartment when the passageway was suddenly filled with silent, running men on their way to battle stations. "Red alert," somebody said quietly as he rushed past. "There's been a red alert."

The tape had kicked in for another brief message. Van Meer started to run for the attack center and passed Schulman standing just inside the door to sick bay, looking confused. He reached out a hand to stop van Meer.

"That's on the tape, isn't it, Van? That's not for real, is it?"

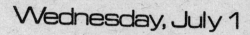

Wednesday, July 1

DAY EIGHT

40

RENSLOW COULD HEAR Cullinane's voice when he was halfway down the main corridor of Flag Plot.

"Dammit, find that leak and put the man on charges. I'll sign them if it's the Secretary of the Navy himself."

Renslow pushed through the door of the Operations Room and found Cullinane sitting in the inner office at the long conference table, a telephone in one hand and a smoldering cigar clamped between his teeth.

"Where the hell do we get our intelligence officers?" Cullinane bellowed. "Out of the Sears catalogue?" He slammed the phone down and glanced at Renslow. "I take it you've already heard the story, complete with interview."

"I know Blandini," Renslow said. "I thought I might be useful and came down."

Cullinane's eyes grew speculative. "How well do you know him?"

"We were in the same class. Friends but not exceptionally close."

Cullinane stood up and motioned to Renslow to follow him. "They're setting up a call with him now. Maybe you can get something out of him that I can't."

Renslow followed Cullinane down the hall and into an elaborate communications room dominated by a huge board with ten video monitors. Renslow recognized several radio installations, including an ELF—extremely long-wave frequency—transmitting board and a bank of computer terminals. At the far end of the room was a glass-fronted booth enclosing a built-in desk divided into five positions. At each position was a video monitor, a jack board for earphones, and a microphone jutting from the panel.

Cullinane caught the look on Renslow's face and smiled. "You should see NORAD someday."

Warden was sitting at one of the positions. "Been waitin' almost half an hour for our little chitchat." His fleshy face was smiling but his voice conveyed thinly concealed annoyance.

The glass doors slid shut behind them at the same time the booth loudspeaker broke in. "Admiral, we've contacted the *Chicago*. Captain Blandini's standing by."

Cullinane eased into one of the open positions and motioned to Renslow to take one of the others. He hunched toward the microphone. "Captain Blandini, this is Admiral Cullinane. Can you read me?"

There was a slight crackle in the loudspeaker. "Loud and clear." Funny, Renslow thought, how electronics could rob a voice of the speaker's personality. Enzio Blandini was a big, robust man who preferred to growl rather than talk. But over the loudspeaker, his voice, although still clear, lacked strength and color. Maybe it was the scramble circuits. . . .

"How long were you on board the *Alaska*?"

"Approximately an hour and a half, sir."

"Any indication of operating difficulties?"

"No, sir. I talked at length with both Captain Harris and Commander Stroop and neither mentioned any difficulty with the mechanical plant."

"Any sign of the *Alaska* now?"

Blandini's voice suddenly sounded strained. "She's not in the area, Admiral." Pause. "Or else she's down. But there's been no sign of debris, no oil slick, no distress buoy or dye markers."

"How did Captain Harris strike you?"

Even with the electronics bleeding Blandini's voice of its character, Renslow could sense the hesitation, the guarded tone. "I'm not sure what you mean, sir."

There was a short chuckle from Warden and Cullinane's face grew tense. "Did he act unusual? Anything about the ship strike you as odd?"

Blandini's voice was now defensive. "Every captain runs his ship according to his own methods, Admiral."

"For God's sake, this is off the record, Captain," Cullinane said tightly. "Save your cop-outs for the board of inquiry."

Blandini's voice became coldly formal. "I'm not sure what you mean, sir," he repeated.

Cullinane looked at Renslow in disgust and Renslow leaned toward his own microphone. "Enzio, this is Al Renslow. We have reason to believe the disappearance of the *Alaska* may be deliberate." He paused just long enough for Blandini to catch the implications of what he was saying. "What was the material condition of the ship? Your honest assessment."

"You're putting me in a hell of a spot, Al." There was a relaxed note in Blandini's voice, a sense of relief that he was talking to somebody besides the admiral.

"I wouldn't ask you if a lot didn't depend on your answer."

There was a brief silence while Blandini struggled with his conscience. Finally: "I run a tight ship, Al. I'd always heard that Harris did, too." Renslow could almost imagine his shrug. "Frankly, the ship was a pigsty. Tools left out of their racks, charts that hadn't been put away, clothes left around the laundry room, . . . most of the men were out of uniform . . . If I'd taken over the *Alaska*, there'd have been a dozen summary masts immediately."

"What about morale?"

There was no hint of hesitation this time. "Good, a lot of tension but, considering the drill, I'd say damned good."

"How about Harris himself?"

"He was very serious about the drill," Blandini said slowly.

Something was being left unsaid. "Can you elaborate?"

"I think the statement stands by itself." Blandini was freezing up once again. He wasn't going to let himself be pushed into denigrating a fellow officer.

"Physical appearance, Enzio. What'd he look like?"

Once more the sense of a shrug. "You know uniform regulations are relaxed on board submarines, Al."

It was Renslow's turn to be slow in responding. "I don't think that's answering the question, Enzio."

Blandini exploded angrily. "He looked like hell. Hair rumpled, the start of a beard, dirty uniform . . . Is that enough?"

"What about the other officers?"

"The same." There was a long pause, then Blandini came back to the subject of Harris. "Harris had the reputation for being evenhanded with his officers and men. This time I got the impression he was building a . . . court. Playing favorites."

Renslow felt pressure on his arm and glanced down. Cullinane had slid a note across the desk. "Enzio, did you see van Meer, the exec?"

"Not for long but he seemed—and looked—like the sanest guy on board." There was sudden relief in Blandini's voice and Renslow guessed it was because he could say something good for a change.

"Nothing peculiar in his actions?"

"Not at all. He seemed so normal, he stood out."

Renslow glanced at Cullinane, who looked surprised, almost shocked. And it didn't make sense to him, either. If anybody had slipped his moorings, it should have been van Meer.

"Could you sum up the *Alaska*?"

Blandini sounded ashamed and angry, as if he were being forced into playing Judas. "It was like one big, sloppy boarding-house that had put to sea, okay?"

Cullinane suddenly growled, "Why the hell didn't you say so at the time?"

Blandini's sigh was clearly audible over the loudspeaker. "What would you have had me do, Admiral? Put the *Alaska* on report? Certainly at the time it didn't strike me that either the ship or the drill was in danger."

Renslow put out his hand to cut Cullinane off. There were still things that were bothering him. "You said Harris was serious about the drill?"

A puzzled note crept into Blandini's voice. "He was deadly serious. He never let up even when we were alone. If anything, he was ... too serious. Considering the nature of the drill, I know that's contradictory."

"Did he seem as if he was on drugs?"

"Jesus Christ, Al ..." Blandini sounded agonized. "No, I wouldn't say that. But he didn't seem ... normal, either." Then, explosively: "Goddammit, none of them did."

Renslow leaned back in his chair. "Thanks for opening up with us, Enzio. It's off the record. You've got my word on that."

A dry "Thanks," then: "Over and out."

Renslow drummed his fingers on the desk top for a moment, lost in thought. It took him a moment to realize Cullinane was talking to him. "Any conclusions, Commander?"

Renslow nodded. "It's got to be the paint. We've got the psychotic captain and crew, a situation undoubtedly caused by the fumes given off by the new paint used on the interior bulkheads."

Warden snorted. "Commander, I still think that's the most crackpot idea I've ever heard."

Renslow swung around toward him. He'd taken a dislike to Warden when he'd first met him and the dislike had deepened since. "We have two alternatives, Mr. Warden. The first is that a paranoid captain and crew are hiding the *Alaska* under a thermal inversion, waiting for further orders. If you don't buy that, then we have to face the possibility that the *Zhukov* may have sunk the *Alaska* in addition to ramming the *Chicago*. If that's so, then it's your problem more than the Navy's."

Warden glanced at Cullinane, who frowned slightly at Renslow. "Those are the alternatives," Cullinane said.

There was a rap on the thick plate-glass wall. Outside, Lieutenant Chavez was motioning to the admiral. Cullinane pressed a button on the desk and part of the glass wall slid to one side.

Chavez hurried in, nodding to Renslow and Warden. "One of the *Hornet*'s sonar buoys has picked up a signature about twenty miles due north of the *Chicago*. They've matched sonic prints and it is definitely the *Alaska*."

"Exact coordinates?"

Chavez spread his hands in disappointment. "There was just the one contact."

"She's gone back to hiding under an inversion," Renslow said quietly.

Warden looked peeved. "You'll have to spell that one out to me, Commander."

"She's ducked into a warm water area trapped under a layer of much cooler water. Any sound from an active sonar will either bounce off the layer or be deflected."

Warden looked questioningly at Cullinane. "Is that standard operating procedure in case of collision?"

Cullinane sounded uncomfortable. "No, I'm afraid it's not."

Warden smiled smugly. "Then I guess it's the Navy's problem after all."

"It's everybody's problem, Mr. Warden," Cullinane said in an angry voice. He glanced at Renslow. "Including yours, Commander. As of right now, consider yourself attached to my staff. There's nobody else who knows as much about the *Alaska* and her crew as you do. The *Alaska*'s still your command, *Captain.*"

Cullinane turned to go and Warden said, "You keep me informed, y'hear? Both of you." The words were almost a threat.

Out in the hall, Cullinane turned to Renslow. "You've made an enemy, Commander. If he wants your gizzards on toast for breakfast, there's not much I can do to keep him from having them."

"I'm afraid I don't like our good National Security Adviser," Renslow said quietly. Then, with more passion: "He's a fool."

Cullinane's voice was suddenly sharper. "Don't underestimate the politicians from Pennsylvania Avenue, Commander. Fools are dangerous because they're unpredictable. But Warden is no fool and for that reason he's doubly dangerous. He's shrewd. He uses his chicken-fried background to throw you off guard. You start to think of him as a naive cracker and you forget his history—the university posts, his presidency at United Motors, his work at the Yonkers Institute . . ." He half smiled in bitter memory. "Once you relax, he sandbags you. That red-neck accent disappears and he becomes as hard as steel. Beneath it all, he's brilliant, logical, demanding—the deadliest political infighter I've ever seen. Don't sell him short just because he sounds like Brer Rabbit."

"You're not running scared, are you, Admiral?" Renslow meant it half jokingly but once again he cursed the lack of proper inflection in his voice.

Cullinane's glance was tinged with frost. "Don't belittle your elders, Commander. I suppose you could handle him?"

"He must have made a lot of enemies," Renslow said stubbornly.

Cullinane suddenly smiled. "Sometimes I forget that. You're right, he's made a whole gaggle of enemies, from the Secretary of State on down. He's got only one real friend—the President— but that's enough."

Renslow grunted, lost in thought once more. Outside the Operations Room, Cullinane said, "You seem rather quiet, Commander. Did Warden bug you that much?"

"I was thinking," Renslow said. Cullinane stared at him politely. "What Captain Blandini said about van Meer. That he seemed like the sanest man on board. From what we know about van Meer, it shouldn't follow."

41

VAN MEER DUCKED into sick bay and closed the door. Schulman looked confused and worried, a frightened Santa Claus with a graying stubble of a beard.

"That was a red alert, Van. A red alert was on the tape. It *is* the tape, isn't it?"

He couldn't assume anything this time; he had to play it very carefully. And there wasn't much time; he was due in the control room. "What do you think, Abe?"

Schulman massaged his temples. "Give me a moment, Van." He finally looked up, his eyes hollow. "All those messages and alerts—strictly on tape?"

Van Meer nodded

"But the collision, the *Zhukov*—"

"Real, very real. But also coincidence."

Schulman sighed. "You're going to have to refresh my memory. It's all there but it's jumbled. It's hard to figure out what's . . . real and what isn't."

Van Meer quickly led him back through the briefings by Admiral Cullinane and then through the taped messages. Schulman nodded at each point, trying to put events into order.

"How come you weren't affected?"

Van Meer shrugged. "The Equavil. Whatever is causing the psychosis, the Equavil acts as a barrier. I didn't take it for a couple of watches and I became just as bad as everybody else." He paused. "I slipped some to you in the bourbon."

Schulman looked surprised, then shivered. "There's only the launch left to be played on the tape."

Van Meer had to fight rising panic. Somebody had to stop the *Alaska* from launching. But there was only him and Schulman.

"That's right. The crew thinks the world is about to go up in smoke—and their friends and relatives with it."

Schulman hastily poured himself a cup of coffee, his hand trembling. "When they get the order, they'll launch the missiles—all of them. And they'll probably welcome a chance to launch, just to get the waiting over with."

"It's a war psychosis," van Meer said grimly. "That's what Washington wanted and that's what they got."

"Washington has to send another cancel order."

Schulman was safe; his terror and concern were real. "The crew wouldn't believe it if they did, Doc. Certainly Harris wouldn't."

"Then what the hell do we do? We can't just sit around."

Van Meer laughed without humor. "It's obvious—take over the ship. Some of the men are affected less than others. Messier for one. Some of the nukes. I might be able to talk to Olson."

Schulman dismissed the idea. "I don't think we'd make very good mutineers, Van. And we'd need something more than just our word against the taped messages and Harris' convictions." He frowned. "Harris went over the edge pretty damned easy."

Van Meer shrugged. He had never really known Harris. A brittle man in some respects, a man who never discussed his personal problems, who kept to himself. The constant patrols, the boredom, the ennui, must have finally gotten to him. And Harris was at an age at which he probably questioned what he was living for, his purpose in life.

Now he had discovered purpose and meaning and he wasn't going to give them up easily. . . .

"There are other alternatives, Doc. Maybe we could slip Harris some of the Equavil."

Schulman huddled in his chair, cradling the cup of coffee between his knees. "It won't be easy. He's suspicious, paranoid. . . . And I think with some of the crew, especially Harris, the psychosis might be irreversible. They've had one severe shock to their beliefs. They won't be willing to suffer another."

"We could still try, Doc. Maybe you could prescribe it as medicine."

"He's too damned healthy. His medical record has been clean for the past five years."

"What about the tape deck itself?" van Meer asked suddenly. "Harris was going to tell you where it is."

Schulman looked guilty. "I don't know where it is," he confessed. "I never asked him again."

"Commander van Meer, lay up to the bridge."

In the control room Harris glared at him and van Meer realized it was another nail in his fitness report. If anybody was left around to read it after all this was over. . .

He checked their position on the DRT. They were well out in the Atlantic now, though still in the general area of their station. Another watch or two, they'd be far away. . . . In one sense it really didn't matter whether Harris stayed in the mid-Atlantic to launch the missiles or went up to the Barents Sea. The Trident III missiles had a range in excess of six thousand miles; there was little of importance that they couldn't hit from where they were. But launching in the Barents would shorten the range and give the Soviets less of an early warning, for whatever dubious advantage that might confer. . . .

Olson suddenly said, "We've got a contact."

A moment later, both Harris and van Meer were looking over his shoulder. "Can you get a signature?"

Olson shook his head. "She's too far away." He hesitated. "I think she's the same one we had before. She seems to be keeping her distance, at the very limits of detection."

"She'll follow us," Harris said thoughtfully. "We're leaving station. They must be wondering where we're heading."

"We can shake her," van Meer said.

Harris glanced up at him grimly. "I'm not so sure I want to."

An hour later, they had secured from red alert and van Meer drifted through the crew's mess on his way to his own compartment. Some of the men were writing letters—letters they really didn't think would be read. Other were playing bridge. Dritz, the first-class radioman, who someday hoped to have his own audiovisual shop, was sitting at one of the tables thumbing through some stereo catalogues and sliding them across the table to Russo, his striker. Russo was probably the only man on board who couldn't grow a beard. Most of the other ops had begun to look hard and warlike. Russo looked merely scraggly. . . .

"It's hard to keep up," Dritz was saying. "They're always in-

troducing new models, particularly in the high end—the esoteric
gear that costs an arm and a leg. Stocking even a small store
would still cost a fortune." He was suddenly quiet, his hands flut-
tering over the stack of four-color brochures. There was a lost
look on his face and van Meer knew he was thinking that the shop
was a fantasy, that tomorrow or the day after there would be no
city in which to open it and no customers waiting to buy. . . .

Dritz glanced around the compartment and slid another
pamphlet to Russo. He looked secretive and lowered his voice to
a whisper. "I don't want you talking about this, Russo. I don't
want anybody stealing my idea."

Van Meer walked over and tapped Russo on the shoulder.
"My compartment in five minutes, Russo." He pretended not to
notice Dritz huddling over his brochures to hide them from view.

In his compartment a few minutes later, van Meer motioned
to Russo to have a seat. "When do you think you're going to
qualify, Russo?"

Russo looked startled and van Meer guessed what he was
thinking. A genuine red alert and the XO wanted to talk about
striking for radioman.

"There's still the routine of the ship, war or no war," van
Meer added. He looked sympathetic. "It's tough to keep up with
the new gear, isn't it?" It was a deliberate echo of what Dritz had
said in the mess compartment and Russo caught the comparison.

"Yes, sir," Russo said uneasily, still not knowing where the
conversation was leading. "Every time you go into the yard they
add something new."

"You know the layout of all the equipment, the cabling, the
antenna systems?"

Russo nodded. "Yes, sir. If anything new is installed, I've got
to know all about it."

Van Meer nodded. That was why he had asked Russo instead
of Dritz. It was a striker's job to familiarize himself with all the
gear in his specialty, to know how it worked, how it was hooked
up, to be able to trace down the cabling in case of emergency.

"Anything new on board this time, Russo?"

Russo looked cagey. The XO was checking up on him. "A
BQQ-six sonar, advanced model, a new . . ."

Van Meer listened politely as Russo rattled down the list.

" . . . and there's some cabling I haven't had a chance to trace down yet." Russo sounded nervous and a little defiant. "Under the circumstances, it didn't seem important."

"Under the circumstances," van Meer repeated, almost to himself. "You sure you hadn't been over it before?"

"Positive, sir."

Van Meer stood up. "Show me," he said.

42

THE AIR in the Flag Plot conference room was thick with cigarette smoke. Renslow twisted nervously in his chair, feeling uneasy surrounded by so much brass. Admiral Cullinane was at the head of the long conference table, chewing nervously on an unlit cigar. Admiral Howland, the CNO, was at his right and Lieutenant Chavez was seated on Cullinane's left. Renslow liked Chavez; a young lieutenant eager for sea duty who would have to fight to get it simply because he was too good in his advisory capacity.

On the other side of the table, like antagonists drawn up on a battlefield, sat Dr. Hardin and several members of his team, as well as Warden and Captain Oxley. Oxley, Warden had told them with barely concealed amusement, had been placed on temporary duty in his office. "The captain will be mah interpreter when you fellas start throwin' those technical terms around."

Cullinane leaned over toward Renslow and whispered, "Were you able to get in touch with your wife?"

Renslow shook his head. "I think she's staying at her parents' home in Alexandria but the maid keeps telling me she's not there."

"Let me know if I can help in any way." Cullinane leaned back in his chair, saw that everybody was present, and rapped for silence. "Dr. Hardin, we'll start with you. You have a report on the paint?"

Renslow glanced across the table at Warden, who was staring at Hardin with a baffled, faintly worried look on his face. Apparently Hardin had refused to leak the results of the tests in advance of the meeting.

Hardin stood up and fiddled a moment with his glasses, then opened a folder on the table in front of him. "We've run several animal tests in the laboratory, exposing rhesus monkeys to both the wet and the dried paint. This included two runs in which we lined the animal box with panels taken from ships on which the paint had been drying for up to a month. All the animals showed psychotic behavior within twenty-four hours."

He hesitated, glanced opaquely at Warden, then down again at the paper. "It will take more extensive testing but there's reason to believe that as the paint dries it undergoes a chemical change. The fumes given off by panels on which the paint has dried a week or two are more toxic." He shot an almost frightened look at Warden.

That was why he hadn't leaked the results earlier, Renslow thought. Warden would hardly welcome any more bad news. . . . Then he stiffened. The *Alaska* had been to sea for a little more than a week. Whatever was happening on board was only going to get worse.

"What about the chemistry?" Cullinane asked.

"We have the formula from New England Pigment and we're fairly sure it's the drying agent."

"Did you check out the workers at Electric Boat?" Renslow asked.

Hardin nodded. "We talked to Dr. Sanchez, who treated them, and he confirmed that they showed all the classic signs of paranoid schizophrenia, although their recovery was fairly rapid."

There was an uncomfortable silence at the table, broken when Cullinane said, "Then I'm afraid Commander Renslow's theory was absolutely correct." He nodded at Renslow. "We owe you a vote of thanks."

"I don't begrudge the commander any thanks," Warden said, annoyed. "But it would seem more logical to discuss what we're going to do now." The look he directed at Hardin was pure ice. Renslow guessed that Warden was already planning how to pull the rug out from under the doctor. If anybody was going to be the fall guy, it would be Dr. Augustus Hardin, not Caleb Warden.

"Can you sum up the situation, Doctor?" Cullinane asked.

Hardin dabbed at his forehead with a handkerchief. "You understand that in the minds of the crew, the taped broadcasts have created the picture of a world on the brink of war, one in which their worst fears have been realized. Their belief that this is reality has undoubtedly been buttressed by the effects of the paint. The tendency for a paranoid mind would be to believe the tapes. Completely."

"What about your controls?" Cullinane asked. "Harris, van Meer, and Schulman? They knew it was a test."

Hardin looked unhappy. "Either they're no longer in effective command or—more logically—the paint has affected them as well as the others. They've already been told the drill has been canceled and that they're to return to Charleston. They refused to acknowledge. Nor did they respond to the request of the *Chicago* for help. Under ordinary circumstances"—he glanced at Cullinane—"that would be unforgivable." He hesitated. "If we assume the *Alaska* is not down, then my guess is that the crew interpreted the collision between the *Chicago* and the *Zhukov* as the opening gun in some sort of hostile action."

"I'm not so sure I agree with you, Doctor," Renslow said.

Everybody was looking at him now; Cullinane and Howland with surprise, Warden with open hostility. For the first time since he had known him, however, Hardin looked as if he welcomed somebody disagreeing with his conclusions. "About van Meer," Renslow added quickly. "I know him personally and consider him solid and dependable. He's suffering from extreme depression because of a great personal loss but that's the extent of it. I've read the transmissions he's signed and under the circumstances they struck me as logical and sane—the man was obviously trying to warn us without at the same time losing his post as second in command of the *Alaska.*"

"I realize the temptation for one officer to protect another," Warden said in mock sympathy. "I sat through it the other day while your Captain Blandini defended Harris. Our situation is too serious to do it again." He nodded at Oxley, who handed him a folder.

"The man's a borderline case under any circumstances," Warden continued, thumbing the pages in the folder. "How the Navy failed to catch him in its initial screening, I don't know. His fitness reports have always been mediocre. There's reason to believe he was responsible for the death of his wife due to his own negligence. He's been under the care of a civilian psychiatrist for bouts of severe depression, and in the last six months he's been popping pills like a ghetto hophead."

"You're missing the point, Mr. Warden," Renslow said. Warden reddened with anger and started to speak. Renslow plunged ahead. "I said I read his early transmissions. They violate proper Navy procedure but there was nothing mad or unbalanced about them. The point I wanted to make was that his medication"—he stressed the word "medication"—"may be keeping him the one sane man on board."

Warden shuffled through the folder and came up with a sheet he passed over to Renslow. "That's your signature, isn't it, Commander?"

Renslow nodded. Warden waved the sheet at the others around the table. "Commander Renslow had a chance to recommend van Meer for his own command." He looked at Renslow. "But you gave him a pass, didn't you?"

Renslow colored. "I don't think that's relevant right now."

Cullinane ignored Warden and turned to Hardin. "Could the medication act as a buffer?"

Hardin shrugged. "We're checking it out. It's possible the drug could bind the organic fragments in the paint."

"I don't care what you find out," Warden said dryly. "I'm not willing to entrust the world to him."

Renslow glanced at Warden sharply. The man must have come to the meeting with some sort of plan. Warden wasn't the type to be caught with his pants down, no matter which way the chips fell.

"The *Alaska* has ignored her recall orders," Cullinane said. "I think that's the only thing that's important right now. Dr. Hardin, you were about to say something?"

"We must get them to reject their programming," Hardin said. "Somehow we have to discredit the taped transmissions. My guess is that the crew thinks the previous recall message was an enemy trick. That would be consistent with their pananoia. Unfortunately, once they've received a red alert it will be extremely difficult to persuade them the world is not headed for war."

"They've already received it," Cullinane said grimly.

"We could still try," Hardin said desperately, clutching at straws. "We might be able to enforce new orders by having wives send familygrams with information contradicting what they've heard on the tape and also containing personal information to verify the identity of the sender."

It was an idea, and it upped Renslow's estimation of Hardin a notch.

"Failing that," Hardin continued, "our only hope would be to enter their fantasy world in some fashion. To somehow write a scenario consistent with the world as they think it actually is, a scenario that might lead them to abandon their mission. Frankly, at the moment we haven't come up with anything that looks convincing."

"It doesn't matter what we decide on," Renslow said. "We have to find the *Alaska* first."

Cullinane nodded. "It's a big ocean, Commander. We've sown sonobuoys and had helicopters lower sonar probes into the area. We've had one contact and that's all."

"What about the *Zhukov*?" Renslow asked.

Cullinane look troubled. "That's been bothering me, too, Commander. The *Chicago* lost track of the *Zhukov* immediately after the collision. We haven't picked her up and that suggests silent running capabilities we didn't think she had."

Renslow looked at Warden. "The State Department lodged a complaint?"

Warden's eyes glittered. "Are you asking me or telling me? For the record, State lodged the strongest possible protest. You may not approve, Commander, but a collision at sea is not the sort of thing you go to war over."

"We're getting off the subject," Cullinane interrupted.

"My apologies, Admiral," Warden said. But he spoke with an effort and Renslow realized he had gotten to him. "I think we ought to talk about what we're going to do once we locate the *Alaska.*"

There was something in Warden's tone that made Renslow catch his breath and brought a sudden hush to the room.

"Dr. Hardin's drill"—Warden nodded coldly at Hardin, who suddenly looked as if he were going to faint—"has backfired. The result is that we have the world's most advanced weapons system loose at sea, manned by a psychotic crew that believes war is imminent. And as Admiral Cullinane is so fond of reminding us, that weapons system is self-contained. It doesn't depend on the President pushing his red button—it's perfectly capable of operating independently."

He glanced at Renslow, his expression patronizing. "Even if there is one sane man on board, I doubt that it would make much difference. Particularly this one sane man."

"You have a suggestion," Cullinane said in a sardonic tone of voice.

"The *Alaska* has refused to return to port or even to respond," Warden continued. "If she carries out her launch, she'll start World War Three."

The silence in the room was smothering.

"Your suggestion," Cullinane prompted.

"When we find her," Warden said harshly, "if she refuses to return, then we have no other choice but to sink her."

43

THE CABLING TRACED back to a Fathometer in the small auxiliary transmitter room off the radio shack proper. Van Meer chewed Russo out lightly for not knowing it had been installed, then dismissed him, hoping that Russo, with other things to worry about, wouldn't dwell on this incident with the exec.

The next watch, he took Schulman aside and they both inspected the Fathometer. "Why didn't Russo know about it?" Schulman asked, puzzled.

"It's an old model. Apparently it was installed as a backup." He smiled slightly, feeling the first sense of relief in days. "If that's the real reason."

Schulman looked dubious. "You sure this isn't wishful thinking, Van? It might really be a Fathometer behind that face plate."

Van Meer made a closer inspection. Presumably the equipment would unbolt from its mounting but he could see a thin line where it had been welded. He clicked the ON switch and a small red dial light came on but the gear itself was nonfunctional.

"Five will get you ten that the tape deck is behind that face plate, Doc, wired into the radio antenna system."

Schulman still looked doubtful and van Meer showed him the weld line. "Then we can hardly take it apart without a torch and there's no way you're going to succeed in doing that without questions being asked."

Van Meer reflected. He could probably think of some reason but there wasn't much time. They could close the door to the equipment room so they wouldn't be interrupted but there was no way they could operate a torch in there.

"Get me a hacksaw, Doc."

"What're you going to do?"

"Cut the cable." It would buy them time, though the sudden absence of any transmissions might indicate the worst had happened. If they were careful, the cut cable wouldn't be discovered. Dritz and Russo were the only ones likely to stumble across it and they were preoccupied. Besides, he thought grimly, it was never meant to work as a Fathometer in the first place. It wouldn't be missed.

Schulman returned with the saw. Van Meer had barely taken the first bite, cutting through the paint on the thick cable, when "Battle stations" sounded once again. He cursed, hid the saw behind a nearby communications receiver, brushed away the few flecks of chipped paint, and ran for the control room.

Harris was standing behind Olson at the sonar console. "Our friend has returned."

"They're closing, sir," Olson interrupted. "I should be able to get a signature soon."

A worried Costanza now joined them at the console. "I've heard rumors the Soviets have a new detection technique. If they're true, then we can't lose her by sending out a decoy."

"I'm not so sure I want to lose them," Harris said. He watched the scope a moment longer, his face hawklike in the green glow. "Let me know when you get a signature, Olson. I want to be sure."

Van Meer watched him walk over to the DRT, once again struck by the changes in Harris. His cheekbones were now etched high in his face, his eyes dark and fierce-looking. There was a suggestion of a trim to his beard and mustache. His collar was open and a handkerchief was knotted around his forehead to keep the sweat out of his eyes.

If he ever got back, he'd have to look into that. Everybody seemed flushed and feverish, sweating even in the constant seventy-two degrees of the forward part of the ship.

Harris watched the quartermasters working over the DRT for five minutes, pacing nervously back and forth, his forehead creased in thought. He suddenly snapped his fingers and walked over to stand behind Spencer, who had the deck.

"Half speed, Mr. Spencer."

Van Meer caught a startled look on Spencer's face and noticed the other crew members glance furtively at one another. He was positive they could have run away from the other submarine with ease but Harris was deliberately letting her creep up on them.

A few minutes later, Olson had a signature. "Contact bearing zero-three-zero, Captain. It's the *Zhukov*."

Harris nodded, smiling slightly, an I-told-you-so expression on his face. "Get a fix, Olson, then plug it into the fire control computer. Range, speed, bearing, angle on the bow . . ."

Suddenly van Meer could feel the hairs on the back of his neck start to stir. What the hell was Harris up to?

Harris turned to his phone talker. "Forward torpedo room, load one and four."

Thursday, July 2

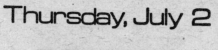

44

IT WAS OVER breakfast at the Tabard Inn that Renslow clarified his thinking about the *Zhukov*. It had been bothering him since his meeting with the brass at Flag Plot, where Warden had dropped his bombshell. Nobody knew what had happened to the *Zhukov;* nobody knew whether she was down or disabled, and, most important of all, if she was still afloat, nobody knew what she was doing *right now*. Significantly, State had yet to receive a protest from the Soviets, who were usually quick to lodge a complaint about any incident involving their submarines. If only to place the blame elsewhere . . .

He had ordered coffee and croissants, and was moodily reading the front page of the paper—Admiral Cullinane had yet to find his leak—about two American submarines and a Soviet submarine involved in a ramming incident at sea: SUBS COLLIDE IN MID-OCEAN. There was a large amount of wild-eyed speculation and a small kernel of hard fact. The sidebar by the science editor devoted most of a column to the rigors of life on board a Trident submarine and the dangers of channel fever. The author neglected to mention that both American submarines involved had left home port less than ten days before.

"More coffee, sir?" He pushed his cup forward and the waitress filled it, glancing at the headlines as she did so. "Y'know, that doesn't make sense. What'd they want to do that for?"

He grunted and she smiled her way over to the next table. She must be just out of high school. Then her words hit him and he realized she had anthropomorphized the submarines. Common usage: A ship was always *"she,"* and "she" did this or that. But submarines didn't *do* anything.

[301]

Captains did.

He thought about that for a moment, then crumpled up the paper and headed for the telephone in the lobby. Some of the federal employees in Washington hit their offices early and he knew from past experience that PeeWee Schwarting was one of them. . . . He rang PeeWee's private number and Schwarting himself picked it up. How soon could Renslow see him? Schwarting sounded surprised and pleased. Ten o'clock would be fine. . . .

He didn't even ask what it was about but, then, PeeWee read the papers, too.

He caught the blue shuttle bus at State and tried to put together what he remembered about PeeWee as it battled the traffic out to Langley. Thomas Schwarting, an Academy graduate one class ahead of his, had served ten years on destroyers and then been recruited by the CIA. They had been good friends at the Academy. . . .

Renslow paused uneasily. Or had they? Time tended to soften events and the truth was that he had never made many friends at the Academy. On the other hand, he couldn't think of any reason why PeeWee should dislike him.

Thirty minutes later, the bus crossed the Chain Bridge and turned north on route 123 into Maryland. Shortly after reaching the small town of Langley, a highway sign read CIA—NEXT RIGHT. Some years before, another sign had announced HIGHWAY DEPARTMENT or something of the sort. The sign had quickly become a standing joke and had finally been replaced.

The building that housed the CIA was not particularly imposing. More what might be termed Federal Modern, Renslow thought, though not nearly the atrocity the FBI Building was. The guards checked his ID in the lobby, then the receptionist called up to Schwarting and gave Renslow a visitor's ID badge with a large number. "Please wear it the entire time you're here," she said pleasantly.

"So everybody will know I'm 'one of them' and not 'one of us'?" Renslow asked.

She smiled politely but said nothing.

A moment later, Schwarting walked into the lobby. He stood nearly seven feet tall and was lean as a broom handle. He had sharp features and sleepy eyes and a perpetual smile drew his lips slightly off center. His brown hair had thinned a great deal since

Renslow had seen him last and what was left was flecked with gray.

"Good to see you, Al." Renslow signed the registration book on the receptionist's desk. "I'm right down the hall. Got a fresh pot of coffee if you missed breakfast."

"You didn't have to come down," Renslow protested. "You could've sent your secretary."

Schwarting smiled slightly. "Don't play games, Al. Visitors are allowed in on a personal-recognition basis only." He walked into an anteroom, waving at the girl pounding an IBM Memory typewriter. She ignored both of them.

In the inner office Schwarting sprawled in a high-backed swivel chair behind a vast expanse of desk. Renslow sat in a chair to his left and looked around the room. Nice office, he thought. Thick rugs on the floor, expensive furniture, and a series of Hogarth reproductions in massive mahogany-and-gold frames on the wall. In the corner there was a computer terminal backed by a printer and a video readout screen.

He glanced back at the desk. A desk set, blotter pad, and phone. Nothing else.

"This one's for visitors, right?"

"You can't expect me to clean off my desk every time somebody drops in." Schwarting smiled a surprisingly boyish smile. "The working offices aren't nearly so fancy, Al." He pointed to a small but professional coffee brewing service against the far wall. "Help yourself to the coffee."

Renslow poured himself a mug of black and returned to his seat. "At least you've got appropriate wall decorations. 'The Rake's Progress.'"

"The one thing I had a hand in picking. Speaking of rakes, I'm keeping regular company now. You'll get the announcement next month." A speculative look. "How's Elizabeth?"

Renslow hesitated a split second, then said, "Just fine."

"Having troubles, huh?"

They stared at each other in silence, Renslow suddenly baffled as to how to get the information he wanted. Schwarting was as friendly and easygoing as he remembered but there was still something of a screen between them. Working for the Company did that, he thought. If they couldn't talk to their wives, they sure as hell weren't going to let their hair down with former friends.

"Look, I'd love to play the game but time's short this morning," Schwarting said apologetically.

"We've got a problem," Renslow said.

Schwarting's smile faded. "I'll go along with that. The whole country will know something's up by tomorrow evening."

Renslow kept his face blank. "What do you mean?"

"Hell, you've got a leak, Al. Every reporter in D.C. knows something's wrong with the *Alaska.*"

"That was on last night's news," Renslow said evenly.

"Is she really down?"

"I'm sorry, PeeWee," Renslow said slowly. "I can't tell you that."

"Well, something's sure as hell wrong with her—you guys in Navy don't piss in your pants for nothing." He leaned over his desk, pointing a bony finger at Renslow. "Look, Al, you're here because you want to know something. So do I. And it's not for idle curiosity's sake, either."

"I thought you guys knew everything."

Schwarting shook his head. "We have our contacts but Navy's been very tight-lipped about this one."

"Dammit, PeeWee—"

"Cut the crap, Al. You want information from me. I want information from you. Fair trade or no game."

"I could go through channels," Renslow said.

"You don't have the time or else you would have," Schwarting said bluntly.

"She's not down," Renslow said quietly. "At least, we don't think she is. We don't know where she is."

Schwarting watched his face for a moment. "You're holding out on me, Al."

Renslow agonized for a moment. "White source?"

"Not even the director will know where it came from."

"All right," Renslow said, resigned. He quickly filled Schwarting in on the situation aboard the *Alaska.*

"Sheee-it. If it was anybody else but you, Al, I'd say he was pulling my leg. How can I help?"

"You have files on Soviet military personnel? Navy?"

Schwarting's eyelids flickered. "More than 'Janes.' Gorshkov's due to retire next year—but they won't let him. Grishanov's been promoted—he used to be chief of the Political Directorate.

That's important to you guys; your order-of-battle people at Navy Intelligence should know all that."

"They don't have what I want," Renslow said. "It's somebody lower down. We think the *Alaska* played a game of chicken with a Soviet Victor Three. The signature the *Chicago* picked up matches that of a Soviet attack sub named the *Zhukov*. I want everything you've got on the *Zhukov*'s captain."

Schwarting got to his feet. "Let's see what Junior knows." He walked over to the computer terminal and unlocked it, then flipped two switches and waited as the terminal warmed up. He pulled over a typing chair and sat down, then drummed his fingers briefly on the keyboard. The words on the screen read CLEAR BUFFER. CODE 1 J. SOONEST.

"There are ten guys in this building who are going to hate me—I just cleared their programs off the buffer assigned to this section. Top-priority code." He typed another line, waited a moment, then muttered, "Crap, let's try something else." He started typing again, then finally leaned back. Lines of type suddenly started appearing on the display screen. "There we are. I should have tried the political files the first thing."

Renslow leaned over his shoulder and Schwarting said, "Use the space bar if you want to see it line by line."

It was all there. Personal life, naval career, political history, psychological profile—even a career prognosis. But what the hell had caused such intense interest on the CIA's part? The answer came up a moment later and he pressed the space bar to stop the scrolling.

"What about that?" he said tightly.

Schwarting read it and shrugged. "Détente, remember?"

The file finally stopped and Renslow said, "I'll need a copy."

"You're asking me to put my ass in a sling, buddy. I was never *that* good a friend of yours." Renslow started to argue and Schwarting suddenly grinned. "Just kidding. What the hell, it's for the cause. Just remember to burn it when you're through with it. I've got ten years to go before I can pension out of here." He leaned forward and typed PRINT #2. The printer began to chatter and Renslow watched as it spit out the long paper form. Schwarting tore off the paper and folded it.

"Stuff this in your shorts and I'll convoy you past the fuzz."

"PeeWee, I really appreciate this," Renslow said.

"Just get the bastard, Al. The older he gets, the more trouble he's going to cause us."

Renslow shook his head. "Uh-uh, this baby I want alive."

Cullinane had reserved a window table at Hogate's for lunch. The admiral was in mufti, looking both uncomfortable and unhappy out of uniform.

Renslow eased into a chair and Cullinane ordered a double martini straight up. It was after one and the dining room was now relatively empty.

"It was a hell of a session at State," Cullinane said after a quick gulp of the gin. "Warden wants to call in the Soviet ambassador and tell him everything . . . well, almost everything."

"We may have to," Renslow said, worried.

"That's not exactly what I want to hear," Cullinane said grimly. "You don't think any number of apologies are going to calm their hawks once the *Alaska* starts launching, do you?"

"You think it will come down to Kahn's trade-off? One of ours for one of theirs?"

"Bernard Kahn had a broad fanny and spent too much time sitting on it," Cullinane said sourly. "Do you honestly think the President would allow an American city to be destroyed for each Soviet city we accidentally vaporize? That's no answer." He drained half his glass. "You said you had something?"

Renslow pulled a brown kraft envelope out of his briefcase and handed it to Cullinane. The admiral opened it and unfolded the long printout sheet. "I take it we've got a real winner."

"Sergei Polnykov," Renslow recited quietly. "Forty years old. Born in Leningrad, raised by foster parents. A member of the Young Pioneers. His early political activity led to an appointment to the Naval Academy. Member of the Tolstoy Society. Married. He was Admiral Golgi's aide for two years after graduating from submarine school and serving three years in a Hotel-class SSBN. Put in a year as XO on a Yankee and then was selected to command the *Zhukov* over seventy-three men ahead of him on the promotion list. Golgi's in political trouble now and they're looking very closely at Polnykov. He's considered a hothead and dangerous—but for the moment he's safe. He's the fair-haired boy of the hard-liners. He has a low opinion of the U. S. Navy and said so at length in several articles for the *Soviet Naval Journal*."

"So he's a nasty bastard," Cullinane said.

"You didn't finish reading his poop sheet," Renslow said, mildly accusative. "He's been involved in rammings before, two of them as the result of deliberately disobeying orders." He hesitated. "There's good reason to believe he was the captain responsible for the loss of the *Blowfin* a few months back."

Cullinane's face hardened. He opened the sheet again and read it slowly. "I had friends on board," he said softly. Then: "What's your point, Commander?"

"Polnykov wasn't interested in the *Chicago*," Renslow said. "My guess is the Navy Ministry assigned him to dog the *Alaska* because he was in the area. They could have picked up rumors that the *Alaska* was involved in some sort of secret drill. It might have been a true collision with the *Chicago* but knowing Polnykov, I'd bet on a ramming. If the *Zhukov* was damaged, that might account for her sudden disappearance. She'd be under orders to return to port."

"We don't even know if the *Zhukov* survived the collision," Cullinane said.

"There was certainly no indication that she didn't. And I'll bet that Polnykov was mad as hell if the *Zhukov* was even slightly damaged. I don't think his ego could stand that. He'd want to get even. And the *Alaska*'s probably still out there and acting very strange. She didn't surface to come to the *Chicago*'s aid and she hasn't returned to port, either."

Cullinane motioned to the waiter to bring him another drink. "So what's your point?"

"I'm betting the *Zhukov* was damaged during the ramming but that Polnykov is still tailing the *Alaska*."

Cullinane shook his head, dismissing the idea. "I'd buy the idea that the *Zhukov* might be damaged. But I think the odds are overwhelming that she's returning to port, probably one of the Baltic Sea ports. That would take her a long way away from the *Alaska*."

"You're assuming the *Alaska* is staying on station," Renslow said. "It's possible she's going in the same general direction."

Cullinane looked thoughtful and Renslow could see him examining a map in his mind's eye.

"That's not what you're driving at. You're not really worried about the *Zhukov*'s intentions."

"My point is that if you find the *Zhukov*, chances are the *Alaska* will be somewhere close by. And if the *Zhukov* was damaged, she's probably making a lot of noise."

Cullinane suddenly smiled. "I'm sorry, Commander, I haven't been thinking—still grousing about Warden. The point, of course, is that it will be a lot easier to locate a damaged *Zhukov* than an *Alaska* that's trying to hide from us."

"Exactly," Renslow said. "As you said, Admiral, it's a big ocean. It'll be a lot easier if we hunt for both of them."

45

VAN MEER BLINKED the sweat from his eyes and stared over Olson's shoulder at the sonar screen. The *Zhukov* had become cautious, cutting her speed to more nearly match that of the *Alaska*, but she was still creeping up on them. The *Zhukov*'s captain must be curious why the *Alaska* had slowed and had suddenly become more prudent.

"We could outrun her," he said quietly to Harris.

Harris shook his head, his eyes glued to the screen. "I have no intentions of outrunning her. I want to find out what she's going to do."

Who's the cat and who's the mouse? van Meer wondered. Then he realized that, of course, Harris was the cat. The *Zhukov* was curious; her captain wanted to play another game of chicken of the sea. What he didn't know was that Harris was convinced a war was about to begin.

"Let's see what they can do," Harris suddenly said. He walked back to the bucket seat directly behind Clinger and Sandeman. "Evasive maneuvers, Clinger. Pattern one."

Van Meer stayed at the sonar screen, fighting the sweat that was trickling down his neck. The *Zhukov* clung tenaciously to them as Clinger "flew" the *Alaska* through a series of sharp turns and then slid it quietly under an inversion. Harris cut the engines and waited. The *Zhukov* seemed to hesitate, then came on. Her captain had guts but he wasn't too smart, van Meer thought; he was revealing too much of the *Zhukov*'s capabilities. . . .Though in a very real sense Harris was demonstrating the *Alaska*'s, too.

"Well, we now know something about their detection and maneuverability," Harris said thoughtfully. "Let's see how fast they can go."

At flank speed, the bright blip on the screen began to recede. The *Zhukov* couldn't keep up; she wasn't nearly so fast as the *Alaska*. But, then, underwater the *Alaska* could travel at freeway speeds. . . .

Once more Harris cut to half speed and the *Zhukov* began to creep up again. If it was really war, van Meer thought uncomfortably, they or the *Zhukov* would have been sunk hours ago.

Harris was by his side now and van Meer said tentatively, "They just want to play chicken."

Harris shrugged. "That's today. Who knows what they'll want to play tomorrow?" Then, almost to himself: "Why wait?"

The *Zhukov* was within a few kilometers now and Harris suddenly turned to van Meer. "Take over in the forward torpedo room. I don't want any screw-ups on this one. We're only going to get one chance."

Van Meer ducked through the hatch and went forward, his heart skipping beats. Harris was going to do it. Harris was going to torpedo the *Zhukov*. . . . He tasted salt at the corners of his mouth and wiped away the sweat with the back of his hand. What the hell could he do? "I don't want any screwups," Harris had said.

In the forward torpedo room Meslinsky was working with two third-class torpedo man's mates, preparing tubes one and four. "How about that, Commander? We'll be drawing first blood."

"That's right, Animal," van Meer said, trying to keep his voice from shaking. He made a pretense of studying the controls on the repeater for the Mk 130 fire control computer, the latest improvement on the old TDC, which fed target bearing, range, speed, and angle on the bow into the small memory banks of the torpedoes themselves. Once Olson flicked the switch on his sonar console it became automatic. But there were provisions for manual override in case of emergencies.

The loudspeaker suddenly blared: "Range two kilometers and closing."

Behind him, a torpedo had stuck in its cradle and Meslinsky

was swearing at the top of his lungs as he tried to break it free. Van Meer glanced around. Animal was too busy to be paying any attention. . . . He quickly started unscrewing the knurled bolts that held one of the drawers of electronics in its frame. If he could break the interlocks, even momentarily . . . He cursed silently at the sweat that dribbled down his forehead and made his fingers slip on the bolts. The last one was tight and wouldn't move. He took a breath, gripped it hard enough so his fingers started to cramp, and tried again. Behind him, Meslinsky was still swearing at the torpedo.

Van Meer winced at the pain in his fingers and twisted once more. The bolt moved a little and suddenly loosened. He eased the drawer forward half an inch. The dials and panel lights abruptly went dead. Van Meer immediately shoved the drawer back in and tightened the bolts. The operator in the control room must have noticed that something had gone wrong. . . .

Harris was now on the loudspeaker, sounding annoyed. "There's a glitch in the computer, Van. This will have to be a manual shoot."

Van Meer's hands flew over the front of the repeater, shifting rocker switches to the manual position. Range, bearing, and depth data were now read over the intercom and van Meer made the settings, deliberately altering them slightly and hoping that Meslinsky wasn't looking over his shoulder.

"It's a down-the-throat shot, Van." Harris sounded calm and unhurried, not at all like a man going to his own funeral.

Then the countdown started.

"Hit the controls, you bastards," Meslinsky roared.

The countdown was taking forever. Van Meer felt faintly sick. Then: "Shoot one and four!"

The *Alaska* lurched slightly as the torpedoes sped away. "It's a bear trap," Meslinsky chortled. "One on each side. She can't turn either way."

Van Meer could hear the heavy breathing of the men behind him, could smell the stink of their perspiration. With a little luck, he had changed the safe run of the torpedoes before they armed themselves. They'd explode behind the *Zhukov*. . . .

There was the distant rumble of an explosion. Half a minute later, there was another one.

He suddenly felt a huge hand on his shoulder, the fingers digging deep into the flesh.

"I can't believe it," Meslinsky whispered. "One of them missed. Would you believe it? One of them missed."

But the other one had hit. Van Meer felt dead inside. Now there would be hell to pay.

46

LIEUTENANT, j.g., Timothy Epping leaned against a winch housing on the edge of the *Hornet*'s flight deck and looked out over the blazing surface of the ocean. The Atlantic was unusually calm, the high July sun painting a hot red streak across the water. In the distance, the three destroyer escorts shimmered, their outlines vague and distorted by the lens of hot air and water vapor rising from the sea.

Where the skies are polished silver and the seas are burnished brass, Epping recited to himself, and wondered who had written the line. He took off his flight cap and mopped the sweat from his upper lip. His shirt was plastered to his back with perspiration and a vague itching under his arms warned of the start of another attack of heat rash. He would settle for being any other place right then, he thought; it didn't matter where just as long as the temperature was on the cool side of ninety. He reached down and touched the flight deck. The surface was like the top of a stove. . . .

The deck crew, stripped down to cutoffs and oblivious of the heat, was busily reloading the sonobuoys for Epping's next pass over the search area. He had seeded several hundred square miles of ocean already that morning and was scheduled to make at least two more flights that afternoon.

The other seventeen Sikorsky Sea Kings had also been dropping buoys, which meant somebody was desperately looking for something in that part of the ocean. Scuttlebutt had it that the *Alaska* was down but Epping didn't buy that. "You don't use sonobuoys to locate a dead boomer," he'd said at officers' mess that morning. "Whatever we're looking for, she's hot and she's moving damned fast."

Epping's private reverie was interrupted by the distant *beat-beat* of chopper blades. In the steamy moistness of the day, it sounded like somebody hitting a wet blanket with a baseball bat. He glanced up and watched another Sea King lumber closer and pause above the flight deck before the flight chief waved it in. It touched the deck and two crewmen ran forward with elastic lines to secure it, ducking low under blades that were already bending down from their rotor as the speed decreased.

Moments later, the ship's PA system announced: "Lieutenant Epping, Lieutenant Talbot, man your chopper."

Epping tugged his flight cap down so the visor shaded his eyes and walked quickly across the deck. Talbot and the two computer techs were waiting for him. They quickly climbed aboard, Epping taking the pilot's seat and Talbot settling into the seat next to him. Talbot pushed back his flight cap and slipped on a lightweight pair of headphones. "Another milk run, huh?"

Epping didn't bother answering; the heat had given him a splitting headache. He checked in with the flight officer on the bridge, then keyed the starter, wincing at the high-pitched whine of the rotor motors. He waited while the deck crew undogged the landing gear. The fume-laden blast from the rotors, blowing through the open side port, did little to alleviate the oppressive heat. Finally he was given the lift-off command and he pulled back on the collective. The chopper angled into the sky, the *Hornet* rapidly dwindling to a speck on the horizon. They beat over the brassy seas to the southwest and fifty minutes later were on station.

"Candy bar?"

Talbot waved a drooping chocolate bar at him and Epping shook his head, nauseated. Talbot shrugged and settled back to enjoy two.

They flew in comparative silence for the next half hour, Epping dipping closer to the waves to drop the sonobuoys. They had turned northeast after the first four buoys and then southwest again, sowing the second set in a parallel line. Occasionally Epping would switch his headphones to the monitoring gear in the rear of the chopper and listen to the clicks and rustle of the ocean noises that the buoys were picking up. An hour into the run, there was the distant beat of a propeller but the techs identified it as that of one of the escort ships.

Talbot was half dozing, his headphones tuned to the monitoring unit. Once, he sat up in surprise and Epping hit the switch just in time to hear the alien melodic wail of two humpbacks serenading each other. He sank back and decided the afternoon was going to be as boring as the morning.

"We're picking something up." Talbot was suddenly alert, gesturing at his headset. Epping flicked on the switch again. The reception from the last buoy was loud and clear. He listened intently to the water-muffled thrumming sound, then switched to the voice circuit. "You guys got that?"

Romero, one of the techs in the rear, said, "Yeah, we're running it now." There was a short pause. "It's a Victor Three class. Sounds like it has some damage to its reduction gears."

Epping called in on the *Hornet's* frequency. "Gray Warrior, this is White Two. Come in, please." The *Hornet* answered almost immediately. "I've got a contact," Epping said, giving the coordinates. "Sounds like a Victor-Three in trouble. Can you monitor number C-seven?"

There was a delay of several minutes before the *Hornet* came back. "Confirmed, White Two. It's the *Zhukov.*"

Talbot struck him lightly on the arm to get his attention. "There's something else. On number six." Talbot almost sounded excited.

Epping switched quickly to number six and then back to the *Hornet.* "We have a second contact, Gray Warrior. On C-six."

"Roger." Another pause of several minutes and then: "An Ohio class, White Two. It's the *Alaska.*"

The crewmen in back confirmed that it was the *Alaska* a moment later and Epping grinned at Talbot, his headache suddenly gone. For a fleeting second he wondered if Talbot had a third chocolate bar on him. He switched back and forth between buoys seven and six, then pirouetted the Sea King in midair and sped back to the search area. The thrumming on buoy seven had begun to fade and buoy six was beginning to pick it up. At the same time, the sound of the *Alaska* remained constant, as if the sub were circling.

"White Two, this is Gray Warrior," the voice in his headphones suddenly said. "Our reception from six isn't clear. Monitor six and tape it."

"Roger." A few minutes later, he frowned. "Gray Warrior, White Two. It sounds like the two boats are closing. I think our boy is being stalked and that he's holding still for it. Doesn't make sense. Hold it—"

He broke off the transmission and concentrated on the sounds from buoy six. There was the thrumming of the screws of the two submarines and then what sounded like two deep sighs, followed by two soft, whirring sounds. Torpedoes, he thought, dumbfounded. *My God, one of them has launched two torpedoes.*

A moment later, a blast of sound made him pull off the headphones in pain. There was a long pause and then another blast from the headphones, cut short as if someone had chopped the end of a sound track.

"Number six is out," Talbot said grimly. "That last one must have got her."

Epping touched the controls and the Sea King tilted around its rotor axles and slowly turned to the east. Through the window he could see the expanse of sea in the area of buoy six. Even as he watched, the sea boiled up in a massive explosion.

"I'm taking it closer."

He dipped the chopper and flew toward the bubbling sea.

"Christ, look at that," Talbot yelled, leaning forward in his seat. Below, the sea continued to churn, then the blunt nose of a submarine broke the surface. Seconds later, the vessel was rolling helplessly in the water. The low, streamlined superstructure and the ports along the side identified it as a Victor III.

Epping quickly donned the headphones and flicked the switch for the *Hornet.* "Gray Warrior, White Two. A Victor Three has just surfaced. It looks like it needs help."

The voice on the *Hornet* sounded excited. "Monitor her position. Do not attempt contact." A short pause, then: "Radio intercept reports a coded distress signal. Reconnaissance indicates a Soviet trawler has just changed course—ETA three hours. Nice work, White Two. Stay on station as long as possible."

"Something on number seven," Talbot said.

Epping switched quickly to the buoy. At first it sounded like the *Alaska.* Then the sound grew fainter and abruptly cut off.

"What the hell happened?" Talbot demanded, confused. "She just seemed to disappear."

Epping stared down at the surface of the ocean as if somehow he could look beneath the waves and see the *Alaska.*

"We weren't tracking her, Ernie," he said, his headache back in full force. "That was a decoy. It must've been launched by the *Alaska.*"

"But where the hell is she?" Talbot said. "Why the decoy?"

"I don't know why the decoy," Epping said thoughtfully. And after a pause: "I don't know where the hell she is."

47

RENSLOW SLAMMED DOWN the phone and fumbled for a cigarette. There were none in his pockets. He opened the top drawer to Cullinane's desk, found a box of cigars, and helped himself to one. He lit it with the lighter on the desk and noted that his hands were still shaking with anger.

He had never liked Elizabeth's father, who had always treated him with contempt. The Talmadges were a Southern military family of impressive pedigree and Harley Talmadge had never hidden his conviction that Elizabeth had married beneath her.

Today was the first time in seven years that Renslow had even talked to him. Talmadge had admitted that Elizabeth was there but, "I've advised her not to speak with you and she has wisely decided to follow my advice." His voice left no doubt of his distaste for Renslow.

Renslow was still staring moodily at his cigar when the door opened and Cullinane said quietly, "Sorry to disturb you but I'm going to have to reclaim my office."

Renslow stood up. "Thanks a lot, Admiral. This is about the only place I could phone in privacy."

"Hand me a cigar before you smoke them all," Cullinane said. Renslow lit it for him and Cullinane sank back into his own chair, his eyes compassionate and speculative as he stared at Renslow. "You fleet officers seem to be able to manage everything but your own lives. Why is it you always marry women who want more of your life than you can give them?"

"Elizabeth won't accept the fact that the Navy has first call on me. She feels . . . shortchanged, I guess."

Cullinane nodded in agreement. "It's the singleness of attention. You live Navy even when you're out for a social evening.

Frequently, your friends and shipmates mean more to you than your wives. It's natural they should resent it."

"I don't think anybody means more to me than Elizabeth," Renslow mused. "But I'm not so sure there's any way I can prove that to her." He smiled faintly. "You're hardly the one to talk, Admiral."

"True," Cullinane said, not at all offended. "But I knew how it would be. That's why I never remarried. If Marilyn hadn't died, we would have divorced. In a sense, thank God she did. I wouldn't be here otherwise."

"You don't really mean that," Renslow said slowly.

"I *do* mean it," Cullinane said, his face sad. "I know what I'm good at and I'm very good at being a flag officer. My whole life has led up to this moment. I would have hated her if she had tried to deny me it." He suddenly looked lost. "I wonder who I'll blame after this mess is over."

Renslow was uncomfortable at Cullinane's confiding in him. "Nobody can fault you for the way you've handled this," he said.

"You're being naive, Commander." Cullinane stood up and paced over to the wall and stared at a chart of the Atlantic. "I'm not the most popular guy with State or with some of the senators on the Hill. Locking horns with Warden won't help me at all." He turned to face Renslow, his expression bleak. "But, goddammit, Warden and his tribe are wrong. They're in love with their megaton toys and their role in history. They don't seem to realize that their policies may ensure that there'll be no history at all."

There was an embarrassed silence on Renslow's part, then the intercom on the desk buzzed. Cullinane reached over and flipped the switch. Chief Matthews in the outer office said, "Captain Oxley is here, Admiral. He says it's vitally important that he see you."

"Jack Ketch has sent his dogsbody," Cullinane mused. Then, into the intercom: "Send him in."

Captain Oxley pushed open the door, his fleshy face wreathed in a self-important smile. "Mr. Warden has asked me to drive you over to State, Admiral."

"I don't suppose he sent a message along with that request," Cullinane said wryly.

"It's at the request of the CNO," Oxley said, trying to mask the pleasure in his voice.

Cullinane was out of favor, Renslow thought. Howland hadn't bothered to call him personally.

Cullinane sighed and turned to Renslow. "This thing is getting more political by the minute, Commander. For the next forty-eight hours I'll be spending a lot of time trying to keep the civilians away from the red button." He hesitated, looking at Renslow thoughtfully. "You're going to have to take over the day-to-day part of the search-and-rescue operation for the *Alaska*. You know more about the variables involved than anyone else. I'll clear it with Admiral Howland."

Renslow stood up. "Yes, sir." He was numbed. It was too much responsibility and it was too soon.

"My car is just outside," Oxley said.

"Captain Oxley," Cullinane said softly, "I have my own car and my own driver and both of us know how to get to State." He took his service cap off the hat tree by the door and snapped it down over his eyes. He glanced back at Oxley with a faint smile of contempt and then he was gone.

"Feisty little bastard," Oxley said resentfully once the door had closed. "They'll cut him down to size before the day is over."

"You're choosing up sides, Captain. Don't forget you're still Navy."

Oxley laughed. He walked over and sat in Cullinane's chair, rocking back on the swivel. "Renslow, the Navy doesn't run this country. In fact, the Navy doesn't run the Navy. If you're trying to ride on Cullinane's coattails, you're playing on the wrong team."

"Admiral Cullinane is my commanding officer."

"That kind of loyalty won't buy you much. Cullinane is hardly the most popular flag officer in the department." His small eyes narrowed. "You know, he could have been CNO if he'd kept his mouth shut."

Renslow said mildly, "You really think so?"

"You should keep your ears open, Renslow. He was passed over once, right after he testified against deploying the Ohio-class ships."

"I never heard about that," Renslow said, interested in spite of himself.

"Of course not." Oxley looked smug. "The Man put a lid on it. Not only was your good admiral against deploying them, he

was against deploying the advanced MARV warheads. He lost a
lot of friends in the sub service then."

"No shit," Renslow said, forcing himself to marvel at Oxley's
insight.

"That's right," Oxley said pompously. "Cullinane advanced
the theory that the new warheads were too accurate for a retaliatory strike. That in an attack they'd be shooting at empty silos—
the enemy birds would already have been launched. He wanted to
spend the money on early-warning and defensive systems, and
depend on broad-saturation warheads." He shook his head
wonderingly. "Can you imagine what his testimony did for the
Navy's position in the overall defense picture?"

Oxley was quoting somebody else's argument, Renslow
thought coldly. And he wasn't smart enough to see where it was
leading. . . .

Renslow's obvious interest was flattering to Oxley and the fat
captain started to warm up to him. "This little emergency is a
great opportunity for both of us if we play our cards right." He
hesitated and became properly humble. "Mr. Warden would be
very grateful for any help you could give." He suddenly smiled.
"You could act as a sort of early-warning system for information
you think it's vital for him to know."

"That should be easy," Renslow said slowly, teasing Oxley
with a grateful smile. "I think the less that son of a bitch knows,
the better."

Oxley jerked to his feet, his face red. "I outrank you, Mr.
Navy. Here or in State, I outrank you. You'll find that out soon
enough."

At that moment the door banged open and Matthews thrust
his head in. "Sorry, Commander, I was looking for the admiral."

"He's left for State," Renslow said. "For the moment I'm in
charge."

Matthews looked both excited and appalled. "Then you'd
better get down to the Situation Room. The *Alaska* just shot a torpedo up the *Zhukov*'s ass."

Renslow started. "Did they sink her?"

"Shook her up and blew all the water out of her ballast tanks.
She's on the surface now, chewed up a bit and mad as hell."

"What about the *Alaska*?"

Matthews' face clouded. "They lost her in the confusion."

Renslow motioned to the chief to follow him and ran for the door, Oxley momentarily forgotten.

Harris had fired the first shot, he thought. The first shot in a war that existed only in his imagination.

48

ONLY ONE of them hit, Van," Harris said, disbelieving. There was sudden suspicion in his eyes. "That shouldn't have happened. Especially not with you in the torpedo room."

They were standing in one corner of the control room, Harris pitching his voice low so the rest of the crew in the compartment couldn't overhear. They couldn't have anyway, van Meer thought; the *Alaska* had struck the first blow and the effect had been the same as several shots of whiskey, straight up. Costanza had a crooked smile on his face and was shouting and slapping Spencer on the back. Sandeman and Clinger were yelling and grinning, and even Gurnee looked happy.

"Well, Van?"

"Are you telling me or accusing me?" van Meer said tightly. He let carefully controlled anger bubble to the surface. He couldn't afford to knuckle under, not this time. "I'm not responsible for malfunctioning computers or faulty torpedoes. We fought half of World War Two with torpedoes that ran too deep or never exploded at all."

He glared back at Harris and the suspicion gradually left Harris' face. "It doesn't matter. That's probably the only time we'll launch torpedoes. The next time it'll be the birds." He stepped over to the chart table and van Meer followed. Harris stared down and spread his fingers over their position at the time of the shoot against the *Zhukov* to where they were now. Immediately after the hit they had made a sharp turn and sought the bottom, a thousand feet down. They could go twice as deep in an emergency, but it would be dangerously close to their crush depth. A pinpoint leak and the ocean would smash in, tearing the *Alaska* apart. . . .

"The *Zhukov* must have got off a message," Harris said, almost to himself. "Some trawler might have picked it up and then the Soviets would know our course." He glanced at van Meer with a sour smile. "The Barents is out after all."

"You have an alternative?"

Harris frowned. "Maybe a better one. Back to station. I don't think they'd expect that."

Neither would the Americans, van Meer thought, depressed. The only plus to come out of torpedoing the *Zhukov* was that it had given away their position to the task force searching for them. Like the Russians, the Americans, too, would think the *Alaska* was heading for the Barents Sea.

Harris had been watching his face. "You don't approve?"

"I think it's . . . logical," van Meer said, keeping his eyes on the chart.

"Your approval is a big help," Harris said sardonically, still studying him. "We're going to go through a lot together in the next watch or two. We're going to need each other's support."

Van Meer was chilled. He had to get to the Fathometer. As soon as possible, he would have to cut the cable, put it out of commission. . . .

A few minutes later, Harris secured from quarters and van Meer hurried to the communications equipment room. Dritz was there ahead of him, opening the drawer of a transmitter and shining a light inside. He'd already spread a white cloth on the carpeted deck and van Meer guessed that he'd have the drawer apart in a few minutes.

"Trouble, Dritz?"

Dritz glanced up, barely concealing his irritation at being interrupted. "Maintenance," he said gruffly. "No time like the present. Right, Commander?"

Van Meer nodded curtly and swore to himself. Dritz was under a heavy strain and he wasn't the type to sit in the crew's mess and play cards or read to forget what was happening. Now he'd probably spend all his waking hours in the equipment room, testing and retesting the equipment.

In crew's berthing a small party was going on. Somebody besides Cermak had smuggled liquor on board and was passing around a bottle. Van Meer hung back for a moment and watched. There was a group gathered by the lockers in the aftersection of the compartment, their faces shiny in the gloom, excited and happy at having fired the first shot.

Scoma, excited but still questioning: "Yeah, but we don't know if the *Zhukov* went down."

Leggett, the gambler, who would bet on the exact minute the world would blow up: "You wanna bet? Ten bucks, Scoma."

McCune, partly drunk, snapping his fingers with glee: "Teach 'em to fuck with us."

And finally Longstreet, sounding oddly curt and depressed: "That's a stupid bet, Leggett. We'll all be dead before we ever find out."

Nobody answered Longstreet but the little group broke up to re-form another locker away, effectively cutting Longstreet out.

"Hey, pass the bottle over here."

"Wait until we launch the birds."

Van Meer started to walk down a side aisle and suddenly felt a tug from one of the bottom bunks. Geranios, who had been confined to quarters since the finger incident, was holding something out to him in the shadows. His voice sounded high and strangled.

"Have some, Commander. It's good shit."

Van Meer reached down and flicked the bunk switch on. Geranios' eyes were heavy-lidded and sleepy. He was clutching a small hash pipe.

"That's worth a dishonorable," van Meer said coldly.

Geranios shrugged, a smile sliding across his face. "If you can guarantee I'll live to get it, I'll take it, Commander."

There was a commotion at the other end of the compartment and van Meer turned to see Harris swaggering up the far aisle.

"Hey, we really creamed 'em, Captain."

Harris answered in a deep, almost laughing voice, "When they tangle with us, they tangle with the best."

"Let's hit 'em again."

"When do we launch, Captain?"

And Harris again: "We'll make them sorry they ever took us on, right?" There was a cheer from the bunks around him.

Van Meer shrank back into the shadows. Harris sounded like a coach in the locker room at halftime. Or maybe more like a throwback to World War II, a latter-day Mush Morton, the idol of his crew.

And the crew, particularly the ops, were manic: They had struck the first blow.

But underneath it all, van Meer could sense the worry and the fear. They knew what was coming; they could go to sleep this watch and wake up to find family and friends had vanished. Then it would be time to launch the missiles and their turn to die.

He turned abruptly and went to sick bay. Schulman had broken out a fifth from medical stores and was pouring himself a shot, neat. His hand was trembling.

"I saw you in the shadows, Van—you stayed longer than I did. My God, did you hear the man? He's not going to wait much longer, whether the launch order is on the tape or not. If he doesn't get it, he's going to assume the top brass were wiped out and launch on his own."

Van Meer took the offered shot and squatted on the little examination stool against the bulkhead. "Dritz is in the equipment room. We won't be able to get close to the Fathometer. He's going to tear apart everything he's got and put it back together again."

Schulman blinked, looking almost sick with strain. "What the hell are we going to do?"

Van Meer shook his head, trying to fight off panic and despair. "Just what we're doing, Abe. I'll have to trace the cabling farther back—or else just wait. Dritz has to sleep sometime."

"He can always start something and tell Russo to finish it."

"We'll have to take our chances." He drained the shot and reached for the bottle to pour himself another, then realized he could probably drink the whole bottle and nothing would happen, that he was too keyed up for it to affect him. "The crew's hot to launch—at least most of them."

Schulman wiped at his sweaty forehead with a dirty handkerchief. "I don't know if they're that anxious. Some of it's probably a reaction to prevent themselves from feeling paralyzed. It was something the brass didn't consider when they thought up the drill. Under normal circumstances the world wouldn't be going to hell all at once. There'd be a buildup over a period of weeks or months. You'd have a chance to get used to the idea. But this crew hasn't had a chance. They've seen everything collapse in a matter of days."

"There're a lot of things the brass didn't take into consideration," van Meer said bitterly. He stood up to go.

"The crew's probably split pretty much in two, Van." Schulman was kneading his knuckles now and leaning forward in his chair, intent on what he was saying. Van Meer had the feeling that Schulman didn't want him to leave, that once he did so the doctor would be left alone with his fears and his thoughts and he couldn't face them. "There are those who are gung-ho because they really feel that way or think it's appropriate. And then there are probably some who can't deal with what they're going to have to do in a day or two."

At the hatch, van Meer turned and looked at the haggard doctor. "When's the last time you got a good night's sleep, Doc?"

Schulman smiled wanly. "Who can sleep, Van?"

Two doors away from his own compartment, van Meer noticed that the door to Okamoto's was slightly ajar and light was streaming from the opening into the dimly lit passageway. The light kept winking on and off as if it were a lantern swaying back and forth.

But the *Alaska* was rock-steady; she was sitting quietly on the bottom.

He hesitated, then knocked on the door. There was no answer and he could feel the hair on the back of his neck start to prickle. He pushed open the door and stood stock-still, watching the body as it swung slowly back and forth. Okamoto had looped his belt around a pipe that ran close to the overhead, then had kicked away the chair he had stood on.

Van Meer stared, frozen, then yanked the chair upright and jumped up on it. He lifted Okamoto with one arm around his waist and fumbled in his own pocket for a penknife. He sawed frantically at the leather and a moment later lowered Okamoto to the deck.

He started to call for help, then took another look at Okamoto's face and let the words die in his throat. Okamoto hadn't broken his neck. He had slowly strangled. It was a low ceiling and Chips had been fairly tall but not quite tall enough. Another inch and the weapons officer would still be alive.

Van Meer leaned against the bulkhead, suddenly sick at the sight and the smell. Chips had belonged to Schulman's second group. The group that not only couldn't stand what had been done but couldn't face what they had to do.

Then: *How long had he stood in the hatchway, doing nothing?*

49

A MASS OF cool air was moving in from the northeast. Now it touched the humid air rising from the Atlantic and loose tatters of mist condensed, coalesced, and drifted across the surface of the ocean. The low sun cut through the growing banks of mist and turned them into clouds of gleaming vapor.

On the cruiser *Halsey* Captain Aaron Oscodar lowered his glasses and murmured, "Visibility's down to a hundred yards."

"Shall I cut speed, Captain?" Commander Downs was at his elbow, a shade too eager, almost obsequious. His manner irritated Oscodar, especially in view of the fact that Downs had recently requested a transfer.

"No, Mr. Downs," Oscodar sighed. "If the Soviet trawler beats us to the *Zhukov*, there'll be hell to pay—and you know it." Out of the corner of his eye he caught the helmsman suppressing a smile, stared the man down, and turned to peer out at the streamers of mist. The *Halsey* broke through one leg of vapor and raced across the bright sea, its bow slicing the water and throwing it to either side in streams of froth. They were doing close to thirty-five knots, Oscodar estimated. The *Hornet* was too far away to beat the trawler; it was up to them. They had picked up the *Zhukov* on radar minutes ago but the fog was still too thick for a visual sighting.

The bridge intercom suddenly blurted into life. "Bridge, this is radar. Vessel dead ahead—range two miles."

"Half speed, Mr. Downs." Oscodar strained his eyes but still couldn't see through the opalescent fog. He thumbed the bridge

"The Hornet's due east at a little over ten miles. There's a blip on the scope at forty that could be the trawler." There was a slight hesitation over the intercom. "It's making at least twenty-five knots."

"That's not an ordinary trawler," Downs offered brightly.

Why had he fought the transfer? Oscodar thought darkly. Downs's replacement couldn't help but be an improvement. . . .

"ETA on the trawler is estimated at an hour and a half," Radar volunteered.

They were breaking through the heavier mist now, cutting across bright expanses of water before knifing into another wall of vapor. The walls were thinner, however, scarcely half the length of the cruiser and more of an inconvenience than a real hazard to navigation.

"Target vessel just off the starboard bow," one of the lookouts announced a few minutes later.

Oscodar brought up his binoculars and swung around to starboard. The dark shape was half shrouded in thin mist but there was no mistaking the low, menacing silhouette.

"Quarter speed, Mr. Downs," Oscodar murmured. "Bring us alongside about five hundred yards and alert the flotation team."

The mist was starting to dissipate and he could make out small figures climbing out of the *Zhukov*'s forward hatch, still wreathed in threads of fog. Then he caught his breath. It wasn't fog—it was smoke. The *Zhukov* was on fire.

Downs had noticed it, too, and sniffed the air. "Electrical fire."

"She's riding low," Oscodar said slowly, putting down the glasses. "Probably shipping water. We'd better get the bags on her quickly."

Downs signaled the bosun and, moments later, the *Halsey* lowered two powerboats, each filled with frogmen. Oscodar watched the boats close with the *Zhukov* and the frogmen bail overboard.

"The blast from the torpedo must have blown all the water out of her tanks," Downs said.

Oscodar nodded, his irritation at Downs momentarily forgotten. "Judging by her list, she won't stay up long. We'll have to call the *Hornet* for floats."

Downs looked smug. "Already did so, Captain."

The intercom saved Oscodar from a sharp reply. "Aircraft due south, Captain. Contact imminent."

That would be the Sikorskys with the floats. Moments later, Oscodar heard the beat of the choppers and a Sikorsky Sea King cut its way through the ragged mists. Four more followed and hovered over the *Zhukov*, then dropped large orange bundles into the water.

The frogmen moved in quickly and shoved the bundles closer to the *Zhukov*, attaching some of them underneath the submarine and throwing lines for the others to sailors on deck. As Oscodar watched, the crewmen lashed them to any available anchor.

"They'd better get on the stick," Downs said nervously. "From the way the stern is sinking, she's taking on water fast."

At that moment the frogmen swam rapidly away from the sinking sub. A series of loud pops echoed over the water. The orange bundles suddenly ballooned, inflating to bright-orange sausages thirty feet long and eight feet in diameter. They wallowed in the water, sinking reluctantly under the weight of the *Zhukov*.

The frogmen now swarmed over the hull of the *Zhukov*. Several remained in the water, inflating the rafts they had towed with them. Smoke was still boiling from the afterhatch but even as Oscodar watched, it feathered and disappeared. The crewmen of the *Zhukov* and the American frogmen were now lifting green-clad figures out of the hatch, men obviously injured or overcome by smoke, and lowering them into the rafts.

"Mr. Downs, get a medic over there and alert sick bay. Who's the officer in charge of the boarding party?"

"Lieutenant Schwann, sir."

Downs disappeared and Oscodar went back to watching the scene around the *Zhukov* with the binoculars. The powerboats had moved back in and were being moored alongside the *Zhukov*. He recognized the short, squat figure of Schwann in his wet suit and arched his eyebrows as a bulky figure, clad, surprisingly, in white, appeared at the bridge on top of the sail. He seemed to be shouting at Schwann, occasionally shaking his fist. A moment later, Schwann jumped into a boat and picked up a walkie-talkie.

The bridge intercom broke in. "Lieutenant Schwann wants to talk to you, sir."

"Put him on."

Schwann's voice sounded tinny and excited over the inter-com. "Captain Polnykov wants to come aboard, sir." A short pause. "He's mad as hell."

Downs was back at Oscodar's elbow, sounding worried. "A number of his men are down in sick bay, Captain. Preventing him from coming on board might be misconstrued."

"I wouldn't dream of it," Oscodar said tightly. He scribbled a short message on a pad and handed it to the bridge messenger. "Tell the radio shack to get this off to the *Hornet* immediately, copies to ComSubLant and the CNO." He turned to Downs. "You'll be the official greeter, Mr. Downs. Show him to sick bay if he wants to see it first, then up here. The rest of the ship is re-stricted." He hesitated. "Have an armed guard standing by."

Downs continued to gape at the *Zhukov*, only a few hundred yards off. "This is really touchy, Captain," he said shaking his head. "One of our submarines attacking the *Zhukov*. . ."

Oscodar looked severe. "Did it now, Mr. Downs? Do you know that for a fact?" He glanced back at the *Zhukov*, where Lieutenant Schwann was helping the white-clad figure into the powerboat. The figure shook him off and jumped into the boat on his own. A moment later, the boat was heading back toward the *Halsey*. Oscodar walked to the other side of the bridge to watch Polnykov board while Downs hurried to greet the Soviet captain.

The powerboat bumped against the side of the *Halsey*. Schwann grabbed at the safety ropes on the ladder and climbed up, Polnykov following. At the top of the ladder, Schwann turned to salute the bridge. There was the shrill of the bosun's pipe and Polnykov stepped on board. He didn't bother to acknowledge the bridge or Downs's salute.

Arrogant bastard, Oscodar thought, and hoped that Wash-ington would reply immediately on guidelines for handling the captain. It was going to be a very sticky wicket, as the British would say.

There were footsteps on the ladder and Downs appeared, standing courteously to one side to make room for Polnykov. The Russian was a squat man, heavier even than Schwann. Oscodar noted the cold, fleshy face, the small eyes red with anger. The face of the enemy. Unsettling, to say the least. Schwann had followed behind him, as had the armed guard. Oscodar shot a glance at Schwann to have him wait, then turned and saluted Polnykov.

The Russian ignored the salute. "You are the captain?" His English was crisp and only faintly accented.

"Captain Aaron Oscodar. My pleasure to have you aboard, Captain Polnykov."

Polnykov's teeth glittered in a faint smile. Steel choppers, Oscodar thought. Appropriate. "Of course you would know my name. You would know whom you are hunting."

Oscodar allowed himself to look faintly surprised. "Lieutenant Schwann told me your name, Captain. But we would know the Soviet order of battle in any event."

Another show of teeth. "You use the right word. An attack on a peaceful vessel of the USSR does constitute battle."

"One of our vessels, Captain?"

Polnykov's face got redder. "You fence, Captain. Our means of identification are quite as good as yours. We had time enough—" He stopped abruptly, then: "Your vessel made an unprovoked attack on my ship with units of the American Navy deployed above to supplement the attack. This is certainly an act of war."

"I believe all vessels were warned away from this part of the ocean," Oscodar said softly. "You deliberately entered an area of U.S. naval operations despite those warnings. The consequences are regrettable but hardly our fault."

"The Atlantic is not an American lake," Polnykov rasped. "Your *Alaska*—"

Oscodar spotted a nervous radioman at the head of the ladder and turned away from Polnykov. "Excuse me, Captain." The radioman saluted and handed him the message flimsy. Oscodar scanned it quickly and hoped his shocked surprise didn't show on his face. He handed the carbon to Downs, putting the original in his tunic pocket. "Please take care of this, Mr. Downs," he murmured. "You and Lieutenant Schwann." He waved them off the bridge, hoping Downs wouldn't read the message until he was on the deck below.

He turned back to Polnykov, locking his hands behind his back. "Captain, we've helped your injured and saved your ship when it seemed in danger of sinking. I should think in a difficult situation like this we should put aside our differences and help each other." He looked sympathetic. "I'm sending over a damage-control party to help your crew salvage your vessel."

Polnykov's teeth showed in a steel-blue smile. "I do not need help. Help is on the way from my own people. You have kidnapped some of my crewmen, forcibly taking them aboard your ship."

Oscodar's face grew harder. "The ship's doctor tells me some of your men may die from smoke inhalation, Captain. If they don't, it's because of our efforts. I'm afraid if we hadn't helped, you would have lost them *and* your ship."

He walked to the other end of the bridge and poured two cups of coffee, offering one to Polnykov. The Soviet captain hesitated, then accepted it, cautiously sitting down when Oscodar motioned him to a seat.

"You mentioned the *Alaska*, Captain," Oscodar said. "Which suggests you were close enough to identify her signature." He hesitated politely. "Perhaps even stalking her?" He waved a hand at Polnykov's protest. "Both sides play chicken of the sea, Captain. I personally disapprove, of course." The helmsman was smiling again. "I thought perhaps you might want to make a statement regarding your encounter with the *Alaska*."

Polnykov looked thoughtful. "Your *Alaska* is something of a mystery. One wonders at this sudden deployment of surface vessels and the activity with your sonar buoys, which I thought was directed at my vessel."

"Just a simple statement," Oscodar said, persisting. "Something that presents the order of events as you see them."

Polnykov studied Oscodar shrewdly. "Your vessel is hardly down, not if she can launch torpedoes. And yet you are obviously looking for something." His eyes suddenly opened wide. "You have a rogue submarine."

It was Oscodar's turn to try to control his composure. Polnykov got up and helped himself to another cup of coffee, suddenly genial and almost smiling. "I wish all my men returned to my vessel, Captain—or to the trawler if the doctor on board thinks it important." He obviously considered this last a concession. "To keep them here is a provocation."

Oscodar couldn't let him leave, and now made the most important decision of his career. Oscodar gestured to the armed guard. "When the trawler arrives, we will tell them that we've offered you sanctuary, that you've defected."

Polnykov's cup crashed on the deck and for a moment Oscodar thought the man would leap at him. "What do you mean?" he roared.

"That you will remain on board until I receive orders to the contrary."

Polnykov took a step toward him, his fists doubled and the coffee dripping down his right pants leg, a dark streak on the white cloth. The armed guard stepped forward nervously but Oscodar waved him back.

"I am a Soviet officer and citizen," Polnykov roared again. "This is an act of war. When my superiors hear—"

"You'll be assigned quarters befitting your rank," Oscodar continued affably. "Your men will be transferred to your trawler. In the meantime, your superiors will be notified that you have asked for political asylum. You will be a guest on board, pending our government's decision."

Downs returned and Oscodar nodded at him. "Will you show the captain to his quarters, Commander?"

Polnykov glared, then turned stiffly and followed Downs, the armed guard trailing after them. Oscodar listened as they descended the ladder, then walked to the front of the bridge, looking out over the ocean to where the *Zhukov* wallowed, supported by the bright-orange floats. The powerboat was at its side again and Lieutenant Schwann was clambering aboard with six armed guards following him. Most of the crew of the *Zhukov* had been transferred to the *Halsey*. Oscodar didn't expect any opposition. And once more there was smoke coming from the afterhatch; Schwann and his men could very well be just a damage-control party instead of the search party that they actually were.

If it were really true that the *Alaska* had torpedoed the *Zhukov*, then Polnykov was correct and it was an act of war. And so was boarding her as Schwann was now doing.

Downs climbed up the ladder, his face pale. "I've put him in my compartment. I wouldn't let him see his men—afraid he'd get a message off." He bit his lip, then suddenly exploded, his eyes wide. "My *God*, Captain, this is insanity "

Oscodar pulled the message flimsy from his tunic pocket and read it again. It was from Captain Allard Renslow, a name he knew only vaguely, but countersigned by ComSubLant and the CNO.

"For once, Mr. Downs," Oscodar said slowly, "I'm in complete agreement."

50

OKAMOTO'S DEATH STUNNED the crew. Within an hour, however, a rumor was circulating that Chips's suicide had actually been a cleverly disguised murder. A Soviet agent on board had somehow arranged it to prevent the launch. The body was wrapped in a plastic mattress cover, laced in canvas, and placed in a corner of the vegetable reefer for burial at sea or at Charleston later. Harris delivered a short sermon in a crowded crew's mess.

"He gave his life for his country as surely as if he had been killed by an enemy shell. But they won't succeed. *They won't succeed.* Chips didn't die in vain. A little of him lives in all of us who are willing to die for our country." There was a minor stir at that, then Leggett sang, in a surprisingly moving way, the Navy hymn, followed by a minute of silent prayer. Okamoto's body would be consigned to the sea the next time they surfaced, van Meer thought, but that might not be for days. And maybe not at all.

The next watch, van Meer asked Olson to see him in his compartment. Costanza had the duty, though Schulman was there, sitting quietly on the lower bunk. Olson came in and van Meer motioned to him to close and lock the door. He did so and van Meer waved him to a chair.

Olson glanced at Schulman, then back at van Meer, slightly apprehensive. "Something wrong, Commander?"

"How long have you known me, Ray?" van Meer asked grimly.

Olson looked relieved. "Five, six years now. I was on the old *Tecumseh* when you were assigned as weapons officer. We came to the *Alaska* together."

"Have I ever lied to you?"

Olson shook his head. "No, sir." A tinge of formality crept into his voice.

"I'm not lying to you now, either," van Meer said. His eyes didn't leave Olson's. A lot depended on whether or not he could convince Olson of what was actually happening. "There's no war about to break out, Ray. All the messages and alerts have been faked. All of this has been a drill."

Olson stared at him for a long moment. He was still in cutoffs and go-ahead shoes, the sweatband tight around his forehead. His dirty-blond beard and mustache gave him the appearance of an aging, skinny Viking. He finally looked away.

"I think you've gone around the bend, Commander."

He stood up to leave and van Meer said sharply, "Sit down, Olson." It was more of a command than a request and Olson sat down, looking uneasily at Schulman again.

Schulman nodded confirmation. "The commander is correct, Ray. It's been a drill and you've been part of it. It's also gotten out of hand."

The play of emotions on Olson's face was complex, but among them van Meer thought he detected a sudden hopefulness, a desperate wish that van Meer was right.

"Ray," van Meer said again, "do you remember a Tuesday, a week before the *Alaska* left New London? Do you remember your special assignment?"

Olson nodded and van Meer started to fill in from that Tuesday on: the nature of the drill, the tape recorder, the messages, the growing realization that something had gone dreadfully wrong. Half an hour later, a dubious Olson was still shaking his head.

"I want to believe—*Jesus*, I want to believe." He hit his leg with his fist, then looked up, shaking his head. "But you've got to prove it to me, Commander. It's your word against everything that's happened so far and I don't know whether what you're telling me is true or if you've just cracked under the strain."

"I can prove it to you," van Meer said with a confidence he didn't feel. "But in the meantime you'll have to keep your mouth shut. Doc and I could end up in irons—or worse."

Olson shrugged. "Nothing's going to change if I forget you said any of this."

After he left, Schulman said thoughtfully, "He wasn't a dead loss, Van. He realizes that everything happened much too fast, that it lacks the logic of a buildup. And a lot of the men will probably want to believe it's a drill, desperately want to believe it. But we'll have to be lucky. Some external event will have to prove you're right. And we run the risk that some of them won't be able to be convinced. They'll think we're traitors."

He didn't have a charisma of a leader, van Meer thought. He didn't have the glamor or the strength of Harris. And sooner or later, it would come down to which one of them the crew wanted to believe. He'd need help then, a lot of it.

Messier was much easier. Maybe it was his innate cynicism; maybe it was his refusal to believe in either God or man that left him open to alternatives. Or maybe, as van Meer had speculated earlier, he was naturally immune to . . . whatever it was. His only reaction was to look thoughtful, nod, and say, "I thought that Tuesday was strange." He had been suspicious all along and seemed oddly pleased that he had been right. At the door he said, "Let me know what you want me to do."

Udall, on the other hand, was surprisingly difficult. He shook his head at the end of van Meer's recital, looking at him with a certain amount of pity. "The *Zhukov* was real, Van."

"It was chicken of the sea, Jeff. It was just a little closer than usual, that's all."

Udall shook his head again. "Look, Van, you don't have real proof of any kind. We've gotten the dispatches; we know the *Zhukov* was trailing us; we know there's been a concentration of ships above us—"

"I've explained all that," van Meer cut in tightly.

"It's your word against the facts, Van."

"It would be my word, too," Schulman said.

Udall turned to Schulman, openly hostile. "Why should I believe you any more than the commander, Doctor? At least I've shipped with Van before."

He was at the make-or-break point. "Jeff—"

Udall suddenly smiled and snapped his fingers. "You've been testing me. It's got to be that. I guess the captain can't be too careful."

Van Meer strained to keep a poker face. He'd been almost sure with Udall. And now he'd have to save the situation as best he could. He forced a smile. "You passed with flying colors, Jeff.

But do us a favor and don't mention this conversation, right?"

Udall was magnanimous. "Sure, I understand. I can keep my mouth shut."

After he had left, Schulman said, "We're going to have to be more careful whom we talk to."

Van Meer shrugged. "He gave us a way out. It's all a loyalty test if they don't believe us."

"And when the word gets back to Harris?"

"We'll have to move fast and live in hope."

The intercom on the desk lit up and he picked up the phone and listened for a moment, then glanced at his watch. "They want me in the control room. My guess is Harris is going to take her up again." He looked at Schulman hopefully. "It'll have to be up to you, Doc. Dritz should be sacked out. You know where the hacksaw is. The door to the equipment room can be locked, so you won't be interrupted. Russo's on mess-cook duty, so the chances are slim anyway."

He left a suddenly white-faced Schulman and headed for the control room. "We're taking her up," Harris grunted when he came in. "It's time for another contact."

When they got close to the surface, the tape would start up again, and this time it would be the beginning of the launch sequence. Van Meer tried to stall for time, to give Schulman a chance to cut the tape-deck cable.

"There were no sounds of breakup of the *Zhukov*. It's possible she's still out there, waiting for us to show ourselves."

Harris looked sardonic. "All right, Van—if you were captain, what would you do?"

"Maintain depth," van Meer said, finding it difficult to meet Harris' eyes and not flinch at what he saw there. "At least until we're well away from here."

Harris shook his head, smiling slightly. "You're not thinking, Van. Any breakup of the *Zhukov* could have been masked by the explosion. And we didn't stay around long enough to search for debris. But at the least she's probably seriously disabled." His face clouded. "In any event, our mission isn't to fight other submarines, Van."

Harris turned and walked over to Spencer. "Depth two hundred feet, Mr. Spencer."

"Two hundred feet, Captain."

Van Meer glanced surreptitiously at his watch. Another five minutes and Schulman should have cut the cable to the tape unit. There wouldn't be any message this time. He wiped away the sweat on his forehead and watched the depth gauge climb. They leveled off at two hundred and van Meer found himself holding his breath.

Weppler, the other radioman striker, brought in the message. His face was ashen. Harris read it quickly, than handed it to van Meer. There were just the code words "Bunker Hill," which meant the *Alaska*. Costanza came over and read the message over his shoulder. Decoded, it was a simple "Stand by" followed by "No time sequence." That meant the firing order could come at any time. They'd have to maintain depth and wait.

A few minutes later, the message was repeated.

Van Meer was sweating. Something had gone wrong. Maybe somebody had walked in on Schulman; maybe even now somebody was coming to the control room to report him to Harris.

He looked slowly around the silent compartment. Everybody was staring at him and Harris. They knew the contents of the message without being told. Van Meer could feel the sweat stinging his eyes and reached for a handkerchief. Even when he knew what was happening, he couldn't help but be caught up in the paranoia of the *Alaska*'s crew. And neither could anybody else, not Messier or Olson or Longstreet.

"Contacts, Captain. Too far away for signature."

Harris glanced at Olson at the sonar console, hesitated, then reluctantly ordered the *Alaska* back down to a thousand feet. But Harris wouldn't stay there long, van Meer thought.

He left the attack center and hurried to the equipment room, cursing to himself. The message shouldn't have come through at all. . . . He ran into Schulman in the passageway, walking back to sick bay. Van Meer told him about the message and Schulman looked blank. "What do you mean it came through, Van? I cut that cable minutes ago."

Van Meer grabbed the doctor by the shoulders and pinned him against the bulkhead. He was trembling, images of Maggie and Okamoto suddenly crowding in on him. It was too much of a disappointment, he was too exhausted, worn too thin. . . .

"It was the wrong cable," he said in a shaking voice. "You cut the wrong cable."

Friday, July 3

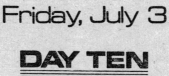

DAY TEN

51

THE BRIEFING ROOM was packed with reporters, the rear dominated by television cameramen. Leaks and rumors had served as appetizers, Renslow thought, but the press was going to be disappointed in the main course. He cleared his throat, read the brief statement in a loud voice, then settled back on his heels for the expected volley of questions.

A thin, lantern-jawed reporter in his thirties caught his eye among the roomful of waving arms and he nodded at him to speak.

"Jeff Spann of the *Post,* Commander. You've just read the official Navy version of the collision of one of our submarines with a Russian sub. Frankly, we all think there's more to the story than that. Just what was our submarine doing in those waters?"

"Routine patrol, Mr. Spann."

Spann looked skeptical. "Why won't you release the name of the submarine, Commander? Rumors are that it was the *Alaska,* yet earlier this week there were other rumors—that the *Alaska* had gone down and that a DSRV had been dispatched to help her."

"No one in the Navy has ever announced any problems with the *Alaska,* Mr. Spann." Renslow forced a thin smile. "If you would identify your sources, perhaps we could deal more realistically with their reports." A ripple of laughter washed across the room and Renslow felt a little more confident. "I can't verify the name of the vessel involved pending official reassurance of the relatives and the debriefing of the crew itself." He ignored Spann's frantic efforts to get in another question and pointed to a graying reporter on his left.

"How badly were the ships damaged?"

"As I just said, both ships are proceeding under their own

power. A Soviet trawler is lending all assistance to the Russian submarine."

Spann was on his feet again, shouting at the podium. "Is it true the Soviets have lodged a formal protest?"

"You'll have to ask State about that, Mr. Spann." Renslow closed the file folder in front of him. "I'm sorry, gentlemen. That's all I'm authorized to tell you." He stepped down from the podium, itching from the sweat trickling down his back and relieved that it was over.

Spann was waiting for him in the corridor outside. "Off the record, Commander, I understand the Soviet submarine is the *Zhukov* and the Navy is holding its captain."

Renslow looked at him coldly. "I won't dignify that by commenting on it, Mr. Spann. I'm not responsible for the rumors you hear." He shook Spann at a branching corridor, thinking, Security is a goddamned sieve. . . .

He found his car in the Pentagon parking lot and drove to Flag Plot, pushing the speed limit all the way. Cullinane was waiting for him in the Situation Room, slumped in a chair at the railing. He was frowning at the shimmering displays below as if for some reason they were withholding information from him. He glanced over his shoulder when Renslow came in.

"How'd it go?"

"Touchy. It'll brighten your day to know that we've still got a leak." Renslow pulled a chair over and sat down next to Cullinane. "A reporter named Spann knew about Polnykov before I even got there."

Cullinane looked sour. "He did a puff piece when Warden got the appointment a few months back. You can guess where the leak is." He went back to studying the displays. "I'm not so sure I approve of holding Polnykov."

For a moment Renslow was mesmerized by the shifting displays. There was still, he noted, no indication of the *Alaska*. "I told Oscodar to offer Polnykov every cooperation—unless Polnykov suspected the true nature of the situation aboard the *Alaska*. Apparently our Soviet friend put two and two together and Oscodar decided to hold him." He hesitated. "If there's any blame, Admiral, it's mine. But I don't think we had any other choice."

"The question is: Can we get away with it?"

Renslow smiled faintly. "It's probably one of the few things we can get away with. Polnykov's out of favor with the moderates. They don't trust him or his political sponsor. If he goes back now, screaming that we detained him against his will, they probably won't believe him. Give him a week to think it over and he'll ask for asylum on his own."

"I wish I could believe you." Cullinane stared at the busy floor, lost in thought for a moment. "Look at that—impressive as hell, isn't it? Ten years ago, it would have been impossible to build. But it's all window dressing, Commander. The really useful Flag Plots are smaller and scattered along both coasts. The politicians like the show and the glitter, though. And they want more. More situation rooms with flashing lights and computerized animation, more and fancier weapons. . . Did you ever see how excited civilians get at a weapons briefing? There's something almost erotic in the way they dwell on the megadeath potential of a new warhead."

Renslow couldn't remember seeing Cullinane this depressed. "It's not just the civilians."

Cullinane looked grim. "You've got a point. I remember the body counts in Vietnam."

Renslow felt vaguely disloyal. "Everybody's frightened of the Soviets."

"The Soviets are just as scared of us. We're unreliable, inconsistent. . . . Their hawks would probably like to solve the problem with a preemptive strike."

Cullinane was under heavy pressure, Renslow thought; he wouldn't be talking like this if he wasn't. "I imagine ours would, too."

"That's rather fascinatin', Admiral." Warden had entered silently and had obviously been listening for some moments. He smiled unctuously. "Forgive me if I find the professional view simplistic."

Cullinane didn't bother to turn around. "Simplistic? The Borgias probably thought so at one time or another."

"And the Borgias were among history's most successful politicians," Warden said lightly. "You're not much of a student of history, Admiral."

"I know the United States isn't exactly fifteenth-century Italy," Cullinane rasped, not bothering to conceal his rancor.

"Would you agree if I quoted Clemenceau when he said that

war is much too important to leave to the military?" Warden put down his briefcase and poured himself a cup of coffee, then stood at the railing and glanced at the fleeting symbols on the walls of the main floor. The room was thick with tension again and Renslow realized that all three of them were grappling with the reality of the *Alaska*, each in his own way. Warden took a noisy gulp of coffee, then turned to face him.

"This Captain Oscodar a friend of yours, Commander?"

Warden's voice was tighter, harder, without accent. Renslow was instantly wary. "I may have met him once. If so, I don't remember."

Warden sprawled back on one of the chairs at the rear of the room and made himself comfortable. His neck disappeared completely into his collar, so that his necktie now started immediately below his chins. He ought to be sitting on a lily pad, Renslow thought.

"Not necessarily criticizing, Commander, though you should've been polite enough to clear the decision through me as well as the CNO. You realize that if and when we return Polnykov, your Captain Oscodar will have to take the blame." He looked innocent. "We don't want another U-Two incident with the President caught with egg on his face."

"There wasn't much time," Renslow said grimly.

"There never seems to be for the tough decisions, does there, Commander?" Warden edged forward in his chair, his eyes suddenly hard and angry as he glared at both of them. "Do you realize—fully realize—what's happened? Both the *Zhukov* and the Soviet trawler reported the attack. Their radio transmissions were monitored. How much longer do you think it will be before the Russians discover that our most powerful weapons system is in the hands of a bunch of madmen? The Soviets are hopping mad right now. What do you think they'll do then?"

Cullinane admitted reluctantly, "We haven't located the *Alaska* yet. There's little that we can do."

"And what are your plans when you do locate her?"

"Dr. Hardin's drafted a special recall message. We also have a number of familygrams we can send that should convince the crew members they've been on a . . . drill."

"Too little and too late, Commander," Warden said with a sneer. "We've received sonar reports on the *Alaska* twice. We should have sunk her then and there." The words came out casually, as if Warden had given no special thought to them.

"Nobody's approved that course of action," Cullinane said in a ragged voice.

"Don't think the President and I haven't discussed it," Warden said threateningly. "If the Russians find out, they'll sink the *Alaska* themselves. Or worse." He stood up and tugged at his coat to straighten it over his bulging stomach. "You haven't received the message yet but you will. The Soviet ambassador is calling on the Secretary at two this afternoon. The Secretary wants both of you to be present."

He smiled affably at the door, once more the country squire. "I objected, of course . . . completely contrary to protocol. But it seems you still have friends in court."

Warden had just left when Lieutenant David Chavez appeared and nodded at Renslow. "Call for you on the scrambler circuit, sir."

Renslow took it in the communications room on the main floor. "Renslow here." He listened for a moment, then felt a sudden wave of relief. "I want a translation immediately. Divide it among translators if you have to but I want it in less than two hours."

He hung up. The Soviet ambassador was due for a small surprise. And so was Warden.

52

HARRIS KEPT THE *Alaska* a thousand feet down through the next watch, edging farther and farther away from the activity above. The next time he took it up, van Meer thought, the rest of the launch order would come through—unless either he or Schulman got back into the equipment room. But both Dritz and Russo were working there now. A transmitter had failed during a routine checkout and Dritz had finally found something to take his mind off what was happening.

Meanwhile, Van Meer enlarged the number of crew members he took into his confidence. To some he later said it had been a loyalty test; to others he talked earnestly in an effort to shake their beliefs.

But it was all "if." If he convinced enough members of the crew, if they stayed down, if he managed to disable the Fathometer and tape unit, if . . . He leaned against the bulkhead in the passageway to sick bay, suddenly exhausted, and tried to blot out Harris, the crew, the *Alaska* itself. . . . He stood there for a moment, his mind blank, then shifted slightly. His hand kept sliding down the greasy bulkhead. He took another purchase, aware that they were a thousand feet down and there'd be some condensation that would make the bulkheads slippery to the touch. But they weren't slippery inside his compartment. Or in the crew's mess.

He ran a finger over the surface. Almost like a film, not slick, not exactly oily, but . . . greasy. On impulse, he smelled the tip of his finger. A chemical odor, a faint, slightly acrid, almost pungent smell.

During the retrofit they had painted the passageways blue, he remembered. It had been a nice shade of blue, like a clear blue sky in late afternoon. He stroked the surface of the bulkhead with his finger once again. The paint must be decomposing, perhaps because of pressure and condensation. . . .

The paint.

The problem had to be either the food or the water—or the air. The crew could have been reacting to a gradual breakdown of the paint, which would release chemicals into the air. And now the decomposition seemed to be accelerating . . . and the crew would get worse.

He smiled wanly. It was all speculation; there was no proof. There might be a hundred different reasons for the crew's paranoia. And what could he do even if it was the paint? Stop breathing? Scrape the bulkheads? Tell Harris "I told you so"?

Maybe he'd check it out when they got back to Charleston. If and when they got back . . .

He went into sick bay. Schulman was sitting at his desk, on which he had up-ended the bottle of Equavil tablets. He was counting them swiftly, two by two, and dropping them back into the bottle. Van Meer closed the door behind him and Schulman glanced up over the top of his glasses. "Who have you convinced so far?"

"Messier, for sure. Possibly Olson. Maybe Moskowitz if I talk to him again. Some of the nukes—Longstreet, possibly Fuhrman and Baker."

Schulman finished counting the pills and capped the bottle. He stared into space a moment, silently mouthing the names van Meer had mentioned, then shook his head. "It's too weak, Van—way too weak. They're with you from wishful thinking, not because they're convinced you're right. We still need some external proof to help us."

Van Meer pointed at the bottle of Equavil. "What about those?"

Schulman grunted and put the bottle back in the safe. "There's nothing worse than a little hope, Van. Anything we tried vis-à-vis the entire crew would be too diluted. I could dream up some cock-and-bull story and prescribe them for some of the men leaning our way but the effects would take a while. And we don't have the time—"

They both heard it then: a thin scream from crew's berthing. They looked at each other and hit the passageway outside on the run. A crowd had gathered at the far end of the compartment by the time they got there and van Meer had to fight his way through. Crouched against the lockers were Clinger and Perez, the commissary man. Perez was clutching a thin paring knife. A few feet away, Longstreet, Baker, and Poletti were facing them. Baker, of all people, was in front, red-faced, his eyes blinking rapidly behind his glasses. The nukes versus the ops, van Meer thought; their thin tolerance for each other on board the *Alaska* had finally broken down. . . .

On the deck directly in front, Meslinsky was kneeling on top of Bailey. The slightly built auxiliary man was bleeding from a slash in his leg just below the bottom of his cutoffs. He was writhing desperately to get away from Meslinsky, who had one hand on his neck. Meslinsky's other hand held a hunting knife, already bloodied. There was a flurry at the edge of the silent crowd, then Olson burst through. He leaped for Meslinsky at the same time van Meer did.

"He's got a mouth—he's got a goddamned big mouth," Meslinsky was bellowing. Van Meer caught the fingers of the hand that held the knife and bent them back, then almost lost his grip when Meslinsky elbowed him in the stomach.

"Let him go, Animal. *Let him go.*"

He could hear Costanza, in the compartment now, yelling, "Break it up. Break it up. Everybody back to their stations."

The crowd started to thin and out of the corner of his eye, van Meer saw Perez slip the knife back into his pocket, silently mouthing something, his eyes never leaving Baker.

Meslinsky tried to elbow him again but his arm slipped on the bloody deck and van Meer slid around his back and got him in a hammerlock. Olson had grabbed his legs and Meslinsky couldn't get a purchase against the lockers and kick out. Meslinsky's fingers abruptly loosened. Bailey lay for a moment gasping for air, then scrambled away.

Meslinsky suddenly went limp. Van Meer let him go and sat up on the deck. Meslinsky turned his face to the lockers and started crying. The compartment was empty now except for van Meer, Schulman, and Meslinsky. Costanza and Olson were at the compartment hatch, turning away a few crewmen who wanted to get to their lockers.

"What happened, Animal?"

The big man found a seat on the bottom bunk and held his head between his hands for a moment. "The prick found out about my ex-wife. Why she filed for divorce." Van Meer waited, signaling Schulman with his eyes to keep quiet and let Animal talk. "We couldn't have kids," Meslinsky finished in a low voice. "It wasn't her fault; it was mine."

Bailey had been knifed but, of the two, Meslinsky had been the more seriously hurt, van Meer thought. He and Schulman helped Meslinsky to his feet. Then he said quietly, "You're confined to quarters, Animal, until we get the launch order."

Meslinsky shook him off. "I won't live long enough to lose another stripe, Commander. Neither will you or anybody else."

Schulman suddenly said, "Where the hell did Bailey go?"

Van Meer saw the small trail of bloody dots and smears on the tiled deck that disappeared at the hatch. Bailey must have run out of the compartment, scared out of his wits, but not so scared that he hadn't first bound his leg with something to stop the bleeding.

Back in the control room, Harris listened to van Meer's report with growing anger. "Both of them should have been at their stations. Why the hell weren't they?" He turned to Costanza. "Have the ship searched. When they find Bailey, bring him and Meslinsky to my compartment."

Harris turned back to the plotting table, motioning to van Meer to join him. "We have to get far enough away so we can get the birds off without interference, Van." He took up a pair of dividers and walked it across the chart. "I figure we'll come up about here." Van Meer studied the chart. They were creeping farther and farther away from the task force above, edging back to their original station. And they were also getting farther and farther away from the ships that must be looking for them.

A little later, Costanza returned, puzzled. "There's no sign of Bailey, Captain."

Harris stared at him. "It's a big ship but it's not that big." Van Meer caught a glimpse of Harris' hands at the side of the plotting table. The tendons were standing out like cables as Harris slowly pulled the dividers apart. "Take the search party and try again, Costanza."

Costanza caught something in Harris' voice and hastily left. Harris stared after him for a moment, then walked over to the sonar console. Olson's hands flew over the controls, adjusting the range. Olson suddenly tensed. "Small targets above, sir. May be destroyers."

Harris had just bent down to look at the display screen when the intercom chattered into life. "Man in the pump room, Captain." Pause. "He's got a flare pistol."

Bailey, van Meer thought. He must have hidden there. Harris didn't bother looking up from the screen. "Drag him out, Van."

Van Meer ran to the next level down, almost colliding with Schulman in the passageway. Schulman was carrying his black bag. "What the hell made him hide there?"

"Nobody goes there that much," van Meer muttered. The hatch to the small compartment just above the pump room was open. Costanza and Fuhrman were standing around the open access port. A steel ladder led down to the tiny room below, which held the IMO and trim pumps, the air compressor and blower, and Fuhrman's miniature machine shop. Van Meer could hear somebody in the room alternately swearing and crying.

"We tried talking him up," Costanza said. "I don't want to send a man down. With the flare pistol he's dangerous."

"You should have gone yourself," van Meer grunted. He grabbed a battle lantern off a nearby bulkhead and shoved his shoulders through the access port. Bailey was crouched at the bottom of the ladder, fifteen feet below, his eyes white with fear. The deep slash on his leg had begun to bleed again and the deck around the bottom of the ladder looked slippery with a mixture of condensation and blood.

"Come on up, Bailey—it can't be that bad."

"Fuck you, Commander. Animal's nuts—he'll kill me."

"You shouldn't have sounded off to him, Glenn," van Meer said quietly.

"You're not going to get me up there," Bailey screamed. He started babbling incoherently. Somebody tugged at van Meer's shirt and he backed out. Schulman brushed past him and started to climb through the port, one hand on the ladder and the other on his medical bag. "You're never going to get him out, Van. Let me talk to him."

Van Meer started to protest but the chubby doctor was already climbing down. Van Meer stuck his head back through the port, aiming the battle lantern so he could see Schulman bending

over the terrified Bailey at the bottom. There was a low murmur
of conversation, then Bailey screamed, "I'm not going." He and
Schulman suddenly became a struggling knot on the deck below.

Van Meer had already started down the ladder when Schulman said, "It's okay, Van—I'm sitting on him." There was a sudden "Screw you!" from Bailey and another brief struggle. Then a
tired-sounding Schulman said, "I've given him a shot. See if you
can help me hoist him out."

Halfway down the ladder, van Meer grabbed a dazed and
flaccid Bailey by the arm. He pulled while Schulman pushed from
below. Costanza leaned through the port above and grabbed Bailey. Van Meer pushed Bailey from beneath, climbing out after
him while Schulman went back down for his bag.

Bailey was groaning but seemed all right. Van Meer leaned
through the port again to shine the lantern on Schulman at the
bottom. The doctor's shirt and face were covered with blood.
"You okay, Doc?"

"It looks worse than it is," Schulman said. "Most of the blood
is his."

He started up the ladder, van Meer holding the lantern so
Schulman could see to get a grip on the slippery rungs. He was
panting and tired. Van Meer leaned through the hatch and held
out his hand. "Give me the bag, Doc. It'll make it easier."

The muffled *boom* and the sudden lurching of the *Alaska*
caught them both by surprise. Costanza said, "Oh, shit!" For a
moment van Meer thought the Soviets were depth-bombing
them. Then he realized that one of the destroyers was probably
dropping small depth charges, trying to locate the *Alaska* through
its sonic shadow.

He was backing out of the hatch, still clutching the bag, when
another charge went off, closer this time. The *Alaska* lurched
again and Schulman, who had just stuck his head out of the open
port, grabbed at the coaming, his sweaty, bloody hands trying
desperately for a grip. Van Meer dropped the medical bag and
grabbed for him but it was too late.

Schulman abruptly vanished, the look on his face one of faint
astonishment. He yelled and a moment later van Meer heard the
thud of his body striking the deck at the bottom of the ladder, fifteen feet below.

Van Meer jackknifed through the port, his hands on the sides of the ladder. His feet barely touched the rungs as he slid rather than climbed down to the bottom.

He felt for Schulman in the darkness. "You okay, Doc?" There wasn't any answer. He realized in a burst of panic that he couldn't hear the doctor breathing. Costanza was leaning through the port, shining the battle lantern down. Schulman was lying at van Meer's feet, facedown on the deck.

"C'mon, Doc, upsy-daisy." He rolled Schulman over. Then he stopped, still in a crouch, the breath whistling out between his teeth.

Schulman had tumbled in midair as he fell from the ladder. He had struck a small pipe jutting up from the deck at just the right angle.

The blow had caved in half of Schulman's skull.

53

WARDEN'S DRIVER PULLED into the basement of New State and drove to the bank of two elevators. Warden leaned forward and said, "Come back for me in an hour, y'hear?" One of the plainclothes guards opened the door for him and then he was in the cool interior of the elevator, being whisked to the seventh floor and the Secretary of State's offices.

Warden felt exhilarated. The shit was hitting the fan and in the corridors of power in capitals all over the world, soft-spoken men were making the decisions that would determine the destiny of the human race.

And he was in the thick of it.

The sweet taste of power . . . It was a greater high than you could ever find at the bottom of a bottle or the end of a needle. The ol' Georgia farm boy was breathin' a rarefied atmosphere these days, he thought. It had been a long climb and he had loved every bloody minute of it. Claw or be clawed. . . . That was the language he had understood since his barefoot days in his daddy's sorghum fields when he had first realized that God had singled him out for a special mission in the world. How right that early vision had been.

He walked briskly down the corridor, savoring the sound of his heels echoing on the parquet floor, and entered the Secretary's anteroom. Miss Hobbs, the Secretary's administrative assistant, glanced up and said, "Oh, Mr. Warden. The Secretary is in the conference room at the moment. Would you like to wait in his office?"

She was a good, solid worker, who had grown grayer and wiser during her years of service. He'd probably keep her around.

God knows she knew where a lot of bodies were buried. That could be helpful in the future.

"Why, thankee kindly," he said. He followed her through the imposing walnut doors to the Secretary's inner office.

"Please make yourself comfortable, Mr. Warden." She touched a button under a portrait of President Monroe and a small bar revolved into the room from its hidden niche in the wall. "Can I fix you something?"

He shook his head. "No, thankee, Miss Hobbs—much too early." As soon as she was gone he walked over to the bar and poured himself two fingers of sour-mash bourbon. No sense letting the world know his fondness for a nip during office hours. Such stories *did* get exaggerated in Washington. He came from a hard-drinking family and the stuff was like mother's milk to him. His enemies would make a great to-do about it if they knew. He'd had some trouble with such gossip during his period at the Yonkers Institute but that fool bluenose had lived to regret his wagging tongue. . . .

He turned and inspected the room. The deep leather chairs by the window, the heavy moiré silk drapes with their exquisitely constructed valances, the Secretary's desk, simple and rich-looking, its wood buffed by the touch of powerful hands over two centuries . . . He walked across the floor and ran a finger over the smooth top. It seemed to ooze history and power. Jack Kennedy had used the desk at one point in the Oval Office. Rosalynn Carter had found it in storage in Blair House and sent it over as a gift to New State and the Secretary's predecessor, once removed. Or so the story went. . . .

He walked around the desk and lowered himself into the great chair behind it. Who-ee, he thought, if the good ol' boys could see me now. Or the Fitzsimmons up on the hill in their great white house with all their nigra help. They'd never had time for the likes of him and even after he became board chairman of First Fidelity Bank, they had sent their lawyers to deal with him. Even when the bank had finally taken over the estate, old Fitzsimmons and his wife had locked themselves in the room upstairs and sent a cousin to handle the final details. Uppity bastards. Where were they now? Where was ol' nose-in-the-air Joshua Fitzsimmons? By God, *he* would never have taken *that* way out. But, then, he wasn't a "gentleman." He was something better. He was a survivor.

Good afternoon, Caleb," the Secretary said in a tired voice as he entered from the side door. "Trying it on for size?"

Warden flushed and quickly got up. "It did seem invitin'ly comfortable. I hope you don't mind my givin' it a try?" Then he frowned. The Secretary was trailed by Admiral Cullinane and Captain Renslow, who closed the door behind them. They were supposed to meet him here but for some reason they had gotten here early. What the hell had they been talking about with the Secretary? That was a bad combination but he had already marked those two for special attention once this operation was over.

The Secretary took the chair Warden had abandoned and leaned back, giving a small sigh. He took off his glasses and rubbed at the pinched spot on his nose. "No man in his right mind would want this office, Caleb," he said. Warden felt his face flushing still more. That was a cheap shot. . . . The Secretary didn't like him, of course. It had nothing to do with his being the potential successor. The Secretary would have to step down soon. His thin face, with the waxy, almost transparent skin, spoke of the silent inroads of his disease. . . .

But he resented Warden. He would much rather that his successor be one of his own kind. Ivy League, soft-spoken, and, above all—a gentleman. The Secretary hadn't been an outstanding success, perhaps because of these traits, Warden thought. He didn't understand the peasant surliness of Soviet diplomacy. He spoke as one gentleman to another, which was appreciated, perhaps, by Gorki, the Soviet ambassador, but was undoubtedly considered a sign of weakness by Gorki's tougher-minded superiors.

Well, he knew how to handle the Russkies. Like one ol' boy to another. Smile and then show some knuckles and they'd back off, all right. . . . Only that wouldn't be enough now. The problem had dragged out for decades. It had to be solved once and for all before Americans could consider themselves secure.

It was a Divine Mandate. Hadn't Providence preserved the American experiment and made it prosper and flower into the one truly democratic system? A system in which a man of humble origins like himself could aspire to the very top? God grant him the chance, he wouldn't muff it. It took only one man with the power, one man with the exciting vision of the ultimate destiny the Creator had decreed for the world. It was obvious to all who cared to look: The Almighty in His Infinite Wisdom had created America with its Christian way of life to supersede the tired old orders of the world. It was a mission that Warden saw clearly, and his work in the vineyard—as he often thought of it—excited him and filled his life with purpose.

They should have declared a Pax Americana in 1946, when American power was incontestable, when only America had the Bomb. But well-meaning fools like the Secretary had frittered away that God-given historical opportunity. . . . Warden looked at the tired old man in the chair much too large for him and thought, Just wait. I know how to fill that chair . . . and I know what to do. In the end, he knew that history would see him as the architect of a future that was the fruition of the American Dream.

"We have only a moment or two," the Secretary said. "The ambassador is always on time. Have there been any recent reports on the *Alaska*?"

Cullinane cleared his throat and Warden watched him warily. The old bastard was up to something; he could smell it. "We know the general area where she's likely to be. Following the present search pattern, we should be able to locate her within the next twelve hours. In the meantime, she may finally reestablish contact in response to our messages."

The Secretary looked disappointed. "I wish I could be optimistic about that."

"When we find her, gentlemen," Warden interrupted, "we'll have to eliminate her right then and there. We don't have time for any other solutions."

"That's one hell of a solution," Renslow said angrily.

"It'll prove one thing, Captain," Warden said, drawing himself up. "It'll show the Russkies that we're capable of moving swiftly against an attacker."

The Secretary looked at him with angry amazement and had started to reply when there was a quiet knock on the door. At the Secretary's "Come in," Miss Hobbs entered and said, "The ambassador is here, Mr. Secretary."

The Secretary hesitated, as if he wanted to say something more to the men in the room, then shrugged and said, "All right, Miss Hobbs, show him in." Warden almost rubbed his hands to-

gether. He was glad he was sitting in. It would keep the Secretary
from giving away the store. He thought of protesting Cullinane's
and Renslow's presence once again but decided that this depar-
ture from protocol could only work to the Secretary's disadvantage later.

"Mr. Secretary," the Soviet ambassador said as the door
closed behind him, "thank you for seeing me so promptly." He
extended his hand as the Secretary rose, then noticed the others
in the room and frowned. "I was not aware you would have aides
present. What I have to say . . ."

Warden bridled at the word "aides." Gorki would learn soon
enough who held the real power here. His lips thinned as he did a
quick study of the ambassador. Thickly built in the shoulders and
stomach, with the sense of vitality that so many Slavs seemed to
have. A tough man, Warden decided. It would take toughness to
handle him.

"Please bear with me," the Secretary apologized. "Admiral
Cullinane and Captain Renslow are here because they have information that may bear upon our conversation. Mr. Warden is here
at the request of the President."

Gorki shrugged. "I *do* object, Mr. Secretary, but that is, of
course, for the record. I will proceed as if we were alone." He
smiled thinly. "We can, under the circumstances, dispense with
the social niceties?"

He took the seat the Secretary indicated, shifting the chair
slightly so his conversation included the others as well. "To get to
the point, my chargé d'affaires has delivered our formal protest to
your protocol section about the completely unprovoked attack
upon a People's Navy vessel by one of your undersea craft. I'm referring to the deliberate torpedoing of the submarine *Zhukov* by a
vessel we have tentatively identified as the *Alaska.*"

The Secretary started to say something and Warden leaned
forward in his chair to interrupt. "Tentatively?" He allowed himself a small chuckle. "I would have thought your detection systems were more capable than that."

Gorki looked silently at him until Warden could feel his face
start to flush. Why, the bastard was trying to stare him down.
"This is no laughing matter," Gorki said at last. "We are speaking
of an act of war."

He turned back to the Secretary, who said, "We have not yet

discussed who was the aggressor in this encounter. It should be fairly easy to establish that."

A note of harshness crept into Gorki's voice and Warden, one eyebrow raised, realized that the man was voicing personal outrage as well as presenting a political viewpoint.

"It has already been established to our satisfaction, Mr. Secretary. Not only has a vessel of the United States committed an unprovoked assault but your surface vessels appeared on the scene a short time later, unlawfully boarded a vessel of the USSR, and took its commander prisoner—all of this in clear violation of international law." He hesitated. "I personally am at a loss to understand the reasoning behind this."

"We regret the incident, of course," the Secretary said. Warden stirred uneasily at the physical weakness apparent in his voice. "I would like to point out that U.S. Navy vessels in the area immediately came to the resue of the *Zhukov* once she surfaced. There was every reason to believe that she was on fire and in serious danger of sinking. The men who boarded her were part of the damage-control parties we sent to help."

"My government cannot accept that," Gorki said coldly. "The *Zhukov* was perfectly capable of making any necessary repairs alone or with the help of one of our trawlers that arrived on the scene about an hour after your ships. We have a very capable navy, as you are well aware." He paused for effect. "We can, if necessary, defend our rights on the open seas."

The brazen son of a bitch, Warden thought. Surely the Secretary wouldn't let him get away with that. He had heard that Gorki was a jovial man, one of the more polished members of the Soviet diplomatic corps, but this man was behaving like a shoe-thumping Khrushchev. The godless bastards were all alike. You just couldn't afford to waffle before a man like that and the Secretary was clearly waffling. . . . He interrupted again.

"Mr. Ambassador, I'm sure the Secretary is refraining out of politeness from telling you that such childish threats have little effect here. But I'm not bound by such rules. Any more than you are, apparently."

Gorki colored, his voice becoming guttural. "This is the first time that a senior line officer has been kidnapped from his command. When do you plan to return Captain Polnykov?"

"We don't plan to return the captain," Warden said blandly.

"He has asked for and received political asylum." It hadn't been his idea but there was no way Gorki would know that. It would be politically advantageous for him to take the credit anyway.

"If you please, Mr. Warden," the Secretary interrupted, a sharp edge to his voice. Then, to Gorki: "What he says is true, Mr. Ambassador. Moreover, with reference to so-called acts of war on the high seas, we have been fortunate enough to acquire the log of the *Zhukov.*" He pulled open a side drawer in his desk and took out a sheaf of photocopies. "These are facsimiles of several of the more interesting pages from that log—the log is on the left, the translation on the right." He handed them to Gorki, who glanced through the pages quickly, his expression becoming darker.

"This is unheard of," Gorki said at last, his voice breaking with anger. "You acquire the classified log of a Soviet submarine under the most illegal of circumstances and turn not a hair at showing me the result."

Warden was stunned. What the hell was in the log? That was why Cullinane and Renslow were here. Somehow they had gotten hold of the log and gone to great pains to prevent him from finding out. Well, that was one he owed them and someday soon he would make them pay.

"As you can see," the Secretary continued in a thin voice, "the entry for May sixteenth reads 'Encounter with an American submarine over the Bermuda Rise at coordinates' such-and-such. Routine dispute over right-of-way decided in our favor. No official transmission.'"

Gorki hesitated, then: "What is this to me?"

There was not a surprising amount of steel in the Secretary's voice and Warden felt annoyed. Once again he was being left out of the deliberations. "Your Captain Polnykov is a dangerous man, Mr. Ambassador, a man with a brutal sense of humor. It was on May sixteenth that the American diesel submarine *Blowfin* was lost over the Bermuda Rise with all hands. Shall we discuss further these acts of war? I'm sure that any public airing of such charges would find your country's image somewhat blackened."

They hadn't told him, Warden thought angrily. They had a lever on the ambassador and they hadn't told him.

Gorki looked rattled. "Nevertheless, we shall demand a full inquiry into the *Alaska-Zhukov* affair."

"That you will have, I promise you," the Secretary said.

"You have, of course, recalled the *Alaska*," Gorki said. Warden caught a hidden barb in the question and was suddenly alert. Watch it, he almost cried out loud. He's laying a trap.

"The *Alaska* will be recalled in due course," Admiral Cullinane said.

"You are in touch with her?"

Admiral Cullinane did a masterful job of feigning surprise. "Of course."

Gorki let another long silence develop, then turned back to the Secretary. "Let me be frank. Our naval units in the area have observed unusual U.S. activity—the extensive sowing of sonar buoys, intensive air searches, repeated transmissions, both scrambled and in the clear, all of them apparently aimed at the *Alaska*."

The Secretary became chilly. "Military maneuvers are internal affairs, Mr. Ambassador. What you're describing is part of a prelaunch drill in which the *Alaska* is involved. You were warned two weeks ago of our intentions to conduct dummy test launches down the Atlantic range."

"It seems to us that the *Alaska* is moving farther and farther away from those waters," Gorki said slowly. "Our analysts are at a loss to determine exactly what is happening but the situation appears alarming."

It was the Secretary's turn to engage in a long silence. "You seem to be driving at something, Mr. Ambassador."

"Rumors have been circulated . . . obviously to alert us," Gorki said gravely. "It would appear the *Alaska* is involved in some operation intended to impress us and that the full details will eventually be leaked." The Secretary glanced ever so briefly at Warden, who reddened and thought, The fool—he knows the leaks themselves are all part of the drill. . . . Gorki swung around and was staring at Warden now. "We believe that the operation is the brainchild of Mr. Warden, which tells us a great deal, since we have read Mr. Warden's past policy writings with great interest."

"I'm merely an observer here," Warden said blandly. The crafty bastard. He was putting two and two together entirely too quickly.

"We believe you've lost contact with the *Alaska*," Gorki continued ominously. "That, indeed, the *Alaska* may be proceeding on her own on a completely unauthorized operation. The strategy groups of both our nations have long speculated on such a possibility and how it might be best countered. I can well imagine what your country would do if the situation were reversed."

"I can assure you that we are in contact with the *Alaska* and that no such situation exists," Cullinane said.

Gorki nodded. "As you wish, but your presence and Mr. Warden's argue against that. We must be assured that our suspicions are incorrect."

The Secretary looked bemused. "How do you propose we do that?"

"We need some visible assurance that all is well with your control of the *Alaska*, that she's not operating . . . independently. A recall or a surfacing and contact with one of your surface ships that could be observed by us should be sufficient." He hesitated. "The failure to implement such actions would force us to conclude something has gone wrong. The situation then would be unthinkable."

"I can assure you—"

Gorki held up a hand. "Please, Mr. Secretary, I wish I could believe you. You must understand me clearly. A failure to demonstrate that all is well with the *Alaska* would cause us to have grave doubts about our own safety, doubts that would be acted upon in an immediate and positive fashion."

Gorki rose and brushed at an imaginary spot on his lapel. "I don't believe there's anything further to be discussed. I shall be in contact with you about our Captain Polnykov." His eyelids lowered for a moment. "I understand your reasoning but he is not in such disfavor that he would defect and desert his rather large family." He started for the door, then stopped and turned back to the Secretary. He smiled wanly. "We have had some pleasant associations during my time in Washington and I have felt that between us we have helped make the world a little safer for both our peoples. I must tell you that my superiors believe Captain Polnykov is being detained because he has discovered something very alarming. My country views this with great concern, Mr. Secretary. I hope you can resolve our doubts very quickly."

"That son of a bitch," Warden said after the door had closed. "He's tryin' to bluff."

. The Secretary slowly shook his head, suddenly looking even smaller and weaker in his large chair. "He's not bluffing, Caleb. I know him. He's terribly frightened. And, gentlemen, so am I."

54

THEY WRAPPED SCHULMAN'S body in sheets and a plastic mattress cover and placed it beside Okamoto's in the ship's refrigerator. Harris decided that for reasons of morale there would be no funeral service. Van Meer paid his last respects crouching in the cold-storage compartment, trying to think of the right words to say. The only thing that came to mind was the image of the sea gull hovering in solitary splendor in the bright blue sky and then flapping majestically back to land. After that all he could think of was his cold hands and he left the compartment feeling vaguely guilty. Wherever Doc was now, it certainly wasn't *there*.

Five minutes later, over a cup of lukewarm coffee, he remembered the bottle of Equavil tablets. The tin in his wallet was empty; he had neglected to fill it when Schulman was counting the contents of the bottle. He immediately headed for sick bay. He knew where Doc kept the keys to his desk; the combination of the drug safe must be somewhere in it.

A poker-faced Leggett was sitting behind Doc's desk, acutely conscious of the power conferred on him by Harris.

"Something I can do for you, Commander?" His voice was bland, arrogant.

"Doc Schulman was holding a personal prescription for me," van Meer said curtly. "It's in the safe; it's got my name on it."

He knew before Leggett said anything that he was going to be given a hard time. "Uh, Commander, Captain Harris said no drugs were to be given out, period."

For a moment the desire to hit Leggett was overwhelming.

He had even cocked his fist when the intercom broke in: *"Commander van Meer, report to the radio shack on the double."*

They were rising toward the surface; he could tell by the angle of the deck. Harris was taking the *Alaska* up to two-hundred feet to wait for the rest of the launch signal. And, of course, it would be there.

Harris was in the radio shack with Costanza, Moskowitz, and Stroop. Dritz was at the on-line cryptoequipment, listening for any signals that might come in and watching the printer at his right.

Dritz suddenly tensed. "It's coming in now." There was a faint whir from the printer and the paper began to inch through. Harris bent forward to read it as van Meer leaned over his shoulder. The code words "Bunker Hill" followed by verification signals, then the message itself: "Stand by. Firing order to follow. No time sequence."

They looked at each other; van Meer could guess what was going through their minds. The last-minute negotiations above had failed.... The ultimatums, the sudden peace overtures, the groundswells for peace, and the mysterious comings and goings of VIPs ... All consigned now to the dustbin of diplomacy. The brief period of waiting for the other shoe to drop had passed. They wouldn't get the launch order until the last minute and when they did, it would mean that Soviet missiles were already airborne, that the first strike was on its way....

The message was repeating itself now. Suddenly Dritz tensed and frowned. "There's interference." He tore off his headphones. "For Christ's sake, something's coming in on voice radio."

Costanza looked shocked. "There's nothing within miles. Gertrude won't carry that far."

"They must have hit a sound channel," Dritz muttered.

It was van Meer who said, "Put it on the speakers."

Dritz flipped a switch and a tinny voice started coming over the radio-shack speaker; van Meer could hear an echo from the speaker in the control room, a few yards away.

"CNO to Alaska. Cancel drill. Surface and report. Operation Fire has been canceled. Surface and report."

Van Meer suddenly felt like laughing. One message more to go on the tape—only one more to go—and the cavalry had arrived in time. He felt weak and wanted to sit down somewhere;

the lack of sleep and the nervous tension were catching up with him. . . .

"They've compromised our frequencies," Harris said slowly. "They're trying to cancel orders to every ship in the fleet."

Stroop and Costanza looked confused, staring first at the loudspeaker and then at Harris.

The voice coming over the speaker sounded vaguely familiar to van Meer.

"Personal messages for members of Alaska crew follow."

"Renslow," Harris said, surprised, identifying the voice. "They must have gotten to him."

Somebody had compromised their frequencies . . . somebody had gotten to Renslow. . . . Harris wasn't going to believe any proof. Harris had committed himself. Then he thought suspiciously, How badly had Harris wanted war in the first place?

The voice was fading now. Van Meer guessed that a hovering chopper had lowered a transducer into the ocean nearby to broadcast the message and was now moving away. Maybe the task force had already pinpointed them.

His next thought was horrifying. If they didn't show themselves now, how far would their own task force go to prevent the completion of the drill? And what would the Russians do if they found the *Alaska* first?

He caught himself listening to the messages as they faded in and out. There was a pattern and at first he was shocked by the intimacy of some of them. Then he realized what was happening. . . . Whatever the content of the message, it was designed to convince the crew member that it had indeed originated with the sender.

All of them stressed that there was no war raging above, that things were much the same as before. . . .

There was a message to Cermak from his teenage son stating that he had been suspended from high school for drinking in the washroom; one for Meslinsky from Jenny, the girl who had told him to get lost, who now was claiming she was pregnant; one for Leggett from his wife about a friend trying to collect a gambling debt; a pathetic one for Okamoto mentioning the possibility of a divorce upon his return; one for Olson from his wife reminding him to take his pills. . . .

And finally one for Harris from Yvonne, his "State Department" date the night they had left New London, saying she had found his lighter with the Academy crest.

The intimate and the innocuous. But, for the most part, incidents the crew would have preferred to keep private. Only Harris, van Meer knew, would have known he had lost his lighter in Yvonne's bedroom. . . .

The transmission became fainter and faded completely. By now the *Alaska* must be on the very fringes of any search pattern that had developed. It had been a fluke that they had received the transmission at all.

A number of crew members had clustered at the radio-room door, staring in silence at Harris, who seemed lost in thought.

When the transmissions had faded, he glanced around and said casually, "Pretty convincing, weren't they?" There were a number of nods. "Most of you men don't remember the Battle of the Bulge in World War Two. German soldiers dressed in American uniforms infiltrated the rear. They looked the part; they even spoke English without an accent. They caused enough confusion to almost win the battle. And maybe even the war." He paused. "This is just the modern version, the Battle of the Bulge brought up to date. Remember, that was a *voice* message. You going to fall for it?" There was steel in his voice now. "We've received an official order—in code—to stand by and that's exactly what we're going to do."

He looked around at the silent men listening to him. His face radiated sincerity. "Add it up. The *Chicago* was crippled or sunk by the *Zhukov*. Then she tailed us and it was probably just luck that she didn't launch a SUBROC. We've been depth-bombed with one fatality that can be traced directly to it. We've also received a dozen transmissions indicating things are ready to blow any minute now—if they haven't already." He smiled again. "You want to believe a voice out of the blue?"

Events were against him, van Meer thought. The *Zhukov* had been all too real and it would be difficult, if not impossible, to make the crew believe the depth charges had been dropped in an attempt to locate the *Alaska* through her sonic shadow. And even if they did believe that, how could he convince them that it was the Americans and not the Russians who were trying to locate them? Although that probably wasn't true—not any longer.

There had been the familygrams but it would take a while for

the crew to realize they couldn't possibly have been faked in that
short a time. . . .

Harris picked up the coded launch message that had come
over the on-line cryptography machine. He thrust it at Moskowitz,
the acting weapons officer since Okamoto's death. "Do you authenticate this launch standby, Mr. Moskowitz?" Moskowitz hesitated only a fraction of a second; Costanza hesitated not at all.

He turned to van Meer and held the paper out to him. Harris'
eyes were blazing. "Do you authenticate this standby, Mr. van
Meer?"

"The personal messages—"

"Fuck the personal messages, Mr. van Meer. Answer the
question." Harris was shouting now, waving the message at him.
"*Do you authenticate this standby?*"

Van Meer glanced around the compartment. There was nobody there who would back him up. Not in front of the captain.
Then he caught a barely perceptible nod from Olson.

"Well, Mister?"

Harris was glaring, his eyes red from lack of sleep, his black
beard and mustache glistening with sweat in the overhead lights.

"I authenticate the standby," van Meer said quietly.

Harris stood there, frozen, the paper shaking slightly in his
hand. "*Thank* you, Mr. van Meer." He abruptly turned on his heel
and pushed through the crowd.

Later, in his compartment, van Meer noticed that the ringing
sensation in his ears was back. It had been one watch since he had
taken the last of the Equavil and already he could sense the shadows pressing in on him. And he would have slugged Leggett if he
hadn't been called to the radio shack. . . . He'd have to fight for
his sanity on his own. He'd have to remind himself constantly that
it was all a drill, that the world really wasn't out to get them. . . .

But that wasn't true anymore. Would their own Navy sink
them if that was the only way to prevent the *Alaska* from launching
its missiles? He knew the answer. And certainly the Russians
wouldn't hesitate.

What was the old joke? That anybody in modern society who
was paranoid had every right to be?

There was a knock at the door. He opened it. Olson glanced

swiftly around to make sure that nobody had seen him, then slipped in.

"The message from Edith," he said simply. "She's the only one who could have sent it." He shook his head, agonized. "And I can't believe the other transmissions were faked. But the captain had a point. . . ." His voice trailed off. Van Meer patiently went over the details of the drill, the missing day in the shipyard, the improbability of everything going to hell all at once. . . . And the depth charges that had been dropped. Did Olson think they were standard depth charges or the smaller, lighter charges designed for locating, not destroying, a submarine? Olson should know; he was on the sonar.

Another knock at the door interrupted him. When he opened it, Moskowitz entered, followed by Messier and Longstreet, with Scoma and Fuhrman bringing up the rear.

"Commander," Moskowitz said hesitantly, glancing at the others, "we've been talking."

"We think the familygrams are real," Scoma blurted out.

Longstreet was more hesitant. "Only we don't understand the standby order. It doesn't figure."

Van Meer repeated what he had told Olson. When he had finished, he paused, then said, with pain, "There's a task force overhead looking for us. If we don't show ourselves soon, when they do locate us, they'll probably try to sink us. And the Russians are looking, too." He saw the apprehension on their faces. "We have to take the ship," he said slowly, "before Harris launches any missiles. God help us and the world if we fail."

It was Longstreet who said, "And if you're wrong, you'll have delivered us into the hands of the enemy."

55

T HE AREA WHERE the sonobuoys had been sown was clearly visible on the display walls in the Situation Room. It would be impossible, Renslow thought, for the *Alaska* to leave the area without being detected. Cullinane and Warden were standing beside him, concentrating on the shimmering displays below. Warden finally pursed his lips, frowned, and gave up trying to decipher the changing symbols.

"How long's it been now that they've been playin' your taped message, Commander?"

Renslow had been wondering when Warden would bring that up. "A few hours."

"They're not goin' to come up, mark my words." Warden walked back to one of the Nelson chairs in the rear and settled down with a sigh. The displays no longer interested him.

Cullinane pressed the switch on the desk microphone. "I want a probability map of the area for six hundred miles around the present position of the *Zhukov*. When can you have it?"

The voice from the small speaker above the desk said, "In a few minutes—we've got a lot of data backed up."

"Make it fast."

Warden clasped his hands behind his head. "It's a lost cause, Admiral. Your Buck Rogers gadgets are about as valuable now as a Ouija board." He looked grim. "If they don't get your message, Admiral—or don't come up even if they do get it—then we've got to face the fact that the *Alaska*, the third most powerful force on the face of the earth, is completely out of control." He found a toothpick in his pocket and started chewing on it. "Sooner or later, Admiral, we're gonna have to send out that kill order."

"Ironic, isn't it?"Renslow said bitterly, turning away from the railing. "The whole purpose of the *Alaska* was to avert war. And now it may be the cause of one."

"Admiral, I've got your plot," the loudspeaker announced.

One of the walls below shimmered and moments later, an expanding nest of lines appeared, superimposed over the previous plot. The *Zhukov* was at the center of the nest of lines, which expanded outward, bulging to the south and constricting to the north.

Renslow looked puzzled and Cullinane explained. "Those are probability isopleths. They connect spots of equal probability—the high-probability lines are concentrated outward."

Warden rolled out of the Nelson chair and walked to the front of the bubble to get a better view. "Your best probability, Admiral, seems to be the blue one. And unless my eyes deceive me, that's a probability of only sixty-five percent." He shook his head wonderingly. "All those gadgets and no better than a sixty-five-percent chance you're gonna find the *Alaska* out there?"

"That probability line encloses a hell of a lot less ocean than we have been searching," Cullinane said angrily.

Warden laughed. "You're gonna put all your eggs in that little blue basket? Your confidence is mighty touchin', Admiral."

Behind them, the doors *whoosh*ed open and a messenger came in for Warden. "Priority call for you, sir."

Warden looked annoyed at having to leave the observation bubble. "Can't you give me a secure line up here?"

"Right away, sir." The messenger left and a moment later, the phone rang. Warden took it, turning his back to Renslow and Cullinane, and lowered his voice.

Renslow drew Cullinane over to the other side of the bubble. "I'm afraid I don't have much faith in the probability patterns, either, Admiral. Steve Harris, mad or sane, isn't going to be there."

"Why not? Given what we know about the torpedoing of the *Zhukov* and figuring the *Alaska*'s probable speed, plus the two contacts, that area of the ocean seems like the most logical place to search."

"I know. That's why he won't be there. He's got a top sonar crew; he has a general knowledge of where our sonobuoys have been sown; and he has a pretty good idea of what we must know."

Cullinane rubbed his jaw thoughtfully. "If you've got a better idea, Commander, let's not keep it a secret."

Renslow turned around to the railing and waved at the wall below. "There are certain areas of low probability—those areas immediately south of where the *Zhukov* was torpedoed. Harris knows they're points of low probability, too."

Cullinane studied the wall. "They're also rather far from the Eurasian land mass."

"With the range of the Trident missile, Harris doesn't have to be right on top of it. More importantly, would you expect him there?"

"No," Cullinane admitted. "I'd expect him to put as much distance between himself and the *Zhukov* as possible."

"And we have no surface units that far south," Renslow pointed out.

Cullinane sighed in frustration. "What you're really telling me is that we can't run a search operation from here. Somebody has to be on the scene." He looked away from the wall and studied Renslow. "You want to go, don't you?"

Renslow half smiled. "Desperately. But it's also the logical thing to do."

Cullinane turned back to the wall again, and Renslow could see him only in profile. "You'll be in charge but there's something you've got to remember. Other people run the country; other people make the top decisions. You have to trust that they make the right ones."

There was something in his voice that made Renslow say, "You'd better spell that out."

"It means," Cullinane said carefully, "that if the *Alaska* is located and won't surface, you can try to make her surface with conventional depth charges—blow the water out of her ballast tanks. But nobody's to launch a SUBROC attack without direct orders from Washington It would mean the death of the *Alaska* and everybody on her."

"You know I wouldn't do that," Renslow said, indignant.

"Unless you're ordered to do so," Cullinane said softly. "Then you'll have to."

Renslow suddenly felt very tired. "I understand."

"There's a Harrier two-seat trainer out at Dulles, fueling for a flight to the *Hornet.* Ever flown on a VTOL?" Renslow shook his head. "Get your gear together and get out there as fast as you can. I'll ask the CNO to detach the *Hornet* and some of her support craft."

"It's a hell of a gamble."

"I think you've read Harris correctly."

Renslow smiled slightly. "I never thought I'd be heading out to rescue Steve Harris."

Cullinane turned away from the wall, the expression on his face one of the saddest Renslow had ever seen. "Don't count yourself his savior too soon, Commander." His voice was strained. "You may be his executioner. His and everybody else's on board."

Behind them, Warden hung up the phone and cleared his throat. When he turned around, Renslow was startled. Warden looked gray. He moistened his lips, then: "That was the Secretary." His voice was strangely hesitant. "The Central Committee left Moscow in a body within the last hour, presumably headed for their main command post. Our satellites report unusual activity at Kapustin Yar, Omsk, at Tyuratam, and several other missile centers."

Neither Cullinane nor Renslow said anything. Warden fumbled for a cigarette, his hands shaking. "I'm suggesting to the President that if we locate the *Alaska*, we sink her immediately. And if we don't find her within the next twelve hours, I'm going to suggest we share our information with the Russians. Between the two of us, we should be able to get her."

"Why twelve hours?" Renslow asked.

"Gorki just delivered another message to us. The Russians demand tangible evidence within twelve hours that the *Alaska* has surfaced and joined the fleet—or has been destroyed."

Cullinane said, "An ultimatum?"

Warden tried for a smile. The effect was ghastly. "They weren't very polite."

56

BY PREARRANGEMENT, van Meer met Olson and the others in the corridor outside the radio-equipment room. He had tried earlier to get at the Fathometer again but both Dritz and Russo were working in the compartment now. There was no longer any choice. He passed the word and, half an hour later, was casually standing in the passageway, lighting a cigarette and waiting for the others to show. The blue bulkhead caught his eye and he touched it, then drew back his hand as if he had been burned. The surface was even more slippery than it had been before; another few days and he guessed the paint would begin to slough. It made him more uneasy.

Olson was the first to show. Van Meer asked nervously, "Did you get the keys?" Olson nodded. Messier and Longstreet drifted up, Longstreet brushing away the remains of the evening meal. He was excited. "How long's it been since there was a mutiny in the U.S. Navy?" he asked in a stage whisper.

Van Meer frowned and didn't answer. He was sweaty and starting to feel sick with anxiety. They'd have to raid the small-arms locker in the auxiliary machinery room, then locate Harris and place him under arrest. After that they'd have to take over the control room and bring the *Alaska* up. It would be Messier's job to handle the main propulsion compartment and the after control room. Moskowitz would take over the radio shack and send out their coordinates once they'd surfaced. After that all they'd have to do would be to hold things together until units of the task force got there.

It all seemed so simple. But there were a hundred things that could go wrong.

Dempsey, an engine man third, a small, compact man who

had been a high-school gymnast, was tearing apart a small motor generator in the machinery room. He looked up as van Meer came in and said without smiling, "Not long now, Commander, right?" Then the others crowded in after van Meer. Dempsey stared in surprise and said, "What's up?"

He didn't get a chance to say anything more. Longstreet grabbed him from behind and Fuhrman slugged him with both hands clasped together. Dempsey went down and, a minute later, was bound and gagged. They turned him with his face to the bulkhead so he couldn't see anything when he came to.

Olson knelt by the small-arms locker, sorting through his keys, his face tense and sweating. Something about his expression made van Meer think he was suffering from a lot more than just strain.

"You all right?"

Olson nodded. "Upset stomach. I'll be okay. First time I've been in a mutiny."

Then he had the lock off and the doors open. Van Meer started passing out revolvers and ammunition. Olson closed the locker and abruptly doubled up.

"What the hell's wrong, Ray?"

"Just sick, sick to my stomach," Olson mumbled. Then, with his eyes opened wide and in a more distant voice: "Jesus, my heart's going wild." He slumped back against van Meer. Alarmed, van Meer motioned to Messier. "Give me a hand—quick."

Messier panicked. "You got to leave him, Van—you can't stay here."

"Have to," van Meer muttered. Both Maggie and Chips were bright in his memory now. He could have saved Maggie, he thought. He might even have saved Chips. . . . He ripped open Olson's shirt and listened for his breathing. There wasn't any. Nor was there any pulse. He suddenly remembered the family-gram to Olson from his wife, reminding him to take his pills. What the hell had made him think he was the only one with a private prescription?

He quickly straddled Olson's body, tilted the head back, and breathed into his mouth with four quick breaths. Then he put the heel of his palm on Olson's sternum and pressed down . . . again . . . again. . . . Fifteen times, then he bent over to breathe in Olson's mouth again.

"Van . . ." Messier said, pleading.

He looked up. Only Messier and Longstreet were there; the others had disappeared. He shook his head. He couldn't leave. Longstreet looked as if he were about to cry. Van Meer leaned over to press down on Olson's sternum again. Press . . . again . . . again . . . He heard Dempsey moan and glanced over at him. They were alone now; both Longstreet and Messier had gone.

He was trying for the last time to revive Olson when a dry voice behind him said, "Don't bother, Van—he's dead."

He gave it up then and sat down on the deck. Harris was standing in the hatchway, Scoma and Fuhrman and the others crowding in behind him.

Harris shook his head. "You're too predictable, Van. I knew you'd try it sooner or later."

57

"FIFTEEN MINUTES, Commander."

Before Renslow could answer, Lieutenant Akadian's swarthy Armenian face withdrew and Renslow watched him trot briskly toward the fixed wing VTOL a hundred yards off across the field. Outside the holding shack, a night mist feathered the distant lights of the control tower. Renslow yawned and looked at his watch. It had taken him an hour to get to the field from the postmidnight meeting at Flag Plot. It was now a little after two and it would take three hours to reach the *Hornet*. After that, time would be at a premium. . . .

He yawned again and took another gulp of coffee, then put the cup down. He was jittery enough; the caffeine would only make him worse. There were shouts from the field and he turned to watch the ground crew service the Hawker Siddeley, gleaming dully under the lights. One of the best of the vertical/short take-off and landing jets, the Harrier could do more than seven-hundred miles an hour. If the pilot knew how important time was, Renslow thought, maybe he'd push it a little. . . .

"Ten minutes, Commander," the duty chief said. Renslow nodded and zipped up his borrowed flight suit. The phone rang and the chief answered in a bored voice, snapping alert when the party at the other end identified himself. "It's for you, Commander."

Over the phone, Admiral Cullinane sounded both tired and paternal. "The CNO has agreed to detach the *Hornet* and two support vessels. Make it good, Al."

"I'd better, Admiral."

Cullinane was hesitant now. "It's strictly against regulations but I've got someone on hold who wants to be patched in to you."

He didn't want to talk to her, not until it was all over. Then he realized he might never have another chance.

"Elizabeth?"

Her voice sounded distant and distorted. It was a bad connection, but there wouldn't be time to put the call through again.

"Father told me you had called."

"That's nice," he said inanely.

"I'm in Washington," she said.

Renslow felt a sudden chill and wanted to tell her to get out of the city, to get as far away from Washington as possible. Then he realized he'd have to explain and couldn't. He'd be sowing panic and perhaps it didn't make any difference anyway.

"There's a lot I want to tell you," he said suddenly. "But I can't right now."

"I'm going to stay here," she said, "until you get back."

The connection was getting worse. "You mean a lot to me," he said, afraid he'd be cut off.

". . and Howie says hello . . ."

The connection was lost then and the operator came on to offer a reconnect. But it was too late. Akadian had already thrust his head back in the holding shack.

"Better build a fire under it, Commander. Bad storm developing over the Atlantic."

Renslow hung up and raced across the concrete to climb the long red ladder into the rear cockpit. He buckled in, tightened the combined parachute, safety harness, and leg-restraint straps, then adjusted the equipment connectors and the oxygen and radio links.

There was a buzz in his headphones. "You all set?"

"Roger." Akadian talked to the tower for a moment, then quickly ran through the checkout list. A moment later, the Harrier shuddered to the deep rumble of its turbofan engine. Renslow could see Akadian pull back on the nozzle lever that adjusted the angle of thrust. Then he applied full power and the Harrier seemed to leap into the air. They couldn't have used up more than a hundred feet of runway, Renslow thought, startled.

The lights on the field faded below his line of sight as the Harrier accelerated through a steep climb. Through the canopy, Renslow could see the clouds boil past and then they were high in the night sky, leaving the lights of Washington behind them. A few minutes later, they were over the black streak of Chesapeake Bay and twenty minutes after that, they were flying above the Atlantic.

Renslow's headphones buzzed again. "You want to catch some shut-eye, Commander, go right ahead."

"I wish I could help you."

"This is a lot easier to fly than a chopper." Akadian chuckled, his voice sounding slightly tinny in the headphones. "Except in low-speed operation. Then it's as easy to crash it as it is to fly."

Once beyond the lights of the shoreline, Renslow dozed off, awakening briefly as heavy thermals shook the plane. The canopy was streaming water. He glanced forward at Akadian.

"Plan to climb above it?"

"We're doing that now. Just pray that things quiet down before refueling."

Renslow tried to doze off again but didn't succeed. He kept thinking back to the Academy and one-time classmate Stephen Harris. Maybe Cheryl had been right, that he'd hated Harris more than he had loved Elizabeth. Or had at the time, he thought wryly. Recent events had a way of putting things in perspective. But his mind kept going back to his Academy days, to the hazing by the upperclassmen, the tea dances, the ragging because he was from the wrong side of the tracks. . . . And always there had been Harris, *número uno* in his class. Maybe Harris had been good for him, like Hertz for Avis. He'd been forced to try harder.

Funny, the examination had been so long ago and was still clear in his mind. He hadn't cheated but he knew damned well a number of others had. . . .

And then: What the hell difference did it all make? But it did. Renslow was sleepy once again. Men lived their lives according to the small things that happened to them. The school exams, the smiles from strangers, the raises from their boss. The major things like earthquakes and floods they seldom worried about. . . .

When he awoke next, the Harrier was bucking violently. It took him a moment to realize they were coming in, preparing to land. He glanced out the canopy at a phosphorescent ocean tumbling beneath them. A light stabbed upward and they quickly sank toward the white X painted on the deck of the ship below.

Seconds later, they were down for refueling. Renslow, still

sleepy, could hear the crewmen around the plane and, after what seemed only seconds, felt the heavy surge of acceleration as the Harrier lifted. Heavy winds buffeted the plane and there was a moment of instability, then Akadian tipped the nose forward and they shot away from the ship.

Akadian glanced back at him with a grin and over the headphones said, "That's one I don't want to try again."

"Touch and go, man," Renslow yawned into his throat mike. "Just goddamned touch and go . . ."

The air was calm the next time Renslow awoke and light was streaming through the canopy. He squinted through gummy lids at the cottony expanse of clouds rising toward him, then the Harrier plunged through the layer.

"Touchdown in fifteen minutes," Akadian called back.

The Atlantic blazed below, reflecting back a thousand suns. There was a tiny speck on the surface that grew rapidly as Renslow watched. The *Hornet*, with two smaller specks that were her destroyer escorts. He looked beyond the *Hornet*, at the vast expanse of ocean that surrounded her. Somewhere beneath the surface, the *Alaska* was hiding, her captain still playing his part in a war that didn't exist. He'd have to find her.

Then he had to struggle with a rising tide of panic. There were so few hours left to do it in.

So little time . . .

58

ADMIRAL CULLINANE COUGHED and cleared his throat as he closed the folder before him. The air in the Flag Plot conference room was blue with smoke that spiraled upward toward the air-conditioning vent. At his frown, the communications yeoman who manned the console in the corner had increased the fan setting to HIGH. But both General Leeland, the Air Force Chief of Staff, and General Smythe of Army were puffing heavily on cigars, and Captain Oxley, sitting in the protection of Warden's shadow, was sucking nervously on a handsomely carved briar.

Cullinane turned slightly and waved at the wall behind him; the panels had been rolled back to reveal a back projection of the main display televised from the Situation Room.

"That's the latest update on the *Alaska,* gentlemen," he concluded. "I'm sorry I don't have more favorable information."

"I'll bet," Leeland said quietly.

Across from him, Warden had been nervously tapping his pencil, eraser end down, on the conference table. "What you took so long to tell us, Admiral, is that you have no idea of where the *Alaska* is and no real hope of locating her before she launches. Is that correct?"

Too many hard decisions were before them for him to waste emotion on anger. Cullinane pointed toward an area on the television display wall. "We have very real hopes of finding the *Alaska* within the perimeter outlined in blue, Mr. Warden."

"Very unreal hopes, I'm afraid," Warden said curtly.

"What I want to know is who dreamed up this harebrained scheme," Leeland said. He fixed on Warden, on the other side of the table. "Somebody from State, no doubt."

Admiral Howland kept a poker face. "There was the question of the credibility of our retaliatory stance."

"Bullshit," Leeland grunted. He rolled his cigar between thumb and forefinger while he talked. "SAC and three hundred Minutemen missiles in hardened sites should be credibility enough."

"You really believe that?" Warden said in a flat voice.

Leeland bit off the end of a new cigar and studied Warden for a moment. There had been rumors of confrontations in the past, and Cullinane could believe them—Leeland was making his dislike of Warden obvious. "Yes, I believe it, Mr. Warden."

"SAC bombers can be shot down, General." Warden was trying to browbeat Leeland as Warden had browbeat him, Cullinane thought. But with Leeland it wasn't going to work. "And missiles in hardened sites can be destroyed by direct hits. The Soviet missiles are far more accurate now than they were a few years back."

"I'm aware of Soviet missile capability, Mr. Warden."

Warden was sweating profusely and Cullinane wondered if the tension was getting to him. Or was he afraid that Operation Fire would finally be laid at his door?

"The President is awaiting your recommendations regarding the *Alaska*," Warden said.

Warden was pushing it too soon, Cullinane thought clinically. Something was bothering him; he was usually smoother than this.

"I know what the President expects, Mr. Warden," Admiral Howland said sharply. "I talk to him, too." He glanced down the table. "What's the alert readiness of our armed forces?"

"It will be twenty-four hours before we have a full alert of NATO ground forces," General Smythe said. He looked worried.

"What about intermediate-range missiles?"

"All on alert within the next hour, Admiral."

"They'll be sitting ducks for a first strike," Warden interrupted bitterly. There was a chilly silence and Warden made a show of glancing at his watch. "We don't have much time if we're going to evacuate Class A personnel to the Mount Weather national shelter. The President's helicopter is on standby to leave for Andrews Air Force Base. Kneecap's seven-forty-seven can loft with the President, his staff, and Cabinet personnel forty-five minutes after his arrival. Once in the air, control of all strategic operations will pass to Kneecap."

Leeland studied his cigar for a full five seconds, studiously ignoring Warden. "We have seventy-five percent of our SAC operational strength in the air right now. Thirty percent of our bomber force is already holding at its fail-safe point with air-to-air tankers within range so it can continue to hold for forty-eight hours. All hardened sites are on yellow alert as well as eighty percent of the mobiles."

Howland looked thoughtful. "What about satellites?"

"Eight Diamondbacks are within the sector where the *Alaska* was last spotted. Six of the Diamondbacks are maneuverable. We're moving them into intercept position with an operational window of twelve minutes."

It was Smythe's turn to interrupt. "I thought all the Diamondbacks were maneuverable?"

Leeland shrugged. "Two have exhausted their inboard propellant. We had to cover the Iranian general strike a month ago and there's been no chance to refuel them."

"Can the lasers on the Diamondbacks interdict the *Alaska*'s launch?" Howland suddenly asked.

Leeland shrugged. "Your guess is as good as mine. We've never had to take out a missile under full booster power. It's a lot different from a re-entry body, even a powered and maneuvering one."

Warden cleared his throat and once again Cullinane found himself studying the man. He was less nervous now and the soft features of his face seemed to have settled into concrete.

"We're straying from the point, gentlemen. Central Intelligence says that all members of the Politburo have disappeared and several major social and governmental functions have been canceled. Second-echelon civil servants are beginning to leave Moscow. I think we can assume that the Russians are bringing all their forces to red alert. Kapustin Yar, Tyuratam, the Smolensk sector—all launch installations are buttoned up tight. Right now we're looking down the barrel of a very large gun."

They were all staring at Warden now and Cullinane thought; He's trying to stampede us into something.

Admiral Howland said quietly, "I think all of us in this room understand the seriousness of the situation. But it won't help to panic."

Warden looked impatient. "I was only trying to impress the Joint Chiefs with the need for speedy decisions." He mopped at his forehead with the blue bandanna and Cullinane suddenly realized it wasn't for effect; Warden looked almost feverish. "We're running out of time in a situation where timing is everything."

Out of the corner of his eye, Cullinane saw the communications yeoman suddenly jerk alert and bend over the console. A message was quietly reeling up on heat-sensitive paper and not even the clatter of keys punctuated the sudden silence. The paper abruptly stopped and the yeoman ripped it out of the machine and handed it to Howland.

The admiral scanned it, smiled slightly, and looked down the table. "The *Hornet* reports two contacts that are definitely the *Alaska*. They haven't pinpointed her exact location but there's no doubt she's within their sector."

There were audible sighs of relief. Then Leeland said quietly, "Once they pinpoint her, gentlemen, I suggest the order to be given to sink the *Alaska*."

"We've got to give them the chance to contact the *Alaska*," Cullinane said. Even to him the words sounded as if they had been torn from him. "They can still stop the drill."

There was an embarrassed silence. Howland imperceptibly shook his head. "We know they're your men, Stew. Some of them are probably your personal friends. But it's a hundred and forty men against . . . millions. We don't have much choice." He turned to Smythe. "General?" A brusque nod.

Cullinane felt sick. Warden had won. He had wanted to sink the *Alaska* almost from the start. But it was for a different reason then: He had wanted to bury his own mistakes. . . .

"Mr. Warden?" Howland asked. It was strictly a formality but Warden had to be asked.

"I disagree," Warden said flatly. There was another sharp silence and Leeland put down his cigar and stared at him. Cullinane felt a brief surge of relief that quickly turned to deep unease. He knew Warden better than the others; he knew what the man was about to suggest.

"Your reasons, Mr. Warden?" Howland asked politely.

Warden stood up and Cullinane watched with fascination as he walked over to the image on the display wall.

"I disagree, Admiral, because it's no longer a viable alternative, although it may have been at one time. Now I think it might be a serious mistake—the *Alaska* is almost ten percent of our seaborne striking force. In any case, we no longer have a choice." He waved at the area of ocean outlined in blue on the display wall. "That's a smaller part of the ocean—but it's still enormous. We haven't pinpointed the *Alaska* and to think we're going to do so before she launches is wishful thinking."

Warden's face was shiny with perspiration, the front of his shirt stained with it. He turned away from the wall projection and faced them, a chubby little man suddenly far larger than life.

"I don't think we should delude ourselves. The *Alaska* is going to launch. And once she does, there are no alternatives left to us. We're not going to trade off targets. That might be a viable option when there's only one but not when there are four hundred. Even if there were only one—where the casualties could be limited to a million, say—it would be grossly immoral when there remained an obvious alternative."

The silence was longer this time. Then Leeland said, "We're waiting, Mr. Warden. I want to hear you say it."

"We're going to have that war," Warden said in a gritty voice, his face flushed and ugly. "We can't stop the *Alaska* from launching and once she does, the fat's in the fire for good. We're going to defend ourselves in any event. Why not take advantage of the one thing in our favor? We *know* what the *Alaska* is going to do. The Soviets are still speculating. Let's use that time. If we're going to have to attack sooner or later, why not sooner?"

Leeland had drawn back from the table as if he were looking at something disgusting. Smythe was frozen, stunned. Howland was frowning, as if he didn't quite believe what he was hearing.

Warden leaned toward them, his eyes glowing. "A preemptive strike, gentlemen. The Trident system has an accuracy the Soviets won't match for five years. With it we can get most of their sea and land-based missiles. It's a God-given opportunity that's been thrust upon us. In one clean wash of purifying flame we can wipe the world clean of these barbarians. The alternative is to take eighty million casualties and see the only true hope of the world reduced to rubble. The choice has been made for us—it would be immoral not to act upon it."

Cullinane stared at Warden, openmouthed. The man was raving mad. . . .

Howland stood up to face Warden. He towered above the chubby adviser by a good six inches and Warden suddenly seemed to shrink. Howland was aware of his stage presence, too, Cullinane thought.

"No," Howland said firmly. "And if the vote goes against me, I'll take it to the President. We've sworn as a nation never to strike first. I cannot and will not support that decision."

Smythe nodded silently and Leeland said, "We still have options. I propose the President open the hotline, ask the Soviets to help us intercept the *Alaska*'s missiles. Their killer satellites are effective. And in the few hours remaining, they might help us locate the *Alaska*."

"And if the Soviets launch first?" Warden demanded. His voice had turned shrill.

"Then we'll strike back with everything in our arsenal."

"I would have sunk the *Alaska* when we still had a chance," Warden shouted. "None of you were with me then—but you are now. Within a few hours you'll wish you had been with me on this one. We're using a weapon with first-strike capabilities in a second-strike system. It doesn't make sense; it's never made sense. We can alert the other Trident submarines at sea. With their warhead accuracy they'll wipe out the Russian hardened sites."

Howland started to gather up his papers. "We'll have to give the order to sink the *Alaska*, Stew. And we'll ask the President to contact the Soviets."

"My God, can't you see what you're doing?" Warden was almost in tears.

General Leeland was looking at Cullinane. "There's no other choice, Admiral. I'm damned sorry."

Cullinane scarcely heard him. He was staring at Warden, who seemed to have lost all control. His face was brick red and a heavy blue vein pounded in his temple. "You goddamned brass hats," he snarled. "You've seen the studies on first-strike losses. We've got them beat almost two to one. Don't you realize what will happen if we allow them to strike first?"

"If they do," Leeland said quietly, "SAC and our Tridents will still survive. They'll pay a terrible price."

"They'll pay practically nothing," Warden said fiercely. "We can eliminate ninety-eight percent of both Soviet sea and land capability if we want to. My God, do I have to spell it out? The Trident missiles are first-strike missiles—they always have been. That's why their accuracy was so essential. They're now zeroed in on the silos. If we let the Soviets strike first, then our Tridents will be shooting at empty holes in the ground. Can't you see that?"

Warden sank into his chair, white and shaking. Cullinane was still staring at him; the pudgy Warden looked weak and desperate. The others in the room were staring, too, with growing revulsion.

Then, for the first time, Cullinane understood what Operation Fire really had been about.

59

I T WAS GOING to be the Mad Hatter's tea party right from
the start, van Meer thought. A wild-eyed Meslinsky had been
assigned to guard him until Harris could have the crew's mess
set up as a courtroom. The final part of the launch order was expected but the last message had said, "no time sequence." Neither Harris nor anybody else could predict when the launch order
would be completed.

Animal watched him closely but didn't talk to him; occasionally he would frown, as if trying to figure something out, mumble
to himself, then shake his head and go back to staring at van
Meer. The big man seemed both afraid and hostile, at times spit-
ting on the deck and muttering, "Commie bastard."

It was an hour, maybe more, before Clinger knocked on the
door and opened it. "Let's go, Animal." He didn't look at van
Meer. Meslinsky grabbed van Meer's arm and dragged him into
the red-lit passageway filled with curious crew members.

Animal cleared a path and shoved van Meer into the mess
compartment. It smelled of sweat and stale food, and was jammed
to the bulkheads with crewmen stripped down to ragged cutoffs
and wearing untrimmed beards and mustaches. Men were crowded together on the benches and sitting on top of the tables and
clinging to the wire grill around the rec locker at the rear. There
were catcalls and shouts of "Hang the bastard!" Halfway through
the crowd, van Meer felt something wet sting his face. He turned
angrily toward the man who had spat on him. Meslinsky grabbed
his arm and dragged him forward.

Then he was facing Harris, sitting behind a table that had
been set up in front of the steam counter. MacGowan, Costanza,
and Udall sat on one side of him and Cermak and Stroop on the

other. MacGowan was obviously hostile; Stroop looked confused. Udall and Costanza were poker-faced and Cermak seemed embarrassed.

Harris rapped on the table with a mallet and the noise in the compartment abruptly stopped. He stood up to face van Meer, reading from a sheet of paper.

" 'You are accused of crimes against the *Alaska* and her crew and, by extension, against the United States of America. They include sabotage, failing to carry out orders, inciting to mutiny, and indirectly causing the death of Chief Raymond Olson.'" He paused, a sly look slipping over his face. " 'Furthermore, the court will seek to prove that you are, as suspected, a Soviet agent.'"

There was a roar from the crowd and Harris looked pleased. He waited until the noise died down. "How do you plead, Mr. van Meer?" The expression on his face was suddenly amiable, friendly. The change in personality was as abrupt as somebody throwing open a set of window blinds.

There would be no right answers. "Not guilty, I—"

"Speak up, Mr. van Meer." Then, without waiting for van Meer to repeat himself, Harris put his knuckles on the table and leaned forward, his face only a few inches from van Meer's. "What do you mean, 'not guilty'?" he roared. "We'll goddamn well *prove* you're guilty. First witness. The court calls Yeoman First Class Dominic Scoma."

Scoma came to the front. Meslinsky pushed van Meer over to a chair. Scoma was smirking and looking self-important. Van Meer guessed that he had been the one who had warned Harris of what was happening. Van Meer glanced at the crowd but at first didn't see any of the others who had been with him in the abortive mutiny. Maybe they were being held for trial later, then he guessed that only he was being tried, as an example. If you could call it a trial. Harris had thrown the Unified Code of Military Justice out the window; he hadn't even appointed defense counsel. *I'll be judge, I'll be jury. . . .*

Scoma detailed the formation of the mutiny. Leggett was next. Somewhere he had found a lab smock and was wearing it proudly—like a badge of office. He testified that van Meer obviously used drugs, that he had used the pretext of a prescription in an attempt to get into the drug safe. Leggett said he had inventoried the contents of the safe and found serious discrepancies between what Dr. Schulman had listed as being there and what he actually found.

Cermak had been frowning throughout most of the testimony and now objected. "We don't know that Van used any of those drugs. And he certainly couldn't have used them all. . . . "

Cermak wilted under Harris' sudden glare. "You're out of order, Mr. Cermak. The court isn't concerned with what the defendant did with them, only with the fact that he had access and most probably took them."

There were more catcalls from the crowd. Russo was next, to complain about being forced to trace cabling when the ship was on an alert. Then it was Longstreet's turn. He glanced several times at van Meer. On prodding from Harris, Longstreet told about the aborted mutiny and van Meer's insistence that what was happening to the *Alaska* was part of a drill.

The line of witnesses lengthened. Van Meer found himself ignoring the testimony and studying Harris. The man hated him, had always hated him, and he didn't know why. Harris had had everything going for him: money, background, what they used to call breeding . . . He had always been a top-flight officer, one who felt strong enough to say what he thought in military life and to do what he wanted in private life.

Maybe that's what had gone wrong, van Meer mused. As an officer, Harris had been too outspoken; he undoubtedly had made his share of enemies. And he had dabbled too long with the role of young-Navy-officer-about-town. Now he was too old to carry it off. Even if he married, the reputation of playboy would stick. The promotion list had come out . . . when? Last month? Harris had been passed over, which wasn't all that unusual, but friends must have warned him it might be permanent.

Harris could probably look forward to only a few more years of active duty as captain, then he would sail a desk in some backwater Navy bureau in Washington, with a chief who drank too much as his aide and a secretary who'd spend most of her time trying to get transferred to Mare Island so she could keep an eye on her boyfriend. . . .

Harris had lost his own future and probably resented him because he thought van Meer still had one, however dim.

Harris was summing up now, shouting and hammering on the table to emphasize his words ". . . and the defendant admitted to breaking radio silence to acknowledge a yellow alert, an act that could have given away our position to the enemy."

There was another chorus of catcalls and boos. The faces in the compartment struck van Meer as grotesque. Something was wrong with the lighting. Even as he watched, shadows were creeping in from the corners of the brilliantly lit compartment. The Equavil. He had gone without it for two watches now and was starting to slip. He wondered what the rest of the crew must be thinking, what they were seeing and feeling. . . .

There was sudden silence and van Meer realized that Harris had asked him something. Harris repeated the question. Did van Meer have anything to say for himself?

"You haven't appointed counsel for me," van Meer said.

Harris snickered and nudged Costanza in the ribs. "You don't need counsel, Mr. van Meer. From the testimony, you've done a great job of talking so far."

Somebody shouted, "Let him speak," and Harris frowned, then shrugged. "You've got the deck, Mr. van Meer. Better hurry it up, though; the rest of the launch order is due any minute."

Van Meer was starting to feel like the accused in a Stalin purge trial. He'd be glad to confess if only he knew what to confess to. . . . He cleared his throat and started talking, stammering at first, then surprising himself with his eloquence. He outlined the purpose of the drill, the "missing day" in the yard and what had been done, the improbability of everything going down the drain so soon, and finally the fact that all the messages and alerts they had received had actually been on an on-board tape.

Harris interrupted. "Who knew about your so-called tape?"

"You," van Meer said bluntly. "Myself and Dr. Schulman."

Harris nodded, clasping his hands behind his head. "Doc Schulman's dead. That leaves you and me. And I'm here to tell you that you're a liar." He waved a hand, scowling. "What the hell kind of proof do you have?"

It was the only break he was going to get. They had asked him, he didn't have to volunteer.

"The Fathometer in the equipment room. It's a standby unit; it's never used. Open it up and you'll find your tape deck."

There was a sharp silence, then McCune, who was sitting in the first row of benches, shouted, "No way. That's a sealed unit."

"Open it up," van Meer challenged.

Harris rapped the mallet again. "Court's adjourned and will

reconvene in the equipment room."

Van Meer and Harris and the rest of the court pushed into the small equipment compartment. Fuhrman arrived seconds later with a torch and a hood. For a moment van Meer was afraid that the heat from the torch would set the plastic tape inside afire, then he throttled his fears and watched as the machinist made an incision all around the face plate. Five minutes later, the plate was loose. Fuhrman snapped off the torch and lifted the plate away.

Van Meer stared in dismay. Inside were the standard circuit boards and scrolling device of a Fathometer. There were no reels of tape, no transport mechanism of a tape deck.

There was a murmur from the crowd in the passageway. Cermak and Udall looked both disappointed and angry. They had been hoping that he was right all along. Now he had deceived them, had dashed their sudden hopes that it had all been a bad dream, a drill.

"The personal messages. . ." He faltered.

". . .were faked," Harris finished succinctly. "We all know that." He shook his head, puzzled. "I don't know why you sold out. I can't figure it. What'd you hope to gain?" He seemed genuinely baffled.

They moved back to the mess compartment. Harris held a long, whispered conversation with the other judges, glancing every now and then at van Meer. Finally: "It's the decision of the court that the next time the *Alaska* surfaces, Lieutenant Commander Mark van Meer will be set adrift in a raft to fend for himself." He smiled. "We're being generous, Van. The penalty for mutiny in wartime is to be shot."

A sudden commotion in the back of the compartment interrupted him. The far fringes of the crowd parted as Dritz forced his way up front. "The rest of the launch order is coming in, Captain."

The crew scattered, hurrying to their battle stations. Harris stood up to leave, then turned back to van Meer. "Come on, Mr. van Meer. We're going to need you one more time."

60

I'LL ADMIT IT'S a long shot," Renslow said slowly, staring at the chart. "Nevertheless, the CNO has authorized us to try it for the next"—he glanced at his watch—"six hours."

Captain Andrews of the *Hornet* shook his head, frowning. "That's a hell of a lot of ocean to cover. The destroyers and the choppers can sow sonobuoys to hem in the area but all we've really done is stake out the boundaries of our haystack. It'll take a lot longer than eight hours to cover the area thoroughly. We can try to speed it up with choppers using dunking sonars."

Renslow felt beat and depressed. His short spell of sleep on board the Harrier had been fitful and he had gone two days before that with not much more than four hours of catnaps. "We'll be spreading ourselves thin but there's no helping it. I'm gambling that the *Alaska* will slowly move to waters south of this point"—he jabbed at the chart—"as she detects the movement of the main search body north."

Andrews studied the chart and nodded gravely. With a neatly trimmed beard that was now a salt-and-pepper gray, he looked more English than most English captains Renslow had met. "Our destroyer escorts are equipped with ASROC missiles and launchers," he said. "The submarines at the northern perimeter are equipped with SUBROCS." He hesitated, not looking at Renslow. "I suspect that this will eventually become a kill operation."

Renslow nodded without replying. He didn't want to think about that, at least not now. There would be time enough later.

"It's a shame," Andrews said. He didn't say it but Renslow knew he felt both uneasy and embarrassed to be around a captain who had been given orders to sink his own ship if he had to.

"We're concerned with locating her right now," Renslow

said curtly. "Any kill orders will come from Washington." He looked up at Andrews to emphasize the point. "You might pass that on to the destroyer captains.".

He finished briefing Andrews and they took the small personnel elevator to the *Hornet*'s flight deck. It was still early morning but the sun was hazy in the east and there was a chill, moist wind whipping across the deck. Renslow zipped up his flight jacket.

Andrews cast a critical look at the sky and said, "The front you came through is catching up to us. It'll be here around noon or so. We'll have to pull the choppers in then."

"They'll stay out as long as they have to," Renslow said in a firm voice.

Andrews raised an eyebrow and shrugged. "What happens if we don't locate the *Alaska* in this quadrant?"

Renslow stared out at the ocean a moment, intimidated by its immensity. The sudden downdraft of a rising Sea King tugged at his hair and he brushed absently at it.

"I don't want to think about that, Captain. And neither do you."

61

THE CODE WORDS "Bunker Hill" had come in by the time van Meer and the others got to the radio shack. What followed was a brief, coded message—"Launch missiles"—along with the necessary verification signals.

Harris turned to Moskowitz, his eyes glazed. "Get your arming key."

Moskowitz nodded and Harris pushed into the passageway to go to the safe in his own compartment, motioning to van Meer to follow. Meslinsky prodded him forward again and for the first time van Meer noticed the .45-caliber automatic stuck in the waistband of his cutoffs. He could try for it but Meslinsky would break his arm before he could grab the gun.

In his compartment, Harris knelt by the safe and dialed the combination to the outer door. Inside was an inner door with another combination lock. Harris stood up and moved away.

"Your turn, Van."

Van Meer held back. "I'm not going to be a party to the end of the world," he said in a husky voice. Meslinsky quickly stepped behind him and grabbed his right arm, forcing it up behind his back. Van Meer grunted in pain and dropped to his knees. A moment later, he felt the cold mouth of Meslinsky's automatic pressed against his temple.

"You're a goddamned traitor," Harris growled. "I ought to have you shot right now." He glanced at Costanza. "Have Fuhrman bring up the torch."

It took Fuhrman fifteen minutes to burn through the inner door. Harris pulled open a small drawer on the inside and took out the two arming keys, still in their plastic wrap. He turned to leave, saying to Meslinsky, "Bring him along."

Van Meer hung back in the passageway and Meslinsky jammed his fist in the middle of his back. He grunted and went down, was yanked to his feet, then pushed into the attack center. Harris had gone straight to the intercom.

"Now hear this. Now hear this. This is your captain speaking. Man battle stations missile. Man battle stations missile. Proceed to status two-SQ. This is not a drill. This is not a drill."

The battle alarm came on. Harris stepped over to the red command box to insert the keys. Without thinking, van Meer lunged forward. Meslinsky caught him in a hammerlock and dragged him back.

Harris opened the command box, inserted the two keys, and turned them. There was something peculiar about his eyes. Harris had looked at him as he turned around but there was no indication that he recognized him or had even seen him.

Harris flicked the intercom again. *"Weapons supervisor, the system is armed."*

It was the litany for destruction.

"Launch depth, Mr. Spencer."

The atmosphere in the control room was changing now, the feeling of tension, of madness, was suddenly gone. There were only the soft whispers from the machinery, and Harris' commands. The crew moved quickly, methodically, concentrating on the task at hand. Van Meer smiled sardonically. The final irony. The crew was performing exactly as they had been trained.

". . . navigation on the line . . ."

". . . engineering on the line . . ."

". . . all stations report manned for battle stations missile . . ."

". . . very well . . ."

". . .navigation is making a reset . . ."

". . . aye, aye . . ."

". . . we are putting a reset into the master . . ."

". . . very well . . ."

". . . all stations, navigation . . .time check . . . on the mark, thirteen-thirty-four . . . three . . . two . . . mark thirteen-thirty-four . . ."

". . . all stations have the time check, sir . . ."

". . . very well . . ."

Van Meer started to struggle. Meslinsky's arm clamped down

tighter. Harris noticed him then and said casually, "Take him below, Animal." Meslinsky forced van Meer's arm up higher and pushed him toward the hatch.

"... *set condition one-SQ* ..."

Van Meer's despair was total. In a very few minutes the *Alaska*'s missiles would be on their way.

62

Y NOON the dark mass of the approaching weather front had started to build on the radar. In the west a low-lying scud of clouds grew on the horizon. Negative reports from the two destroyer escorts and the submarines posted to picket duty came into the operations room with depressing regularity. There was still no sign of the *Alaska*. The transmissions from the air-sown sonobuoys were equally negative.

Renslow sagged back in his chair and stared at the operations chart on the table. A thin sheet of plastic had been pinned over it and a quartermaster was entering new data on its face. Search patterns had been drawn in grease pencil and Renslow kept coming back to them. Something was nagging him about the patterns but he wasn't sure what.

Andrews fished out a cigarette, lit it, and took a few puffs, then snuffed it out with a dozen others in the nearby ashtray. "We've only got a few more hours and then we're due to return to the main search area," he said quietly.

Renslow only half heard him, still staring at the chart. "We don't know when the *Alaska* will get its launch order," he mused.

Andrews shrugged. "We have to assume she received and ignored her recall."

Renslow gave him a sharp look, then realized that Andrews undoubtedly knew at least part of the story about the *Alaska*. Probably so did most of the captains in the search team. There would be hell to pay for the Navy when more of the details leaked out. It was a little too large for the Navy brass to retreat behind a "No comment" or to pull the "security" routine. A rogue submarine was too important a story for the press to pass up. . . .

But, then, he was assuming that they would find her before

she launched and that there would still be an America and a press to worry about such things.

"I want to see the search pattern from the air," he said.

Andrews glanced at him, startled, then looked compassionate. It was Renslow's ship and Renslow's friends were in the crew. "You'll have to hurry. The last wave's due to leave any minute."

Renslow found a flight jacket and helmet, and a few minutes later, he was on deck, bracing himself against the stiff wind that had blown up. One of the choppers was being serviced in the refueling area of the flight deck. A young pilot was standing nearby, talking to the deck officer. Every so often, he waved his hands and pointed to the west.

"That my pilot?"

Andrews nodded. "Lieutenant Epping. One of the best."

Renslow trotted over. Epping held out his hand. "You Commander Renslow?" A quick handshake. "I just got the message from the bridge." He smiled, showing a small gap between his two front teeth. He looked too young. If Epping had been wearing street clothes, he might have taken him for an undergraduate.

The fueling crew finished and dragged away their hoses. Renslow started to climb aboard, then hung back, inspecting the undercarriage of the helicopter. "You've had some armament changes."

The Sea King ordinarily carried two Mark 46 acoustic torpedoes along with its sonobuoys and chaff dispenser. Now, four Agile heat-seeking rockets were suspended from the bottom.

Epping had to shout to be heard above a chopper setting down nearby. "They're in case of company—you can never tell these days."

Renslow nodded and climbed in behind Talbot, the copilot. Epping started the engines, then suddenly cut them. He pointed out the windscreen, frowning. "Something's up."

Renslow craned around to look. Andrews was on the flight deck, hurrying toward them. Epping slid open the window and Andrews handed up a message flimsy. He looked unhappy. "Bad news, Commander."

Epping passed along the flimsy and Renslow quickly scanned it. It was signed by Cullinane and left no room for argument.

The *Alaska* was to be sunk as soon as she was located.

63

"*TURN FIRING circuit power on . . .*"

"*. . . supervisor, prepare to fire. . .*"

Meslinsky pushed van Meer down the ladder, holding his right arm high behind his back. Animal was taking him to the forward torpedo room, van Meer thought, his mind dulled with the pain in his shoulder and arm. It was too late to try to stop the launch now.

"*. . . all compartments, hold on countdown . . .*"

It had to be strictly a temporary hold. Van Meer noted that the passageway was clear of personnel—everybody was at battle stations. Without thinking, he dropped to his knees and whirled, wrenching his arm free from the surprised Meslinsky's grasp. He caught Meslinsky just below the knees and rolled, tucking Animal's legs beneath his own. The big man grunted and hit the deck, the .45 skittering across the tiles. Van Meer lunged for it. Meslinsky scrambled to his feet and caught van Meer's arm, yanking him back.

Instead of pulling away, van Meer went with the tug, bringing up his knee and knocking the air out of Meslinsky. He darted for the gun again and almost had it when Meslinsky grabbed his ankle. He fell full length on the tiled deck, his fingers clutching at the .45, now only inches away. Meslinsky dragged him closer, then momentarily loosened his grip to get a better purchase.

Van Meer kicked out, grabbed the gun, and rocked to his feet. He slugged Meslinsky behind the ear. The big man dropped to his knees, both hands going to his head, which showed an ugly bruise and torn skin. Blood oozed between his fingers.

He still hadn't said a word.

Van Meer raced down the passageway to the forward torpedo

room, an idea forming. He bolted in and skidded to a stop. The three crewmen at battle stations gaped. One of them started moving toward him.

Van Meer cocked the .45 and held it with both hands to take steady aim. He nodded toward a shelf of yellow dye markers. "The dye markers—launch one." His chest was heaving and he felt as if his words should be coming out in little puffs of steam.

The man who had started toward him paled. "That'll give away our position."

"Launch one. *Now.*"

"He's a commie spy," one of the other men muttered. "Don't—"

Van Meer began to feel hysterical. *"Now. Do it."*

The crewman moved slowly to the rack of dye markers, glancing nervously at van Meer over his shoulder.

". . . *resume countdown* . . ."

". . . *firing order one* . . ."

The crewman had the dye marker now and was walking slowly toward the signal-ejector tube. Van Meer panicked. The man was stalling.

". . . *erection is completed on firing order one* . . ."

Van Meer straightened up. His voice was calm, brittle. "On the count of three, I'm going to kill you. One . . ."

The torpedo man slammed the dye marker into the ejector tube. A moment later, it was on its way to the surface.

". . . *muzzle hatch is locked open, tube is in automatic breathe* . . ."

Van Meer abruptly turned and bolted for the control compartment.

64

THE EARLY-AFTERNOON sun had become a dull yellow glow behind the layers of clouds that scudded in boiling ferment across the sky. There were still ragged patches of blue, Renslow noted, but these were becoming increasingly rare as the tattered cumuli slowly knit into a solid blanket. A sudden spatter of raindrops rattled across the windows.

They were going to have to go in soon. The Sea King was bucking in the sudden gusts of wind and the air itself felt thick and heavy. Below, the sea had become frosted with whitecaps. It was going to be a real blow, and a bad one. He squinted and glanced at the horizon, where the *Hornet* and its destroyer escorts were mere specks.

"We're going to have to head back in a few minutes," Epping said. "Flying a chopper in this weather is asking for it."

"I can think of other things I'd rather be doing," Talbot said nervously.

Renslow squinted again at the ocean below. By late afternoon the ships would be wallowing in high-running swells. By evening they'd be weathering a first-class storm. He looked at his wristwatch. A little after one-thirty.

"Let's see the navigation chart."

Epping handed it back. The sector they were patrolling, sector eight, was outlined in red felt pen. Renslow studied it. The display wall in Flag Plot was suddenly sharp in his mind, as was the chart on the table in the *Hornet*.

"Take her farther south."

Epping partly turned his head. "That'll take us out of our sector, Commander."

"Yeah, I know."

A sudden updraft seized the Sea King and she soared alarmingly. Renslow felt the acceleration pull at his stomach and tasted the harsh bite of acid in his mouth. It took him a moment to bring the motion nausea under control.

Up front, Epping fought the controls and the chopper slowly turned, the rotor blades slicing through mist streamers that curled down from an overhanging cloud bank. In the distance, another Sea King was riding heavy side winds near the weather front. It bucked and weaved in a sudden gust, then rose into the low clouds and was lost to sight for a second.

Their own Sea King started bucking again, one of the sonar technicians in back yelling in protest as the sudden maneuvers threw him against the bulkhead.

"This is crazy," Epping yelled.

"White Five is in trouble," Talbot shouted, pointing.

The other Sea King had appeared again. It seemed to wallow in the air, then plunged seaward, its rotor blades beating erratically. Epping pulled out a pair of binoculars and peered through them for a moment. "He's one lucky son of a bitch. Stabilized her before they hit the water."

They continued south for another ten minutes. "This about it, Commander?"

Renslow left his seat and held on to the back of Epping's to look through the windscreen for a better view. The Sea King bucked once again in the wind, then tilted, and the whole expanse of the ocean was spread out before them. Epping swore quietly and struggled with the controls; Renslow had to fight to keep from being thrown through the windscreen. The sun blazed through a rift in the clouds. The sea below looked like one huge sheet of beaten brass. . . .

Renslow suddenly caught his breath. "Give me your glasses." He almost tore them from around Epping's neck. It took only a moment to focus, then he had the distant splash of color in clear view.

He thumped Epping on the shoulder and the young lieutenant swung the chopper toward it. A few moments later, there wasn't any doubt.

"Christ, it's a dye marker," Epping said, his voice unsteady with excitement. "It's a submarine dye marker."

65

ONE-MINUTE standby . . ."

 "*. . . optical Charlie shift to remote control . . .*"

 Van Meer gripped the pistol tightly in his right hand and raced down the passageway. He skidded around a corner. Five feet away, Perez was walking toward him. The commissary man's eyes widened and he took a deep breath to yell. Van Meer stiff-armed him in the face and Perez went down, clutching at his mashed nose.

 "*. . . ten seconds and counting . . .*"

 Van Meer jolted to a stop at the hatchway to the control compartment. He waved the .45 and shouted, "*Stop—*"

 Somebody hit him from behind and he tripped over the coaming, the .45 flying across the deck. He tried to scramble for it but somebody was sitting on his back. To judge by the weight, it was probably Meslinsky. Animal must have followed him.

 Harris looked down at him with mild curiosity, then glanced up at the meters on the bulkhead to make sure that the *Alaska* was rock-steady for the launch.

 "*. . . eight . . . seven . . . six . . .*"

 "Stop it. For the love of God, it's only a drill." It sounded as if somebody else were saying the words then van Meer realized it was himself, screaming at Harris and Costanza and the others. He tried to lunge again for the .45. Somebody stepped on his hand.

 "It's too late," Harris said casually.

 "*. . . two . . . one . . . fire!*"

 There was a *thump* as the ocean poured into a suddenly deserted missile tube.

 "*. . . missile one away . . . missile one away . . .*"

66

THE RAIN WAS getting heavier, beating in sudden gusts against the side of the Sea King. Renslow found an auxiliary strap and fastened himself in his seat frame. Epping was too busy fighting the controls to notice. Talbot looked around once and gave Renslow a sickly grin. He was scared stiff. Epping's strain showed in the corded muscles of his neck. A heavy downdraft pulled the chopper sickeningly toward the sea below before releasing it.

"I'm taking her back to the *Hornet*," Epping yelled.

"No, you're not. Get me closer to that dye marker," Renslow ordered.

"Commander, you're crazy. You know that? You're roaring mad."

"If she gets away from us, you won't have to worry about getting back to the *Hornet*—ever," Renslow shouted.

The air was thickening around them but Renslow could still make out the dye marker ahead of them. He tapped Talbot on the shoulder.

"Radio the coordinates to the *Hornet*. Do an estimate if you have to. And ask for an acknowledgment."

They were five minutes away, maybe more, before they'd be over the exact position of the marker. But once the *Hornet* got the coordinates it would be all over. The tiny specks on the horizon would turn and race to the position he had given. The destroyers would close in and launch their ASROCS or maybe it would be a submarine with a SUBROC. In any event, that would be the end of the *Alaska*. A hundred and forty men, many of them close friends, would die.

And so, of course, would Stephen Harris.

Cullinane had been right after all. The admiral had known all along that he was sending him out as executioner. But Renslow couldn't blame Cullinane for that. He had asked for it.

They were closer now to the yellow smear that was spreading out from the dye marker. Suddenly Talbot shouted, "My God, look at that."

Several hundred yards away from the border of the yellow slash on the ocean's surface, the water heaved and boiled. A great bubble seemed to rise from the depths and churn itself into foam. In the next instant, an ominous, cone-shaped object cut the ocean's skin and hovered for an instant, fire erupting from its base. Clouds of steam billowed out over the surface of the water. The missile poised unmoving on its tail for what seemed endless seconds. Then it began to accelerate slowly. It gathered momentum and arced into the gray sky, disappearing into the low ceiling. Flames flickered through endless layers of clouds, gradually growing dimmer, then vanishing altogether.

"We're too late," Epping said in a flat voice.

Renslow stared at the clouds where the missile had disappeared, his mind momentarily blank.

He had just seen the start of World War III and he felt nothing, nothing at all.

67

"MISSILE TWO AWAY . . . *missile two away* . . ."

The men in the control compartment were frozen, their eyes fastened on the gauges and meters, their feet feeling the *thump* as the bird left its nest, their ears hearing nothing but the monotone voice on the intercom. Sweat glistened on their skin and dampened their T-shirts, running down Clinger's face, shining on the thin gold loop hanging from McCune's ear.

Van Meer stared steadily at Harris. There was a strange flicker of emotions on his face and van Meer guessed that memories were floating to the surface under the stress of the actual launching. But it was too late. The point of no return had been reached. The drill had become a horrifying reality. There would be no more waiting for the signal from SAC; no more worrying by the brass hats about brushfire wars; no more jockeying for position among the powers of the world, both great and small; no more speculating about who had the Bomb and who didn't. . . .

And no more worrying about the kids' teeth or the mortgage payment or how long you'd have to wait in line at the disco or whether or not you'd get laid that night.

By nightfall Paris would be a memory, London would lie in ruins, Moscow would be a fused plain and Manhattan a burned-out island with steel skeletons jutting up like so many stumps after a forest fire.

Harris shook his head, a trace of disgust on his face. "Quit struggling, mister. The Russians will range in on us in another fifteen minutes. That's all the time any of us have to live."

Van Meer lay on the deck, frozen, still staring at Harris but for the first time in days not thinking of the *Alaska* or the drill. How long had he stood at the edge of the clearing watching Maggie burn? Ten minutes? Fifteen? Her screams had gone on for-ever. . . . Suddenly he realized that Rosenberg's therapy could never have worked, that he could never have been convinced that he couldn't have saved her, that he had stood there for only sec-onds. Odd . . . The whole world was now going to die in the same length of time it had taken to snuff out a single human life. . . .

He summoned up strength he didn't know he had, coiling up on the deck and kicking out at Meslinsky. He caught Animal in the stomach with both feet and yanked free, diving over him into the passageway beyond.

There were still a few minutes to go. The next two missiles were also dummies, which meant there was still time. . . . He heard the *clop* of go-ahead shoes behind him and knew that Ani-mal was running after him. He dropped down the ladder at the end of the passageway and flew up another corridor. . . .

He had a plan. It wasn't much of one but it was better than none at all. The missile compartment in the *Alaska* was on three levels. The controls and the technicians who manned them were concentrated on the first level. The third level down housed the bottom of the missile tubes and also served as emergency crew's berthing; it was virtually deserted.

Van Meer passed a damage-control locker in the next pas-sageway, darted in and grabbed an ax off the bulkhead, then burst into the missile compartment. Everything was a shining white un-der the overhead fluorescents—even the insulated tubes, march-ing in two rows down the center of the compartment. Tree trunks, eight feet in diameter, with piping and cables twining around them like so many snakes . . . One lone technician at the far end was taking down readings on a bulkhead full of meters; he turned and stared openmouthed at van Meer.

There was another *thump* and the *Alaska* shivered slightly.

". . . *missile three away . . . missile three away . . .*"

He swung the ax at some of the thinner cabling that swarmed up the side of the nearest missile tube. The cabling parted with a shower of sparks and van Meer scurried over to the next one. He was in a frenzy now, frantic with despair. At the other end of the compartment, the missile tech was screaming into his intercom. Then he came running forward, waving a spanner wrench. Van Meer turned and swung upward with the ax when the man was within reach. There was a scream and the wrench went flying against the bulkhead.

The crewman was on his knees, whimpering and holding his slashed arm, from which blood was spurting. Van Meer blotted the technician from his mind and hacked at another clump of cables, switching immediately to the tube next to it.

"*I'll shoot, van Meer.*"

Harris had come in the opposite hatchway, Animal crowding in behind him. Van Meer ducked behind a missile tube, giving away his position by the shower of sparks from a group of severed cables.

The roar of the gun shattered the quiet of the compartment and a large chunk of insulation flew off the side of a tube, just above van Meer's head. Van Meer darted across the aisle between the two rows of tubes. Something grazed his shoulder but he ignored it, slashing at the next tube over. He was halfway down the compartment, heading directly toward Harris, who fired sporadically at him. The strangely silent Meslinsky had disappeared.

Van Meer managed to damage another tube and slash at still another when he caught a glimpse of Meslinsky behind one of the tubes at his rear. Animal had circled around to stalk him. An odd forest, an odd beast. But there was no time to dodge. He was hacking at another cable when Meslinsky lumbered out from behind a tube, trying to tackle him. He sidestepped and cut at the next tube. Animal scrambled after him. His T-shirt had been torn off and his cutoffs hung by a thread. He was huge—a superhero from a comic-book cover. He was dirty, his body slippery with sweat and blood where he had torn his skin coming through a hatchway too small for him. The stink of his perspiration mixed with the acrid odor of burning electrical insulation and ozone from the sparking cables.

Meslinsky rushed him again. He turned and slashed at Animal with the ax. At the end of the compartment, Harris was trying to get a clear shot without hitting Meslinsky. It didn't make much sense, van Meer thought. Millions were going to die and Harris was worried about hitting Animal. . . .

"*. . . missile four away . . . missile four away . . .*"

For a split second van Meer was distracted. *The next one will be for real.* . . . He slashed downward one more time with the ax, realizing too late he had again lost sight of Animal. The next moment, he was grabbed around the waist and hoisted off his feet. He tried to flail around with the ax, and was hurled to the tiled deck. Meslinsky promptly smothered him with the weight of his body. ". . . son of a bitch," Meslinsky was mumbling, "son of a bitch, son of a bitch . . ."

Van Meer lay for a second on his back, the wind knocked out of him. He could hear Meslinsky panting in his ear and feel the slime of his skin. His own hands were trapped between their bodies. He suddenly clawed upward and squeezed. Animal hunched in pain and van Meer drove his right knee into the same weak spot. Meslinsky howled and scraped at his face, leaving bleeding welts in his cheek. Van Meer jerked away. Meslinsky kicked out, catching him in the side and hurling him against one of the tubes.

Van Meer grunted with pain and tried to dance out of reach. Then Animal had him by the arm and yanked him close. Van Meer stiffened his fingers and drove them deep into the big man's stomach. He wrenched loose again and dove for the ax, beating Harris to it. He yanked the blade from under Harris' feet and whirled to the sixth tube, slashing wildly at its side and hoping he had done some damage, then turned to face Harris and a now stark-naked Meslinsky crouched in front of the fifth tube.

Animal's eyes were puffy and almost closed. Blood was streaming down one side, covering his right leg and dripping onto the deck. Harris was glaring at him, too much white showing around his pupils, his shirt torn and his black beard and mustache dripping with sweat. He pointed the .45 at van Meer's stomach.

"Give it up, mister," Harris screamed. But there was another scream that van Meer knew only he could hear, one that was a long way away in both distance and time. He lunged forward with the ax.

The *Alaska* lurched slightly for the fifth time and the bullet grazed his side, stinging as it plowed through the slight roll of fat around his waist.

". . . *missile five away* . . . *missile five away* . . ."

Number five was the only live missile they'd get off, van Meer thought, feeling himself start to break apart on the inside. But one was enough.

It didn't help to know that this time he had really tried.

68

"ERE COMES another one," Epping said in a tight voice. The deadly shape burst into the air above the boiling waters. There was nothing he could do, Renslow thought, helpless. They were closer now but still too far away. . . .

Talbot was saying something, ". . . acknowledged by the *Hornet*. They want us to clear the area."

Renslow squinted at the horizon and imagined he could see the tiny specks turn and start toward them. They'd be planning an ASROC attack; they'd want the choppers away from the mushroom cloud.

He suddenly hunched forward in his seat. "Get us in there, *fast*." He pulled off his wristwatch and hit the second timer. The launch pattern below would depend on the weather conditions above, the periodicity of the crest and trough of the waves; the missiles would have to hit the surface at just the right moment so as not to be toppled. . . .

"Number three," Epping yelled. Renslow pressed the START button and stared in silence as the deadly cycle of ignition and acceleration played itself out. Number five was the bird that would start World War III. But they were still too far away; it was still too much of a gamble. . . .

"Can't you make this crate go any faster?"

"I'll try but we'll never make it," Epping shouted back. His face was so tense the cheekbones stood out in high relief. He looked as if he were trying, by sheer concentration, to coax extra speed from the bucking craft.

Below them, number four broke the surface and arced upward into the darkening sky. Renslow pressed the button on his watch again and noted the elapsed time.

"Arm the rockets," he yelled at Epping.

"What?"

"Arm the rockets, dammit."

Epping hesitated, then pushed back the firing guards on the instrument panel.

"Start firing when I tell you."

They were closer now, much closer, the smear from the yellow dye marker spreading out over an immense area of the ocean. Renslow watched the ticking hands of his watch, then: "*Fire!*"

Epping pressed the first firing stud. From beneath the airframe of the chopper, the heat-seeking Agile swished out on a rolling tail of vapor, its velocity building rapidly. Five seconds later, a second Agile roared from its pod on the port side. Renslow counted and watched the third rocket streak away.

Ahead of them, the first Agile traced a long, curving path toward the general launch area and passed through it to disappear into the low clouds. Too soon. Renslow was in agony as he watched its vapor trail arc downward toward the sea. The second followed, entering the launch area just as the fourth rocket arrowed from its rear port pod and streaked after the first three.

The sea below erupted in boiling steam. "*Goddammit.*" His timing was off. . . . The third rocket curved in toward the site as the cone of the number-five Trident missile broke the surface of the sea. The Agile was passing to the starboard as the missile hung in space for a moment. Then the missile's motors ignited with a roar, their exhaust gases half obscuring the area.

"Look—baby sees her," Epping shouted.

The long white trail of the third Agile was curving dramatically as its infrared sensor locked on the heat of the Trident's motor. The missile was dancing on a tail of flame, its exhausts flicking back and forth as its motors labored to hold the bird vertical during the critical first second of flight. The Agile was swooping in a wide catenary, its target the wash of flame from the missile. But the missile was already starting to surge upward . . . slowly . . . painfully balancing on its bright exhaust.

Renslow held his breath. It was a long chance at best. The fourth Agile was still seconds away. It would never get there in time.

The Agile vanished into the boiling white exhaust clouds. For a moment nothing happened. Then the missile shuddered as an explosion blasted the white exhaust plume to tatters. A large section of nozzle flew upward in a long arc. The motor still flamed but the missile was rising now at a forty-five-degree angle.

It suddenly tumbled, turning end over end, the thrust of its motors skewed sideward by the loss of the nozzle section. It was nosing downward, accelerating. The nose touched the water and the missile plunged out of sight, its engines still under full thrust. Above, the fourth Agile soared past, then faltered and turned back, seeking a target amid the hot gases drifting above the surface of the ocean.

"*Bull's-eye,*" Talbot yelled, pounding on his seat.

Renslow stared down at the sea, feeling drained. There were no more Agiles; there was no way they could knock down missile six or seven or the ones that would come after. . . .

He wasn't prepared when the ocean in front of them suddenly erupted, throwing a huge plume of water high into the sky. The plume rose silently and became a geyser. Then the sound hit them. It was a rumbling, tearing blast that caught the Sea King and threw it upward.

69

THE FIFTH MISSILE left its tube and van Meer crumpled to the deck, holding his side. For a long moment he and Harris and Animal were celluloid men trapped in a freeze-frame tableau.

Then it happened.

The *Alaska* rocked slightly as something massive hit the water near them, making a heavy, churning sound like that of a giant torpedo. Harris' eyes widened in surprise. The next instant, the *Alaska* shuddered as if struck by a giant hammer. The ship twisted, its seams screaming in protest. A huge hand swatted van Meer against the bulkhead. Pipes wrenched free of their moorings. Needles of high-pressure water suddenly laced the compartment.

The ax nearby abruptly started sliding across the deck. Van Meer had to clutch at some piping to keep from sliding with it. The bow was angling upward at an impossible forty-five degrees.... Then they were rising rapidly. The next instant, the compartment vibrated with a low-pitched thrumming, subsiding to a gentle swaying from side to side.

They had broached the surface of the rolling sea. And they were mortally wounded. Van Meer scrambled out of the compartment, glancing back once to see Harris in a corner by an equipment console and Animal standing over him.

The passageways above were clogged with men struggling toward the forward hatch. Minutes later, van Meer had worked his way up the slippery rungs of the hatch ladder and was standing on the hull, pulling crewmen out of the open hatch behind him. The sea was filled with struggling men and small bundles that popped into orange escape rafts.

"It's going down, Mr. van Meer." A frightened Clinger was

grasping the coaming around the hatch. He was drenched with seawater. Then Clinger was pushed into the water by those behind him. Van Meer watched, as he struck out frantically for a nearby raft.

Scoma was the next into the water and van Meer tried to remember the others he had seen in the last few moments. Longstreet, Sandeman, Russo, Udall, Stroop, Moskowitz . . .

There was nobody waiting to come up the ladder now. And he hadn't yet seen Harris or Animal.

They were settling lower in the water. He made up his mind then and took a last, quick look around. The swelling sea, the overcast sky, the small shape of a helicopter overhead . . . He took a deep breath of the chill salt air and dropped down the ladder. The *Alaska* was settling fast but he couldn't abandon Harris or Animal. He could never repeat the scene with Maggie again, ever. . . .

In the passageway at the base of the ladder, somebody grabbed his arm.

"For God's sake, Van, where the hell are you going? This baby will be underwater in another five minutes."

Cermak, blood oozing from a cut on his forehead, his shirt soaked by the occasional wave that crashed over the open hatch. Clutching a bottle in his right hand. The Lafite-Rothschild . . .

"Harris and Animal—they're still below."

Cermak gripped him tighter, his pudgy face suddenly fierce. "Youll never get to them, Van. We're going under. Jesus, Van, don't be a hero."

Van Meer shook him off and raced down the passageway. The lower decks were now deserted, he noted with relief. Then he was conscious that the *Alaska* was moving more sluggishly in the waves and that the deck had developed a steeper slant.

Harris and Animal were still in the missile compartment. Harris had been caught by a heavy equipment drawer that had rolled out of its console and pinned him between it and the deck. Animal was bending over him, trying desperately to shift the drawer. Van Meer ran forward to help. The drawer wouldn't budge.

The ax, lying a few feet away, caught up in the severed cabling of a missile tube . . . Van Meer scrambled for it, Animal watching him apprehensively.

"Out of the way, Animal."

He drove the ax head between the side of the drawer and the frame, then twisted. The heavy drawer shifted slightly. Again. It shifted more this time and van Meer suddenly realized the increasing angle of the deck was helping. They'd have to hurry.

Another drive with the ax and the drawer suddenly rolled easily back into the console. Harris was free. Animal pulled him out. Harris was unconscious, with a broken arm and an ugly bruise along the side of his head. Van Meer took one arm and Animal the other and they hurried out to the passageway.

Water was running along the tiled deck. It occurred to van Meer that not only were they shipping water through ruptured seams in the pressure hull, but from the increasing tilt of the deck, the afterhatch was probably underwater.

They were at the base of the ladder and about to go up when somebody screamed for help.

Van Meer glanced hastily around. The scream had come from crew's berthing. He looked at Animal. "Who the hell's that?"

Animal didn't meet his eyes. "Bailey," he mumbled. "We put him in restraint."

Crew's berthing was still rigged for red. It looked, remarkably, as if it were on fire. Van Meer stared, fascinated, then slowly let go of Harris. "Can you handle him, Animal?"

Animal nodded, an agonized expression on his face. "The Russians," he said in a husky voice, "they'll kill him."

Van Meer whirled and glared at the naked giant standing ankle-deep in the water sloshing over the deck. "Look, mister," he said, his voice suddenly fierce, "it was all a drill. Do you understand that? It was all a drill and I don't want to hear anything more about it."

He turned and ran for crew's berthing. He hesitated a moment inside the shadowy compartment, trying to get his bearings. Then he could hear Bailey moaning in a corner bunk. His arms were at his sides and a plastic mattress cover, stretched over the bunk up to his neck, was lashed to the bunk frame.

Bailey mumbled something but van Meer wasn't sure whether or not Bailey recognized him.

He worked frantically at the lashings, his fingers slipping on the tightly corded knots. A knife . . . He ran his hands through his pockets and came up with a small penknife. Once the cord was cut he quickly unlashed the bindings.

"Let's go, Bailey."

Bailey rolled out of the bunk and van Meer had to hold him up to keep him from falling. The deck was sharply tilting now; it was difficult to stand. He pushed Bailey into the corridor outside and they ran through the water for the ladder. When they were halfway up, the lights flickered and went out.

Bailey screamed, "We're going to die."

"Get up the goddamned ladder, Bailey."

Bailey scrambled up and van Meer followed. It was like struggling up a small mountain. Then they were in Officers' Country and van Meer could see the ladder that led to the forward hatch just ahead of them. He could even make out a patch of dirty sky at the top.

Bailey was halfway up when the angle of the deck abruptly increased and the clouds outside moved slowly past the hatch opening. For a second the water coming in over the coaming was only a thin stream. Then it was a solid torrent. Bailey lost his grip on the rungs and screamed, and van Meer thought dumbly that the poor bastard wasn't going to make it.

And neither was he.

70

THE FIRST STAGE of the missile had exploded underwater. Somewhere in the ocean, at what depth Renslow didn't know, at least twelve tons of nitroglycerine and nitrocellulose, mixed with aluminum and perchlorate-HMX, a mixture far more powerful than dynamite, had abruptly switched from smooth burning to uncontrolled detonation.

The chopper bucked in the blast as Epping struggled to bring it under control. They hovered in the thick air, waiting. Seconds passed. One minute. Two. How long had it been between missiles? Renslow had timed it but now couldn't remember. . . .

"Hey, look." Talbot pointed out the starboard windscreen and Renslow glanced down. Gouts of air were boiling up to the surface. A dark shape a hundred feet below was now rapidly coming up, huge bubbles of air churning alongside it. A moment later, it had almost leaped from the water to pancake back on the surface, huge waves rolling away from either side.

"It's the *Alaska*," Epping whispered.

They slowly circled the wounded submarine. Her bow was crumpled and Renslow guessed she was shipping water. But for the moment she was buoyant. As he watched, the forward hatch popped open and men began to scramble out. One of them threw a bundle over the side that exploded into a raft.

There was a rattle of transmissions coming over the radio now. Renslow said quietly, "Tell the *Hornet* that the *Alaska* has surfaced, that she's badly damaged. Cancel the SUBROC attacks. They're no longer necessary."

Epping said, "How close do you want me to get?"

"As close as you can," Renslow said slowly.

The chopper dropped lower to the surface and Renslow

could make out the details of the crippled submarine. The sea about her was thick with swimming men and brightly colored life rafts. They circled for perhaps five minutes, Renslow trying hard to keep from counting the number of crewmen floundering in the ocean. Then he tensed. The *Alaska* was settling lower and lower in the water, its bow rising sharply. In seconds the afterhatch was underwater. Then the sail slipped slowly from sight. The bow plunged after and a great bubble rose from the depths.

Epping turned his head slightly. "Commander, what—"

He abruptly shut up and concentrated on controlling the chopper in the sudden gusts of wind.

Behind him, huddled in his seat, Commander Allard Renslow was silently crying.

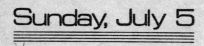

Sunday, July 5

71

RENSLOW GOT THE call for the meeting of the Joint Chiefs of Staff forty-eight hours after the recovery of the *Alaska* personnel. They met informally in the conference room at the Pentagon. Cullinane and Hardin were present, as was Warden. Cullinane looked grim and preoccupied, nodding slightly when Renslow walked in.

Admiral Howland opened the meeting, then nodded at Hardin to give his report. Hardin shuffled the papers uncertainly and Renslow noted that he hadn't glanced across the table at Warden for support.

"This is the interim evaluation," he said nervously. "We will, of course, continue to monitor the men in the hospital and for at least a year after they return to duty."

"Monitor?" Cullinane asked.

Hardin waved a hand. "Nothing really obvious. At present we have twenty-four-hour monitoring on their wards at Bethesda—"

"In other words, you've got their ward bugged," Cullinane interrupted.

Hardin looked offended. "Their reactions immediately after the drill are crucial. There's also an element of security involved. Fortunately, we have an assist in that respect. Their memories seem to be rather sketchy about the exact sequence of events. Judging from our past experience with Chief Gradow"—his eyes sought out Renslow's for a moment—"the amnesia may become complete."

"I should think the admiral would be happy with the outcome of our little problem," Warden said in an airy tone of voice. "Believe me, gentlemen, the President sure as hell is."

"That problem was just about as big as you can get," Cullinane said slowly.

Howland read the danger signs. "We've got a lot to cover today, Stew."

Cullinane shook his head. "There's something that has to be discussed, and I think it has to be discussed now." He paused. "I know my future plans as far as the Navy is concerned. There's little that Mr. Warden can threaten me with now."

Renslow was watching him closely. What had Cullinane meant by "future plans"?

"Threaten?" Warden said indignantly. "I've never threatened the admiral in any way."

"You threaten all of us, Mr. Warden." Cullinane was now standing on his side of the table. "You threaten not only your country but the world."

Warden turned to Howland. "Suh, the admiral is one of your men."

"I think you're out of line, Stew," Howland said in an uneasy voice.

Warden straightened in his chair and Renslow could sense him shifting roles once again. The man was a chameleon; he could flow from one personality to another effortlessly.

"I've devoted my career to this country's security," he said in a steely voice. "Now that the Secretary of State has resigned, and God and the President willing, I can do even more."

There was a surprised silence in the room. Nobody had known about the Secretary's resignation, Renslow thought, even though it had been expected. Only Cullinane didn't seem shocked.

Then Renslow knew what was happening. If Warden was now Secretary of State–designate, then his power was even greater. There would have to be a scapegoat. . . . As ComSubLant, and an officer who had deliberately offended the White House, Cullinane was the logical candidate. It would be a month before the board of inquiry met but any Navy man could foresee the outcome. The early press releases on the "*Alaska* incident" were already focusing the blame on Cullinane.

Cullinane was sacrificing himself. And everybody knew it.

"Congratulations," Cullinane continued heavily. "Though

I'm afraid it's appointing the fox to guard the chickens."

Howland looked shocked. "Admiral—"

"I assume everybody here now knows the true nature of Operation Fire," Cullinane continued in a silky voice.

They were staring. Howland said, "What are you driving at, Stew?"

"The drill wasn't to test the crew at all, Admiral. It was intended as a provocative act, one fraught with risk and peril. It would have prepared the way eventually for an American preemptive strike. Events quickly got beyond Mr. Warden's control but hardly beyond Mr. Warden's desires."

Warden jumped to his feet, red-faced. "That's a lie—an insult to my office and an insult to me personally. Operation Fire was conceived by the Navy Department, presented to the President's security advisers by the Joint Chiefs, and approved, with the Navy being given full authority to plan and carry out the operation. I will not be made the villain in this."

Cullinane waited a moment, then: "Operation Fire was conceived and planned by you, Mr. Warden. With the aid and assistance of Dr. Hardin, who perhaps remembers the record better than you do."

Hardin went white and for a moment Renslow thought he was going to have a seizure.

"I—"

"If you're giving testimony," Warden cut in swiftly, addressing his remarks to Hardin, "then a witness stand is the only place for it." He turned back to Cullinane. "If you want a full-dress hearing, Admiral, you can have it. But neither your career nor your reputation will survive it."

Hardin abruptly shut up. Warden glanced at the others. He looked more like a wolf than Renslow could imagine a fat man ever appearing.

"You wanted a first strike, Mr. Warden," Cullinane said.

"I was one of several voices," Warden admitted.

"You were the only voice," Cullinane said harshly.

"You're accusing me of wanting to start World War Three," Warden said. "That's a ridiculous accusation on the face of it. Utter nonsense."

"It's not nonsense," Cullinane said. "It's insanity."

He had gone beyond the point of no return, Renslow thought with a kind of horrified fascination.

Warden was starting to straighten his papers. "I'm afraid the meeting has degenerated into one of personal attacks," he said grimly.

"Admiral Cullinane," Howland said formally, "you're excused from this meeting."

Renslow trailed him out. Nobody looked at either the admiral or him.

In the hallway outside, Cullinane said, "That blows it, Al. I'm sorry. You're tarred with my brush now. Warden will be after your scalp as well as mine, you know."

For a moment Renslow wasn't sure how he felt about that. Then he suddenly realized he didn't give a damn. Something of himself had followed the *Alaska* into the depths of the sea.

"What are you going to do?"

Cullinane shrugged. "Play a lot of golf. Catch up on my reading. This isn't my battle anymore."

He hadn't known van Meer very well, Renslow reflected, but he had liked him. And Doc Schulman and Okamoto . . . Chips had been in his own crew once.

"It's still mine," he said.

Cullinane suddenly stopped. "Don't stick your neck out, Al. You've still got friends in the Navy. Keep your nose clean and you can outlive Warden. Four years in exile and you could go on with your career."

Renslow smiled. "I should keep my mouth shut and just give up? That's strange advice from you, Admiral." He took a breath. "I'm not staying in the Navy. For a lot of reasons."

Cullinane gave him a searching look, then nodded. "You still want to fight, you might look up some of the independent lobbying groups. One of them contacted me yesterday. I've got the name in my office."

At his door, Cullinane said, "I'm leaving for the day. Can I give you a lift?"

"I was going to Bethesda," Renslow said slowly. "I wanted to see some of my men."

"Our men," Cullinane corrected. Then: "I'll drop you off."

Renslow delayed seeing Harris until the last. Finally, since it was almost three o'clock, he walked to the private room assigned to Harris. He paused in surprise as he entered the small waiting room.

Elizabeth rose from the chair in which she had been sitting. She looked very handsome, he thought, very neat and self-contained. But, then, she almost always did.

"I can come back later," he said.

"I've seen the others I know," she said quietly. "I couldn't very well not see him."

He managed to smile. "You make it sound like a duty." For once he spoke without the inflection of challenge.

"It is," she said simply.

There was the slight sound of a door opening and Harris walked in. He was wearing white-linen pajamas and leather slippers and a dark-blue robe. Harris had pinned the silver oak leaf of a commander on his right lapel. He nodded at both of them, curiously distant. "It was nice of you to come." He sat down on a couch, placing a thin file folder on the small table in front of it.

Nobody said anything for a moment, then Harris cleared his throat. "Have you two had lunch?"

Renslow said no and Elizabeth shook her head. She seemed withdrawn and Renslow wondered if he had interrupted anything by showing up when he had. Then he thought she might be put off by Harris' appearance. His hair was long, his beard full and black. For some reason they hadn't shaved him yet. If anything, he thought, it made him appear more handsome.

"They've got a pretty good mess here," Harris said. "They can bring something up if you'd like."

"That'd be fine," Elizabeth said in a small voice.

Harris got up and went into his room to place the order. When he came back, Renslow said slowly, "They're taking pretty good care of you."

"Yeah." Harris stared at him for a second, thoughtful. Then: "I'm pretty important to them." Bitterly: "Now."

Renslow glanced at Elizabeth. The expression on her face was enigmatic and he wondered how many of the crewmen she had talked to and what they had said.

"How do you mean?" Renslow asked.

Harris shrugged. "I'm a hero, ol' buddy. A genuine, gold-plated, bona-fide hero."

Elizabeth looked as shocked as he imagined he did. A white-jacketed mess attendant wheeled in a serving cart and began arranging dishes on the small table.

"No offense intended, Steve," Renslow said hesitantly," but that's not the way I heard it. It wasn't your fault, of course," he added hastily.

Harris looked at him blankly. "To be absolutely honest, Al, I don't remember a goddamned thing. But it's all in there." He tapped the folder on the table. "Take a look."

Harris picked it up and thumbed through the half-dozen typewritten pages. The Navy needed a hero, badly, and they had picked Harris. The reports of the other men had been confused, fragmentary. There had certainly been nothing they could hang a court-martial on. So they had reversed field and designated Harris as Hero for a Day.

Elizabeth said in a fading voice, "I understand that van Meer—"

Harris picked up a knife and began to saw at a steak. "I heard a little about that." He shook his head and smiled. "Poor Van. I can't imagine a less likely guy to be a hero. Neither could the brass."

He didn't remember, Renslow thought blankly. He shouldn't hold it against Harris because he couldn't remember.

Elizabeth suddenly stood up. "I'm sorry, Steve, I have to leave." She held out her hand. "I'm so pleased that you . . . survived all that." Harris started to say something but she didn't wait to hear. Renslow stared after her. He couldn't be sure but he could have sworn there had been tears in her eyes. The woman of steel, he thought, amazed. The only emotion he thought she was capable of was anger.

"Women," Harris laughed.

"You're going to like being a hero, aren't you?" Renslow suddenly said.

Harris carefully put down his knife and fork, and wiped his mouth. "What the hell do you expect me to say to that, Al? Should I turn it down? I was washed up before, or didn't you know that? Ten years of my goddamned life and I was slated for a desk in D.C. Well, I'll tell you something. I don't know what the hell happened down there—and I don't want to know. They'll scratch my back and I'll scratch theirs. Wearing sackcloth and ashes won't bring back the dead, buddy. And when were you such a great friend of old four-eyes van Meer?"

Renslow bolted to his feet, his plate and cup scattering over the floor. Harris flinched and pushed away from the table. Renslow looked down at him coldly, then turned and walked out.

Maybe *that* was what he had really wanted all those years, he thought. The sudden look of fear in Harris' eyes . . .

"Al . . ."

She had been waiting in the corridor outside. He turned and she was suddenly in his arms. "I didn't know whether to cry or scream," she said.

"You never knew him," Renslow said. "Not really."

She shook her head. "It's not that." It took her a minute to get control of herself, then she pushed him gently away. "I talked to everybody I knew. Most of them didn't remember much. But Animal did." Her expression was pained. "He remembered everything. He couldn't forget." She glanced back at Harris' room. "I couldn't stand what he was saying about Van."

"Harris doesn't care," Renslow said.

"He's never cared about anybody, has he?"

Renslow hesitated. "I don't know, Elizabeth. Has he?"

She shook her head and smiled sadly. "Not really, I guess." She pulled on her gloves. "Would you have the desk call me a taxi?"

"We can share one," he suddenly said.

"I thought you had a meeting." She didn't look at him and he thought she was hiding a smile.

"Nothing that can't be canceled or postponed."

"I think I want to go home," she said. Then: "Howie said to say hello. He wanted me to give you his love." She looked up at him and Renslow put his arm around her protectively.

"We've got a lot to talk about," he said.

She was silent for a moment. He could feel her gradually relax in the crook of his arm.

"We've got a lot of catching up to do," she said quietly.

Epilogue

OOF THE *ALASKA'S* complement of one hundred and forty men and officers, seventy-two escaped while she was still on the surface. Subsequently, the submarine settled beneath nearly one thousand feet of water. Four days later, the submarine rescue ship *Ortolan* and the deep-submergence rescue vehicle *Avalon* located the sunken *Alaska* and discovered that two groups of men had sealed themselves in airtight sections of the pressure hull. One group was rescued, including the engineering officer, Lieutenant Earl Messier, and radio man, first class, Michael Dritz, bringing the total to ninety-six. The *Avalon* was unable to rescue the second group before the air supply was exhausted. Among those who perished were commissary man, first class, Joseph Perez; Lieutenant William Spencer; Lieutenant Commander Michael Costanza; Lieutenant Frank MacGowan; chief machinist's mate Frederick Fuhrman; hospital corpsman, third class, Nicholas Geranios.

Two months after the sinking of the *Alaska*, a Navy board of inquiry met at New London and in Washington to determine the cause of and the responsibility for the loss of the ship. The deliberations were closed to the public and the press. The body of the report was classified top secret, though portions were released three months later. The report was generally favorable to Lieutenant Commander Mark van Meer and Lieutenant, j.g., Abraham Schulman, both of whom received posthumous decorations. Commander Stephen Poindexter Harris, captain of the ill-fated vessel, was singled out for particular praise and awarded the Navy Cross. Four months after Captain Harris received his decoration, he unexpectedly resigned his commission and announced for United States senator from Massachusetts. Despite his well-financed campaign, he was defeated by a significant margin—a defeat political analysts ascribed to his failure to win the labor vote.

Commander Allard Renslow resigned from the Navy and joined the staff of Citizens' Alert, a political-action group. He was a prominent witness during the Citizens' Alert challenge to the appointment of Caleb Warden as Secretary of State. After the hearings, Renslow and his wife, Elizabeth, adopted Jimmy van Meer and moved to Chevy Chase. Jimmy van Meer is now honor man in his high-school class and hopes to attend West Point upon graduation.

Caleb Warden was not confirmed by the U.S. Senate as Secretary of State. Though he successfully defended himself against charges stemming from the *Alaska* incident, Citizens' Alert subsequently presented the confirmation committee with extensive documentation of a conflict of interest in which Warden had profited heavily on the purchase of Bulger Engineering common stock just prior to the award of a major government contract to that company. Mr. Renslow of Citizens' Alert testified that Mr. Warden had been aware of the impending contract award and may have influenced the decision to award the contract to Bulger. Mr. Warden then returned to Columbus, Georgia, where he is reported to be writing a book on politics and religion for a six-figure advance.

Admiral Stewart Cullinane accepted early retirement after a Navy board of inquiry returned a report critical of his performance during the *Alaska* crisis. He entered New York State politics and won election to the Assembly.

Captain Jacob Oxley testified extensively for Caleb Warden during the confirmation hearings. Unfortunately, a slip of the tongue by a confused Oxley during interrogation by the committee's counsel confirmed the charges of conflict of interest by Citizens' Alert witness Allard Renslow. Captain Oxley is presently serving as procurement officer at the naval air station in Agana, Guam.

Lieutenant Anthony Cermak left the service to open an exclusive restaurant, the Turf and Tipple, in Carmel, California. In a glass case by the door is a bottle of Château Lafite-Rothschild, 1959. Just outside the glass is a small hammer and the legend BREAK IN CASE OF EMERGENCY.

Torpedo man's mate, first class, Caesar Meslinsky was assigned to the SSBN 727 *Michigan*. He went on the wagon and is reported to spend most of his liberty time in museums and libraries. His most prized possession is a small book of poems that once belonged to his executive officer on the *Alaska*, Mark van Meer.

Chief petty officer Ernest Gradow was discharged from the hospital a week after the sinking of the *Alaska;* his wife, Florence, was released a week later. Gradow was charged with theft of government property but was allowed to plead guilty to the lesser charge of misappropriation. He received a suspended sentence of ninety days, with forfeiture of all pay and allowances during that period. Despite the black mark on his record, he elected to remain in the Navy.

Lieutenant, j.g., Jeffrey Udall resigned from the Navy and joined the Bechtel Corporation. He later accepted a position as project engineer with Consolidated Reactors and was mentioned prominently in the news stories of the near-meltdown of the Camden reactor. Heavy exposure to radiation during the disaster precluded any further employment as an on-the-job engineer and he reentered government service with the Nuclear Regulatory Commission as a GS-15.

Cheryl Leary moved from New London to her parents' home in Chicago. She married an advertising account executive in the Chicago office of J. Walter Thompson and currently lives in Glen Ellyn with her husband and his two children.

Sergei Polnykov, former commander of the USSR submarine *Zhukov*, requested political asylum during the diplomatic maneuvering following the loss of the *Alaska*. The Washington *Post* published an exclusive by reporter Jeff Spann accusing the *Zhukov* of ramming the *Alaska*. It was widely regarded as an official government leak and accepted as the true story of what had happened to the *Alaska*, with resulting unfavorable publicity for the Soviets. Polnykov was debriefed for four months by Navy Intelligence before being turned over to the CIA. It is rumored that he is living in Nevada under another identity.

On the fifth anniversary of the loss of the *Alaska*, SSBN 742, also called the *Alaska*, was launched in a small ceremony at the yards of the Electric Boat Company in Groton. Of the officers who had served aboard the original *Alaska*, only Stephen Harris attended. Photographs were taken and his manager distributed them widely during his new but unsuccessful campaign for the state legislature.

Also attending was Caesar Meslinsky, who stood, unrecognized, at the rear of the crowd. Once the ceremonies were over, for the first time in five years Meslinsky stopped by the Groton Motor Inn and got falling-down drunk.

OUTSTANDING READING FROM WARNER BOOKS